D0560251

CONDORS

also by Ray Rosenbaum
Falcons
Hawks

CONDORS

a novel by
Ray Rosenbaum

LYFORD
Books

The characters in this novel are fictitious. Any characters (except historical figures) resembling actual persons, living or dead, are purely coincidental. The dialogue and specific incidents described in the novel are products of the author's imagination and creativity. They should not be construed as real.

LYFORD Books
Published by Presidio Press
505 B San Marin Dr., Suite 300
Novato, CA 94945-1340

Library of Congress Cataloging-in-Publication Data

Rosenbaum, Ray, 1923–
   Condors : a novel / by Ray Rosenbaum.
      p. cm.
   ISBN 0-89141-478-9
   1. World War, 1939-1945—Veterans—United States—Fiction. 2. Palestine—History—1929–1948—Fiction. 3. Arms transfers—Palestine—Fiction. 4. Air pilots—United States—Fiction. 5. Jews—Palestine—Fiction. I. Title.
PS3568.0777C66 1995
813'.54—dc20   94-32681
                                          CIP

Typography by ProImage
Printed in the United States of America

For RWR

CONDORS

Prologue

12 October 1917
London, England

Sir Arthur Balfour fixed the assembled members of Great Britain's House of Lords and House of Commons with a steely glare. What he had to say would not rest well with many of them, he knew. Overhead lights, turned on early to dispel the afternoon's fall gloom, accentuated the Parliamentarians' furrowed brows. The text of Balfour's "white paper" to Lloyd George was common knowledge; this reading of its contents into the record was a mere formality.

The dapper foreign minister smoothed his guardsman's mustache with a crooked forefinger and commenced speaking in crisp, measured tones. "The British Empire has stood before the world as the champion of oppressed, persecuted, and enslaved peoples since the adoption of the Magna Carta. The democratic principles of self-government, and freedom to pursue a religious belief of choice, are held to be self-evident. We are presently engaged in a great war to demonstrate our dedication to these ideals.

"It is consistent, therefore, that His Majesty's government recognize the plight of the Jewish people. Persecuted in eastern European and Asian countries, they are without sanctuary. Be it known by all men that the British government is in sympathy with Jewish Zionist aspirations, and views favorably the establishment in Palestine of a national home for the Jewish people. This expression includes a pledge that the best endeavors will be extended to facilitate the achievement

1

of this object, it being clearly understood that nothing shall be done which may prejudice the civil and religious rights of existing non-Jewish communities in Palestine, or the rights and political status enjoyed by Jews in any other country."

Sir Wilford Champion, Earl of Sussex, muttered to his neighbor from behind a concealing hand. "Noble words. I wonder, though, if the man fully understands the implications of what he has set in motion."

Chapter 1

20 July 1946
Des Moines, Iowa

Ross Colyer repositioned the sweat-stained headset over his blond crewcut, its left earpiece firmly in place and the right earpiece resting on his temple. Standard procedure when flying the DC-3, this position allowed the pilot to hear what his copilot said without missing a radio transmission. Colyer's youthful features reflected weary disgust as he regarded tongues of lightning flickering ahead, causing spits of static in the earphones.

He removed the handheld mike from its hook and drawled, "Des Moines radio, this is Nan Six-Niner-Three, position, over."

"Nan Six-Niner-Three, Des Moines radio, go ahead."

"Roger, Des Moines. Six-Niner-Three over your station at four-one—six thousand feet, IFR. Estimating Kansas City at two-one-one-four central. Do you have Kansas City and en route weather, over?"

"Roger on your position, Six-Niner-Three. Stand by for K.C. weather, over."

Ross shifted his attention from the black expanse of windshield—relieved only by random eruptions of electrical discharges—to Alex Taylor, flying as copilot. Leaning toward the slumped figure in the right seat, Ross snarled, "Why the hell can't he just look out the window? Even I can tell him there's a line of thunderstorms between us and K.C. Just hope to hell Fairfax holds up. Otherwise that bunch of drunks in the back is gonna have to hoof it home—from maybe Omaha."

Alex's square, sun-browned face was illuminated briefly as he lit a cigaret. He inhaled deeply, then muttered, "It'd serve 'em right. That big one—Max something—I could get to dislike that bastard real easy. I warned 'em all to take it easy on the booze, that we might have a bumpy ride home. Max told me to stick to airplane driving—that he'd gotten drunk on better airlines than this one."

The radio came to life. Ross raised a hand to silence his disgruntled copilot. "Nan Six-Niner-Three, Des Moines radio with your weather. Ready to copy?"

"Roger, Des Moines. Six-Niner-Three ready to copy, go ahead."

"Kansas City Fairfax forecast for your arrival is prevailing twenty-five hundred broken, visibility seven miles, lowering to twelve hundred feet and three miles in scattered rain showers. Wind southwest at ten, gusting to twenty-five. Altimeter two-niner-decimal-seven-four. Under comments: heavy thunderstorms in north and northeast quadrants. Your en route weather shows thunderstorms in progress south of the Missouri line at Saint Joe, Maryville, and Chillicothe, over."

"Roger, roger, Des Moines. Weather copied, much thanks."

"Roger, Six-Niner-Three. For your information, Braniff Six-Seven just reported northbound. He experienced severe turbulence in the vicinity of Lomona, over."

Ross acknowledged the transmission and turned to Alex. "This goddamn charter was bad news from the beginning. It's not enough that we couldn't use the Norseman to bring them back from International Falls, but there's no assurance that we'll even get to land at Fairfax with this one. And just the gas bill for this bird wipes out the profit—not to mention the bus tickets to get them back to K.C. Shit."

Alex limited his response to a morose grunt. The future of Allied Air, Inc., was an unspoken worry between them, outweighing the prospect of busting through a cold front larded with towering cumulonimbus. The loss of a profit on this fishing charter meant a missed loan payment—again, Ross mused. As it was, Alex had been sleeping on a cot in their twelve-by-twelve office and eating pork and beans from a can. The Norseman was grounded with serious-sounding engine problems. This could well be their last gasp.

Ross tripped off the autopilot and lowered his seat as a spectacular bolt of blue-white lightning illuminated the cockpit. "Okay," he said wearily. "Better go back and tell that bunch to buckle up. And tell 'em to put the goddamn booze away. If they give you a hard time, just tell 'em I'm prepared to turn around, land at Des Moines, and boot their asses onto the ramp. It's against company rules to drink on board, y'know."

Alex flashed a tight smile as he unbuckled his seat belt and eased his chunky frame to a standing position. "A pleasure, Captain, sir. Do you want me to stop and write that rule in the book as I go through the nav compartment?"

"If you can spell all those big words," Ross replied with a chuckle. Turning his attention to configuring the cockpit for the rapidly approaching ordeal, he flipped the cockpit lighting full on to help keep the searing lightning flashes from blinding him. Next, he nudged the prop controls to 2,100 revolutions per minute to provide a bit of added gyroscopic stability, plus an instant response if he needed climb power. With mixture controls set to auto-rich, he reduced indicated airspeed to 145 miles per hour, the '3's best turbulent air–penetration speed. He caged and reset both gyrocompasses; the magnetic compass would dance like a fart in a whirlwind when they hit heavy weather.

Last, he tuned the number one automatic direction finder (ADF) to two hundred kilocycles and the number two to four hundred kilocycles. A TWA pilot had passed along that tip. Most lightning discharges seem to emit maximum electrical disturbances on these frequencies, the guy explained. If you averaged out the deflections on the ADF direction-indicator needles, the odds were that you'd pass between the biggest cells. Ross had never tried the technique, but what the hell. He'd just keep his fingers crossed and hope that the storms weren't loaded with hailstones.

Alex slipped into the right seat, fastening his seat belt just in time to catch the first jolt dealt their laboring craft. It was as if someone had cut the cables suspending an elevator. Only their seat belts prevented both pilots from rising clear of their seats as the bottom dropped out. Ross, his eyes glued to flight instruments suddenly gone crazy, watched the rate-of-climb indicator hit the bottom peg, unable to record their rate of descent. The altimeter unwound, its hands a blur.

Watch the artificial horizon, the veteran instrument pilot told himself; don't chase altitude fluctuations. Keep the little airplane centered, straight, and level; maintain 145 mph as closely as possible. If you start jockeying the wheel and power, you'll either stall or exceed the plane's structural limits when you hit the updraft that will inevitably follow.

They were well into the storm. Its raging currents shook the twenty-ton airplane like a terrier mauling a rat. Blinding flashes of lightning created an eerie, flickering background to the cockpit lighting. The props spun in a blue ring of Saint Elmo's fire. Ross—sweat rings already darkening the armpits of his short-sleeved blue shirt—removed his headset and hung it on the hook; even the VHF was unreadable through constant static. The ADF indicators wandered aimlessly; so much for the TWA pilot's theory.

A respite. As suddenly as it had begun, the slashing rain and bone-jarring turbulence ceased. Ross risked relaxing his concentration on the flight instruments to take a quick peek outside. Stars overhead. Friendly lights winked from a small town below. But not ten miles ahead lurked an untidy heap of dirty, boiling clouds, their tops back-lit by dancing pink light. "My God," he muttered to Alex, "that mother must go to seventy thousand feet."

A resounding thud, as though a gigantic rubber mallet had struck the straining DC-3, blanked out the copilot's response. "Lightning strike," Ross yelled. "Check for damage."

Alex's terse response was immediate. "Radio's out. The mag compass, too, I think. I'll wait till it settles down, but I wouldn't trust it. You want me to check behind?"

"No," Ross grated. "Stay in your seat. God *damn!* Can anything else go wrong? Look, I'm diverting to Omaha. We're VFR now; I'm going underneath and try to pick up the highway from Des Moines to Omaha. Damned if I'll blunder into that mess up ahead with no radio and a compass I can't depend on."

"Don't look to me for an argument," Alex replied fervently. "Let's get out of this shit."

Ross stood by the steps leading from the DC-3's rear door and watched the dazed, ashen-faced fishing party deplane. "Sorry about the diversion, folks," he said, fighting to keep weary dejection from his voice. "I have a cab on the way. It'll take you to a hotel for the night. We'll have new radios installed and be ready for an eight o'clock takeoff—have you home in time for lunch."

"Bullshit," the one named Max rasped. Ross drew a small measure of satisfaction from seeing the man's shirt front damp with vomit.

"You're not getting me back inside that pile of junk," the irate Max continued. "Trains run all night to Kansas City. If you'll throw our bags into that cab, you'll have seen the last of us."

Ross bit back the retort that sprang to mind. Instead he replied, "Sorry you feel that way, and I'm sorry we had to put in here. It was for your own safety, you know. But if you're getting off here, there's the matter of three hundred dollars for the balance of your charter fee."

Max uttered a rude guffaw. "You're out of your mind, flyboy. You agreed to return us to Kansas City. You didn't. You can take a flying fuck at a duck. I'm headed for the train station."

Ross's voice was tight with anger. "If you read the terms of your contract, sir, I think you'll find that the carrier is not responsible for delays due to weather or other acts of God."

Max picked up his carryall and turned toward the lighted terminal. "So sue me," he shouted over his shoulder.

Ross restrained Alex, who stood with a clenched, cocked right fist. "Stow it, fella," he muttered. "We barely have money for a new radio, much less a fine for assault."

"That horse's ass," Alex said through gritted teeth. "Just one good punch, that's all I ask." Ross eyed Alex, who was a third shorter than the belligerent Max, with concealed amusement. "But"—Alex shrugged—"you're right. Now what?"

"We spend the night here," Ross said soothingly. "Tomorrow, we'll take off VFR without a flight plan and follow the river to K.C. Then we'll fall back and regroup. We can't afford to lose that three hundred. Oh well, I still have enough for hamburgers and Cokes. Then it's welcome to the Douglas Hilton, sir." Ross waved toward the parked airplane.

Alex opened his mouth to speak, then bit his lip. "This is the last straw, isn't it? That goddamn fire last winter—we lost our ass and it's been downhill ever since. We'll be lucky to stay out of bankruptcy court."

Ross cuffed his despondent partner on the shoulder. "Never in hell," he said. "Things are gonna turn around; I can feel it."

24 July 1946
Kansas City, Missouri

Uncomfortable in his best double-breasted gray suit and his last pair of army low-quarter shoes, highly polished for the occasion, Ross ended his presentation. "And that's the situation, sir. When the customer refused to pay the balance of the charter fee, it left us without funds to replace the radio. I'll get that three hundred bucks," he added from between clenched teeth. "I'll get it if I have to turn that arrogant bastard upside down and shake it out of his pockets.

"However, we have to get that bird back in the air by Friday or miss a good cargo run to D.C. The other thousand is to hang a new engine on the Norseman. The engine's in the surplus yard, and it's available at a good price. We need it to get the plane ready for deer season in Minnesota, to follow up some good connections we made with a couple of resorts on this trip."

Sam Katzenbaum ran a pudgy pink hand over his hairless scalp. The portly, middle-aged bank vice president gave Ross's single-page financial statement a last doleful look, then removed rimless glasses and regarded the owners of Allied Air, Inc., with a pained expression.

"Ross, Alex—First National is in the business of loaning money. We *want* to loan money. Your VA loan is insured. Why, then, I imagine you're asking yourself, can't I extend your line of credit indefinitely?

"You're both hard workers. I believed when we made your loan that it was a sound investment. I still believe that. You'll pull out of your financial reversals, loss of that second DC-3 notwithstanding. But the harsh facts of life boil down to this: we have bank examiners to contend with; even VA-insured loans must be serviced."

Ross noticed Alex's face take on that angry, pugnacious look that signaled an outburst, and he laid a restraining hand on his arm. The byplay didn't go unnoticed. Katzenbaum spread his hands beseechingly. "To be blunt, gentlemen, the loan committee is tightening the purse strings. Right now your assets roughly equal your loan balance. An extension of your line of credit places you in a deficit situation."

"Look, Mister Katzenbaum, we know you've bent over backward to help. We appreciate it," Ross said. "But the air freight business is just beginning to boom; it's the way high-value cargo is going to be moved. Another year and we'll be solvent, I'm sure of it."

"Ross," the banker responded sadly, "you're right, the air freight business does have a good future. But look at what's happening. Big business is getting into the act. A group of wealthy investors just started an outfit called Flying Tigers on the West Coast. They're picking up four-engine planes. Right here in Kansas City, Southern Railways is branching out into air freight.

"Soon they'll start cutting rates. You small operators are going to face some real tough times. Those who are in good financial condition can maybe hang on, but having to repay big loans will sink you."

"Are you suggesting we sell out while we can?" Ross asked, a harsh note of complaint in his voice. "Alex and I have every dime we came out of the army with in this business, Mister Katzenbaum. You say our assets equal our loan balance. Okay, we sell out and we're stone broke! It's a grim outlook."

Katzenbaum leaned back in his chair. He fiddled with the gold watch chain draped across his ample midsection. A frown creased his forehead. Finally he leaned forward and, crossing his arms on the polished desktop, said, "Ross, Alex—what I'm about to tell you has nothing to do with the bank. I want that clearly understood. I'm talking to you now as a friend, completely outside my association with First National. Okay?"

The two airmen responded with nods and puzzled expressions. The still-frowning banker chose his words with unaccustomed care. "I can put you in touch with a person looking for a reliable air freight operation. You may find some of the aspects of your contract to be, shall we say, unorthodox. I can say with reasonable assurance that there is nothing illegal involved. Beyond that, I'll try not to influence your decision. Would you like to meet with this person?"

Ross shrugged. "What's the alternative? Are you saying you'll shut down Allied Air if we don't take this mysterious contract?"

"Your loan application exceeds my personal approval authority," Katzenbaum replied firmly. "It must be referred to the loan committee and, as I believe I implied, I'm not optimistic regarding their decision."

Alex uttered a short, barking laugh. "But if we do take this contract, then the committee is just going to open up the vault to us—right?"

"I believe your contract would include a loan guarantee," the banker replied stiffly.

Ross's eyes widened. He gave a low whistle. "I think we'll listen."

"Very well. First, I'd like you to attend a meeting tonight." He scribbled an address on a sheet of notepaper and passed it to Ross. "Just go and listen. Then, if you're free for lunch tomorrow, I'll meet you at noon in the Kansas City Club."

Ross paid the cabdriver and examined his destination with bemused surprise. He was alone. Alex had begged off, claiming that the DC-3's right engine needed attention. Ross had expected a sparsely furnished hall with folding chairs and a plywood podium. Instead, he stood in a wide circular driveway beneath a porte cochere that would accommodate a Greyhound bus. The house, a three-story structure of pink brick with white columns, could serve as a hotel—or a museum—he decided. Had he copied the address incorrectly?

He shrugged and followed a smartly dressed couple just emerging from a chauffeur-driven Caddie. A frock-coated butler eyed Ross's corduroy sports coat and open-necked shirt and nodded stiffly. The increasingly curious pilot joined perhaps a hundred other people in an ornately appointed ballroom. He accepted a cocktail from a passing waiter and found an obscure observation post.

Ross's attention drifted to a tableau alongside a small podium. A woman wearing khaki shorts matched by a military-cut shirt with button-down pockets and epaulets was engaged in deep conversation with a matronly brunette dressed in a severely cut evening gown of green velvet. A man in a tuxedo, his mane of iron gray hair contrasting with his florid complexion, hovered nearby.

The background of murmured conversation projected social status, power, and wealth. Ross guessed that most of the group could buy his entire business from their personal checking accounts.

Their hostess—the matronly brunette—clapped her hands and conversations subsided. In modulated, finishing-school tones, she asked the audience to find seats. Ross's interest waned after only minutes of the woman's gushing description of their latest drive to collect warm, sensible wearing apparel. From his vantage point in the rear row of chairs, he randomly selected members of the group for study. He settled on one man, two rows forward and at a slight angle.

The man didn't belong here, he decided—no more than he did. First, his tux was not of the quality and fit of the others—undoubtedly a rental. Another thing he noticed, the man's face revealed no trace of emotion. Everyone else reacted to the speaker's words with enthused expressions, feigned or real.

Okay, Katzenbaum sent me to some kind of a fund-raiser, Ross said to himself, but why? He continued to study the man in the rented tux. Ross searched unsuccessfully for some distinguishing feature. All the other men in the audience had some unique characteristic. One was completely bald; another had large, bat-wing ears; another had a birthmark. The object of Ross's study had none. He was the type of person whom witnesses would describe as having average build, average looks.

The fellow periodically diverted his attention from the speaker to survey those seated around him. When he did, the expression in his deep-set black eyes resembled a snake's inquiring look. It was during one of these moments that Ross saw him shift an object inside the breast pocket of his ill-fitting jacket.

Ross's attention returned to the front. The khaki shorts–clad woman was being introduced. Young? Middle-aged? he wondered. It was hard to tell. Straight black hair that hung nearly to her shoulders framed strong, olive-toned features. Square-cut bangs gave her a faintly prim appearance. Her eyes belied that first impression. Round, brown, and somewhat widely spaced, they swept the room with restless, probing glances. With a generous, curving mouth, the overall effect was one of sensuality.

"Ladies and gentlemen," the elegantly dressed hostess announced, "I have the great pleasure of introducing Miss Ariel Shamir. Less than two months ago, Miss Shamir resided in the Kibbutz Ramat Hakovish, near the Upper Galilee. She will describe conditions there. Miss Shamir . . ."

Just before Ross began to concentrate on the woman's opening remarks, a thought flashed through his mind. That guy has a pistol under his jacket. Now who the hell would come armed to a dull event like this?

He didn't dwell on the matter, however. Ariel Shamir's first words captured his undivided attention. "Ladies and gentlemen, when you return to your comfortable beds tonight, just before you go to sleep, take this thought with you: Palestine, our promised homeland, lives and sleeps with a dagger at its throat."

Ross's boredom disappeared. He couldn't take his eyes off the speaker. Her muscular, compact body radiated magnetic intensity. Her eyes burned with a fervor matched by words that battered the sleek, well-fed listeners like storm-tossed waves. "Roving bands of Arab outlaws raid our farms and villages. In the cities, shops are burned and looted. Not a day goes by that doesn't see our people savagely beaten or killed in the streets—yes, even raped.

"No hand is raised against the perpetrators." Ariel's icy tone froze expressions of even the most blasé. "How can this be? you ask. Palestine is a protectorate of the British—a highly civilized people. Where are their forces of law and order? We are told they have a peacekeeping mission numbering more than one hundred thousand men."

After a pause to allow her audience to digest her grim message, Ariel continued. "The truth is, ladies and gentlemen, that the Arabs already control our so-called homeland. They do so because the powerful nations that defeated Adolf Hitler fear the millions of undisciplined jackals who control the oil, the Suez Canal, and the latent savagery that is the Middle East.

"Arabs openly boast that once the British withdraw from Palestine—and they will—the streets will be awash with Jewish blood. They say this with the full knowledge of, and absence of protest by, our protectors. Even more frightening is the refusal to provide the Jewish citizenry with a means of self-protection—all the while selling guns, tanks, ships, and planes to our sworn enemy.

"But, a steel ring of British ships and planes prevents our importing defensive weaponry. Even our refugees from the death camps are excluded from their rightful homes. They languish in detention camps where living conditions are little better than those they left behind. The reason given? To allow more than token immigration would upset the Arab-Jewish balance of population! This—in a land supposedly ours!"

Ross was among the first to leave. The fish-faced butler grudgingly agreed to call a cab for him. Leaning against a rococo pillar outside, Ross pondered the fiery woman's parting words to her electrified audience.

"Mrs. Kastor showed me the gratifying sum of money pledged here tonight," Ariel had concluded. "It will be put to good use, I assure you. But, my friends, our people cannot eat money. They cannot hurl it at an invading horde, and they cannot purchase peace and security the way one buys meat and vegetables at the marketplace. Those precious commodities come only, as Winston Churchill put it, with an expenditure of blood, sweat, and tears.

"We require young men and women along with the actual hardware to guard our homes. That is our true mission: to defy, circumvent, bribe—to do anything necessary to prepare for that rapidly approaching day when we must protect ourselves."

Them was fightin' words, if ever I've heard 'em, Ross observed to himself. But why the hell did Sam send me to hear some broad carrying on about a squabble between Jews and Arabs?

The expressionless man Ross had studied inside emerged from the entryway. He glanced at his watch and paced the driveway in quick, irritated steps. "You waiting for a cab?" Ross asked. "I have one on the way, if you'd care to share."

"No. I have a car coming for me," was the curt response.

Well, up yours, too, Ross thought. And thank *you* for offering a lift. He realized that the man had turned and was scrutinizing Ross's casual attire. "Are you involved in this business?" the man asked abruptly.

"Business?" Ross asked. "I didn't realize this was a business meeting. No, I'm in the air cargo–hauling game. I'm Ross Colyer." He extended a hand. "I have a little two-plane operation flying out of Fairfax."

The lean, tuxedo-clad man ignored the outstretched hand. "I didn't think you belonged to this crowd," he said. "You an ex-GI?"

Ross's first impulse was to tell the man to go to hell with his rude manner. He settled for withdrawing his hand and giving a brief reply. "Right. I was a P-51 pilot in the Pacific theater this time last year."

The man grunted. "My advice is for you to stick to throttle bending. These people, that speaker especially, are a bunch of radicals."

Ross's jaw set. "I don't recall asking for your advice, whoever you are, but since we're offering it for free, *I* suggest you find a different tailor—and a better place to wear that artillery you seem to find it necessary to carry."

The man's dark eyes blazed. "You're not only stupid, you have a smart mouth. Like I said, you'd best stick to driving airplanes."

Before Ross could frame a fitting reply, a dark gray Chevy sedan displaying U.S. government license plates stopped beside them. A hard-faced youngster wearing slacks and a dark sports jacket slipped from behind the steering wheel and opened the car's rear door. His passenger entered and slammed the door behind him, leaving Ross without a recipient for his angry retort.

Chapter 2

25 July 1946
Kansas City

Ross and Alex entered the Kansas City Club's elegant gray marble and mahogany-paneled foyer at exactly noon. A concierge, resplendent in black serge with blue and white trim, looked down his nose at the pair and greeted them with an icy, "Yes?"

Ross grinned. His one and only gray suit wasn't exactly what the well-dressed executive would select, but Alex's scuffed leather A-2 jacket, plaid shirt, and khaki work pants drew glances. "We're to meet Sam Katzenbaum for lunch," Ross told the disapproving minion.

After consulting a list, the man nodded at Alex. "If the gentleman would like a tie, I can provide one from our selection in the cloakroom."

Alex gave every indication of turning on his heel and leaving. Ross placed a hand on his angry partner's arm. "If you have something subdued, my friend would be most grateful," he replied, deadpan.

Suitably attired, Ross and Alex emerged from an elevator into the dining room. A stony-faced headwaiter steered them to a corner table. Sam Katzenbaum looked up and gave them a warm smile. "Ah, Ross, Alex—so glad you could make it."

Ross looked at the woman seated beside Sam. He recognized the intense speaker from the previous night's fund-raiser. She now wore a well-cut suit made of a dark blue silky fabric with just a touch of lace at the throat to relieve the masculine image.

14

Katzenbaum turned to her. "Ariel Shamir, I'd like you to meet Ross Colyer and Alex Taylor, owners and operators of Allied Air, Incorporated."

Ross accepted the proffered hand, noting the strong, blunt fingers with plain, close-cut nails. She didn't wear more than a hint of makeup, he observed. Her husky, "I'm so pleased to meet you," reinforced his first impression—here was a no-nonsense woman. Why then, he wondered, did the word *sexy* come to mind?

Sam ordered lunch for the party without looking at a menu. Ross found himself studying the woman to the exclusion of the other two. As they sipped martinis, she smoked long brown cigarets. She spoke in clipped, direct sentences, emphasizing her words with hand movements. But his gaze always returned to her eyes. Close up he could see that gold flecks in the brown irises gave them a penetrating intensity that couldn't be ignored.

"What is your view of the Palestine situation, Mister Colyer?" she asked partway through lunch.

Ross, caught off guard, stammered, "Why—uh—seems the British have their hands full. There appear to be more displaced people in Europe wanting to emigrate than the country has room for."

Ariel chewed a bite of sole without shifting her direct look. After swallowing, she asked, "Do you know that part of the world?"

"Only vaguely," Ross replied. "I flew for a time out of Benghazi, Libya—then a short stay in Turkey, and a stopover in Syria."

"What were you doing there?"

"Well"—Ross gave a deprecatory laugh—"it was during the war. I was a B-24 pilot. We had to divert to Turkey after a bad mission over the Ploesti oil refineries. We were interned. We—my crew and I— conned the Turks into letting us restore the airplane to flyable condition. One morning we just flew away—landed in Syria at a British base, refueled, and returned to Benghazi."

The woman's expression didn't change. "I understand you were based in England for a time. How did you get on with the British?"

Ross chuckled. "Well enough, I guess. They're different."

"Different in what way?"

"Oh"—Ross frowned slightly, annoyed at her persistence—"they drink their beer warm, eat at odd times of the day or night, are stubborn as hell about a lot of things, and"—he grinned—"where we were at least, the girls didn't shave their armpits."

His attempt at humor fell flat. Ariel stirred her coffee, pushed her clean plate aside, and lit another cigaret. She stared intently at Ross. "Are you available for an exclusive freight-hauling contract?"

Before Ross could respond, Katzenbaum stood. "Look, I have a board meeting shortly and must leave. Why don't you finish your business discussions over coffee and dessert? I've taken care of the tab; feel free to stay as long as you want and order anything else you'd like."

Ross expressed his thanks for the lunch.

"About that business we discussed yesterday, Ross," Sam said in parting. "Call me tomorrow, okay?"

They watched the pudgy banker waddle toward the elevator, then Ross returned his gaze to Ariel. "Freight hauling is our business, Miss Shamir. And, yes, we're available."

"Very well. We pay prevailing ton-mile rates and guarantee a net return, after all expenses, of a thousand dollars per month. For that, we require first option, on twenty-four-hours' notice, for use of your airplanes."

Ross glanced at Alex, who grinned hugely. "I'd say your terms are highly satisfactory, ma'am," he said. "Do you have your own contract form, or would you want to use our standard agreement?"

Ariel extended her hand. "This is my contract, Mister Colyer. A handshake is good enough for me; I hope it is sufficient for your needs."

"We-l-l," Ross demurred. "It's a departure from our usual procedure. Then there's the bank. We need an extension of our line of credit. Mister Katzenbaum, I'm sure, would prefer to see a signed contract."

"Mister Katzenbaum will have our assurance immediately upon your acceptance."

"I see. Look, Miss Shamir—"

She held up a hand. "Ariel, please, uh—Ross, Alex."

"Okay, Ariel. I hate to appear hesitant, but who—what firm—do you represent?"

"It's a large charitable foundation, Ross."

"Its name?"

A slight frown flickered. "The Jewish Relief Foundation."

"I see. And what, generally, will we be carrying? You mentioned a freight run—passengers as well?"

"Very infrequent, if any, passengers. Your loads will be mixed. There will be no manifests or bills of lading, by the way."

Ross raised his eyebrows.

"There's no need." Ariel's voice carried an edge. "The cargo will consist of clothing, medicine, and the like for refugee families. The foundation is both shipper and consignee, so rules covering interstate shipping don't apply. Most of your flights will be from collection points to New York—Teterboro Field, New Jersey, to be more specific."

"Ariel," Ross responded, "I attended that meeting you spoke at last night." He ignored Alex's startled look and continued. "I received the distinct impression that there is more involved in your agency's activity than just collecting old clothes."

The woman's expression remained impassive. "I hope you enjoyed the meeting, Ross. I didn't see you, I'm sorry. Do you disagree with what I said?"

"No-o-o, can't say I did. But I don't want any misunderstanding. I operate within the law, and rules laid down by the Interstate Commerce Commission."

"You will not be asked to violate the law."

Ross paused while the waiter refilled his coffee cup. "I'm glad to hear that, because *someone* seems concerned about the legality of what you're doing."

Ariel's gaze sharpened. "I'm not sure I understand."

"I spoke with a man as I was leaving—a rather nasty type, I might add—who seemed very interested in your speech. He left in a car that had U.S. government license plates and he carried a pistol under his tux."

Ross watched Ariel closely as he spoke, and saw her catch her breath slightly. "I imagine he was with the Federal Bureau of Investigation," she said, recovering quickly. "Their agents have taken an interest in our fund-raising efforts of late. Given the publicity the Jewish situation in Palestine is creating, I suppose it's inevitable. However, I repeat that you will not be asked to take part in any illegal operations."

"That seems to cover everything, then," Ross said somewhat skeptically. "Do you have a date for the first run?"

"No, but it will be probably six weeks to two months from now. Tomorrow morning I'll arrange an extension of your line of credit with your bank. Then I must return to Palestine. I will give you a check for one thousand dollars as a retainer before I leave."

Ross blinked, then turned to Alex. His saturnine partner shrugged. Deciding he'd had enough surprises for one day, Ross stood and extended his hand. "Deal. I look forward to doing business with you, ma'am—uh, Ariel. See you in six to eight weeks."

Ross eased the battered '34 Ford into traffic and turned to Alex. "Well, what do you think? Was that action fast enough for you?"

Taylor rode in silence for several moments, staring through the windshield. "I don't think I like it," he said finally.

"What? Jesus Christ, man, any operator would drool over a can't-lose deal like this. We're back in business. Can't you see?"

"You've put your finger right on it. It's what I *can't* see that has my Scotch-Irish ancestors nudging me," Alex said morosely. "I can't see Katzenbaum's motive in this little deal. Did you notice how he jumped up and ran when she started getting down to specifics? Something tells me he doesn't *want* to know what's going on.

"I can't see some charity outfit laying out the kind of money she's talking about for a bunch of secondhand clothes and the like. Hell, they could send the money to Europe and buy new stuff with a lot less effort. And the goddamned FBI—that scares the hell out of me. No, there's something off color about the whole thing. Plus, I don't like the woman."

"Aha!" Ross exclaimed. "Now it comes out. Big, macho Alex doesn't like the idea of taking orders from a woman."

"Not that one, at least," was the prompt rejoinder. "Do you?"

Ross sobered. "To tell you the absolute truth, no. But, damnit, this is a sink-or-swim thing. I'll live with it. Can you?"

"I'll stick around for another upcard, and I'll keep my mouth shut—after one more piece of advice."

"What's that?"

"You've heard what a black widow spider does after she mates, haven't you?"

"Yeah, she kills the male."

"Right. Just keep that in mind."

"What the hell is that supposed to mean?" Ross snapped.

"You got the hots for that woman. You show all the signs of a man about to do something stupid."

Ross opened his mouth to speak, then, fishlike, closed it. The picture of Ariel Shamir he carried in his mind was constructed around those disturbing, gold-flecked eyes, full red lips, and a generous bosom that her blue jacket couldn't conceal.

Parked in front of their cubbyhole office back at Fairfax, Ross found time to wish he'd pressed that matter of FBI interest. Damnit, if we just didn't need this contract so badly. . . . He pushed the disturbing implication from his thoughts.

28 July 1946
Washington, D.C.
Colonel Ted Wilson and his wife were already ensconced at a corner table when Ross entered the hotel dining room. He gave them a friendly wave, noticing that two young men wearing natty uniforms of army pinks with dark green Ike jackets—gold bars on their shoulders and sporting silver wings—sat between them. Declining the hostess's effort to seat him, he joined the middle-aged couple. "Morning, Colonel Ted, Doris," he said in greeting.

"Hi there, Mister Airline Executive," the craggy-faced colonel responded. "You're looking disgustingly hale and hearty this morning. Take a seat—we're only having our first cup of coffee. I want you to meet our son, Kyle. He's just out of Randolph and on his way to Muroc Field in the Mojave Desert to fly one of the new jet-engine fighters. And this is Matt Yost. He's staying with Kyle—they were roommates at VMI. Guys, meet Ross Colyer."

Ross gave Kyle a swift appraisal as the youthful officers sprang to their feet. Of average height and build—something less than Ross's own six feet two—he was good-looking, Ross observed as he accepted the young man's outthrust hand. He had a mop of curly black hair, and dark eyes—Doris's, Ross decided. They had that perpetual sparkle of sardonic amusement. I'll bet the San Antonio mothers are breathing easier now that Kyle's leaving Randolph, Ross said to himself.

Yost could have been the clone of any one of the thousands of young, handsome graduates produced by the prestigious Virginia Military Institute. Ross returned his firm handshake and suddenly felt old. Good God, was he ever this young and eager?

Kyle gave Ross an engaging grin. "Major Colyer. A real pleasure to finally meet you, sir. I've heard so much about you. My parents have told the story a hundred times of how you led that cadet down after Dad had his heart attack."

"Greatly exaggerated, I'm sure," Ross responded lightly. "And please, drop the 'major' and 'sir' bit. That's history." He moved to Doris's side, and she turned her cheek for a friendly peck of greeting.

"You are permitted one cup of coffee, then I want to hear how your reunion with Janet went last winter. All of it, too, you hear?" Doris stated firmly in the way of greeting.

"That's enough, Doris," Ted chided. "You're embarrassing the poor guy. I want to hear how the air charter business is going and why we haven't seen or heard from you for more than six months."

Ted turned to Lieutenant Yost. "Don't let anyone kid you. But for Ross, I wouldn't be here today. In fact, if not for a rotten bit of luck, you're looking at a guy who could have been chief of staff one day—still might, by God."

"See what I mean about exaggeration?" Ross told the raptly attentive pair of fledgling officers. He smiled fondly at the shapely, full-bodied brunette, her dark eyes sparkling with unconcealed glee. "To answer your question, Doris, we went to a movie, had a steak dinner, and reminisced about the old days at Hickam Field before the war. A delightful evening."

Doris responded with a most unladylike raspberry. "You damn men," she said. "You're all alike. Don't tell me a handsome couple like you and Janet sat through a movie, had dinner, and just talked about the 1941 army-navy game. Are you trying to tell me that's *all?* I want the juicy stuff. Did she wear a sexy dress? Was there any smooching? Did either one of you bawl?"

"*Doris!* Ye gods, is nothing sacred with you?" Wilson asked, affecting a shocked tone. "Ross, tell her to mind her own damn business."

"No, it isn't," Doris protested good-naturedly. "When it comes to my favorite flyboy, the one who saved my guy's life, I am a very proprietary female. Don't worry, I'll get the really interesting dope straight from the babe's mouth," she added with a salacious leer. "Janet wrote me she's going to be in town next week to cover some Arab sheik's visit. I'll find out what went on, never fear. You know what they say about truth and the mouths of babes."

Ross waited until the waitress had deposited cups and a carafe of coffee on their table before he spoke. "Doris, your horrible puns grow steadily worse, if that's possible." He grinned and poured coffee.

"It was a somewhat surprising situation," he continued. "Frankly, I believe we both expected to pick up where we left off before she married BT. It didn't work out that way, but you won't get the 'salacious details' from me, Miss Nosy. And if you're hinting for an invitation to a wedding, forget it. We shook hands when we parted and agreed to see each other again sometime—as good friends."

Doris's flippant air disappeared. "I'm sorry, Ross, truly sorry," she murmured.

As Kyle topped off everyone's coffee cup, he nodded at Ross. "Matt and I wanted to talk to you about fighter school—er—Major. Do you mind?"

Ross shook his head. "That's okay—shoot. But if you're gonna be flying jets, I'm afraid anything I can tell you is obsolete."

"Is it as rough as they say?" Kyle asked eagerly. "Should we have maybe asked for bombers?"

Ross laughed, his mood lightening. "Yeah, it's tough, but it can be fun, too. And as for asking for a particular plane, just let nature take its course. If you have a genuine love of flying, it doesn't make any difference in the end. But then, I'm not exactly in a position to offer expert advice."

"That's a bunch of you know what, Ross Colyer," Doris snapped. "You always were, and always will be, one of the best pilots in the business. Now, you say you're leaving today? I'd hoped you could stay over. You look in need of a party. We're having some people in tomorrow evening to meet Kyle and Matt, including some unattached females, naturally—hint, hint."

"Sorry." Ross made a rueful grimace. "I gotta get back. This hasn't been a good month for me all around. The Norseman is down for an engine change, and Alex wants to put the bird we're flying in for overhaul before we get into a big contract."

"Well, I can see why you're anxious to get back home," Wilson conceded. "Look, Doris, why don't you and the boys grab a cab. I'll wait for Ross to pack and run him to the airport."

"No way," Doris yelped, then caught her husband's direct look and ended with a muttered, "well, I *do* have things to do at home."

Good-byes were exchanged and Wilson followed Ross to his room. The sober-faced colonel cleared his throat, then mumbled, "Wanted to talk with you a bit without the boys around."

"Sure. You have a fine-looking son there, Colonel. I like him—and his friend, too."

"Yeah, I have to admit to a bit of pride. Kyle graduated at the top of his class, you know."

Ross looked up from stuffing dirty laundry into his battered B-4 bag. "Hey, how about that?" he enthused. "I'll bet Doris all but blew a gasket."

"That she did." Wilson smiled briefly. Then, looking mildly embarrassed, he changed the subject. "I hear you weren't called to testify at the Ploesti hearing. Is that right?"

"Yeah. The board recorder looked at my deposition and said he didn't feel I had anything new to add."

"That whole business was a farce," Colonel Wilson grumbled. "Senator Templeton used his position as chairman of the Military Affairs Committee to have it convened. He wasn't interested in the high loss rate; he just wanted to get his name in print—and maybe pin the blame for his son's death on someone. Do you know if that subject came up?"

"Janet attended every session, and she says not. She was able to sit in only because Templeton used his influence. 'She's my son's widow, you know. She has every right . . .' Bullshit. He's spoken with her only once since BT got himself killed.

"I guess he wasn't satisfied with just blocking my application for a regular commission. Hell, he should have known I didn't have anything to do with that affair. *He's* the one who smuggled the bribe money to BT; he as much as told Janet about it.

"Anyway, about Allied Air. We're struggling. We lost one of our two DC-3s in a hangar fire. The outfit doing the maintenance had let their insurance lapse, and promptly declared bankruptcy. We'll be lucky to collect ten cents on the dollar. But things are looking up. We just signed a juicy contract with some charitable foundation, and this run to D.C. with a rush shipment of optical equipment will put bread on the table until that job kicks in."

Wilson's face tightened in an empathic grimace. "It almost makes me ashamed to tell you my *good* news."

"What's that?" Ross looked up, showing new interest.

"Well, this ol' hoss had his physical exam last week. Not only do I *not* qualify for total-disability retirement, the old ticker has healed to the point that I can stay on active duty without a waiver. Not on flying status, of course, but now I'm at least good for twenty."

"That's great news! Hey, congratulations. I know you weren't looking forward to early retirement. Where will you be assigned?"

"Hard to say right now. Things are very much in a state of flux. Being in personnel has its advantages, of course, but the tables of organization are still being hammered out for a postwar force. Then the air force is putting on pressure to form its own independent service—separate and equal to the army and navy. Now *that* will be worth staying around to watch."

"Oh, man, will it ever," Ross replied excitedly. Then his expression dulled. "I guess I'll just have to be satisfied flying cargo to and from places like Dubuque and Little Rock. Let Kyle and his friend Matt have the fun."

"It's a goddamn shame," Wilson said. "With your record, the decorations you racked up, you should be commanding a fighter squadron. Ross," Wilson chose his words carefully, "would you consider coming back on active duty—as a reservist?"

Ross laughed, a bitter, barking sound devoid of merriment. "To do what? I was told once that—as a reserve officer—I'd never get a command job. I was asking myself after V-J Day: just what does a fighter pilot *do* during peacetime? It could be a pretty dull existence, you know. At least in the air cargo business I'm flying."

"I can't blame you for being pissed off, Ross. But don't think for a minute that there's no need to maintain a strong military force. I sat in on a briefing just last week where potential hot spots around the world were discussed. Take China, for example. This guy Mao Tse-tung has in mind putting all of China under communist rule; you saw that during your tour in the CBI. The Russkies are sending out signals that they're getting set for a land-grabbing poker game. Even in your old stomping grounds—the Middle East—the Jews are demanding that Palestine be declared their homeland. They're not only trying to drive out the Arabs, they've squared off against the British, who have an old League of Nations mandate to administer the country."

Wilson sat on the edge of Ross's bed and tapped his open palm with one finger. "But look at what's happening: there's a blind, hysterical movement to demobilize. The damned politicians. Some of the older military heads, men like Eisenhower and Marshall, are quietly moving to fill the void that's taking shape.

"First, there's little doubt that we'll get an independent air force. It'll take time, but it's coming. Then there's the matter of manpower. The skills our veterans have will be obsolete within another year or two, especially in aviation. So here's the thinking: take people like yourself, in the standby reserve, and create a *ready* reserve. Give them some airplanes to fly, keep them up to date on new developments;

pattern the thing after the National Guard. Hell, it could even include guard units."

Ross screwed his face into a thoughtful frown. "Congress will have a field day. When they finish with the idea, you'll never recognize it."

"Maybe"—Wilson's expression was grim—"but we *can't* sit back and let our armed forces drift into the sorry state we were in before Pearl Harbor."

"What are you trying to tell me, Colonel? That I should forget about Allied Air and come back on active duty—*if* his royal highness, Templeton, deigns to let me do even that?"

"Just planting a seed, Ross—just planting a seed. If—no, not *if, when*—this comes to pass, it will take good men to make it work. Think about it."

Ross gazed into the darkness as the now empty DC-3 droned homeward through the clear night air. Concern for their floundering little company was crowded aside, however, by the memory of Colonel Wilson's last words: ". . . need for a strong military force . . ." and ". . . you belong in a uniform. . . ." A picture of Kyle Wilson's trim, youthful figure flashed across his mind—a kid like that flying *jets*. Screw 'em all, Ross thought savagely. I'll get by.

Chapter 3

7 August 1946
Kibbutz Kafir Haviv, Palestine
Issy Fein's sharp, hooked nose and flashing dark eyes made her look every inch the Arab she pretended to be. She stood only inches from a man wearing the uniform of a British army captain and examined his appearance with a critical eye. "Papers," she snapped. After a close look at the captain's identity card, she continued. "When did your regiment move from Haifa?"

"We were never stationed at Haifa, ma'am. The 16th has always been at El Azir."

Issy nodded and moved to the next man, her quick, birdlike movements belying her sixty years. "Papers," she said, this time to a man wearing the chevrons of a lance corporal in the Royal Artillery. After a glance at the scrap of paper, she threw her hands into the air. "Ayiee," she wailed. "Where in the Prophet's name did you come by this worthless piece of camel dung?"

"Uh—I got it with my uniform, ma'am," the red-faced youngster replied.

"This is an *off-duty* pass, you imbecile. The Brits issued new identity documents with diagonal green stripes more than two weeks ago." She turned back to the man posing as a captain. "Dov, we *must* improve upon this matter of papers. You would all be sacked if Yoel had flashed that pass."

Dov Friedman removed the red beret from his close-cropped blond hair and hiked himself onto the tabletop behind him. Although he was a Polish refugee, few took his fair complexion and blue eyes as evidence of Jewish ancestry. He lit a cigaret and grinned at the fiery woman. "I don't know what we would do without you, Issy. Is there anything about the Brits you don't know? We stole that pass less than two weeks ago. The devils keep changing procedures, ID, and the like more often than they take baths. How do you do it?"

"I keep my eyes open and my mouth shut." The dark-garbed woman sniffed. "The British miss their fresh eggs more than their wives. A crazy old Arab woman, roaming their camps selling *beyyd,* can go anywhere. Now, who are your drivers? They must each have three permits. I wish to inspect them."

"Ariel will drive the officers' scout car. Jack will have the truck."

"Well, at least you'll have someone with brains behind the wheel." She turned to where Ariel Shamir stood watching, her generous lips parted in amusement at the old woman's caustic comments. "My dear, how are you? I understand you've just returned from a journey."

Ariel's brown eyes twinkled. "I'm well, Mother Fein. Yes, I was away." She didn't elaborate. "And you?"

"My bones ache, my stomach rumbles, and my mind plays tricks on me," Issy grumbled. She eyed Ariel's military garb and chuckled. "You look absolutely fetching, my dear. Just take care this loutish person"—she nodded at Dov—"doesn't make indecent advances. This is a raid into enemy territory, not some romantic lark." She scanned Ariel's pass, and added softly, "Now be off with you. *Abi gezunt.*" Faces softened at the woman's traditional benediction, meaning, "'S long as you have your health," bestowed on soldiers going into battle.

Ariel concentrated on holding the scout car away from the treacherous ditches as she negotiated the winding, muddy track. Fine rain, not heavy enough to make the wipers work properly, made vision difficult. Dov, slouched in the passenger's seat, asked, "And where did the Palmach discover you? Pretty girls are not often found in these parts."

"I grew up in Haifa," Ariel replied without taking her eyes off the road. "Of late, I've lived in a kibbutz near the Sea of Galilee."

Dov's eyes crinkled at the corners. "Please don't regale me with a long dissertation covering what *must* be your thoroughly fascinating life."

"I shan't."

"I'm sure you won't," Dov responded good-humoredly. "Is this your first raid? I have a right to know that, you see," he added hastily—"an official inquiry into the qualifications of those in my unit."

Ariel shot him a sidewise glance. Looking straight ahead once more, she answered, "It's my first raid for arms. But I—I—well, I can use that Bren gun clipped to the dash there, as well as the Webley revolver you carry. Does that satisfy you?"

"Marginally," Dov replied. He turned in his seat to confirm that the stolen British army truck, its altered markings having received the approval of Issy Fein, was still following. It was. A half-dozen British-uniformed Palmach troops crouched inside the tarp-covered bed with Bren guns ready. The weapons they carried represented his unit's entire arms inventory. Only three of the automatic weapons held full magazines—hence their carefully planned sortie against the heavily guarded Royal Air Force (RAF) armory.

The rain was increasing, Dov noticed with a frown. Twice he'd seen Ariel downshift to negotiate deep, mud-filled potholes. The inclement weather would make the guards less alert; that was good. But it would also slow down their escape; that was bad. He shrugged. One couldn't have it both ways. "Another ten minutes, I judge," he told Ariel. "Remember, park your vehicle alongside the truck, facing the gate. If you hear two blasts on my whistle, get the hell out. Don't wait for me or anyone else. Floorboard it and crash the barrier. Forget about unlimbering that gun—just go."

Ariel nodded. "There's the main entrance just ahead," she said matter-of-factly.

She expertly swung the little scout car between two rows of coiled barbed wire and negotiated the concrete pylons, strategically placed to force vehicles to proceed at a walking pace. She halted at the striped-pole barrier and watched a slicker-clad soldier leave the gatehouse and trot toward them through the swirling rain.

Dov passed folded documents to the red-faced guard, whose military-style mustache was already dripping rainwater. "Rotten day, no?" Dov asked cheerfully. "I think I'll be glad to get back to the desert."

The guard slung his weapon onto his left shoulder and examined Dov's papers, shielding them beneath his slicker. "From El Azir, eh? After small arms and ammo, I see. Wot 'appened? The bloody Jews steal 'em all? Har, har, har."

"Not likely," Dov answered, seemingly piqued.

"You happen to spot any of the buggers on the way here?" the guard asked. "Potted two of our chaps last week, they did—on the road you just came over."

"You don't say?" Dov asked, an anxious frown on his face. "I don't suppose you could spare one of your armored cars to escort us back when we get loaded."

"'Fraid you'll have to see the major about that, sir. Doubt it mightily, though. The great bloody lot of stuff in our warehouses makes a tempting target. Security is top form just now. My orders are to check papers on everyone entering. Sorry, I can't just take your word."

Once both the car and truck were inside the compound, Dov directed Ariel. "Straight ahead to the third turn. Our warehouse is the last building on your left." He grinned. "Now you don't suppose I could talk that major out of an armored car escort, do you? What a prize! Imagine . . ." His voice trailed off wistfully.

"You would conceal it in the ablutions tent, I assume?" Ariel asked tartly.

"You do have a sense of humor after all," Dov replied. "Droll, but . . ." His manner changed abruptly. "Reverse into that parking row. Remember, keep the engine running and listen for the whistle." He leaped to the ground and waited for the soldiers from the truck to join him.

A uniformed guard, his rifle held at port arms, barred Dov's entrance to the warehouse. "Morning, sir," he said. "May I see your identification?"

Dov scanned the area swiftly—no one seemed interested. "Of course, Corporal." He withdrew the Webley and pointed it carelessly at the guard's midsection. "I am Lieutenant X, of the Jewish Defense Force— the Haganah, you know. Terribly sorry, but my Palmach troops are about to relieve you of some of your toys inside. May we come in?"

The young man's eyes bulged; his rifle remained pointed uselessly into thin air. "Sir—sir," he pleaded, "is this a joke, sir?"

"I couldn't be more serious, Corporal." Dov waved to the semicircle of hard-eyed Palmach troops, Bren guns leveled. "Now, will you summon your officer, or will you be next to die for king and country?"

An ashen-faced captain watched helplessly as the Jewish raiders swiftly transferred cases of Bren guns, Lee Enfield rifles, ammunition, and hand grenades into the waiting truck. "Small arms only," Dov snapped at one man hungrily eyeing a bin filled with four-inch mortars.

The truck, rated at one and a half tons, settled on its springs. Dov guessed they must have loaded close to two tons before he could bring himself to abandon the treasure trove. He ordered his men to tie the captain, the corporal, and two warehouse technicians with electrical wire, and took one more wistful look before giving the order to mount up. Exactly fifteen minutes after entering the arsenal, Dov returned the gate guard's snappy salute. Ariel led the way onto the now soggy roadway.

"Can't we go a bit faster?" Dov asked.

"The truck's having trouble keeping up," Ariel replied shortly. "Loaded as it is, Jack must be using its lowest gear."

"Damn." Dov struck his knee with a clenched fist. "Those men are going to be discovered any minute, and all hell's going to break loose." The words were no sooner out of his mouth when the *whoop, whoop, whoop* of an alarm siren ripped the rain-drenched air.

"That does it," Dov grated. "Take this next turn. We'll have to use back roads; they'll have armored cars on this one in minutes. Thank God the weather will keep their spotter planes grounded."

"Those roads are little more than goat tracks in places," said Ariel. "The truck will never make it."

"It will have to," Dov responded abruptly. "Too much work went into this raid to give up now."

Ariel shrugged and skidded the scout car onto a narrow, brush-lined track. She saw the truck lumber onto the slippery red-dirt surface and slowed to let it catch up. Minutes dragged as forward progress slowed to a crawl. Dov contained his impatience with visible effort. They once saw the soldiers leap to the ground and push the laden vehicle through a particularly difficult stretch. Steam formed an ominous plume from the truck's overheated engine.

Ariel braked to a stop. Dov looked up with a muttered, "What's . . . ," then stared ahead without completing his question. The track dipped into a wadi and crossed what was normally a dry wash. The channel now carried a sizable flow of swirling, reddish brown water.

Depression seemed to reduce the stature of the members of the little task force. Huddled in the rain, ankle deep in sucking mud, they regarded the dingy stream with stooped shoulders and dull eyes. Dov was the first to throw off his apathy. "Can you get the scout car across?" he snapped at Ariel.

"Perhaps—it's a tough little machine."

"Try," Dov directed. "The rest of you unload the truck. If we can get the car on the opposite bank, we can attach a cable and help pull the empty truck across. Then we'll carry the cargo over by hand. Move it now, let's go."

The Palmach troops recovered their former excitement and started heaving crates of arms onto the sodden roadway. Ariel shifted to low gear and eased into the murky stream. She felt the wheels slither, slip, then finally spin uselessly. The entire unloading crew jumped from the truck and ran into the knee-deep water. With every muscle straining, they inched the vehicle to firm ground.

The unloading completed, two mud-smeared, dripping men ran a cable from a drum attached to the truck's front bumper to the scout car's trailer hitch. Jack selected the ton-and-a-half truck's lowest gear. With the engine howling at top revs, the big vehicle waddled into the rushing water like a reluctant hippo. Ariel took up the slack in the cable and floorboarded the accelerator. With overheated tires spitting mud, steam, and smoke, the procession inched forward.

Reaching midstream, the big cargo carrier settled to a halt with an air of finality. Dov, panting and nearly exhausted, leaned his bedraggled frame on the scout car's fender. He snatched the sodden wool beret from his head and hurled it into the mud. "The lives of nine people placed at risk—a flawless operation—and because of this damn rain it's all been for nothing," he raged.

Ariel wanted to cry from frustration. "Dov," she called dejectedly, "load as many crates in this car as we can handle. The men will have to make their way back on foot, but we'll salvage something. There will be other opportunities. You did a magnificent job."

Only the whites of Dov's eyes were visible on his mud-caked face as he looked at Ariel. The glance was fleeting, but a bonding, sparked by shared danger, transcended mere words.

13 August 1946
Tel Aviv, Palestine

Dov Friedman stopped speaking in midsentence and held up his hand for silence. Larry Perlberg, slouched in the hotel room's only armchair, formed his lean, pockmarked features into an unspoken question. "Listen," Dov muttered. "There's a helluva lot of activity out there. Curfew was an hour ago. It has to be a roundup. Only the damn Brits would be driving around and talking in loud voices this time of night."

Perlberg unfolded his slightly built frame from the chair's depths and strode to the window. Standing to one side, he peered through a crack in the drapes. "You're right, it's a sweep. Street's blocked at both intersections, and they're in the buildings across from us. Wonder who they're after?"

Dov shook his head. "I don't see that it makes much difference. They're bound to go through this hotel, room by room. Do you have some inspired story to explain that suitcase filled with coffee sitting over there? Turkish coffee is almost never sold with percussion caps for pistol cartridges packed in it."

"Of course I have an explanation." Perlberg flashed a wicked grin, exposing unnaturally white teeth—replacements for those lost during a long-ago interrogation. "It belongs to you."

Dov laughed despite the gravity of their plight. "And who would believe an ugly, bald-headed bastard like you, when a clean-cut type like myself says otherwise? No, I'd say we have about thirty minutes to be elsewhere. Look, I'll throw our stuff together while you nip down to the desk and see what old Benny has to suggest."

Dov had just finished scooping up their scattered articles of clothing and stuffing them into a duffel bag when Larry rapped softly on the locked door. Dov let him in and queried, "Well?"

Larry shook his head. "It doesn't look good. Benny says this isn't just a spot check for papers. He's heard of at least a dozen other search parties out. They have pictures of Palmach leaders. It looks like a general roundup. Those coffee beans are the least of your worries, my friend."

Dov scratched his chin reflectively. "As far as I know, my name isn't on any of their lists. You can't ever be certain, though; their secret service never sleeps. We can't slip out and leave that suitcase behind, either. Benny would be arrested, and the hotel would be lost to us forevermore. No, we've got to get to the flying club, hole up until daylight, then take off just as planned."

"I can't wait to hear how you plan to do this vanishing act, Mister Houdini—with mirrors, maybe? Smoke?"

"Nope," Dov replied. "With coffee beans."

Thirty minutes later, Dov and Larry were crouched beneath Benny's reception counter. Movement was impossible. Dov cursed aching muscles and muttered, "What's taking so long, do you suppose?"

"Should happen any time now," Larry wheezed. "It's taken a while for that wood to catch and get hot enough. Any action on the street, Benny?"

The elderly, moon-faced proprietor mopped perspiration from his brow and adjusted horn-rimmed glasses. "They've finished across the street. I can't tell how close they are to this building. I still haven't counted more than six of them, by the way."

Dov heard it then. A series of crackling detonations ripped the silence and filtered through the open doorway. He grinned. Forty pounds of percussion caps filled with fulminate of mercury did set up a racket. The roof-mounted trash incinerator's heavy walls directed the magnified explosion up its brick chimney. All in all, it produced a most gratifying result.

Benny ran onto the street, yelling, "Fire! Fire on the roof. Help—people will be trapped inside their rooms. Help me get them out!"

The search party of British soldiers could no more resist rushing toward the disturbance than a rat can resist cheese. Dov heard booted feet pound past the desk. The soldiers weren't interested in saving lives, however. An explosion could only mean some type of hostile action.

At the last moment, he heard a hasty order for one man to remain behind and guard the gaping doorway. Benny promptly seized the man's arm and dragged him toward the stairs. "Come on," he urged. "Up these steps. You take the first floor, and I'll go to the next one."

The man broke free, protesting, "I can't leave my post, you old fool. You'll have to do it yourself." The exchange consumed possibly a half minute—by which time Dov and Larry were strolling along the sidewalk.

They crouched in a recessed entryway and scanned the empty street. Two armored cars sat crossways at either end of the block with their hatches open. Curious heads protruded, engrossed by flying sparks punctuated with random sounds resembling muffled pistol shots.

Dov grasped Larry's shoulder and spoke softly. "We must get across the street," he said. "They've searched those buildings. We can go through one and come out in the alley. Once we're away from this block, we're home free."

"How can we cross the street without being seen?" Larry muttered.

"Good question. A cat couldn't get across that street without being spotted by one of those cars."

"What if they were distracted?" Larry asked.

"It'd have to be a big distraction."

"Okay, look, Dov, I'm clean. True, I've been picked up and inter-
rogated a few times, but no arrests, nothing in the way of a record.
I'll go back to the hotel and act like a terrified guest. During the
commotion, maybe you can work your way around the back side of
that nearest car. They'll probably give me a bad time, but they're after
big names. They surely won't hold me. I'll plan to meet you at the
flying club tomorrow morning. If I'm not there"—he shrugged—"I'll
be in good company."

"No," Dov rasped. "We do this together."

"Don't be an ass. You know too much about the inner Haganah workings. The only things I can tell them, they already know."

Dov's grasp tightened until Larry winced. "You crazy bastard," he
said, his voice choked with emotion. "Don't get yourself shot."

A half hour later, Dov had covered the first stretch of his five-mile
hike to the airport. Memory of seeing two British soldiers drag Larry
into the rear of a covered truck burned like a consuming flame. Dov
eased around a corner to check the remote street for patrols. They were
conspicuously absent. He concluded that every available soldier was
involved in a big operation.

Dov's complacency caused him to move too far; he came face to
face with a man dressed in dark trousers and a pullover. They confronted each other without speaking. The other man brushed past and
continued his furtive progress. I'm not the only curfew violator abroad
tonight, Dov thought with a wry grin.

Dov throttled back and let the grimy little Piper Cub drift lower toward
the haze-enshrouded kibbutz. He searched for the all-clear signal—
a white sheet draped from the water tower. He was late. He'd dragged
out his preflight at Tel Aviv as long as he dared waiting for Larry.
After an hour he gave up and filed his flight plan for the Kibbutz
Ramat Hakovish.

The sentry waved to him from the water-tower platform, but he decided
to land anyway. He sideslipped the Cub to kill airspeed and altitude,
then let the little plane touch down alongside the plank-and-dirt perimeter fence. He immediately regretted his decision to ignore the missing
all-clear signal. It wasn't old Hiram driving the ancient, battered truck
jouncing out to meet him. It was two uniformed British soldiers wearing
dark berets.

Dov stepped to the ground, stretched stiffened muscles, and waited with an easy smile for his grim-faced greeting party. A burly NCO leaped from the truck and strutted toward him. "Hello, Sergeant," said Dov. "What brings you to this godforsaken place?"

"I'll ask you the same question," the man snapped. "And I'll trouble you for some identification."

"Sure thing." Dov fished for his wallet. "I'm with the flying club in Tel Aviv. We got a call last night that there's a very sick child here—needs hospital care. Are they on their way?"

The stolid-faced NCO took Dov's ID and returned to the truck without answering. Dov saw him consulting a clipboard and involuntarily held his breath. He relaxed as he saw the man shrug, toss the clipboard to the seat, and return. "I understand the child is out of danger," he said. "You are free to return to Tel Aviv."

"Just a minute," Dov protested. "I haven't had lunch. I have mail on board. The people here will have mail for me to take back."

"I'll take the mail you brought. There isn't any outgoing mail," the stony-faced sergeant responded. "As for lunch"—he shrugged—"it will be a late one for you today, I fear. Now, I emphasize, you are free to go—immediately."

Dov chewed his lower lip. Instinct told him to get the hell out—something was very wrong. Concern for Ariel surfaced. She was to meet him here—the meeting with the man from the United States. A stubborn streak resisted. "Look," he pleaded, "I don't know what's going on—and I don't really care. But I have between two and three hours flying ahead of me today, and I'm starved. Can't you at least let me pick up some bread and cheese and eat it in flight?"

The truculent NCO grunted. "There's no harm in it, I suppose. Man can't go without grub all day. Jump into the back. We'll run you to the dining hall. You eat and leave, however," he added sternly.

Dov strode into the empty dining room and seated himself at a long plank table. The soldiers took seats near the door. A gaunt-faced, elderly woman entered from the kitchen and stopped at Dov's table. "Good-morning, Dov," she greeted him. "You'll be wanting something, as usual. There's hot bread just coming from the oven. Did you bring mail?"

"I gave it to those two." Dov nodded toward the grim-faced soldiers.

"I see. You'd best wash those filthy hands while you wait for the bread to finish." The woman gave him a direct, piercing look and nodded almost imperceptibly.

Dov stood and casually told his two guards, "Going next door to wash up." He received a sullen nod in reply.

The washhouse was empty. Why was the old woman so insistent he come here? He poured water into a basin and rinsed his hands.

"Dov?" a hoarse, indistinct voice called.

He realized it came from the thin partition that separated the men's and women's facilities. "Yes," he replied.

"Quickly, we don't have much time," the invisible woman continued. "Last night was a disaster. They seized the entire stock of arms hidden here. Six hundred rifles, two cases of pistols, grenades—everything. They've arrested perhaps a dozen of the senior Haganah leaders—"

"Ben-Gurion?" Dov interrupted.

"No, thank heavens. He's in Paris. But find Issy. The meeting with the man from America is urgent. Set up a new place and time. Go! Now, while you can."

19 August 1946
Haifa, Palestine

Dov greeted David Ben-Gurion with a warm handshake, but with words rendered inane from shock at his old mentor's appearance. That indomitable confidence, normally radiating from the Haganah leader, was missing. His powerful features were gray and sunken; even the piercing gaze was reduced to a smolder.

"Dov, I'd like you to meet Julius Mantz," the weary Ben-Gurion rumbled. "Julius is our emissary to America. He is to solicit support from the Jewish community there."

Dov exchanged greetings with the distinguished-looking Mantz, then took a seat. The man could be either the owner of a small but thriving business or a midlevel executive, Dov thought. Mantz appeared to be in his early fifties. He was lean yet large-boned and powerfully built. He could well have been a football player. A mane of gray hair capped the evenly proportioned features of his oval face. Smudged pouches beneath gray-green eyes told of stress.

Dov recognized only three of the six other men seated around the white linen–draped table. The private dining room, separated from the main restaurant, was comfortably but not ornately appointed. Heavy drapes concealed the floor-to-ceiling windows, and heavy double doors, with unobtrusive guards positioned outside, ensured their privacy.

Ben-Gurion waited until a white-jacketed waiter served tea and pastries before launching into the meeting's agenda. "Gentlemen, the British raid two weeks ago was a terrible blow to Zionism." He paused and regarded his folded hands somberly. "The implications go far beyond just the loss of some of our finest leaders and most of the Palmach's supply of arms.

"It should be clear by now that we will never *force* the British to leave through acts of senseless violence. Their ability to retaliate is formidable. Worse, we are eroding world opinion. An independent Jewish nation can be realized only with overwhelming support from the powerful nations, including the United States and Russia."

"Are you saying we should cease our resistance?" a rugged-looking, middle-aged man asked. Without waiting for an answer, he continued, his voice heavy with bitterness. "I am fed up with the traditional Jewish attitude of forgive and forget. It has brought us nothing over the centuries but humiliation, contempt, and persecution. We rely overmuch on decency and good sense in others to prevail over evil. I say spit back with machine guns, answer the oppressors with steel. That is the language they understand."

"Spoken like the brave man you are, Yousef," the aging leader said sadly. "But where are your machine guns? Where is your steel? Listen well, my trusted friends. Our people will never cease to resist. The struggle will go on, but along different lines, and with a longer-range view.

"Just now, the British Empire is our antagonist, but the English will never again rule by their old colonialist doctrine. Their shattered economy will eventually lead them to conclude that they cannot *afford* Palestine. They will go. Then we will face a horde of well-armed, vindictive members of the Arab Legion.

"That is the day we must prepare for. Tomorrow, we shall declare ourselves opposed to the violence we joined with the Irgun in precipitating. With our pledge of nonviolence, the British will relax their vigilance. We will then arm ourselves in secret and be ready to face our natural enemies.

"There is one matter, however, in which we will continue overt efforts. The British are denying our people entry into their rightful homeland. That right will never be negotiated or abrogated."

Respectful silence followed Ben-Gurion's somber words. After several moments, he continued. "Julius brings encouraging news from the United States. He will return to create a clandestine pipeline of arms, young men with whom we can build a fighting force, and funds. The struggle goes on, gentlemen, have no fear. But reality must prevail." He turned to the intently listening Mantz. "Julius, will you provide these gentlemen some insight into the American situation?"

Mantz stroked his chin as he searched for appropriate words. "The 'steel' you refer to, Yousef, exists in the United States—a profusion. Warehouses and storage yards bulge with surplus armament. Young men of Jewish descent, some of whom are veterans, are eager to take up arms in the name of Zionism. More important, funds with which to augment and equip Palmach troops exist.

"A certain rabbi—David wishes him to remain nameless—holds forth hope that he can organize a group of wealthy Americans and induce them to create a war chest."

Dov joined the other serious-faced leaders in muttered expressions of delight. His mind reeled at the prospect of entire shiploads of modern arms and regiments of trained, fresh troops. He couldn't contain his excitement. "When?" he called out.

Mantz wore a wry smile as he replied, "Ah, that depends upon many factors. Obtaining these assets is one thing—to move them is another. The British blockade is formidable. So, as you know well, is their secret service's ability to ferret out their destination. Another obstacle is, ironically, the Irgun. Mister Begin has a following in America who even now competes with the Haganah for funds and war materiel. I cannot promise an early solution, gentlemen. But I have unlimited faith in our ingenuity, and that of our American collaborators."

A babble of excited voices erupted as Mantz finished. Dov wormed his way through the now standing audience to where Julius stood talking with Ben-Gurion. He extended his hand. "Mister Mantz, you've given us some badly needed hope. Give us a few thousand rifles and men to use them, and we'll create a true Jewish homeland. And airplanes— what I wouldn't give for a squadron of British Spitfires."

Ben-Gurion nodded and laid a hand on Friedman's shoulder. "Patience, Dov. Julius has just donned a mantle of great responsibility, don't make it heavier than it already is."

Chapter 4

27 August 1946
New York City

Julius Mantz paused, sipped from a glass of ice water, and formed his closing words after careful thought. "When I tell you that the fate of a free homeland for the Jewish people is in grave jeopardy, I speak from great conviction, gentlemen. Each of you has a letter from our leader, David Ben-Gurion, asking for your support. My task is to convert that support into sufficient men and arms to defend the borders of Palestine, to establish a steel ring as protection against certain invasion by the Arab nations. An invasion will come, I assure you, within twenty-four hours following the withdrawal of British troops. That day, gentlemen, can come as early as eighteen months from now."

Emotionally drained by his impassioned plea, Mantz moved to the open window of Rabbi Avraam Rabinovitch's twentieth-floor penthouse. He stood there, allowing the inadequate breeze to wash over him, while the eleven sober-faced men considered his words. Eleven—of the twelve receiving Ben-Gurion's assessment of potential disaster. A good sign, Mantz mused—only one absentee. Nate Green, publisher of the Chicago *Globe,* was not a Ben-Gurion fan. In fact, the previous month Green had written an editorial that hinted of support for Menachem Begin's radical Irgun tactics inside Palestine as opposed to those of the more conservative Haganah.

Between them these eleven men controlled enough money and resources, not to mention influence, to make the difference. Mantz listened closely for their reaction as he studied the restful green foliage in New York's Central Park.

The rabbi—wisely, in Mantz's opinion—refrained from speaking. Not without a measure of influence in his own right as chairman of the World Jewish Congress and senior member of the Yishuv, a group forming Jewish representation in Palestine's mandatory government, the rabbi was nevertheless allowing events to evolve. Members of this group had not risen to their positions of wealth and power by making impulsive decisions.

They would think, they would question, the rabbi had told Julius; only then would they act. Alfred Meyer, president of Globe Movie Studios; Willard Cohen, chairman of the board for International Bank; Benjamin Swartz, chief executive officer of Mace Manufacturing, Inc.; the others were equally endowed with resources and leverage. The birth or death of the Zionist dream could well hinge on their decision—that and Mantz's own resourcefulness in asking them for a sum of money beyond most men's comprehension, Julius conceded ruefully. Could he expect them to throw their weight behind schemes that just possibly were illegal?

Plus, what did even the rabbi know about Mantz? He'd never met him before this week. In his letter, Ben-Gurion had given Julius high praise—citing his accomplishments with the Aliyah Bet, that shadowy organization on the Continent engaged in arranging clandestine transportation for thousands of displaced Jews trying to enter Palestine. But then, Ben-Gurion was hard-pressed to attract highly competent people to the Haganah cause. Even Rabinovitch, himself a devout Zionist, had expressed doubts. *Was* the task impossible?

The rabbi and Mantz turned their attention to the hard-faced man who broke the silence. Gus Meecham of West Texas Oil cleared his throat and rasped, "What position is the United Nations taking?"

Mantz, hands thrust in his hip pockets, strolled to his former position in front of the marble-mantled fireplace. "The UN's selection of Lake Placid as a headquarters is apt, gentlemen. They will talk, they will vacillate, and, in the end, they will follow the lead of the great powers—Great Britain, the United States, France, and Russia. Expect no support from that quarter, not in time to save Palestine from Arab domination, anyway."

Alfred Meyer, a dark scowl on his face, his voice angry, erupted. "What you and Ben-Gurion tell us defies belief, Mantz." He waved the three-page letter. "What of the Balfour Declaration of 1917? The English clearly took the position that their government 'favored establishment of Palestine as a home for the Jewish people.'"

"And that is still their position." Mantz's voice was tinged with bitter mockery. "I talked with their Foreign Office representative, Donald Ashton-Smythe, just last month. In a few hundred words of garbled, diplomatic language, he made it clear that although he personally was sympathetic to our cause, the British would not support Zionism at the cost of inflaming Arab opinion."

"Oil," Meecham spat. "The bastards see the sun finally setting on their goddamned empire. There's no way they're going to let Suez and the largest oil reserves in the world slip through their fingers. The sickening aspect is that jackass Truman's support of their inhuman blockade of our so-called homeland. And although they refuse to provide arms for *our* defense, they blithely sell the goddamned Arabs anything they want."

Mantz's weary sigh expressed his own frustration. "Ashton-Smythe's explanation is that those arms are being provided under agreements made during the war. They feel bound to abide by their commitment. An influx of a half-million Jews into Palestine would create an unacceptable Muslim-Jewish population ratio. The inevitable result would be bloodshed."

"Bullshit," the doughty oil magnate snorted. "Most of the goddamned Arabs supported *Hitler* during the war. How does that striped-pants limey explain that little fact of life?"

Mantz noticed slight frowns forming in response to the former oil field roustabout's profanity. Rabbi Rabinovitch's lips tightened into a thin line. No rebuke was forthcoming, but the Jewish patriarch deftly changed the conversation's direction.

"Gentlemen, your taking time to come here today gives me much pleasure and satisfaction. It shows you care. But Mister Mantz has presented us with a monumental challenge. Can a scattered people join forces to defeat the combined might of the Western and Arab worlds? The implications of what Mister Ben-Gurion proposes are staggering. Arm an isolated nation in the face of a determined embargo and blockade? Place an impoverished citizenry, one without a formal government, on a war footing? And within slightly more than one year's time?" He paused and made eye contact with each of the eleven serious-faced men. "The alternative to making an attempt, at least, is to see the dreams of the Jewish people for a place to call home go up in smoke; perhaps the word *flames* is more apt.

"The ugly word is *war:* undeclared, with no bugles, no drums, but a war nevertheless—the outcome of which is very much in doubt."

Mantz held his emotions in check with difficulty; he felt his nerves stretched to the point of emitting a loud twang if touched. It was all on the table. Tension was palpable. Could he have made a more convincing presentation? Had this collection of industrial giants sized him up, as a man, and found him lacking in the ability to spearhead such a gargantuan undertaking?

Julius managed to stifle a mighty release of pent-up breath as Meecham interjected disgustedly, "Count me in, Rabbi. Those damn Arabs remind me of a trapwise coyote stalking what he thinks is a crippled rabbit. Well, let's show them this rabbit has some teeth. Where do we start?"

Rabinovitch concealed his reaction equally well, but his smile was anything but benign. "We start with what may be the most potent weapon in our arsenal, gentlemen—*your* checkbooks."

4 September 1946
44 Water Street, New York

Julius brushed a layer of dust from the top of an abandoned packing crate and seated himself in the cleared area. Ariel Shamir gave no indication of ceasing her restless pacing. Lighting a cigaret, she asked, "What exactly do you wish me to do, Mister Mantz? Mister Ben-Gurion was somewhat vague in his instructions."

Mantz returned her gaze with a wry smile. "Would you believe I don't know? I was impressed with the speedy manner in which you arranged for a contract for air transport. I asked David to send me someone who could do anything—could be everyplace at once. There is so much to do. I have a plan, but the execution involves a formidable array of details. It is a tribute to your ability, Miss Shamir, that he selected you."

Ariel's eyes shot indignant sparks. "I suppose you're disappointed that he didn't send a man."

"Not at all," Julius responded promptly. Then a hint of Mantz's inner steel core surfaced. "But if your being a woman gives you any feeling of insecurity or resentment, or poses any other emotional obstacle to doing your job, then you'd best take the next boat back to Palestine.

There's too much to be done to waste time dealing with personal problems."

Twin spots of crimson flared briefly in Ariel's olive-complected cheeks; her full lips compressed to a thin line. "I . . . " She swallowed and her ire subsided. "I was out of line. I apologize. What's to be done?"

Julius grinned and cleared a space next to him. "We'll get along, Miss . . . Ariel. Sit down and stop that infernal stalking about. Let's start with this building; it isn't much, but the location is ideal for our purpose. It's remote, close to the waterfront, and has storage. We need office furniture, telephones, and utilities connected.

"David gave me a shopping list almost fifty pages long. I plan to appoint team leaders for specific projects. The organization will be completely compartmentalized, no one manager knowing details of another's operation. I learned that from the French underground. We will encounter stiff opposition to our efforts to ship items having potential for military use past the British blockade."

"What about the Americans?" Ariel asked with a puzzled look.

Julius sighed. "The Americans are in an awkward position. Most support our Zionist ideal; most sympathize with our homeless. Still, international agreements, both written and implied, exist for mutual support among wartime allies. I think we must assume determined effort by the U.S. government to prevent arms from this country reaching Jewish Palestine."

"We *will* be dealing in arms, then," Ariel observed matter-of-factly.

"Very much so. Arms, especially personal firearms and ammunition, are at the top of David's list. Their procurement presents no problem. The American War Assets Administration has warehouses full of everything the Palmach badly needs. The items sell for scrap prices. Our challenge lies not in buying them, but in getting them past the blockade."

"That is the real reason I was told to retain a reliable air freight operator, then," Ariel said with a slight frown.

"Yes. I'm sorry we couldn't have been more specific."

"But I gave my word to the owner of Allied Air that he wouldn't be required to carry illegal cargoes."

Mantz nodded. "And he won't, unless it becomes necessary; then he will be given the opportunity to refuse. His flights will be within the United States. Shipment of firearms, not for resale, *within* U.S. boundaries is permitted. The nature of his cargoes, however, can raise official eyebrows. Best they be handled with—ah—circumspection.

"Now," Mantz's voice grew crisp and authoritative, "when you get this office running, work up letters to Zionist volunteer organizations all over the U.S. The Jewish Relief Foundation will collect and ship articles of clothing, medicine, and farm equipment for the displaced Jews in European camps, as well as in Palestine. We will use that conduit to ship the other prohibited items as well."

"Where will I—" Ariel stopped in midsentence. *This man doesn't expect to answer questions,* she realized. *He is concerned only that you* do *what needs to be done.* She listened intently as Julius continued.

"I've acquired some tools for turning out agricultural machinery, but one of them can be altered to produce three-oh-three ammunition. The items are being picked up in Connecticut next week and moved to a warehouse in the Bronx. As soon as they are crated for overseas shipment, we'll need export permits, shipping documents, and the like. If you will see to those, and—oh, yes—funds.

"I have checks to deposit. Set up a number of accounts; I'll leave you a list of banks the steering committee gave me. You can start in Kansas City. They have a strong fund-raiser there and a building full of donated equipment ready for shipment. Open an account with Sam Katzenbaum there, at the First National Bank.

"I'll also give you a folder with a list of names—people who have volunteered their services, people we'll need for project managers. Vet them and give me names of those you think are worth interviewing." Julius stood and gave Ariel a winsome smile. "I'm on my way to Washington now to contact some Jewish members of Congress. I'll be back Friday and we'll get that first shipment on its way. If you have any problems . . ." He made vague motions with his hands and strode toward the door.

Ariel watched him go with a half smile of bewildered amusement. She recalled David Ben-Gurion's last words: "Julius is a dedicated, dynamic man, Ariel. Be prepared to spend long days—and nights."

7 September 1946
44 Water Street

Ariel poured another cup of coffee from a battered pot she kept on a hot plate that had also seen better days. Six laughing, chattering teenagers carried a scarred oak desk off the creaky freight elevator; one of them called, "Where do you want this, Miss Shamir?"

"Put it here by this open window," Ariel instructed. "I want to get every bit of breeze I can." She mopped perspiration from her brow.

Another youth, grinning proudly, extended an ancient Westinghouse electric fan. "This should help some, ma'am. We didn't really need it at the boys' club. I—I sort of borrowed it for you."

"Arnold, you are a jewel," Ariel crowed delightedly. She gazed around the transformed suite of offices with open admiration. Involving the Brighton Street Zionist Boys' Club had been her greatest coup to date. Windows, minus ten years or more accumulation of grime, sparkled. All visible surfaces were dust-free. Donated office furniture had materialized as if by magic—knocked about and mismatched, but serviceable. The boys indignantly refused to accept payment.

She basked briefly before the squealing fan, then transferred the used Underwood typewriter to the desk from its former home atop a packing crate. Its presence alongside the gleaming black phone, the only new item in the building, gave the place a distinctly businesslike air, she thought.

The phone's jangle sounded foreign and overloud in its newly renovated surroundings. Ariel scooped up the receiver and caroled, "Jewish Relief Foundation, Ariel Shamir speaking. May I help you?"

"Ariel." Julius Mantz's usually smooth voice had overtones of anger. "Are you still in touch with that crew of kids from the youth club you were telling me about?"

"Very much so, Julius. A dozen or so are busy unloading office furniture right now."

"Good. I have another job for them."

"I'm sure they'll be glad to help. What do you want them to do?"

"They can begin by clearing out that warehouse space on the ground floor," her employer barked. "I'm sending over that shipment of machine tools from Connecticut."

"The first-floor storage room?" Ariel asked. "Julius, that place is a disaster. Windows boarded up, trash all over, even rats. Surely you can't be planning to use that?"

"I am. I'll explain later. Just get enough floor space cleared to hold three truckloads of crated machinery." He hung up abruptly, leaving Ariel staring at a silent instrument.

Ariel stood alongside Julius Mantz and watched the crew of sweating, straining youngsters manhandle bulky wooden crates onto 44 Water Street's loading dock. Gleaming metal parts were visible through open-slatted shipping containers. She winced as one crate, weighing what must have been hundreds of pounds, missed crushing a boy's foot by inches as it slid from the truckbed.

"What happened that the tools had to be moved?" Ariel asked.

"Thieves," Julius snapped. "Blackmailers. A man commended to me as a good Jewish sympathizer."

Ariel remained silent, although Mantz was making no sense whatever. She was learning her boss's mannerisms—he would explain in his own way and at his own pace.

"I went to the warehouse this pirate operates to see the cargo unloaded—check to make sure that it was all there. The place should be condemned. The wheel of one truck had broken through a rotten floorboard. Its load was ready to topple. When I complained about the sorry condition of a place I was paying good money to rent, he said he would need another thousand dollars a month. 'Why?' I asked him. 'The building isn't worth what I'm paying now.'

"Do you know what he said then?" Mantz gave no indication he expected a reply. "'The FBI would be interested in knowing what you're up to,' he had the nerve to tell me.

"I decided to use this space. It's too close to our headquarters and in bad condition, but at least we can keep track of what's going on. We'll hire these boys to repack the stuff for shipment. That alone will save several hundred dollars."

"Julius, these boys are little more than children. Surely you don't expect them to do the job of skilled workmen."

"They're Jews," Mantz retorted. "They will learn—and rapidly. Their counterparts in Palestine are carrying guns."

10 September 1946
44 Water Street

Ariel marched into Mantz's office, her eyes glinting dangerously. "Julius, the shipping operation isn't working," she said, ignoring her boss's irritated frown. "Those boys are just too young and inexperienced. I've gone through enough first-aid supplies to equip a hospital. They have yet to finish one container that can be safely placed on board a ship. Even if they had, I haven't even been able to discover what shipping documents we need. More items arrive every day. We will soon be out of storage space."

Mantz's frown deepened. "Well, what do you propose to do about it?" he asked.

"I propose to hire a professional."

"And where do you intend to find this person?" Julius asked with raised eyebrows.

"He's sitting in my office right now," Ariel shot back. "I went through that list of names you gave me. This man knows the shipping business inside out, and two of the committee members vouched for him. Will you talk with him?"

Scarcely waiting for Mantz's assenting nod, she placed a folder on his desk and stepped to the door. "Mister Mantz will see you now, sir," she called.

Julius waved his visitor to a chair, then absorbed the contents of the buff file folder before speaking. "Eddie Kotch," he said with a reflective tone. "Are you Jewish, Mister Kotch?"

"No, sir."

"I see. Then what prompted you to offer your services to our organization?"

"I don't like what I see happening to those people in Europe. The English are selling guns to the damn Arabs in Palestine, but they won't let the Jews there buy so much as a cap pistol. Then our lily-livered government holds up our own ships—*American-owned ships*—while it fusses about things like, can these paper clips be straightened and put to military use?" The big man snorted in disgust. "Three bottoms sat in the harbor for more than two weeks while customs haggled with shippers. There needs to be some heads broken, if you ask me."

Mantz studied the outspoken man with new interest. What he saw wasn't impressive. Kotch's heavy-set figure strained the seams of his suit jacket; his bulk filled the chair. He looked soft, an impression heightened by a round, almost cherubic face. Brown hair, thinning on top, barely concealed a pink scalp.

"What has Miss Shamir told you about our needs?" Julius inquired.

"She says you have a shipping problem—crating, paperwork, and the like."

"And you know this business?"

"I've been in it all my life. I know the waterfront like the back of my hand, and I know most of the people who work down there—the ones who matter anyway. I know all about getting export permits, and I know how to get cargo on the right ships."

"I see," Julius mused aloud. "And you're willing to give up your present employment and work for us?"

"Well, just now, I don't have a job."

"Oh?"

"I quit. Quite frankly, I met a guy in a bar who started spouting off about Jews being the cause of all our problems. I punched him. Turns out the slimy bastard was a fed of some sort—working undercover trying to nose out illegal shipments. My boss panicked, so I walked before I got fired."

Mantz scratched his chin as he reflected on Kotch's explanation. "What would you expect in the way of remuneration, Mister Kotch?"

"A thousand a month and unaccountable expenses."

Mantz winced. "Quite out of the question, I'm afraid. This is a charitable organization. Our funds are severely limited; you can see the type of facilities we must operate from. You ask more than my own salary."

"Look, Mister Mantz. I know what you're doing. I looked around that warehouse downstairs. There's stuff there that can't be shipped openly without being impounded by the Brits. If you haven't already, you're about to violate U.S. laws when it comes to export permits. You try to get this job done with a bunch of Boy Scouts, you're gonna wind up in the courts. Worse than that, those poor bastards waiting for the stuff in Palestine are gonna be left empty-handed."

"I simply can't pay you a thousand dollars a month, Kotch. I don't disagree with what you say, and we dearly need your expertise, but that sum is out of the question."

"Okay." Kotch released a gusty sigh. "I'll work for whatever you feel you can pay me. I can maybe make it up later on—I'm sure to find some good contacts. But I'll insist on that expense account."

"For what purpose?"

"Look, Mister Mantz, there's two ways you can do this. You can get the big money shippers behind you, or you can get the boys who work the docks behind you. You got no bargaining chips with the shipowners, so that leaves you with the dock crews. There's a system down there. A foreman gets so much, an inspector gets so much, even the customs guy gets a share. It isn't an expense you can put on the books, Mister Mantz, but if you want your cargoes to move on time, and intact, it's one you gotta bear."

"And it doesn't bother you that some of our shipments contain items that may not—er—be strictly legal for export." Again Julius posed a statement instead of a question.

Kotch turned both hands palm up. "You got your rules, I got mine, and the government has another set. What you're planning hurts no one and helps many, so who's to say what's right and what's wrong?"

Mantz's lips twitched in a faint, ironic smile. "How soon can you have those items downstairs crated and on their way?"

"Give me money for a crew, and I'll have those machine tools on board the *Helen of Troy* when she sails next Thursday."

Mantz's eyes widened. "The job is yours."

Kotch nodded and stood. He turned toward the door, then paused. "There's one other thing," he said.

"Which is? . . ."

"I run my own show. You tell me what you want done, and I'll do it—my way. No long-winded explanations, no asking for permission to use the bathroom, and no one to tell me I can or can't do something. In return you'll get no excuses from me. Deal?"

"Deal," Julius replied promptly.

"Okay. By the way, could your people use about ten tons of TNT?"

"*What?*"

"TNT. The stuff that goes bang. Well, not the pure stuff, actually. Demolition blocks. The Corps of Engineers has them coming out of their ears. If you have the right people over there, they'd make nifty mines, pipe bombs, even grenades."

Mantz gulped, then croaked, "Ten *tons?* How—how on earth would you ever get that much hazardous cargo inside Palestine?"

Kotch smiled for the first time since entering the room. "I don't know myself right now. But even if I did, I don't think you'd want to know."

"Uh, yes, I expect you're right. At any rate, my people would be *very* interested in obtaining such an item. How will you pay for it?"

"Just tell Miss Efficiency out there not to ask any questions when I tell her I need cash—lots of it."

"I'll do that."

Kotch nodded, then ambled toward the doorway. "I'll be in touch— boss," he said over his shoulder.

Mantz crossed to the still-open door and watched his newest employee stride toward the stairs. Ariel gave him an inquiring look. "An amazing man," Julius told her with a brief nod of his head.

"Did you hire him?"

"Yes." He chuckled. "At least I think that's how you could describe what just went on in there."

Ariel refrained from voicing her confusion. Instead she ventured, "Julius, I've worked up an itinerary through the Midwest. Would you like to look at it? I'm hitting major cities where volunteer organizations have reported stocks of clothing, medicine, and the like."

Julius waved a hand in dismissal. "You know what has to be done," he said absently. "Just let me know before you leave."

Chapter 5

18 September 1946
Fairfax Field, Kansas City

Ross let the DC-3 roll straight ahead briefly, locked the tail wheel, and set the parking brake. "Ah, good to get home," he said, pulling the mixture controls to idle-cutoff. "I just hope all the runs we get from this contract are as quick and easy."

Alex grunted. "I'd feel better if I knew more about the outfit. That Shamir woman gets under my skin."

"Don't be such a grouch, Alex." Ross unbuckled his seat belt, slid out of his seat, and slapped the dour copilot's shoulder. "The pay is good. We damn near cleared enough this trip to buy an engine for the Norseman. Look, I don't know of anything coming up for the next couple of days. Go downtown, get drunk, get laid, and things will look better."

Busying himself making entries in the logbook, Alex didn't respond. Ross grinned and made for the rear exit. For the first time in weeks, things were looking up. Ross dropped to the ground, stretched, and glanced at the parking ramp. Two familiar shapes drew his attention. I'll be damned, he muttered to himself. Wonder where *those* came from?

The objects of his interest were two army training planes—North American–made Texans, the army's AT-6. He recalled the speedy little trainer from his days as a cadet at Kelly Field—his first love affair. The planes perched with saucy impudence alongside a hulking Kansas City Southern DC-4. They had apparently just landed; four men wearing flight suits were huddled beneath the nose of one examining the engine cowling. Ross strolled impulsively in their direction.

He paused by the wingtip. "Hi, fellows. Got a problem?"

A youngish looking man, with silver bars on the shoulders of his green flying suit, stood. "An oil leak. Doesn't look serious, but I'd like to have a mechanic look at it if there's one about."

"No problem. My partner is over there by that DC-3. He's a grouchy cuss, but he'll take a look-see—and he works for cold beer."

The young lieutenant flashed a wide smile. "Now that's what I call an accommodating mechanic. I'll sure buy if he'll show us the way." He extended his hand. "I'm Dan Frazier."

"Ross Colyer. Where you fellows from?"

"Mitchell Field, Long Island. Down here for a couple days' TDY. Come over and meet the others. Colonel," he called, "I've done found us an angel of mercy. Guy's going to take a look at that leak for *beer*, would you believe?"

A chunky figure wearing a battered green service cap with an authentic fifty-mission crush straightened to his full five-feet eight-inch height. "Frazier, don't you go making deals with no angels," he growled, wiping his hands on his flight suit. "You don't have the right credentials—angels is good, clean-living folk." He turned and allowed a smile to spread across his moon-shaped, cherubic face.

Ross's jaw dropped. Frazier was saying, "Colonel Deckard, meet . . ." He stumbled to a halt as he saw Ross's and Deckard's expressions. "I take it you two already know each other," he concluded dryly.

"You might say that, Frazier—you might say that," the colonel said softly. "Ross Colyer, what a sight for these old, tired eyes."

Ross strode toward Deckard and enveloped the colonel's outstretched hand with both of his own. "Colonel Deckard," he said, his voice husky with emotion and astonishment. "My God, I can't believe it's you."

"You always were a stubborn, hard-to-convince so-and-so, Colyer. This, by God, you can believe." He slapped Ross's shoulder with his free hand and cocked his head to one side. "You know, I didn't remember you being this ugly. . . ." He turned to the other pilots. "You guys are looking at one of the best goddamn pilots in the entire air force—next to me, of course. He glanced at Ross's attire—short-sleeved light blue shirt and dark blue trousers. "What outfit you with these days, Ross?"

"I'm on my own, Colonel. I didn't stay on after V-J Day."

"*What?*"

"Yeah, it's a long story. Look, Lieutenant Frazier said you were planning to RON here. I'll take you to one of the best barbecue places you've ever seen. It also has the best jazz combo around. In fact, they have a *good* trombone player, not that you'd recognize one, Colonel. Does he still make those god-awful efforts to play 'When the Saints Go Marching In'?" Ross asked Frazier.

Frazier smirked. "Badly, but yes. I don't know about the others, but I'm a candidate for some good barbecue and cold beer, and I'd like to hear a decent trombone solo as well."

"Lieutenant, I'll remind you that you have an efficiency report coming up," Deckard snarled. "I didn't come down here to be insulted by a couple of wiseasses. Ross, if your angel services extend to steering us to a decent hotel as well as that eatery you mentioned, lead on. I want to get caught up on what you've been doing."

"Done. Let me give you the keys to my car. You can go ahead to the hotel while I get Alex, my partner, to have a look at that oil leak. Then I'll check my office and have Alex drop me off at your hotel— I suggest the President—and we'll take it from there, okay?"

Deckard wiped greasy fingers with a napkin, took a long pull from his mug of beer, and sighed contentedly. "Ross, those have to be the best ribs I've eaten since leaving Texas. And that music—I've heard worse in New Orleans, especially the vocalist. What did you say her name was?"

"Patty Lynn. She's big time. Makes the nightclub circuit in places like Chicago, Atlanta, New York, even New Orleans. Supposedly, she got her start right here in this restaurant—drops by whenever she's in town."

Deckard looked at the junior officers. "I know you three have plans for a night on the town. Why don't you stop fidgeting and take off? Ross and I have some serious catching up to do."

The two men waited silently while a beaming waiter removed the heap of rib bones and used plates, then brought fresh, frosty mugs of beer. Deckard lit a cigar. "Okay, flyboy, fill me in. How come you're out of uniform?"

"Whoo, boy," Ross exclaimed. "Where do I start? Benghazi, after the Ploesti mission?"

"That'll do. I know you were under a gag order then. I also know you and General Sprague crossed swords, and there was a big dustup about you and your crew escaping from internment in neutral Turkey. I was transferred to Italy about then and never heard anything more."

"Okay. Do you remember Captain Templeton, Sprague's aide?"

"Yeah, a smug little prick, if I remember correctly."

"The same. Well, you know that Sprague used my plane to lead White One on the Ploesti raid—BT flew as copilot. We got shot up pretty bad and had to put down in Turkey. We didn't give our parole to the Turks, so I decided, what the hell, why not escape? My engineer figured we could make the plane flyable.

"BT refused to get involved—said we were nuts. He secretly contacted a Turkish hoodlum and arranged to be smuggled out aboard a fishing boat. Papa—Senator Templeton, the chairman of the Military Affairs Committee, you know—"

"Who didn't?"

"Well, he smuggled in money for BT's escape—right through the damned embassy, no less. BT got killed by a pipe bomb the night he met this Turk. The irony was that they weren't after BT; it was some rival gang after BT's contact."

Deckard shook his head. "Now *that's* irony with a capital *I*."

"When we got back to the States, I had orders to B-29 school. I was really fired up until I discovered that Sprague, of all people, would be my wing commander. I couldn't swallow that. I managed to get transferred to fighters and flew a tour in the CBI, ending up as commander of a P-51 squadron on Iwo Jima. After the war, I found that most reservists were being involuntarily released from active duty, so I applied for a regular commission. That's when I discovered that Senator Templeton had put a political interest flag in my master two-oh-one file. The old bastard thought I was responsible for BT getting killed.

"End of story. I hooked up with Alex Taylor—we met in Texas— and formed a little three-plane air freight outfit, Allied Air, Incorporated.

"Now, it's your turn. How come you're in Kansas City—flying a trainer, of all things?"

Deckard signaled for refills and pursed his lips in a mannerism Ross recalled as the colonel's favorite way of starting an ass-chewing session. "What a low, goddamn blow," he said. "It seems that Ploesti didn't do either of us any favors. That mission derailed a lot of careers. *Anyone* who had anything to do with the planning or who flew in a lead position was tainted. We just got quietly reassigned to a back-water job. I was made a staff operations officer in Fifteenth Air Force headquarters in Italy.

"After the war, I was assigned to the Fourth Air Force plans office at Mitchell Field. I'm still there. I've thought several times about chucking it all, but, damnit, I don't think I'd make a good civilian. I'll make full bull by the time I retire; maybe then I'll do something like you've done. How do you like being a civilian?"

Ross lit a cigaret and pondered the question at length. "It has some good aspects, and some not so good," he said finally. "I like being my own boss, and there's opportunity to make a lot more money than an officer's pay. I miss the kicks of flying high-performance air-planes, though. And civilians don't talk the same language. . . . Ah, shit, Colonel—I won't try to kid you. I'd give anything to be back on active duty."

Deckard chuckled. "Sort of what I suspected. Any women in your life?"

"A few one-night stands is all. I thought BT's widow, Janet, and I had something going. We dated at Hickam before the war, before she married BT. It fizzled out; we still see each other now and then, but just as old friends. BT gave her a rotten deal, too, by the way."

Deckard gave Ross a long, speculative look while he stripped the cellophane from a fresh cigar. "Maybe I can help do something about getting you back in uniform, Ross. Interested?"

"Depends. Doing what?"

"Don't be so damn picky. You interested or not?"

"Well—yeah."

"Okay. Let me bring you into the picture. The War Department is concerned about the wholesale disarmament being pushed by Congress, not to mention some of President Truman's own cabinet. The liberals are saying that we'll never see worldwide war again, that there's no need for a big standing army and navy, so they won't appropriate money for them." A scowl wrinkled Deckard's pudgy features. "They're dreaming."

"Colonel, do you happen to know a Colonel Ted Wilson?" Ross asked. "He's in personnel at USAAF headquarters."

"Can't say as I do."

"Well, he was telling me the same thing not long ago. I'm sorry, go ahead."

"The planners have come up with an idea to keep some of our combat veterans, especially aircrews, in at least a minimum state of preparedness by forming reserve training units. Give them some airplanes to fly, hold ground school, and keep them from getting out of touch."

"Will Congress provide funds?"

"Probably. They're getting pressure to cancel some of the base closings; they may see it as a cheap way to save some votes back home."

"Will it work? Do you think you can keep civilians ready to go right into combat overnight?"

"Maybe not overnight, but a helluva lot quicker than we did in '41."

"Yeah. Okay, you said you had some idea that might get me back on active duty. Is this it?"

"I said 'back in uniform,' not active duty. But it could lead to that. This is what I was getting at. We're here in Kansas City to set up a Reserve Flying Training Detachment. We'll provide a couple of AT-6s, and Beechcraft AT-11 bombardier trainers for twin-engine pilots. You'll meet periodically for ground training, and the airplanes will be available to fly anytime, anyplace."

Ross laughed. "Hell, you're talking about a country club—a flying country club. You call that 'getting back in uniform'?"

"It can, and must be, more than that. If these 'clubs'—as you call them—are run in a military manner and the aircrews stay proficient, then we'll see more up-to-date airplanes, even pay for training periods. Seriously, it's the best chance we have to avoid slipping back to where we were before the war. Some state National Guard outfits are already forming air units."

"Okay, I'll sign on. I'd like to get some time in the old AT-6 again—it'll be fun."

Deckard's pale blue eyes twinkled. "Well, I had in mind asking you to do a bit more than just 'sign on.'"

"Oh? Like what?"

"We'll need a strong detachment commander—someone who can recruit veterans and whip them into a flying unit."

"Me?"

"The thought crossed my mind. Lieutenant Frazier will be the detachment's active duty adviser, but the rest is up to you."

"Colonel, I don't have time. I have an airline to run, remember?"

"You also hold a commission in the United States Army, Ross," Deckard responded with a note of mild admonishment.

"You don't have to remind me of that," Ross flared. "But after the way I was treated, I don't owe the army a damned thing; my dues are paid up."

"Then why don't you resign your commission?"

"Because, damnit . . ." Ross paused and glared at his old squadron commander. "Okay, I get your point. Let me think about it."

Deckard looked up at the black waiter, impatiently shuffling his feet in the otherwise empty restaurant. Pulling bills from his pocket, Deckard responded, "Sure. Now, let's go look for a honky-tonk. Maybe I can find a band that'll let me play the trombone."

4 October 1946
Fairfax Field

Ross stood at rigid attention and listened to Lieutenant Colonel Deckard's unemotional drone echo within the cavernous sheet-metal hangar. "Headquarters, Fourth Air Force. General Order Seventeen, dated 1 October 1946. Pursuant to provisions of USAAF Regulation ten-dash-two, Reserve Flying Training Detachment 7017 is hereby activated at Fairfax Field, Kansas. . . ."

Ross's attention wandered as Deckard continued with the litany of mission, authorized personnel, and equipment, then drifted into a pep talk. Could my forest green Ike jacket have shrunk in less than a year's time? Ross wondered. He stole a sideways glance at the six other officers lined up to his left—yeah, some of their buttons were straining, too. He gave a mental shrug. Admit it, he thought, it feels good to be wearing a uniform again, even if it is sort of reminiscent of kids playing soldier.

Hearing Deckard use the word *militia,* Ross frowned. It made them sound like a ragtag band, dressed in homespun, wearing coonskin caps, and carrying flintlock rifles. But, he conceded, that pretty well describes us—civilians, prepared to defend our country. Modern-day Minutemen. His ruminations were interrupted by a scattered round of hand clapping from the little group—mostly women and children—seated on folding chairs behind him. He realized that the colonel had concluded his remarks and was asking him to step to the microphone.

Ross threw a self-conscious glance at the array of ribbons he wore below his wings as Deckard boomed, "Officers and men of the 7017th, you are fortunate indeed to have a man who has distinguished himself in combat as detachment commander. I served with Major Colyer during the war in Europe and know him as a courageous, dedicated officer. Major Colyer . . ."

Ross grasped the microphone stand and favored the audience with a bashful grin, totally at a loss for words. He recalled his previous reflections; the comparison to Minutemen seemed apt. He spoke briefly on the subject, then glanced at his watch. "Colonel Deckard and his staff have laid on an impressive ceremony for this occasion. In addition to the airplanes on static display on the ramp, they pulled some strings and arranged for a flyover in about five minutes. I suggest we go outside and watch."

Deckard joined Ross as the chattering group straggled through the rolled-back hangar doors. "Hey," he muttered, "that Minuteman thing was inspired. I may have you do some public speaking. Don't be surprised if you see that theme on our recruiting literature."

"It was desperation. Why didn't you tell me I was supposed to give a speech?"

Lieutenant Frazier fell into step in time to hear the exchange. "It made an impact," he said. "I was watching faces. . . . Okay, stand by for the flyover." Frazier trotted to a parked truck and vaulted onto its flat bed. He held a bullhorn to his mouth and bawled, "All right, folks. The tower is in contact with the flyover formation and has cleared them for a low pass. They will approach from the southeast; you'll have to look quick."

"Why all the mystery, Colonel?" asked Ross. "My God, you wrangled a B-29, an A-26, a B-25, a Jug, and a Mustang for static display. What else do you have to show off?"

"Wait and see. I think you're gonna like this," Deckard added with an enigmatic smile.

Ross's fighter pilot–trained eyes were first to pick up the two black dots, low on the horizon and approaching with unbelievable swiftness. He tried to identify the speedy craft as he listened for the thunder of engines at max power. This is going to be a flyby to remember, he thought.

A pair of sleek, deadly-looking shapes flashed across the twenty-foot dike separating the field from the broad Missouri River. The sight of planes hurtling toward him in total silence raised goosebumps. The engine noise, when it came, was strangely muted—more like a giant cat purring than the nerve-shattering roar of unmuffled exhaust stacks.

Ross gaped, too awestruck to speak, as he realized that the two streaking silver darts were jet-powered fighters. The formation was overhead and gone before half the people in the audience realized what they had just witnessed. "My God," Ross whispered finally, "*jets!* How on earth? . . ." He shook his head in disbelief.

"They're out of the training squadron at Muroc," Deckard replied smugly. "They'll be part of an air show at the SAC base in Omaha tomorrow. The pilots wanted to RON close enough to make it without refueling en route. An old friend of a friend was glad to return a favor."

"I'm impressed." Ross paused, then asked, "Did you say they were going to RON here tonight?"

"That's right. They should be in the pattern any minute now."

"I gotta see one close up. Any problem, do you suppose?"

"They asked us to keep 'em roped off from the general public, but later I'm sure we can get a peek inside one."

Ross and Frazier joined the parade of onlookers forming a circle around the parked jets as they shut down their whining engines. "What I wouldn't give . . ." Frazier let his wistful expression trail off.

"After me, you'd be next," Ross remarked. "I sure want to visit with those pilots. I wonder just what the hell they were indicating when they crossed the field."

"I hear they're redlined at about Mach point eight—that's roughly five hundred fifty miles per hour. You can bet they were right on it."

Ross whistled softly, watching the pilots dismount and strip off flying gear. He stared at one—a black-haired youth who was laughing at something his buddy said—and mumbled to Frazier, "That guy looks familiar. It looks like . . . good God, it is! The tall, black-haired one's the son of my old CO at Thunderbird Field. His name is Kyle Wilson."

Ross strode through the milling throng toward the approaching pilots. "Lieutenant Wilson, over here."

Kyle stared at Ross for several seconds before he grinned in recognition. "Major Colyer. What a surprise this is. Hey, you're in uniform. You back on active duty?"

Ross extended his hand. "Hardly. I just signed up in the ready reserve. This is our activation ceremony."

"Oh, I see. Major Colyer, I'd like you to meet Major Biddle, our training flight commander."

Biddle eyed Ross's display of ribbons as they shook hands. "Did I hear you say you were in the reserve outfit here?"

"Right," Ross replied. "This is quite an event. That airplane looks like a real flying machine. Kyle, do you mean to tell me you're checked out in it already?"

"Just barely. I only have about thirty hours—ten of that solo, though. They let a student fly wing for this air show at Offutt tomorrow; I lucked out." Kyle turned to Major Biddle and added, "I'll go close our flight plans, sir, and call a cab—okay?"

"Wait a minute," Ross interrupted. "Hold up on that cab business. You people are my guests tonight, understand?"

Kyle looked at the major, who nodded, then strode toward the hangar.

Ross watched ruefully as the young man—with just a bit of a swagger—departed. Who the hell can blame him for being proud? he thought. "Kyle Wilson will make a good officer," he observed to Biddle. "His dad is one of the best."

"Kyle is a natural-born pilot," said Biddle. "What he didn't mention is that only the most outstanding students get to come along on these boondoggles. But, speaking of pilots, I notice you carry a few medals they don't give out for perfect attendance."

Ross chuckled. "I'd trade 'em all for your job."

"Yeah," Biddle observed, "I consider myself a very lucky man. Look, I can't give you a ride, but I can let you have a close-up look, if you like."

"You're on. Beggars can't be choosers."

Ross eased into the cockpit and drank in the array of instruments. "My God, where did some of these come from—and what happened to the ones I *do* remember?" he asked.

"Well, to start with, you have a different power cluster. You see, a jet gets its thrust from what amounts to a continuous explosion. It's the old law of physics that says for every force, an equal force is created in the opposite direction—remember?"

Ross nodded.

"Okay. Most people believe that it's pressure of the jet coming out the rear that propels the plane. It isn't really. What happens is, you squirt part of the force generated by the explosion out the tailpipe, and the opposite force drives the plane forward. Simple, huh? And it accounts for the fact that performance actually improves at altitude:

the explosive force remains about the same, but the thinner the air, the less air resistance. Fuel consumption goes down to less than a fourth of what it is at sea level."

"Yeah, how about that?" Ross marveled. "And just think—no torque, no vibration, and no noise inside the cockpit, I'm told."

"Right. So we measure power by tailpipe temperature instead of mani-fold pressure and, since rpm's are measured in the thousands, the gauge is calibrated in percent rather than actual revolutions."

"How does she handle? You know, takeoff, landing, and acrobatics?"

"Like a dream. It really eats up runway on landing rollout, though. The thing is so clean, there's no air friction to slow 'er down. They've come up with new brakes, however—discs that clamp against a rotor. Heat doesn't build up as rapidly, and they wear longer."

Ross extracted himself reluctantly from the cockpit. "One day," he breathed. "One day."

Chapter 6

15 October 1946
Headquarters, Central Intelligence Group
Washington, D.C.
Timothy O'Shea pitched a ten-page typewritten report toward his desktop and watched it slither over the edge. He mentally debated retrieving it. Punching his intercom, he barked, "Judy, get Hank Wallace in here, will you?"

Without waiting for an acknowledgment, he hung up and allowed his six feet of wiry muscle to slump into the depths of an oversized executive chair. He loosened his conservatively figured tie, then laced his hands behind his head and contemplated the ceiling. A frown creased his already profusely wrinkled features.

Not even the most ardent spinster would call the forty-five-year-old Central Intelligence Group (CIG) agent handsome. Tailors despaired of fitting suits to a body whose chest, waist, and hip measurements were virtually identical. Ears protruded from a skull devoid of fatty tissue. A visitor once observed, "No wonder Rick is a top agent. With those ears and wrinkles, he even *looks* like a goddamn bloodhound."

One picture graced the spartan office. It portrayed the Scarsdale High School football team of 1921. State Champs, a proudly displayed football proclaimed. O'Shea was the scatback. Fearless, and fleet of foot, he passed through defensive tackles like a greased ghost. His stock-in-trade was a twisting, shifting run—bouncing, ricocheting off the opposition—that earned him the nickname "Rick" O'Shea. The name he once carried proudly was inked out on the picture; now, coworkers, especially subordinates, used it at their peril.

He shifted his glance as Hank Wallace knocked once, then entered without waiting. He clutched a bulging file folder under his right arm. O'Shea lowered his gaze and waved his top agent to a seat. Wallace's gray slacks, white shirt, and highly polished black shoes constituted what amounted to a government agent's uniform. Hank's clothes fit his slender, youthful figure as they were advertised to look but seldom did—and without benefit of alteration. Taking one look at O'Shea's outthrust jaw and blazing eyes, Wallace assumed an attentive demeanor. "Morning, Tim. You wanted to see me?"

O'Shea pointed to where the errant ten-page report had landed on the floor. His voice was deceptively mild. "Hank, within the hour I'm supposed to brief the director on the Palestine situation. I was given a briefing paper from which I am supposed to extract certain facts— or at least I assumed that. Is this briefing paper a joke? Are you holding back the real report just to irritate me?"

Wallace scooped up the report and leafed through it. "It's all in there, Tim. Everything we've dug up during the past six months."

"Which amounts to zero, insofar as the director is concerned. The president's chief of staff expects us to give him answers to two questions. One: can the Jews stave off the Arabs when England pulls out of Palestine? Two: who is the strongman over there—Menachem Begin or David Ben-Gurion? President Truman has to get off the fence sometime in the not-too-distant future, and we have a history of backing losers. There isn't a damned thing here I can use."

"Tim," Wallace answered doggedly, "to answer those questions, we need a reliable source inside Palestine. We don't have one—not a *reliable* one at least—just finger pointers."

"Then get one, goddamnit!" O'Shea's gaunt features took on an apoplectic hue. He regained his composure and added, "Okay, here's a possibility. The director showed me a personal memo from Hoover to the president—wouldn't even give me a copy. I had to read it in his office. Anyway, the FBI is nosing around a charitable foundation in New York. Some rabbi up there has gotten together a bunch of monied Jews, and they're supposedly smuggling arms past the British blockade to the Jews inside Palestine.

"In this memo, Hoover claims that the operation is breaking a bunch of laws. That may be horseshit—J. Edgar doesn't like Jews on principle. He thinks in straight lines. Jews control much of the money in this country. People who have money stole most of it. Ergo, they are guilty and should go to jail. But it occurs to me that if that bunch—the organization is called the Jewish Relief Foundation—*does* have a pipeline inside Palestine, they have a good idea of what's going on."

"I say, more power to 'em," Wallace observed. "That blockade is stupid. Good Christ, those people have been slaughtered in Hitler's ovens, and now they're living in refugee camps not much better than what they left. Why not help them settle a country of their own?"

O'Shea gave his angry agent a wintry smile. "Stick to learning to write a decent report, Hank. Leave mind reading to the gypsies. Now, I'm going in there and tell the director you'll have a man in that New York headquarters at"—he leafed through Wallace's report—"Forty-four Water Street within the next two weeks. I don't want to know who, or how you do it. Get with the State Department, Commerce, Health, Customs—hell, anyone else you can think of. Call in some markers. We're going to come up with something to take the chief off my back."

29 October 1946
Victorville, California

Ross cradled the phone between his chin and shoulder while he lit a cigaret. He surveyed the stretch of barren desert landscape visible through the motel room's grimy window with a disgusted scowl. He'd probably been stupid to think he could track down Kyle during a weekday morning. About to give up, he heard a brisk, "This is Lieutenant Wilson."

"Kyle, this is Ross Colyer. Wasn't sure I'd find you at this time of day. I'm stuck here in Victorville and thought I'd at least try."

"Major Colyer! Hey, this is great. What're you doing in this part of the world? Lose your airplane in a crap game?"

"Not quite. We were on a cargo run to Los Angeles and had to divert in here with a fuel leak. The bird is out of commission for a goddamn fifty-cent O-ring seal. They're sending one from Burbank, but it will be tomorrow before we can be up and running. I was wondering if you might join me for dinner tonight. My map shows Muroc isn't more than about an hour's drive."

"Aw, gee, Major. I have a flight schedule this afternoon and ground school first thing tomorrow morning."

"I see. Well, I thought it was worth a shot. I'd like to hear how the flying is coming along—and please, just call me Ross."

"Uh, okay, uh, Ross. The '80 is the sweetest thing in the air, and I sure would like to talk to you. Look, we don't compare with L.A. for nightlife, but I'll show you what we have if you can make it down here. Can you arrange a ride in this direction?"

"I'll try to rent a car. I'd sure like to see the setup; I've never been on a jet fighter base."

"Well, we can sure take care of that. And fighters aren't all we have here. I'll tell you more about it when I see you. Listen, I'll give your name to the guard shack and they'll direct you to the officers' club. I'll look for you there around five, okay?"

Ross squinted into the noonday sun and let the desert warmth that cascaded into the open car window wash over him. He reluctantly conceded that mechanical delays weren't always unwelcome. It'd been a rough week. He stretched stiffened muscles and savored the idea of an afternoon of prowling around the desert, maybe finding an old mining camp to explore. Alex had wrinkled his nose at the invitation to come along, muttering something about checking on the airplane. It was a patent lie; Alex hated to walk, and was even less fond of the desert.

Ross saw a rest stop with a picnic table up ahead and eyed the cooler of beer and carton of sandwiches on the floor. Why not? I've got an entire five hours to kill, he thought. Walking around the rest area to scare off any slumbering desert rattlers, Ross stopped in his tracks as a jarring peal of thunder rent the stillness. "What the hell?" he exclaimed aloud. *Thunder?* On a cloudless day in the desert? It couldn't be, but the rumbling detonation sounded exactly like a typical Missouri thunderstorm.

He pondered the phenomenon as he washed down bites of a ham sandwich with the cold, tangy beer. Minutes later, he heard the distinctive whining burble of jet aircraft engines. Donning sunglasses against the glare, he spotted three swiftly moving planes streaking toward where the desert wind was beginning to dissipate a glob of black smoke, half hidden by a range of low hills. Okay, he thought, that's what I heard; they have a practice bombing and rocket range over there. He tidied up the area, returned the beer cooler to the rental sedan's rear seat, and steered onto the deserted highway.

It was after four o'clock when Ross turned off the main road. He'd almost missed the modest sign that pointed toward Muroc Field. They sure as hell don't advertise the place, he grumbled to himself. And that eight-foot security fence isn't exactly a welcome mat. This should be interesting, he thought. He drove through a tiny cluster of buildings bordering the narrow blacktop roadway—one service station, one combination grocery and drugstore, and four bars. He grinned. Easy to see what the law of supply and demand dictated in the local economy.

Another sign identified Gate No. 4 to the airfield. A barbed wire–crested gate barred the entrance. Ross pulled even with a white-painted sentry booth and smiled at the occupant, a nattily uniformed corporal. "Hi, my name is Ross Colyer. I'm visiting a Lieutenant Kyle Wilson. He's expecting me."

The unsmiling sentry scanned a clipboard. "Yes, sir, Mister Colyer. The lieutenant advised that he was expecting you. But I'm sorry, sir, the base is temporarily closed to all civilian visitors."

"Oh? Then can you call Lieutenant Wilson and ask him to meet me here? I'd appreciate it."

"Yes, sir, I'll call him. But the lieutenant isn't listed as being an authorized escort officer."

Ross wore a puzzled frown as he pulled into a graveled parking area. *Authorized* escort? What the hell was all this? We were never this strict during wartime, for Christ's sake, he complained to himself.

He'd finished a cigaret and was eyeing the cooler of cold beer when he heard the barking thunder of a powerful motorcycle engine. A machine he recognized as one of the big Indian Scouts rumbled to a halt inside the gate. He saw Kyle Wilson's trim figure dismount. The young pilot waved and waited for the sentry to open the locked gate.

Kyle strode toward the car wearing a broad smile. "Major Colyer— uh, Ross. Damn, I'm glad to see you. Look, I'm sorry about the cold reception, but—well, we got a flap of sorts."

"So I guessed. An exercise? Surprise readiness evaluation?"

"Uh, well, you might say that. Anyway, I can't take you on base to the O club. Do you mind if we go to the Jetwash Bar and Grill in town? One thing you can count on is a super steak and good drinks."

"Sounds great. You want to park your bike and ride with me?"

"Sure. I'll just be a minute."

"That's quite a hunk of machinery, Kyle," Ross observed, following him to where the gleaming red and black Indian leaned on its kickstand. "Is it new?"

"Yeah." Kyle flashed a pleased grin. "This is terrific country for bikes. With that four-thirty-five overhead-cam twin engine, she'll really fly. My mom gave it to me when I graduated from flying school."

"What do you hear from your folks?" Ross inquired as they settled into the rental car.

"Nothing much that's new, except dad has his next assignment. He's going into the judge advocate general's office. He has that old law degree, you know. Mom—well, she's just mom."

Ross studied the young man as they exchanged desultory conversation through the first mug of ice-cold beer. Kyle seemed tense, not worried tense, but excited. "So you're in love with the P-80?" Ross asked.

"Oh, man. I can't get enough of it. Five hundred fifty miles an hour straight and level—faster than the P-51s we flew in school could *dive.* Climb to twenty thousand feet in five minutes, and these models are already out of date. The new ones will have bigger engines, more firepower, better radios—I can't wait."

"I'd sure like to fly one," Ross said enviously. "I just can't imagine how a jet would, you know, feel."

"They're different all right," Kyle conceded with a wry grin. "That engine, for one thing. It's kinda touchy—you add throttle too fast and you have an over-temp. And engine life is short, although it's a little better now—we're getting twenty hours or so before an engine change. At first it was two or three. And the acceleration and deceleration are slower than with a prop. For instance, if you let your airspeed on final approach get low, you don't just make a small adjustment; you add climb power, hold the nose down to let your airspeed build, then raise the nose.

"You land like a streak of shit. The bird is so clean that I'll bet one would roll for five miles if you let it. It has speed brakes that you extend into the slipstream before landing, but you still have to get on the binders as soon as the nosewheel makes contact."

Ross realized that he'd been listening so raptly, he was neglecting his beer. Raising the mug, he saw that the little bar was filling up rapidly. Sure a quiet bunch, he thought. Everyone wore a long face and conversed with neighbors in muttered monosyllables. He looked at Kyle and again noticed the youngster's agitated state. "What the hell is going on, Kyle? Everyone around here acts like they're attending a funeral."

Kyle bit his lip and hesitated. "Something like that, you might say. Something big happened here today, Ross. I'm sorry, but we—we're under orders not to discuss it." His eyes revealed how difficult he found it to observe the ban.

"Oh." Ross nodded. "Hell, I can understand that. But I'm putting two and two together and coming up with a major accident. I saw a flight of '80s going toward a pall of smoke on my way here. I thought at first it was a bombing-rocketry range, but that smoke was from a crash site, I'm betting now. And from the security measures I see, I'll add another stack of chips on it being a highly classified prototype." He sipped his beer and watched for Kyle's reaction.

Kyle looked miserable. Ross grinned and waited silently. "Oh, shit, Ross." The youthful pilot cast worried glances at the subdued group crowded around the bar. "Listen, you shouldn't say a word about what you saw and heard here tonight. A lot of people could get their asses burned. But since you've figured it out pretty much anyway," he leaned across the table and hissed, "we lost a plane that got too close to the sound barrier."

"Come again?"

"Mach one—the speed of sound. It's like an invisible wall; the engineers call it the sound barrier."

Ross stared. "You mean he let his airspeed get beyond the plane's structural limits. They're calling that a 'barrier'?"

The excited youngster could contain himself no longer. "Look, sir, you're in the army—you have a security clearance—you know this has to be kept under wraps—"

Ross raised a hand, palm out. "Whoa, don't get your ass in a sling for divulging classified information. I'll admit I'm curious as hell. We lost planes during the war in power-on dives: the controls freeze and you can't pull out. The Germans lost more than we did trying to outdive our Mustangs, however. Their '109s and '190s weren't built as ruggedly as ours. Hell, any fighter pilot knows that if you exceed design airspeed, you'll start shedding parts. But an invisible wall?" He shrugged.

Kyle leaned toward him, his voice crackling with excitement. "That's just it, Ross. They're trying to design an airplane that *won't* come apart at high speeds. And it isn't a matter of a stronger airframe; it's designing a wing that will punch through that barrier. You see—and this *isn't* classified, it's just plain engineering fact—at the speed of sound, seven hundred plus miles per hour, the plane's surfaces compress the air in front until it becomes solid."

Ross blinked. "Yeah," he breathed. "I see. At some point it's just like trying to fly through a wall of water—it won't give." His eyes gleamed. This time, he made no move to halt Kyle's outpouring.

"Exactly. That's what happened today. The plane was a prototype, Republic Aviation's XP-84. It was sent here for evaluation as
a high-speed dive-bomber. It's bigger and faster than the '80, and has
a lot more range. Well, I was in one of those '80s you saw. We were
flying chase while the factory pilot recorded performance beyond Mach
point eight five; that's as far as their wind-tunnel data goes. He'd
previously made progressive runs up to point eight nine, and today
he was to go past point nine.

"It was spooky. I was monitoring his radio transmissions to ground
and heard the whole thing. The guy was cool and collected the entire
time. He said, 'I'm getting some buffeting at point nine one, Wally.
It's getting more severe—think we're just about at the limit of the
envelope.'

"The ground controller said, 'We think it's a bit early for severe
buffeting. Max says the bird should be good for point nine five, but
break it off now and we'll analyze the barograph readings tonight before
we press on.'

"The pilot comes back with, 'Uh—well, there's a small problem
there, Wally. I'm having a control surface reversal. Stick forward causes
a pitch *up*. Stick back makes her want to tuck under.'

"'Jesus Christ! Max says to pop speed brakes *now*. Drop the gear
if you have to. You'll lose it, but just get that bitch below point nine.'

"The pilot actually laughed. He comes back with, 'Tell Max I already thought of that. The barn door lasted all of thirty seconds—some
lucky jackrabbit now has a new place to hide.'" Kyle drank thirstily
and finished with an unemotional, "That was his last transmission. We
were orbiting beneath him at thirty thousand and saw him tumble down
in two pieces."

Ross sat transfixed. Finally, he asked, "He couldn't bail out?"

Kyle shook his head. "No, sir. Not at those speeds. They're working on a high-altitude, high-speed pilot escape system, but it's way
down the road."

Ross waved his hand impatiently. "Kyle, damnit, forget that 'sir'
business. That must have been a really bad experience. You okay?"

"Yeah, I am now, but I was pretty shook up for a while. First time
I've watched a man die. You sure feel helpless."

"I know what you mean. But I'm wondering, do they always seal
the base after a crash? Hell, this is a place where you expect accidents."

"Well, sir—Ross—not exactly. I've already talked too much," he
gave Ross a wry grimace, "so I may as well tell you the rest. There's

another experimental airplane on the way out here. It's built by Bell and called the X-1. This baby is supposed to be hot—*really* hot. It has rocket engines, and they think *it* can bust through that sound barrier.

"But a lot of people in Washington say it's impossible and want to scrap the project. They point to the English program. The Brits built a high-speed test model—the *Swallow*—and it broke up at somewhere around point nine five. Their government trashed any further research into supersonic flight. Our engineers are afraid that if this XP-84 crash gets played up too much, the same thing might happen here. I'd say that this accident investigation might take as long as a year to determine the actual cause."

"You seem to know a lot about what goes on for just a buck pilot," Ross teased with an amused, questioning squint.

Kyle blushed. "I guess I'm an eager-beaver sort, but this business is so fascinating—the things we don't know, and have to find out. I spend most of my spare time bugging the engineers and test pilots. There isn't much else to do around here, anyway.

"I'm gonna be a test pilot, Ross. It's the most exciting job in the air force—and the most important just now," Kyle added defensively. "You see, you guys had a war to prove yourselves. Well, there isn't any war just now. The men who'll rise to the top have to be damn good at something. I'm a pilot. I intend to be the best damn pilot in the air force. I'm on a list being considered for reassignment to a test pilot training program at Wright Field. Whoever is selected will be doing suitability tests on the new model P-80. I'm gonna be on that list—I've just got to be."

Ross formed interlocking rings on the tabletop with the condensation from his beer mug. "You're already a top-notch pilot, guy," he said softly. "That Major Biddle you were with at Kansas City told me that much. Go for it; you have what it takes—a lot of your dad's blood in your veins. Just don't—" he realized what he was about to say and finished with—"consider being anything but the best. Now, it's my turn to buy. This is a night I'll remember for a long, long time."

Ross watched the ribbon of blacktop unwind ahead of the car's probing headlights. He suddenly slammed his fist on the steering wheel. Damn you, Broderick Templeton, he raged inwardly. But for you . . . He relaxed and thanked the god that watches over people with big mouths. He'd been about to tell Kyle Wilson that, sometimes, outstanding performance of duty doesn't seem to make a damn bit of difference.

Chapter 7

Moshe Barnett threw an annoyed glance at his secretary as she escorted a visitor into his neatly organized office. The athletic, suntanned president of Seaboard Manufacturing terminated his telephone conversation with a curt, "I'll get back to you."

Folding his hands atop the desk's walnut surface, Barnett nodded an acknowledgment, then waved his visitor to a chair. He regarded the intruder with gray eyes, almost the exact shade of his well-barbered hair. His easy smile of greeting was unusual, however, in that the lips didn't curve, some muscular quirk causing him to smile in a straight line. Wrinkles forming parentheses at the corners of his mouth gave him the appearance of a friendly jack-o'-lantern.

"Mister Sweitzer says he has an appointment with you, Mister Barnett." The birdlike woman pursed her thin lips, painted a garish orange, in disapproval. "I don't have the appointment listed in my book, Mister Barnett," she stated in icy tones.

Moshe flashed his peculiar straight-lipped grin. "I'm sorry, Winifred, I made the appointment by phone yesterday and forgot to tell you. I apologize. I'm glad to meet you, Mister Sweitzer. Would you care for coffee?"

Winifred expressed her displeasure with an indignant sniff. Checking to see that her lacquered, blue-tinted hairdo was intact, she twitched her bony hips into the outer office, not deigning to follow up on her boss's offer of refreshment.

Sweitzer settled his diminutive, figure into an armchair and declined coffee. Middle-aged, he had an unruly shock of snow white hair; that and gold-rimmed eyeglasses gave him a distinguished, faintly foreign appearance. "Thank you for seeing me, Mister Barnett," he said primly. He deposited a canvas carryall on the floor beside him; it gave off a metallic rattle as he released his grip.

"My—ah—friend said you had a matter to discuss that I might find of interest," Moshe responded.

"If you are in the business of making guns, I think you will be interested—yes, Mister Barnett."

"Guns?" Moshe's features reflected mild surprise. "I'm sorry, Mister Sweitzer, someone has misled you. I manufacture and broker machine tools, not guns."

"Same difference," Sweitzer announced airily with a casual wave of a neatly manicured hand. "I wish to manufacture a gun. This requires certain machine tools. You make the machines I require. We can do business, no?"

"Possibly. What type of gun are we talking about?"

"A handheld machine gun, Mister Barnett. One similar to those provided to the French underground during the war."

Barnett sat bolt upright. "*Machine gun?* You propose to set up a plant to make a fully automatic weapon? I believe you must explain a great deal to me before we go further, Mister Sweitzer. Do you have a patent on such a weapon? Do you have a government contract, or a permit to make this gun? What firm do you represent? Where is your office located?"

Sweitzer repeated his wave of dismissal, this time with an air of irritation. "So many questions. It is a simple matter. I am Swiss. I am not connected with any business firm. I have invented a firearm superior to any in use. The war ended before I completed my design, and now no one is interested in making guns—except, I hear, the Jews in Palestine. I understand they desperately need personal firearms. I will make and sell them what they need."

Moshe gulped. "Mister Sweitzer, what you propose borders on being impossible. First, ownership of fully automatic weapons is illegal in the United States except for law enforcement agencies and the military, and the manufacture of such weapons is closely controlled. The process requires highly specialized machinery and is terribly expensive. Second, and most important, shipment of arms of any type to the Jewish Defense Force in Palestine is prohibited by a British mandate—and enforced by an airtight blockade."

"This I know, Mister Barnett," Sweitzer responded in tones reserved for explaining difficult matters to a child. "I will take the machines you sell me *to* Palestine and make the guns there."

Moshe, at a loss for words, rubbed his face with both hands. Lowering them, he stared at Sweitzer with a suddenly suspicious gaze. "Who suggested you come to me, Mister Sweitzer?"

"A Mister Berkowitz in New York. A man in Vienna who is in the arms-manufacturing business suggested I come to America; he gave me Berkowitz's name. Berkowitz called someone, then told me to see you today. I am growing impatient, Mister Barnett. I was told everything in America would be easy. Is no one here interested in even *seeing* my invention?"

Barnett watched, horrified, as Sweitzer calmly started to remove items from the canvas carryall. They could only be parts of a disassembled firearm. Barnett leaped to his feet, then raced to the open door and closed it. Winifred would have some caustic remarks about that unprecedented move he knew, but . . .

"Mister Sweitzer," Barnett uttered in hushed tones, "have you been carrying that thing around in public? In *New York,* of all places? Don't you know that just possessing an unregistered firearm is a serious violation there? And fully automatic weapons are illegal *anywhere.*"

Sweitzer appeared unruffled by Moshe's outburst. "I am a businessman," Sweitzer stated stiffly. "What, may I ask, is wrong with displaying the merchandise one offers for sale? How else is one expected to sell? See, the gun easily breaks down into three parts: barrel, stock, and firing mechanism—none longer than sixteen inches. Assembled, it fires seven hundred rounds per minute, is virtually jam-proof, uses the standard three-oh-three cartridge, and weighs only five pounds."

Moshe, still nearly in shock, was drawn to the black matte-finished components much like a mouse facing a cobra. He stroked the ugly, sinister-looking barrel. Fragments of discussions he'd had with a Julius Mantz two weeks ago flashed through his mind. Could this be "The Gun" Mantz had told him was badly needed by the Jewish Defense Force in Palestine? Easily concealed, a deadly rate of fire,

chambered for readily available .303 ammunition. Could it be manu-
factured in existing underground munitions production facilities inside
that beleaguered country?

Moshe was looking at a precision-made weapon, one requiring hours
of work by skilled hands. What if the firing mechanism could be housed
in a stamped receiver, much like the famous "grease gun"? What if
the hand-tooled stock could be replaced by a skeleton of steel rod?

Barnett's instinct for bartering surfaced. "What would you expect
to be paid for your invention, Mister Sweitzer?" he asked idly.

"Thirty thousand dollars for these drawings," the little Swiss replied
promptly, extracting a roll of blueprints from his carryall, "plus another thirty thousand for designing the dies peculiar to the firing
mechanism. You see," he added in confidential tones, "most of the
gun can be turned out on standard milling machines. I am a tool and
die maker by trade and will have to design dies for the parts I made
by hand. Then I would expect to participate in the profit realized from
its manufacture."

Moshe nodded. His mind raced. "I would, of course, be interested
in furnishing machine tools to a legal arms manufacturer," he said off-
handedly. "I suggest you go back to this Mister Berkowitz and tell
him you can arrange for the necessary machine tools." He glanced at
the stack of War Assets Administration circulars on his desk; they were
filled with lists of such equipment. "Do you anticipate investing funds
of your own in the project?"

"I have no funds, Mister Barnett, only a dream."

"I see. I warn you that prospective investors will have some sharp
questions. Has the prototype been test fired? Proof fired? How long
will it take to produce the necessary dies? What are your qualifications as a production manager?"

"Test fired? Yes. Proof fired? That requires a production model to
have any validity. Provide me with an assistant who can meet my
tolerances, and I can furnish dies within six months. I *will* produce,"
Sweitzer stated in firm tones.

"Very good. Now, I suggest you leave your prototype with me. I
have a secure vault and will give you a receipt for a sealed container.
You risk arrest and a prison term if you're apprehended with that firearm
in your possession."

"Never. This is the only item of value I own. It will not leave my
sight until I have a check in my hand." Sweitzer's pale blue eyes took

on a mischievous twinkle. "The man in Vienna—he told me, 'Karl, go to America yourself. Do not send a fool to do your negotiating; already they have many of their own.'"

Moshe chuckled, then sobered. "Good advice, but I can't intercede on your behalf unless you leave the gun with me. I will not risk being involved as an accomplice if it becomes known that I have knowledge of an illegal firearm and failed to report it to the authorities."

Sweitzer reluctantly agreed and watched Moshe deposit the canvas carryall inside the vault. Barnett waited until he was certain the little Swiss had left the outer office, then he dialed the phone connected to his private line. "Miss Shamir," he barked, "I must talk with Julius Mantz—today if possible. And, oh, yes, tell him I accept his ah—proposition."

17 November 1946
Toronto, Canada

Eddie Kotch's fleshy features bunched in a dark scowl. The train from Detroit had been crowded, the club car overflowed with thirsty passengers, and they were two hours late. He turned to Moshe Barnett as they elbowed their way through the press of exiting passengers toward a cab rank. "I still say the guy sounds like a nutcase," Kotch growled, his breath creating spurts of vapor in the subfreezing air.

Moshe flashed his straight-line smile. "Many things Karl Sweitzer may be, Eddie, but a nutcase is not one of them. His motive is simple and straightforward; he wants to be rich. I had only the briefest look at his gun, but the workmanship was first-rate. If it will work half as well as he claims, it could be our answer."

"The son of a bitch wouldn't even let me see the thing or arrange for shipment." Eddie snorted in disgust. "I had to leave the refrigerator with him, show him how to conceal the parts in the insulation, and let him arrange for shipment by Railway Express all by himself. Dumb bastard was convinced he could just stroll into Canada carrying the damn gun in that canvas bag." Eddie shook his head. "How come Julius wants to handle this operation in Canada, anyway?"

"A man named Clifford is the only member of the rabbi's steering committee from Canada. He's been complaining that there isn't anything for him to do." Moshe smiled. "Plus, the guy has access to money—big money."

Eddie glowered at a cold-faced, fashionably dressed matron trying to cut ahead of them and appropriate the sole available cab. Ignoring her icy, "Well . . . ," he slid into the rear seat. "Damn foreigners—none of 'em got any manners," he observed. Then he said, "Good to hear we have a project without money worries. Is this apt to be expensive?"

"Could be. Sweitzer estimates six months to turn out dies for the firing mechanism. Add a twenty percent optimism factor, time to test and proof-fire a production model, disassemble and ship the machinery, and we're talking a full year. That won't cut it. The Arabs will have covered Palestine like locusts by then. We've got six, maybe seven months. Pushing up the schedule like that will drive costs out of sight. As it is, we need a pipeline into Europe someplace so the machine components can be put on small boats and smuggled in."

The cab halted in front of their hotel, and the driver went to the rear to remove their bags. Eddie paused, his fingers on the door handle. "You just worry about getting that factory put together. When you give me the word, old Eddie will have those machines in place and running before you know it. Trust me."

Clyde Clifford was a big man, and energetic. His round pink face was unlined by middle age and seemed set in a perpetual smile. He bounced when he walked, his ample girth reminding Moshe of Clement Moore's description of Santa Claus. Unable to sit for more than a few minutes at a time, Clifford paced as he talked. "I can't wait to hear what you fellows have in mind for me. Julius said it was big, and essential. That's what I've been waiting for. Thought I was destined to be a wallflower at the party, har, har, har."

Moshe read Eddie's thoughts: Another goddamn clown. "It is big, and it is essential," Barnett assured the portly industrialist. "Now, we're going to be joined shortly by a man who claims to have invented a compact, fully automatic weapon. It is the type of gun our Palmach troops are clamoring for, and one almost impossible to smuggle past the blockade.

"The solution is to equip their underground factories to *produce* these guns. That, in a nutshell, is what we propose to do—put a factory together here, then disassemble it and ship the pieces to Palestine."

Clifford's demeanor changed abruptly, erasing the garrulous, glad-hander image. "You say the man *claims* to have invented a gun. Have you seen it? I know inventors—deal with them all the time. I find most of their 'inventions' exist only in their minds." He peered intently at Barnett.

"I've seen a handmade prototype," Moshe responded. "He says it will shoot. I believe him; it's first-class work. The only unfinished aspect is the making of dies for parts unique to the firing mechanism."

Clifford stood staring into space. Talking more to himself than his audience, he muttered, "I don't offhand know a master gunsmith. I do have a master tool and die maker, however. As for space, there's the old warehouse on Marlboro Street. We can use the inactive charter for Acme Metal Fabrication, Limited, as a vehicle. Organize a fundraiser . . ." He wheeled and asked Moshe, "Machine tools—basic lathes, horizontal drilling machines, planers, screw machines, and so forth—you have a source?"

"The best. Our War Assets Administration has them coming out their ears—at scrap-metal prices. There's no problem getting export permits for Canada."

Clifford nodded. "This inventor. What kind of person is he? What's his background? What does he want from all this?"

Barnett frowned, a thoughtful look on his face. "He's Swiss. Says he was told to come over here and sell his invention to the Jews; other markets for military arms are glutted. He's—well—he's odd in some ways. Terribly naive when it comes to doing business here. He's a tool and die maker himself, by the way—estimates six months to make the dies. His motive? He likes money."

"Well, that's in his favor," Clifford responded in dry tones. "Anything I can't abide is a starry-eyed zealot bent on saving the human race." He paused as the phone rang. "He's on his way up," Clifford stated as he hung up.

The Canadian slumped on a sofa, all traces of joviality gone; he appeared to be half asleep. Karl Sweitzer sat in a chair facing the trio, his feet barely touching the floor. "These gentlemen tell me you have a gun for sale, Mister Sweitzer," Clifford drawled. "May I see it?"

"My demonstration model is in a safe place, Mister Clifford," the little Swiss responded warily.

Clifford gave Sweitzer a long, level look. "Now let's see if I have all my facts straight. You've invented a gun. You want to manufacture the thing and sell it. You require capital and a factory. Is that substantially correct?"

"It is."

"I'm the man with the resources you need. I'm interested. But a couple of things need to be settled up front." Clifford's tone grew icy. "I won't waste your time or mine. Number one, I run this fucking show. Number two, don't play games with me, like that coy, 'My demonstration model is in a safe place.' When I ask questions, I want straight answers."

He ignored Sweitzer's efforts to voice his indignation. "Step one," Clifford continued, "I want to shoot that gun. My car will pick up you and your gun at your hotel tomorrow morning. We'll go to my place in the country and see if it fires; these gentlemen will be there too. *If* the thing works, we'll go on from there. Is that understood?"

Barnett tried to ignore Eddie Kotch's smirk as they waited for the elevator.

17 November 1946
Teterboro Field, New Jersey

Ross watched three straining young men manhandle four-foot-square cartons from the DC-3 into the bed of a ton-and-a-half truck. Ariel made her presence felt, issuing orders like a drill sergeant. She obviously knew the crew—addressing each man by his first name.

Ross felt good. A smooth flight, no mechanical problems, and, best of all, money in the bank. The past few months had netted Allied Air, Inc., more income than the preceding year. As soon as he returned to Kansas City, he'd buy that engine for the Norseman and look for another pilot. The sturdy, fabric-covered craft was slow, ugly, and ungainly, but she was a proven moneymaker.

Ariel approached with swift, purposeful strides. "Well, Ross, I suppose you'll spend the night?"

"Yeah, it's been a long five days. I think we'll lay up here and go home tomorrow. What do you have in mind for our next run?"

"I'll have to call you, perhaps Sunday. The solicitation crew was working on a drive in the Dallas area when I left."

"We'll be ready," Ross told her cheerfully. "Enjoy your weekend."

Her voice contained no hint of emotion other than business: "I have a week's work to catch up on. My schedule leaves little time for recreation."

Ross's mumbled, "We'll have to do something about that sometime," drew a dark look.

Alex placed his knife and fork on the empty plate and signaled for the waitress. Ross leaned forward and grinned. "Okay, out with it. You've been in some sort of huff for the last two days. What's eating you?"

Alex ordered a bottle of beer, then, at Ross's nod, made it two.

"I don't like this setup, Ross."

Ross sighed and refilled his beer mug. "I know, I know, Alex. She's pushy. She has the airplane loaded at night when we aren't there. But she has the weight and balance computed, accurate to the nth degree—and we get a good night's sleep. After all, she *is* picking up the tab. She's just a compulsive doer. She can't sit and do nothing for more than about ten minutes. And, I might remind you, we're eating regular and making loan payments on time."

"Ever wonder why she doesn't want us around those nights?"

"Alex, I don't think I really give a damn. These are her cargoes, from onloading to offloading. She and Katzenbaum assured us that we wouldn't be carrying illegal goods, like untaxed booze or stolen merchandise. As far as I'm concerned, those cartons contain just what she tells us: used clothing collected for the DPs in Europe."

"Ross, I had to go back to the airplane the other night in Tulsa. I wanted to check a hydraulic leak after the bird had been parked awhile. That cargo was already loaded."

"So?"

"There was a guard on it. I had to prove I was crew before he'd let me on board."

"Okay."

"Don't you wonder why she'd be guarding a bunch of old clothes?"

"No, I don't wonder. She doesn't want the stuff stolen. Paranoid, maybe, but none of our business."

"Well, *I* wondered. I opened a couple of those boxes."

"You *what?*"

"Look, all we know about this woman is what she and that shifty character Katzenbaum told us—which isn't much. Don't worry, I resealed them so no one can tell they were ever opened." Alex sipped his beer.

"Okay, okay." Ross spread his hands. "I can see you're dying to tell me. What was in the boxes?"

"Well, it must be a strange bunch of women and kids they're helping. They all wear GI army boots, sizes nine to eleven."

"Is that right?" Ross's voice was cold.

"And they all keep their pants up with GI web belts."

"Alex, unless the stuff was stolen—which I doubt, since the surplus warehouses are running over with that sort of thing—it's legal."

"That's bullshit. Can't you see? This so-called charitable foundation is equipping some kind of army."

"Even if they are, so what? We aren't breaking any laws."

"Damnit, Ross." Alex realized he was shouting; he looked around quickly, then continued in more moderate tones. "The woman is lying to us. Doesn't that bother you in the least? Even if the cargoes *are* legal, is your obsession to make a buck keeping you from wondering *why* she's lying?"

"That's a low blow, Alex." Ross's voice was ominously level. "Allied Air is the only future either of us have. Do you want to spend your best years hanging around airfields, grabbing at a chance to pick up a few bucks doing odd jobs?"

Alex lowered his gaze and concentrated on making circles in the pool of condensation left by the chilled bottles. "I want out, Ross. I don't want any more to do with this operation."

Ross stifled an astonished outburst and lit a cigaret while he collected his thoughts. "I think you're overreacting, Alex."

"Maybe, but I've thought about it for the past two days. I won't leave you flapping in the breeze; I'll stick around until you can find someone else. I know you don't have the cash to buy me out, so I'll take your note for the book value of my share. But I want out."

"I—I don't know what to say, Alex. I have no hold on you—you're free to do as you please. I'd offer to cancel this contract if that'd make you change your mind, but we need it just to survive."

"I know that, and I don't blame you. You probably won't understand, but . . . it's just that I don't like Jews."

Ross gaped, unable to speak.

"I can't help it, Ross. I grew up in a neighborhood where Jews owned all the good stores, including the only small loan business. They drove shiny new cars; their women wore fur coats and fancy jewelry. My dad worked in a meatpacking plant. Mom took in washing. They blamed the Jews for the way we had to live. Maybe they were wrong, but I can't be around people like Katzenbaum or this Shamir woman without getting riled. If I had my way, we'd be doing this for the Arabs."

"I'm flabbergasted, Alex. I had no idea you felt this way. What these people went through—what they're calling the Holocaust—that doesn't change your thinking one bit?"

"I've said all I'm going to. In my own mind, I know these people

are up to something besides kindly acts of goodwill. I won't be part
of it."

Ross stood and counted out bills, placing them alongside the check.
"We'll talk about it tomorrow, Alex," he said.

"I won't change my mind."

"I'm sure you won't," Ross replied bitterly. "I won't even try to
make you." They walked toward the exit, faces tight and drawn with
inner turmoil.

An hour later, in the darkness of the hotel room, Ross untangled
himself from sweaty, twisted sheets and sat upright. Bone-tired though
he was, sleep evaded him. He flicked on the light, swung his feet over
the edge of the thin mattress, and lit a cigaret.

Damn Alex for being a rednecked, bigoted fool. Why hadn't he noticed
the guy's bias before? Then he recalled a night in the Kelly Field officers'
club when Alex had lashed out at a loudmouthed lieutenant, saying,
"Everyone knows Jews won't fight." Ross should have known.

The defection of his dour, taciturn partner was maddening, but at
the same time, saddening. They had been close. They had shared some
trying times. Now, just when things were beginning to look up, Alex
had to pull this crap.

Sure, there was more to their contract than met the eye, Ross acknowledged. So why didn't it bother him? Well, maybe it did. Maybe
Alex had more faith in his convictions—had the guts to investigate
his suspicions. Did that mean he, Ross, was blinded by the lure of juicy
profits? No, he told himself savagely, Alex was motivated purely by
anti-Semitic feelings. I'll put it squarely to Ariel tomorrow, he thought.

The telephone's raucous clamor interrupted Ross's introspection.
He answered after the second ring. "Room three-seventeen."

"Ross?" He recognized Ariel Shamir's precise tones.

"Yeah, this is Ross."

"I hope I didn't wake you, but there's been a change in plans."

"I see. What changed?"

"Tomorrow. I must go to Chicago. You can drop me off on your
way to Kansas City. Any problem with that?"

"No problem. What time is departure?"

"Let's make it noon; I can't get away before then."

"We'll be ready. Oh, any cargo?"

"No, just me."

"You have any objection if I call one of the freight forwarding outfits—see if I can pick up something to pay expenses?"

After a moment's hesitation, Ariel said, "No, none at all. Just so it doesn't make us late."

"I'll see that it doesn't," he assured her. "Good-night."

Ross sprawled back on the bed and rearranged the snarl of blankets. Chicago. What rang a bell about Chicago? he asked himself. Of course—Janet. She'd gone there to take a job. How would she react if he called? He replayed the scene in his mind of that night last winter in D.C.—in the hotel room. She had been sitting at the window gazing into the winter dawn when he awoke. Reluctant to break the silence, he finally asked, "Shall I call down for coffee?"

"I'd like some, yes," Janet replied without turning. "Ross, what's wrong with me?" she added abruptly.

"Wha? . . . Wrong? What are you talking about?"

"BT told me I was frigid. I'm *not*." Janet turned, and Ross saw her eyes glisten with tears. "I'm a kind, warm, loving person. I wanted more than anything else to make love with you. But . . ."

"Janet." Ross swung his feet over the edge of the bed. "It was a perfect—"

"Don't lie. You felt it too. We went through the motions, but there was no—no *togetherness.*"

Ross stubbed out his cigaret and crossed to the bathroom for a glass of water. The parting had been amicable, Ross rationalizing that perhaps the ghosts he'd joked about *had* been in the Willard's antebellum room. Not only those of past presidents, but the ghosts of BT, and maybe Ruth Lasher—the girl he'd lost in China. He and Janet had promised to keep in touch—would always be good friends, they vowed—but they'd never written. Yeah, he told himself, I'll look her up; I'll be there overnight—if she'll see me. The thought of discussing his screwed-up situation with the levelheaded Janet brightened his outlook. He fell asleep within minutes.

Chapter 8

18 November 1946
Midway Airport, Chicago, Illinois
Ross handed Ariel's bag to the cabbie and leaned through the rolled-down rear window. "Enjoy your stay. I'll wait for your call in K.C. You think Dallas, huh?"

"Yes, it may be a two-day trip. They said something about my speaking at a rally one evening."

Ross nodded. "See you in Dallas then." He gave her a soft, two-finger salute and watched the cab slide into the afternoon traffic. Wonder how many GI boots and web pistol belts she'll raise this time? he asked himself. Damnit, he'd had an opportunity to confront her with the business Alex laid in his lap the night before—why hadn't he? He scowled and turned toward the terminal entrance.

He found Janet listed in the directory and dialed the number. After letting it ring five times, he hung up. Oh, well, he told himself, she does have a job. Not likely she'd be home this time of day. He collected Alex and they headed for a nearby hotel. Alex, who seemed relieved that Ross hadn't mentioned the previous night's conversation, made an unnatural effort to engage in small talk. Ross replied in monosyllables, and they completed the ride in silence. At the hotel, neither suggested sharing a room or meeting for dinner.

The name came to Ross in the shower. The *Chicago Globe*—that's where Janet had said she was going to work. He toweled himself dry, slipped into a pair of shorts, and opened the telephone directory. Two calls later, he was rewarded by that voice he remembered so well—laughter always seeming to lurk just below the surface. "Mrs. Templeton. May I help you?"

He grinned. "Why, yes, ma'am. You see, I'm a stranger in town and don't have anyone to eat dinner with tonight. Are you available?"

A pause. Then a cautious, "Would this be Ross Colyer?"

"None other. I'm surprised you recognize my voice. How on earth are you?"

"Oh, Ross. My God, it's good to hear that Upper Peninsula twang. In all your travels you never lost it. And you're in town? Where are you calling from?"

"A hotel near the airport. I was passing through and had to look you up. Are you free this evening? I know it's a Saturday night, but thought I'd try anyway."

"Oh . . ." He sensed indecision. Then a firm, "Absolutely. Where shall we go?"

"You name it. Anyplace where we can talk without having to yell at each other."

Janet chuckled. "I remember the type of restaurant you don't like. I know just the place. The food's good, the drinks are passable, and nothing but Glenn Miller in the background."

"Fantastic. What's the name?"

Janet gave him an address. "Apartment Four-C. Ring the bell—my name is on the mailbox."

Ross smiled to himself. "Hey, sounds like a high-class joint. Shall I wear black or white tie?"

"Anything except that awful number with the hula girl and palm tree on it you used to have. Sevenish?"

"It's a date. You still like that god-awful California burgundy?"

"Just bring yourself; I'll select the wine. Don't be late."

Janet took the flowers and, after a long, searching look, gave him a chaste peck on the cheek. "Oh, they're lovely. Come on in; I'll quick put them in a vase."

Ross watched her flowing stride with open admiration as Janet moved to retrieve a vase from atop the buffet. Her tailored black slacks and a V-necked white blouse emphasized a perfectly proportioned figure. She was clearly a classy, fourteen-karat dish.

"I wasn't sure you'd want to see me," Ross said.

"Don't be silly. I was wondering about you just the other day."

"You didn't write."

"Nor did you," Janet replied shortly as she concentrated on arranging the flowers.

Ross stood, at a loss for a response. Finally he blurted, "You still have the sexiest walk of anyone I know—especially from behind."

Janet turned—her cheeks flaming but her voice frosty. "More so than that nurse in China you told me about?" She saw Ross's face flush and clapped a hand over her mouth. "Oh, my God, Ross. That was a terrible thing to say. Forgive me. I—I—why do I always say the wrong things—things I don't mean?"

Ross forced a shaky laugh. "Aw, forget it. I was out of line."

"Let's forget the whole stupid business, shall we?" Janet responded. "Now, makings for drinks are in the kitchen. We can talk while I finish dinner."

Ross perched on a stool at the breakfast bar and swirled gin and vermouth over ice. He noticed that Janet wore her rich mahogany-hued hair piled atop her head. I wonder if she remembers I always liked it that way? he asked himself. He poured the drinks into chilled glasses. Handing Janet hers, he raised his own. "To all the good times."

Janet met his gaze, a wistful smile causing her gray-green eyes nearly to close. "There were some good ones, weren't there?"

An hour later, Ross, comfortably stuffed, stretched his legs beneath the table and watched Janet rinse and stack the dinner dishes in the sink. "Enough reminiscing," he said, "and enough talk about the air freight business. Tell me about your work."

Janet returned with coffee, and a bottle of brandy and glasses. "I love my work." Her features curved in an enthusiastic smile. "It's nothing great just now; I'm only an assistant on the international news desk. I read all the foreign releases, sort them for the appropriate departments, and flag the ones I think are hot. I'm taking a night course in journalism at the university, though. I'll move into a real reporter's slot when I finish. It's exiting, Ross—to be the first person in the entire country to know what's going on."

Ross stirred his coffee and lit cigarets for both of them. "I'm glad for you," he said cheerfully. "You'll make a great newshound. You were always curious."

Janet sipped her brandy and her expression sobered. "Ross, we've talked around it all evening. I *am* curious—is there any chance you will ever get a regular commission? I know how much an army career meant to you."

"Funny you should mention that. As a matter of fact, I am back in uniform—sort of."

"Really? Tell me; and what do you mean by 'sort of'?"

"I'm in the ready reserve now, instead of the standby. That means I take training in my spare time, in return for which I agree to report for active duty immediately in case of an emergency. My old B-24 squadron commander blew into town a couple of months ago—he's in charge of setting up these reserve training detachments—and conned me into signing up as detachment commander.

"It's quite a setup. We already have six officers and four enlisted men assigned and four airplanes—AT-6s and AT-11s—that we use for training. Our detachment orderly room, operations, and a room for ground school are in the hangar right next to my office, and we're even forming an officers' open mess!"

"Oh, Ross! That's wonderful. Does this mean someday you'll be back on active duty?"

"Not in the foreseeable future. But if I do a good job, it sure won't hurt my chances. According to Colonel Wilson, word around the cocktail circuit has it that Senator Templeton is going to make a run against Truman in '48. If he does, it's likely that the damn political interest flag on my records will be pulled."

"Oh, m'God," Janet exclaimed. "Broderick Templeton—*president?* That's downright scary."

"Anyway, things have turned out okay. Running my own airline, I don't have a lot of bureaucratic red tape to put up with."

Janet gave Ross a long look. "That's crap, Ross Colyer. You're down. Don't try to fool me; you're as low as I've ever known you to be."

Ross emptied his brandy glass and gave her a rueful smile. "Like I said, you'll make a first-class reporter. Okay, I was pissed—mad as hell, in fact—that I couldn't go back on active duty. But after this guy I met at Kelly showed up and wanted to start an airline, I discovered I couldn't get flying out of my blood."

"But you hate civilian flying."

"Not so," Ross protested. "It's just—well, that DC-3 we lost last winter ate up most of our operating capital. This summer has been a real struggle. To top it off, last night Alex told me he wants out. You see, we landed a contract with a Jewish relief agency that's been a lifesaver, and it turns out he hates Jews. Let me tell you about the deal, see what you think. . . ."

The mantle clock chimed softly. Ross counted twelve and leaped to his feet. "My God, I didn't realize the time. I'm sorry—you're a working gal and you have Sunday duty."

Janet regarded him from the corner of the sofa, where she lounged, bare feet tucked beneath her, like a lazy cat. "The farthest thing from my thoughts. You don't know how I've enjoyed this evening. It takes me back to Hickam. Remember those nights on the beach? You'd tell me your dreams and I'd tell you mine. Mix me another drink—so I'll *be* a zombie tomorrow."

Ross talked as he made refills. "So what do you think? Is Alex right? Am I getting into something I'll regret?"

Janet chewed her lower lip. "I'd like to meet this Shamir woman. You sure you aren't letting a pair of swishy hips and big boobs screw up your thinking?"

"Oh, Janet. For Christ's sake. I'm not some dumb, calf-eyed sopho-more."

Janet laughed. "No? Tell me about men, Ross," she teased. She sobered. "Okay, so what are the alternatives? What happens if you tell her to take her business elsewhere?"

"Allied Air would be out of business within thirty days," Ross replied glumly. "But if she's setting me up for—for God knows what—something that could land me in jail . . . Well, better broke than behind bars."

"Ross, the money—why didn't you tell me? BT carried a big, re-ally big, insurance policy. He left me a rich woman. Let me help—maybe buy some stock in your company?"

"No way," Ross snapped. "Two reasons. First, I wouldn't risk your money. Second, I wouldn't touch money that Broderick Templeton III had anything to do with—under any circumstances."

"You're a stiff-necked ass, Ross Colyer. That isn't BT's money; it's mine."

"Maybe, but it's a closed issue."

"Okay then, Mister Know-it-all. What will you do?"

Ross finished his drink, stood, and reached for his jacket. "Like Alex said the day we accepted the job against his wishes, 'I'll stay in the pot for another upcard.' But the first whiff of something illegal, and I'm dumping her."

"Sometimes that's easier said than done," Janet replied sagely. "But I agree that it's about the only logical thing to do, for now." She followed him to the door, then gave him another peck on the cheek. "Don't stay away for so long next time. And, Ross, I'm dying to know what happens, okay?"

Ross punched her lightly on the shoulder and grinned. "Count on it. I need all the people in my corner I can get. Janet, we parted friends . . ."

Janet hugged herself with crossed arms and cocked her head to one side. "What's the alternative?"

"Enemies? Lovers?"

"Is there no middle ground, Ross?"

He responded with a dry chuckle. "We seem to be standing in it. I'll keep in touch." He heard the door close softly behind him as he walked toward the elevators.

21 November 1946
Kansas City

From behind his battered wooden desk, Ross regarded Ariel with a skeptical glint in his eye. The slacks-clad woman had shown up without notice at his office in one corner of a hangar at Fairfax. His gut feeling told him he wasn't going to like hearing whatever prompted the surprise visit.

Ross greeted her, then made introductions. "Miss Shamir, meet our new pilot, Jake Trask. Alex left to try his fortunes elsewhere."

Ariel proffered her hand, seemingly immune to Trask's wicked smile, his dark features split by flashing white teeth. The big man was a good pilot; Ross had taken to him from the first when Jake had applied for entry into the reserve detachment at Fairfax. A second-generation Greek—his father had shortened the family name from something unpronounceable—Jake had a fun-loving disposition that was a far cry from Alex Taylor's. Like Ross, Jake had been a fighter pilot in the Pacific. Their experience differed in that Jake had flown F4U Corsairs off a carrier for the marines.

Trask excused himself as Ariel lit a cigaret and sipped Jake's idea of coffee. "Ross, I'd like to change your itinerary," she said. "Instead of Denver, I'd like you to go first to Albuquerque, then to Nashville, and on to Teterboro."

"I see no problem," Ross replied. "I'm curious, though. Why come here to deliver the message when a phone call would have served?"

"You'll be carrying a different kind of cargo. I thought you might prefer my explaining the change in person."

Alarm bells rang faintly in Ross's subconscious. His gut tightened. Ariel's *asking* him to change his itinerary instead of *directing* the alteration was a warning. "What *kind* of different cargo are we talking about?"

"Ross, I told you from the beginning you would never be asked to break the law. If you examine the items you'll be picking up in Albuquerque and Nashville, well, you might believe I misled you."

"But I won't be—breaking the law, that is. How about letting me be the judge of that?"

"Of course. But first some background. Are you familiar with the term *Haganah?*"

"Yes, it's a Jewish organization inside Palestine, I believe."

"Right. Specifically, the Jewish agency's defense force. Possession of any type of firearm is prohibited by the British. The Haganah must therefore keep their weapons carefully concealed."

"That's understandable," Ross agreed. "But who is this Haganah defending? Why do they even need guns?"

"Spare me your sarcasm," Ariel snapped. It was only then that Ross noticed how tense she was—more so than usual. "At any rate, a disaster occurred some time ago. The police made coordinated raids on our weapons caches. They confiscated more than six hundred guns of various types."

Ross gave a low whistle. Ariel ignored him and continued, eyes focused on her tightly clasped hands. "At the same time, they arrested the entire leadership of the agency. Mister Ben-Gurion, the head of our organization, avoided arrest only because he was out of the country." Her voice trembled slightly.

"I see," Ross said, not knowing what comment was called for.

"I'm not sure you do," Ariel responded with a weariness she didn't often display. "What it amounts to is that those firearms must be replaced—quickly. You see, a split exists within the Jewish population. The Irgun favors violent reprisals against the British. The Haganah advocates more deliberate preparation against the inevitable conflict with our Arab neighbors.

"There is little doubt that the Irgun provided the police with information leading to the raid. They figure to eliminate the Haganah as an obstacle. Without arms and leadership, we are most vulnerable."

"I'm beginning to see where this is leading. There are crates of firearms waiting at Albuquerque and Nashville. You want me to fly them to Teterboro for you."

"Yes."

"Ariel, you know I won't carry contraband. That was understood from the beginning."

The tight-faced young woman leaned toward Ross. "But this isn't illegal cargo. That's why I wanted to talk with you in person. The National Firearms Act doesn't restrict movement of personal firearms. Interstate shipments via common carrier require a permit. But these are *my* guns aboard *my* chartered airplane. I can take them anyplace I please, as long as I comply with state and local laws at destination."

"Whoa—wait up just a damn minute now," Ross protested.

Ariel ignored his reluctance and continued. "There are no prohibited weapons in the shipment—no fully automatic machine guns, no sawed-off shotguns, no grenades. It's an assortment of personal weapons donated by people during clothing and fund-raising drives. Not knowing exactly what to do with them, we just allowed them to accumulate. Well, they are desperately needed now."

Ross frowned. "You seem to be well versed on our laws, Miss Shamir. Conceding you may be right, how do you plan to get them inside Palestine?"

"That step needn't concern you, Ross. I don't mean to imply you aren't to be trusted, but limiting the number of people who know all aspects of the operation is essential. The Irgun has active members here in the States also.

"There is one pitfall, however. Do not under any circumstances land this load in New York. Their Sullivan Act makes it a felony to have an unregistered handgun in private possession."

Ross leaned back in his aging, creaking swivel chair. Folding his hands across his stomach, he regarded Ariel with a long, contemplative look. His thoughts surfaced in jumbled segments. To Janet, he'd said, "The first whiff of something illegal, and I'm dumping her." To Alex, something about an overactive imagination. He quickly suppressed the picture of the previous month's gratifying bank statement that flashed before him. That picture was replaced by one in *Life* magazine: gaunt, hollow-eyed faces peering through an eight-foot-high chain-link fence— one of the faces belonging to a six-year-old girl.

He sighed. "Okay. Give me times, places, and names," he told the suddenly radiant Ariel.

Ariel reached across and folded both his hands inside her own. "You'll never regret this decision, Ross Colyer," she said with unaccustomed warmth.

Ross freed his hands and reached for a pad of paper and pencil. "That's questionable at this point," he responded dryly.

26 November 1946
Fairfax Field

Ross tossed his briefcase on the desk and stretched tired muscles. Mild irritation crossed his face as he heard the door open behind him. He turned to see a good-looking man wearing tan gabardine slacks and an open-necked white sport shirt. "You looking for somebody?" Ross asked ungraciously.

"Are you Ross Colyer?"

"Could be. Who wants to know?"

"Hank Wallace. I'm a private investigator. My credentials." He held out a leather folder containing a gold badge.

Ross flashed a cursory glance at the ID card and said wearily, "Then you didn't have to ask; you already know who I am. Come on in and take a seat. I'm about to have a cold beer—just landed after a rough ride. Join me?" He cocked a quizzical eyebrow.

"Sure, if only to prove that this is a friendly visit, not an official one." Wallace returned Ross's chiding look with a wide smile.

Ross removed two brown long-necked bottles of beer from a little refrigerator, uncapped them, and seated himself behind the desk. He slid one bottle and an open pack of cigarets toward Wallace. After taking a long pull from his beer, he said, "Okay, I'm all atwitter. Why, out of the blue, am I favored with this social call?"

"It's just that you interest me. I'd like to talk—off the record."

"Good. *You* talk while I listen."

"Very well. I've had a look at your war record—impressive. I couldn't help but wonder why you got out."

"You *what?*"

"Don't get all riled. I'm doing work for the government. Your secret, private life is safe." Wallace drank from his beer and added, "But, like I said, I'm off duty now, just wanted to visit. And I'm still curious as to why you left a promising career in the army."

"That's easy. They turned down my application for a regular commission; I didn't have a choice."

"But you kept your reserve commission."

"That's right."

"Why?"

"That sounds very much like a question. I'm just listening. Remember?"

Wallace chuckled. "Sorry. Asking questions is my business. It gets habit-forming—ask my wife."

"I doubt I'll ever have the opportunity."

"You can never tell. Who knows? You may be spending some time in D.C. one of these days—answering, not asking, questions."

"That sounds very much like a threat."

Wallace didn't reply, just looked out the window. Taking in the parked DC-3, he changed the subject. "Nice airplane."

"Business is pretty good."

"I know. I've seen your bank statements. Colyer," he went on hurriedly, as he saw Ross's face turn crimson, "we're just jacking around. I know what you're doing—I just wonder if *you* know."

"What the hell is that supposed to mean?"

"This contract you have with the Jewish Relief Foundation. How much do you know about the outfit?"

"They pay on time and they keep their nose out of my business," Ross snapped.

"Admirable qualities in an employer."

"The foundation is *not* my employer. I'm a private contractor. You seem to know one helluva lot about me to be nothing more than a private investigator, and I think this 'friendly visit' has gone on long enough."

Wallace set his empty bottle on the floor alongside his chair and sighed. "Okay, so I lied to you." He grinned. "If you had checked my ID closer, you'd know I *do* work for the government—but as an employee, not a PI."

"Get out."

"Please, like I said, this is only a friendly visit. I may be the best friend you have, by the way. Those people you say 'pay on time' are also breaking the law. It could be said that you are a conspirator—that's what the FBI is thinking, at least."

"*What?*" Ross opened his mouth to further vent his outrage, then closed it. He remembered that man at Ariel's fund-raising rally—the guy Ariel suspected was FBI. He'd had cop written all over him, and had driven off in a car with government license tags. Ross settled for a clipped, "*I'm* not breaking any laws. My cargoes are all legal under interstate shipping regulations."

"As far as you know—no, damnit, you *do* know that some of the stuff you're carrying isn't for people in the displaced persons' camps. Now, my first thought was: okay, the guy's a hustler; he's getting rich. But you aren't—getting rich, that is. And your war record points to you being a law-abiding citizen; that's why I was curious as to why you left active duty. So let's change your last statement to read: I'm not knowingly breaking any laws *yet*."

Ross stared at his unwelcome visitor at length, then asked, "Could I see that ID card again?"

"Sure." Wallace extended the opened leather carrying case.

"Central Intelligence Group," Ross read aloud. "A spy, for Christ's sake? What pray tell is your interest in me or what I do?"

Wallace chuckled. "I like talking to you, Colyer. You're suspicious, *and* you're cagey. Okay, you know the rules regarding classified information. Anything we discuss doesn't leave this room. Interested in hearing what I have to say?"

"No."

"You play poker?"

"Some."

"All right, the cards are dealt. It's my open. Your girlfriend's visa is in danger of being revoked. I can maybe prevent it. Call, raise, or fold?"

Ross's face turned granitelike. "Jesus," he said, his voice low but harsh. "You people play with other people's lives like they were tiddledywinks. I assume you're talking about Ariel Shamir. She's not my girlfriend; she represents my customer. But let's say I call."

"Then you have to put something in the pot."

"What if I decide to raise?" Ross asked.

"Then I'd have to match you—if I wanted to play, that is."

"I'll remember that. What the hell are you after?"

"Ross . . . may I call you that?"

Ross nodded grimly.

"The president decided his intelligence-gathering operation needed an overhaul. The FBI has a branch, the military services have their own—there are others. It's all specialized, and the White House has a helluva time getting timely information. So, Truman ordered a new

Central Intelligence Group, strictly for overseas information gathering and analysis."

"That's nice. You still haven't told me why you're interested in me, however."

"The situation in Palestine—it's a powder keg. We don't know enough about the active parties to advise the president on his options in case it blows. The FBI tells him that the Jewish Relief Foundation is smuggling arms past the British blockade to the Palestinian Jews. We'd like to know more about it. Not that it's our job to stop it, but how much success are they having?"

"Assuming they are smuggling arms, how would *I* know? Wallace, you're dreaming. I'm just a truck driver."

"So you say. You have access, however. We'd like your help."

"*Me?* A government snoop? You're out of your mind."

"Maybe. But you're a patriot, Ross. You're a hero who got put out to pasture. That inconsistency bothered me, you know. I discovered that you got screwed by a politician but, deep down, still have hopes of returning to active duty. That's dedication. I can give you a chance to render a service to your country. It may make a difference someday."

"What would this 'help' consist of?"

"The White House asked the agency to prepare an analysis. Simply put, if it should come to partitioning Palestine, can the Jewish government defend whatever territory they end up with?"

"I can answer that right now. No—not without help. Hell, anyone who reads the paper knows that."

"How about some facts and figures? How much help are we talking about? Who will get the nod as leader—Begin or Ben-Gurion?"

Ross extracted a cigaret from the pack lying between them. He lit it and tried to blow a smoke ring toward the ceiling—without success. "I think you'd best talk with my customer," he replied finally.

"Nope, they're foreign nationals and have an ax to grind."

"And I don't?"

"Sure you do." Wallace smiled wolfishly. "But you aren't going to put their interests ahead of Uncle Sam's."

"You sure of that?"

"Pretty much. Anyway, I think you'll end up seeing it my way. You can't afford not to. The FBI has this foundation—and you—squarely in its sights; you're on borrowed time. Besides, after you think about this offer, you'll see that it's an opportunity to get their case before the president—under the table. Sooner or later he'll have to take a position: support partitioning—yes or no. If yes, do we provide a new Jewish nation with the means to defend itself? Follow me?"

"Perfectly. But I don't like this under-the-table business, the cloak-and-dagger aspect. You're asking me to spy on the very people I'm under contract to help. Why can't I level with them? Bring them into this analysis you talk about?"

"You already know the answer to that."

"Yeah. Any guarantees of all these favors you're tossing out?"

"None. But our director has clout; trust me."

"*Trust* you?" Ross's laughter bordered on hysteria. "*I* know about clout, believe me. Senators have more of it than civil-service types have."

"You're referring to your regular commission. I'll say only this: the OSS used a few sneaky tricks during the war; some of their people now work for us. What if this senator suddenly, and without explanation, changed his mind?"

Ross examined his beer bottle, saw it was empty, and set it down. "What you're asking would lead to breaking the law. I'm trying to build an airline. I'm slowly accumulating some equity, but I can't build anything looking out from behind bars."

"What if I can offer immunity from prosecution?" Wallace asked idly.

"In writing?"

"No. You gotta trust someone, Ross. I trust *you,* and I stand to lose my job—or worse—if you feed me a line of bullshit."

"I don't think I like this game, Wallace. The rules stink. I think I'll take my chips and go home."

Wallace stood and extended a hand. Ross shook it briefly. "Think about it, Ross," the CIG agent said. "You'll be doing a favor for the Jews and performing a service for your country at the same time."

"Yeah? Then why is it I have a sudden urge to go wash my hands?" Ross replied.

"That feeling goes with the trade," Wallace said, a note of sadness in his voice. "Here's a New York telephone number. Leave a message with whoever answers if you want to play. If not—well, you can always file an appeal."

Wallace's parting words stuck in Ross's mind. He had to agree with the man's assessment; you don't buck the largest, most sophisticated law enforcement agency in the world and escape unscathed.

Okay, you need this contract in the worst way, he mused. Assume you ignore this guy's warning and get caught—indicted. Prison? A fine? Perhaps, but the inevitable loss of his reserve commission and Allied Air loomed larger. The most disturbing aspect, however, was that after paying the price for his actions, would he have accomplished anything of significance?

Chapter 9

23 March 1947
Above Pittsburgh, Pennsylvania
Ross watched dirty gray mist sweep past the DC-3's side window and scowled. Damnit, where had this weather come from? *Snow?* This late in the season? The forecast he'd picked up from Nashville radio called for no more than broken stuff. Teterboro was to be three thousand feet and light snow.

Jake leaned toward him. "Just heard an Eastern flight divert from Cleveland—below minimums there. Whatta you think?"

"Shit!" Ross pounded the control wheel disgustedly. "I'll be damned if I'm going to haul this stuff all the way back to Atlanta. Call Philly radio and recheck that Teterboro forecast."

Trask reached for the microphone, then hesitated. "La Guardia's still open and forecast to stay that way," the copilot said with a questioning look.

"Negative," Ross retorted brusquely. "It's either Teterboro or return to Atlanta—Newark, maybe, in an emergency." He put on both earphones and listened while Trask obtained a marginal weather forecast for their arrival at Teterboro.

The weary pilot deliberated a while. "Okay," Ross said at last. "We're picking up ice and using fuel like crazy; Atlanta would run us real close to dry tanks. We'll make a decision at Philly. If Teterboro goes down, we'll divert to Newark."

Jake considered Ross's decision for several minutes. "You're the boss, but why this hell-bent attitude?"

Ross hesitated. "This is a priority cargo. They're waiting for it. Besides, the landing and tie-down fees at La Guardia are higher than hell."

Trask shrugged and added more carburetor heat. "I get the message," he said. "Ain't no way this here airplane is gonna land in New York today."

Ross threw an icy look at his copilot. "Don't speculate, Jake. Give me a new estimate for Teterboro. We must be ten minutes or more behind flight plan. Just hope we don't get put in a stack in the New York area. And get that injured look off your face."

Thirty minutes later, Jake, peering into the swirling white vista from his half of the windshield, called, "Runway in sight—one o'clock— standing by flaps."

Ross sighed with relief. The altimeter showed minimum-approach altitude—three hundred feet. Another half minute and he'd be forced to go around and head for the place where discovery of their cargo would cause all hell to break loose. "Set full flaps," he called tersely.

Ross leaped from the DC-3's cargo door and pulled the zipper on his lightweight jacket up to his neck. Christ, a balmy sixty-two degrees in Atlanta. Here in Teterboro, a slate gray sky warned of heavy weather later in the day.

He watched a young man slide a wooden crate from the DC-3's cargo door into the maw of a covered ton-and-a-half truck. He punched the boy lightly on the shoulder and shouted, "Have a good weekend, Ben."

"Thanks, Mister Colyer. You too. You were damn-near overgrossed this trip, weren't you?"

"She complained a bit on takeoff. Those crates sure as hell aren't filled with old clothes."

Ben grinned and rapped a stenciled label on the one still to unload. "Used farm machinery—heavy stuff."

Ross shrugged. "If you say so, Ben—if you say so. Well, see you next trip. I have a train to catch. Tell Jake I've gone ahead to close our flight plan. I'll see him in the coffee shop after he buttons up the bird."

Ross leaned across the chest-high operations counter and called to a pert attendant, "Nan Six-Niner-Three—down at one-four. Would you close me out, please?"

"Will do, Captain Colyer. There's a message for you, by the way."

Ross scanned the scribbled note and scowled. "Call me as soon as you land. Ariel," it read. He glanced at his watch. Damn. Trains to D.C. will be filled to overflowing later, this being Friday night and airline schedules shot to hell. He strode to the bank of pay phones and fumbled for change.

Ariel answered on the second ring. "Ross? Glad you made it in ahead of the storm. The weatherman says it will be a big one. Everything go all right?"

"Yeah, but those guys in Atlanta better check their scales. I figure we were six to eight hundred pounds heavy on takeoff. I know they want to see that stuff moved, but it sure won't do anyone any good scattered all over the landscape."

A pause, then, "I'll speak to them about it. The reason I asked you to call, Ross—are you free to attend a meeting tonight, here, in New York?"

"Not really. I was on my way to catch a train to D.C. I have an invitation from friends to spend the weekend and celebrate a birthday."

"Can you cancel? This is an important meeting—for me, certainly, but I'm sure it can be important for you as well."

"What's it all about?"

"I'm sorry, Ross. I can't tell you that. Just trust me; it's a serious matter."

"Oh," Ross said disgustedly. "Well, I guess I'd better call my friends and make apologies."

"Before you do, the meeting shouldn't last beyond ten or eleven. You could take the airplane and still get there yet tonight. The foundation will reimburse you; we owe you that much."

"Look outside, Ariel. This airport will be below minimums by dark—Washington National, too, I would guess."

"I'll arrange a car. It's only a four-hour drive."

Ross laughed mirthlessly. "Ariel, that's with dry roads, no traffic, and when I haven't just landed from a six-hour flight with weather all the way."

"It's important, Ross."

"Okay, okay. I'll be there. Where and when?"

He scribbled down directions, hung up, and dialed the long-distance operator. "Let there be an open circuit," he muttered.

Luck favored him. A cheery, "Richards's residence, Janet speaking," brought a smile to his tired face.

"Happy birthday, gal. This is Ross."

"Hi! Where are you?"

"Teterboro. Look, something has come up. I can't get away from here until nearly midnight. I'll try a sleeper, but at this late date, well . . ."

"Oh, how awful." A pause, then, "Ross, give me an hour or so, then call the INS New York bureau. Maybe I can get them to help; I know someone there from the San Francisco office; they have connections. Mother and Daddy do so want you to be here."

Weary and disgusted, he hung up and headed to the coffee shop to break the news to Jake Trask.

Ross's watch read eight o'clock. The cabbie groped his way through eddies of wet, blowing snow, his headlights and the feeble yellow street lamps doing little to improve visibility. "This has to be it, Mister," the harassed driver grumbled. "Forty-four Water Street. Don't look like much of a place; not a light showing that I can see. Want me to stick around in case it's locked up?"

Ross eyed the deserted street and dark, lifeless windows as he counted bills into the driver's hand. "Would you? I'd hate to get stuck in this godforsaken place without a ride." He stepped into the unbroken covering of snow and proceeded toward a barely visible entrance to 44 Water Street. Nearly there, he saw a dim light glowing through dirt-encrusted glass. The door opened at his touch. He turned and waved for the cabbie to leave.

The building was old. A musty odor told of long disuse. A naked, low-wattage bulb dangled above a flight of open stairs with deeply worn wooden treads. There was no hint of warmth in the dank air. What the hell have I gotten into? he wondered. As if in answer, boards creaked overhead. Light, rapid footsteps signaled human presence.

He recognized Ariel's dimly lit face peering over a wooden railing. "Oh, it's you, Ross. I thought I heard someone. Come on up."

Ross joined her in the gloom of a narrow hallway and uttered a shaky laugh. "I feel like I stumbled into the spook house we used to have at the fair. What do you have here, a secret laboratory for making monsters?"

"It looks dilapidated, I admit," Ariel replied. "But we have some of the offices pretty well fixed up. Follow me."

Ariel opened a wood-paneled door and led Ross into surprisingly cheery surroundings. Some long-forgotten executive had embellished his office with golden-oak window and doorframes with matching wainscoting. An ornately carved fireplace mantle of the same mellow-toned wood graced one wall. Dusty bricks, with carelessly applied mortar, prevented any attempt to utilize the grate for its original purpose. Cherry red coils of a portable electric heater provided welcome warmth, however.

Ross's gaze settled on the figure sitting behind a shiny, walnut-veneered desk. The man's attire, more so than the ultramodern piece of furniture, provided sharp contrast to the room's antebellum decor. His tuxedo, with its starched white collar and black tie, was of a vaguely foreign cut. It fit his powerfully built shoulders perfectly. A benign expression seemed to conceal inner fire. He stood and extended his hand as Ariel said, "Ross Colyer, meet Julius Mantz."

The man's handshake was brief but firm. Mantz said, "I greatly appreciate your interrupting your plans to meet with us. May I call you Ross?"

Ross murmured permission, and his host continued. "As you probably gather from my dress, I, too, must make an appearance at a gala later this evening. Please have a seat." He waved toward a comfortable-looking armchair. "I'm sorry we have neither food nor drink to offer, but we seldom entertain here." An easy chuckle accompanied the words.

Ross noticed, for the first time, that another man was present. He sat just on the fringe of the pool of light created by a green glass–shaded banker's lamp on Mantz's desk. "This is Moshe Barnett," said Mantz. "I asked him to join us for reasons I'll make clear in a moment."

Ross quickly sized up the figure in the shadows and extended his hand. Then he shifted his attention from the well-dressed, middle-aged Barnett as Mantz explained, "I am titular head, chairman, president, whatever, of the Jewish Relief Foundation, with which you presently hold a contract. Miss Shamir serves as my most able right hand."

Ross shot a glance at Ariel and raised his eyebrows. Her placid expression told him little.

Mantz's smooth, powerful voice continued. "We have in mind offering you a commission to perform extra services for the foundation, which is the reason for this urgent invitation. Are you in a position to take on other duties, in addition to your charter flying?"

"I'm not sure," Ross answered warily. "I believe I'd have to know more about the situation than Miss Shamir has seen fit to divulge so far."

Mantz stroked his chin. "Yes, Ariel is rather tight-lipped, isn't she? Believe me, you will be fully apprised of the details, should you accept. There are reasons for our circumspection, however. I ask your indulgence while I pose a few questions before we go into those details. Is that agreeable?" He threw a quizzical look at Ross, who nodded.

"You have an illustrious military record, Major Colyer. It would seem that you were in line for a brilliant career. Why did you leave the army?"

Ross frowned. "Would 'personal reasons' be sufficient?"

"I'm afraid not."

"I didn't leave under a cloud, if that's what you're driving at. It's simple, really. My commission was in the army reserve. We reservists had served our purpose, so they released us."

Mantz regarded Ross with a direct, thoughtful look. "You volunteered for hazardous duty. On more than one occasion you placed your life in jeopardy. Why? You were close to an engineering degree; you could have served in relative safety."

"Someone had to do the fighting," Ross replied curtly. "Look, you've obviously checked my background pretty thoroughly. If you don't trust me, then we'd better forget whatever it is you have in mind. I won't pretend that this contract hasn't put me on my feet financially. I'm grateful. I know that other outfits could have done the same job, probably for less money. But . . ." He stood.

Mantz held up a restraining hand. "Please. Your integrity is accepted; it's the reason we wished to have this conversation. I'll move on. Tell me, if you were a Jew, living in Palestine today, what would you consider your duty to be?"

Ross returned to his seat and pondered the question. "Well, from the little I know, I'd offer my services to the organization trying to win independence for the Jewish people."

Ross caught surreptitious nods between Mantz and Ariel.

"Exactly," Mantz responded. "What if this meant breaking the laws of the land?"

"Mister Mantz, I believe I see where this conversation is headed."
"I read the papers. I listen to the radio. I also know that the cargoes
I've carried for Ariel—you—these past months are not all intended
for the displaced persons' camps in Europe. Today's load, for example—
'used farm machinery'—not likely. I've asked myself many times: why
pay air freight rates to move cargoes that could be shipped by truck
or rail for a fraction of the cost?

"Sam Katzenbaum and Ariel gave me their word that all my cargoes would be legal under interstate commerce laws. That's good enough
for me. But I'm not a Jew, living in Palestine. I'm Ross Colyer, reserve army officer, still sworn to uphold the Constitution of the United
States. Don't ask me to violate that oath."

"Well put, Mister—Major Colyer." Mantz's voice carried a note of
weary resignation. "I'd perhaps rather hear you say you'd be willing
to break the law if the price was right, but you are a man of principle,
with the integrity I mentioned. I respect your position. And I desperately need men I can trust."

The somber-faced Mantz studied his clasped hands for several moments.
"If I assure you that you will never be pressured to violate the laws
of your country, what then? Are your considerable talents still for sale?"

Ross flushed. "I'm not sure I like your choice of words, Mister Mantz.
I'm not a mercenary."

"What, then, has been your motivation?"

"I'm trying to keep my airline out of bankruptcy. But I listened to
a speech Ariel made in Kansas City. I believe that plans for a homeland for Jews face heavy odds. Americans traditionally favor the underdog
in a fight, especially if freedom is the issue."

Mantz cocked his head to one side. Smiling, he asked, "Do I take
that as an acceptance speech?"

"It means I'm willing to listen," Ross replied.

"Excellent! Moshe, will you outline what we have in mind for Mister
Colyer?"

Barnett drew his chair into the circle of light. "I won't waste time,
Colyer. Early this year, the British asked the United Nations Security
Council to resolve the Palestinian situation. They are drafting a proposal that calls for dividing the land between Arabs and Jews, with
independence for each. British peacekeeping forces will withdraw. The
Arab Legion has already announced that on that day, they will drive
the Jews into the sea.

"David Ben-Gurion, leader of the Zionist movement, has charged Julius with the task of arming the Haganah—equipping a few thousand people to stave off an invasion by a determined invader, superior in both numbers and armament. This is where I come in. I am in the business of manufacturing machine tools. Julius has enlisted me to obtain equipment necessary for Jews living in Palestine to manufacture arms—clandestinely, as long as the British are in control."

Ross smiled and looked toward Ariel. "Used farm machinery?" he asked.

Ariel compressed her lips and remained silent. "Exactly," Barnett continued. "How those items find their way to Palestine is not, and will not, be your concern. Only this is: the British blockade is formidable. They seize on sight anything resembling machine tools for producing arms or ammunition. The amount of procured goods reaching the underground factories is dismal."

Ross lit a cigaret. "Wait a minute," he interjected. "Are you telling me you plan to equip and train an *army* under the nose of the British? An army that can fight off—how many?—maybe a million Arabs? You're out of your mind."

"*We must.*" Mantz's voice crackled. "We must, and we will. I'm sorry, Moshe. Go on."

"It's the sea blockade, Ross," Barnett continued. "We have to find a way to bypass it."

"You're thinking of airplanes. If you can't get through, you go over. Good thinking," said Ross, "but airplanes have to land, unload, refuel, undergo maintenance. . . . Is the British army just going to sit idly by and pick their aristocratic noses while you do this?"

"Highly unlikely." Barnett flashed a straight-lipped smile. "We will resolve that situation when we have airplanes, however. Your new job? Search for war surplus airplanes that can airlift crucial items to bases in Europe and Africa, then locate other airplanes that can take smaller loads into unprepared strips inside Palestine. After you find the planes, buy them and arrange for crews."

Ross felt his lower jaw drop. "That has to be the craziest idea I've ever heard. My God . . ." He shook his head in disbelief.

Barnett went on as if Ross hadn't spoken. "Mister Ben-Gurion also wants a means of countering the Egyptian and Syrian air forces—you know, some fighters and bombers of our own."

Ross stood, then paced the shadowy confines of the suddenly silent

office. Running fingers through his blond crew cut, he stopped in front
of the massive desk. "Mister Mantz," he said in his firmest voice, "I
don't think you realize what you're asking. Creating an army from a
bunch of civilians is one thing. To create an entire damn air force from
nothing is something else. Do you realize—" He fell silent as Mantz
raised a hand.

"Yes, Major, I do know what we're asking—the impossible. I recall a motto coined in one of your military services during the recent
war: 'The difficult we do immediately. The impossible takes a little
longer.' I estimate we have one year, slightly less, perhaps."

Ross watched Ariel maneuver the battered Chevy through the near-
deserted streets, slippery with wet snow. She had insisted on driving
him to Penn Station, where he would pick up the Pullman reservation
Janet had finagled.

"Where did a gal raised in the desert learn to drive in snow?" Ross
teased as Ariel negotiated a tricky stretch with deft manipulation of
gearshift, clutch, and accelerator.

Ariel's features were dimly visible in the glow of the Chevy's dash
lights. "I attended school in Switzerland for a time," she replied briefly.

Ross nodded, then asked, "Just what the hell did you tell this
Julius Mantz about me? You *did* suggest he make this stupid offer,
didn't you?"

"I did. I told him you were scrupulously honest, reliable, and highly
observant. And the offer is not stupid; the job must be done."

"I don't know why I even agreed to consider it," Ross mused aloud.
"It *can't* be done, in spite of your blind faith."

Ariel swung the car onto a major thoroughfare. The street was better
lighted, so she accelerated. Stores had only recently closed, and the
sidewalks were thronged with package-laden shoppers and clerks. Ross
discovered that the events of the past two hours had driven any thought
of a festive birthday party from his mind. The gaily wrapped gift in
his suitcase for Janet suddenly seemed tawdry and meaningless. He
tried, unsuccessfully, to recapture a holiday mood.

Ariel interrupted his thoughts. "Your next pickup is in Burbank, California," she said. "There are two fields close by crammed with surplus aircraft. It would be a good place to start your search."

"Damnit, woman. Didn't you hear what I just said? Or are you simply
ignoring me? This business Mantz talked about is insanity."

"Ross, when you were flying bombers, were you ever frightened?"

"Damn right. Only a fool isn't afraid of flak and fighters on all sides."

"But you kept going."

"There wasn't much choice, really," Ross replied with a short laugh.

"I'm frightened now, Ross. Terribly."

"Of what?"

"If the Jewish people fail to form a free, independent homeland now, the opportunity may well be lost forever. Like you, we really have no choice but to fight our way out of an impossible situation."

The untidy heap of stone that was Penn Station loomed just ahead, its rococo lines blurred by the unseasonal storm. He was glad for an end to Ariel's disturbing comments. "You can drop me anywhere along here. I can walk."

Ariel eased the Chevy to a halt, then turned to face him. "Burbank. Next week. Please, Ross."

He grasped the door handle, then paused. Her habitual stiff expression was gone. Her eyes seemed to plead. "I'll give it serious thought, Ariel, really I will," he assured her. Impulsively he laid a hand on her shoulder. He started to warn her to be careful, but the words died in his throat.

At the first touch of his fingers, Ariel jerked like a startled doe. Cringing against the door, she hissed, "What do you think you're doing? Don't *ever* try that again!" He felt her muscles turn rock hard beneath the hand he'd laid lightly on her shoulder.

Nearly as startled as she, Ross withdrew. "I'm sorry. I—I—oh, well." He wrenched his door open and stepped outside, then extracted his bag from the rear and marched toward the brightly lit entrance.

Behind him, he heard, "Ross . . . Ross . . ." He ignored the voice.

Chapter 10

Ross pulled Janet away from the curb as a passing car drenched the sidewalk with muddy slush. Clear skies and bright afternoon sunlight would make short work of the previous night's snowfall. Janet examined her silken-clad calves and muttered, "Damn, my last pair of hose. You would insist on a stroll without giving me time to change."

Ross grinned. "That could have taken until dark. It was either a walk or a nap for me after that dinner."

"What were you and Daddy talking about earlier—the time you both grew suddenly quiet when I walked into the room?" Janet threw him a derisive smile.

"Oh, nothing, really. He keeps in touch with his old army buddies; I just wondered if any of them were involved with this Palestine business. I understand that ex-officers with command experience can about name their own price over there."

"*You're* not thinking of going, are you?" Janet asked, frowning.

"Oh, no. I was just curious how the army looked at retired officers taking jobs overseas."

"Then you *are* considering it," Janet stated in firm tones. "But you aren't retired."

"No, damnit, I'm not. I have an airline, remember? An airline that's showing a profit, for a change. I've made a bid on another DC-3. I now employ five people and will hire another crew. Why in hell should I want to go chasing off to that miserable part of the world?" He steered Janet onto a crosswalk bisecting a small neighborhood park, now deserted and silent under warm, lazy sunlight.

Janet tucked her arm into the crook of his elbow. "I'm sure I don't know," she replied sweetly. "Tell me."

"Oh, for Christ's sake, Janet." Ross halted and faced his red-haired companion. "You get some idea in your mind and . . . Ah"—he waved both arms—"here I am, walking through one of the most beautiful cities in the country, with the best-looking girl in that city, and what do we do? We argue."

"Ross Colyer, you are about as devious as a six year old trying to explain an empty cookie jar. And your efforts to change the subject are equally transparent. The expression on your face when you were talking to Daddy, the guilty look when I interrupted. . . . Tell mama all, Ross—give." She made beckoning movements with four fingers of her right hand.

"You're impossible," Ross grated. "Very well. This outfit I have the big contract with—"

"That Jewish relief organization," Janet interrupted. "Go on."

"Yes. Well, they've asked me to take on another job, not a part of my charter contract. I'd be sort of a purchasing agent for them."

"Oh? And you were talking with Daddy because he's an expert on how to be a successful purchasing agent?"

"No, damnit. I'm not sure of the legal aspects of the job because of my reserve commission. Even though I'm not on active duty, I'm not sure what I can and can't do under army regs. I thought he might know. After all, he spent thirty years in the army."

Janet spotted a concrete bench and led Ross toward it. "You're doing fine, for starters," she said, seating herself. "Now the rest of it. What is it they want you to buy?"

"Surplus airplanes. They seem to think they'll need them when things are settled over there. I'm supposed to find good ones in the army surplus lists and buy them."

"Is that illegal?"

"Well, the laws are all mixed up. There's federal law, state law, international law, United Nations resolutions, and, equally important to me, army regulations."

"I still don't understand what could be illegal about what they're asking you to do."

"Probably nothing. The War Assets Administration has all kinds of airplanes for sale; anyone can buy them. The tricky thing is, the relief organization wants some fighters and bombers along with transports. Now, it's obvious they don't want those combat planes for display. They foresee fighting with the Arabs—maybe even the damn British."

"So what? You won't be flying the planes—or will you? Good God, Ross, surely you don't plan on doing something that stupid."

"Of course not. The legality issue arises from a federal law that prohibits enlisting or entering into any foreign military service. I won't be doing this as a part of my air charter contract; I'll be on the foundation's payroll. Is the Jewish Relief Foundation an arm of a Jewish underground army? Is the Haganah in Palestine a foreign military service? See my problem?"

Janet shrugged. "Sounds to me as if you need a lawyer. You haven't agreed to do it, have you?"

"They want an answer when I go back to New York to pick up the airplane."

"What if you refuse?"

Ross drew a deep breath. "Well, for one thing, they can suddenly discover another airline that provides better service. But it isn't just that, even though Allied Air *is* depending on this contract to stay in the black. It's just that, damnit, those people are getting a raw deal. I *want* to help them. You should hear some of the stories."

"I do, Ross, every day," Janet said quietly. "You forget that reading news dispatches is my job. And I read stories from both sides."

"What do you mean?"

"The Arabs say they are being driven from land they've lived on for centuries. The British say they are responsible for ensuring stability for the entire Middle East, not just Palestine."

"That's crap!" Ross exploded. "The English are looking out for their own interests—oil, the Suez, the hundred million or so Muslims in India. The Arabs, well, they're a bunch of fanatics. Who knows what they want?—other than to finish what Hitler started."

Janet, appearing not to have heard Ross's outburst, gave her furious-faced companion a long, thoughtful look. "Ross," she said hesitantly, "please don't mistake my motives, but my editor has offered to let me do my first real feature article."

"That's great. What's the subject?"

Janet uttered a mirthless chuckle. "Remember that rumor you told me was floating around about Senator Templeton running against President Truman in '48? Foley, my editor, wants me to do an in-depth piece on him."

Ross erupted in laughter. "That's a hot one—that's a real whoop-de-do," he said, wiping his eyes. "What did you tell him?"

"Nothing, yet. Ross, this is my chance to break into serious journalism. Would you think it terrible if I went ahead?"

"Why not? You can emasculate the old bastard."

"I—I don't think that's what Foley has in mind. You see, the *Globe* is a Democratic paper through and through. But Mister Green, the publisher, hates Truman."

"They want an endorsement of Templeton, in other words."

"Foley didn't actually say that, but it's pretty plain."

"Won't the fact that you're his daughter-in-law sort of raise a question in the readers' minds? I hardly think the last name connection will go unnoticed."

"We discussed that. He proposed a sidebar—said he'd explain the situation to give me credibility."

"So you'd write a fluff article—maybe help put that conniving sonofabitch in the White House?" Ross asked, an amazed look on his face.

"If I do go ahead, it won't be a 'fluff' article, Ross," Janet said stoutly. "And I don't have to let my personal dislike creep in—I'll just write about what I dig up and let people make up their own minds. That's the democratic process, isn't it?"

"Will the man buy that?"

Janet stood and paced restlessly. "I don't know. If I don't write the piece, Foley will assign it to someone else. Even if my version is edited down, it will be closer to the truth than a stranger—knowing the *Globe*'s political affiliation—is apt to write. Anyway, an article on the presidential candidates is timely, and I want very much to grow as a reporter."

"It sounds like you've already made up your mind. Now you're rationalizing, and wanting me to agree with you," Ross said with a sardonic grin.

"I have not!" Janet exploded, "I'm still trying to decide what's right."

Ross shrugged. "Well, far be it from me to advise you; you're calling your own shots. I know what *I'd* do, but I also see your predicament. So just what *do* you intend telling them, Miss Political Affairs Expert?"

"The truth as I see it. I don't even know myself yet what picture will emerge, but it will be honest, I give you my word. And that was a nasty and uncalled-for question, Ross Colyer."

They walked in silence for several minutes. Finally Janet said, "More than ever, I'd like to meet this Ariel person. Are you sleeping with her?"

Ross's lips tightened as he glared his reply.

26 March 1947
Teterboro Field

Ariel Shamir listened closely as Ross spoke between bites of ham and eggs. They sat at a corner table in the nearly deserted Teterboro Field snack bar.

"Tell Barnett I'll scout the fields around Burbank like you suggested. I need to know how much money I have to spend and what I'm supposed to do with the planes I buy. If you give me Barnett's number, I'll call him when I have something positive to report."

"Uh—Moshe Barnett isn't often close to a telephone, Ross. You can call me; I'll have answers to your questions by tonight."

Ross grinned crookedly. "It's like that, huh?"

"It isn't what you're thinking at all," Ariel said. "Moshe is out of touch right now. He's traveling somewhere in Texas, but he calls every day. Security *is* tight, but Julius promised that you would have all the details you need. He was greatly impressed by what you said, by the way. He'll be pleased to hear you've accepted. I am, too, Ross." She blushed ever so slightly.

"I'll do my best." Ross shrugged. "I don't think you have a prayer, but never let it be said we didn't try."

"We?" Ariel asked with a questioning look. "Did you say *we?*"

"Well, yeah. I'm on the payroll now, aren't I? Or am I?"

"As of this minute. But there's more to it than just that, and you know it. Otherwise you would have refused our offer. Speaking of which, why did you accept? Barnett was certain you wouldn't."

Ross wordlessly extracted a newspaper from his briefcase and slid it across the table. The previous day's edition of the *Washington Post* was folded to expose a headline: ARAB LEGION TO DEFY UN. The story, datelined Nicosia, read:

> Top-level Arab leaders meeting in Cairo today reportedly adopted a resolution to defy any effort by the United Nations Security Council to partition Palestine.
>
> The British Foreign Office has denied knowledge of the meeting. According to spokesman Sir Donald Ashton-Smythe, "We regard the story as an effort on the part of reckless and irresponsible members of the Jewish leadership to influence world opinion."

Ariel glanced at the headline and nodded. "That meeting took place," she stated in grim tones. "The resolution was adopted; we knew about it the same day."

"I talked with a retired army officer about this article while I was in Washington," commented Ross. "He said, 'We sat around negotiating in '39—for two years. See what happened? Our politicians will never outnegotiate the Arabs. When they start to annihilate the Jews—to shut off Middle East oil—we'll be drawn into another war.'

"The way I see it, if you don't get arms, we'll be over there anyway. Right now, you need airplanes. I'm the person who can help you get them; airplanes are my business, and this is just another business deal. I've had my belly full of politicians. It's time for someone to stand up and do something besides talk."

"The Haganah agrees with you," Ariel said. "We can't let it happen." She leaned across to stare directly into Ross's eyes. "I will return and resist an Arab takeover to the bitter, bloody end—fighting with my bare hands if necessary.

"The British"—the corners of Ariel's mouth turned down in a grimace of disgust—"they are putting extreme pressure on your President Truman to support their blockade. Julius talked with a man high up in your government. Ours is one of several Jewish organizations the Brits say are buying war materiel for illegal shipment through the blockade. Your State Department goes only as far as promising to prevent our violating American arms control. They watch us, yes."

"*Are* you buying arms?" Ross asked, unrelenting.

"Buying is one thing, Ross. Shipment is something else. Your buying airplanes is not illegal, if that bothers you."

Ross rubbed his forehead. "Okay. I've known for some time that I was hauling more than old clothes and medicine. But these airplanes I'm buying—what do I tell the crews who fly them? *They* are sure as hell going to be breaking the law."

"Perhaps. Perhaps not. By the time the planes and crews are ready, America may change its policies."

"That's not—" Ross broke off the conversation as he saw Jake Trask striding toward them, his copilot's swarthy features resembling a thundercloud.

"Ross, you better get out there. Some government jackass who says he's from the Civil Aeronautics Administration just grounded the airplane."

"What?" Ross exclaimed. "Is he crazy?"

"Your airworthiness certificate expired yesterday."

"Oh, for Christ's sake." Ross shoved his chair back and stood. "Excuse me, Ariel. This shouldn't take long. The damn paper is waiting for me back in K.C. I had the inspection before I left on this trip."

Ariel sighed. "Don't count on it, Ross—it not taking long, that is. They've tied you and Allied Air to the foundation."

30 March 1947
Burbank, California

Ross stood, arms akimbo, and surveyed the rows of parked airplanes. He turned to Jake Trask and muttered, "Christ, what a bunch of junk. We're expected to get these things in the air again? We're talking upper-grade miracle, friend."

Jake nodded and turned to Rogers, the portly, middle-aged man from the War Assets Administration. "Where's the paperwork on this bunch?" Trask inquired. "You know, time on airframes and engines, maintenance records, and such."

Rogers removed a Panama hat and mopped his shiny pink scalp with an oversized bandanna. "If we have them, they'll be in boxes stacked in that hangar over there." He waved vaguely toward a corrugated-steel building, barely visible above row upon row of drab, dust-covered airframes. "You want to look at any others?"

"Not until we get an idea of what condition these C-46s are in," Ross replied, concealing his disappointment. "And what do you mean, *if* you have them?"

"Mister Colyer, these birds was brought here straight from the Pacific more'n a year ago. You know what paperwork was like at the end of the war. All them crews was interested in was getting the hell home and into a set of civvies."

"Yeah, I know," Ross said reflectively. He studied the nearest of the twin-engine transports, the Curtiss Commando—workhorse of the China-Burma-India run over "the Hump" into China. Designed to carry upward of eight thousand pounds of cargo, its twin R-2800 supercharged Pratt & Whitney engines could boost the aircraft to seventeen thousand feet. Its design range was twelve hundred miles when cruising at 180 miles per hour.

"I know this plane from my tour in the CBI," Ross said. "She has some real cute handling characteristics, although she's a bitch on the ground in gusty crosswinds, and she's a gas guzzler. Besides that, she's the ugliest fucking airplane made." He turned to Rogers. "How about spare parts?"

"You'll find engines down at Riverside. Other spares you'll have to find in a depot in Oklahoma City."

"I see," Ross mused. "Okay, show us some short-haul stuff. How about the Norduyn Norseman? We already have one."

"Uh, I don't have any lists with them. Think you'd have to go to Canada—or Europe maybe."

"Well," Ross said, "I'll have to think about it. Thanks for showing us around." He and Trask strode back to their parked car with Rogers wheezing to keep up.

Driving toward the exit, Ross suddenly stomped on the brake pedal; the rental sedan's wheels slid to a stop. Ross waved to his left. "What the hell are *those* doing here?" he asked Rogers.

The War Assets man's gaze followed Ross's pointing finger. "Them Connies? Neat lookers, aren't they?"

"Don't tell me they're surplus," Ross said, hungrily eyeing the sleek, four-engine Lockheed Constellations. The slender, aerodynamically designed fuselage and distinctive triple-fin tail assembly seemed insulted by their coats of olive-drab camouflage paint.

"Sure thing. Lockheed built a prototype for TWA before the war. Hughes wanted a coast-to-coast, high-altitude airliner. When the war came along, the military took 'em. Lockheed has already started production on a bigger, faster model, and the airlines are waiting for them. TWA got theirs back, but they don't want any more of these 'Baby Connies.' They were built strictly to army-navy specs, and it'll cost an arm and a leg to get 'em certified for civilian use."

"How much?" Ross asked softly.

"Upward of two hundred grand, I hear. But hell, they're listed for only fifteen."

Ross put the car in gear and drove off, his thoughts in turmoil.

Ross cradled the phone against his shoulder and waited for Moshe Barnett to come on the line. He regarded the motel room with sour distaste. Christ, had the same designer done them all? Worn blue carpet; limp, flowered drapes with purple roses; sleazy spreads, of a color that defied description, covering lumpy mattresses; imitation tile bathroom; and wall lamps casting sickly yellow puddles of illumination. The picture of a mounted cowboy, back turned to a raging blizzard, provided the final depressing touch.

Ross straightened as Barnett's voice crackled over two thousand miles of telephone wire. "Ross, sorry to keep you waiting. Ariel said you needed to talk with me. What's up?"

"Well, good news and bad news, Mister Barnett. First, I found airplanes—acres of them. C-46 transports for five thousand each. I'd rather have C-47s, but they don't have the range we need. By adding a fuselage tank, the '46 can make the two-thousand-mile haul from Natal, Brazil, to Dakar. Better than that, though, are some four-engine Constellations. A steal at fifteen grand."

"Sounds great. What's the bad news?"

"The C-46s have virtually no records. It'll mean a complete IRAN to get them certified."

"IRAN?"

"Sorry—army term for inspect and replace as necessary. They'll need a hangar, a crew of specialists, and maybe four weeks per bird. The Connies are something else. They require modifications to include toilets, seats, and such to meet passenger-carrying specs. We're talking maybe seventy-five thou each if the local Lockheed plant does it. They're the ultimate answer, though."

"I see. How about the other planes; the—uh—tactical types?"

"Most of them are in Tucson, Arizona—all you can carry for scrap-metal prices. A big—really big—cache there. However, you can't get one certified unless it's converted to a 'sports' model by removing every last screw of its armament. Even then, export permits for combat airplanes are out of the question."

"Hmmmm." A long pause. "You had time to check into crews?"

"Jake and I did some barhopping this afternoon," Ross replied with a chuckle. "Besides getting half loaded, we agreed that an ad in the papers will bring more prospects than we can handle."

"Sounds like you've been busy. About the crews, Ross." Barnett seemed to be choosing his words carefully. "We'll have to talk about this. For what we have in mind, I'm sure Julius will insist on Jewish Americans."

"Oh, for Christ's sake," Ross protested. "You can't run an ad like that; it'd draw too much attention. Plus, the best prospect we ran across is a TWA Connie captain out on strike. He's looking for another job. We got most of our info about the planes from him. His name is Murtaugh, and Jewish he ain't."

"I see. Look, something else has come up. Let's plan on meeting with Julius when you get back. When will that be?"

"We're loaded and ready to go. I'd like to spend tomorrow arranging for a crew to start on one of the '46s. Give us two days to get to New York—that will be Tuesday."

"Sounds great. Write an Allied Air check for the plane and overhaul. I'll see that the money is wired to your bank tomorrow morning."

"Whoa," said Ross. "I don't want that bird on *my* inventory. What the hell will I do with it?"

"Uh, Ross," Barnett replied hesitantly, "we'd prefer that a chartered operator acquire the planes. It won't raise questions. Later, I assure you, you'll receive an offer to purchase from a third party. You'll show a margin of profit on the transaction of course."

Ross scowled. "I wish this had been mentioned earlier. Okay, but I want to sign a note for the extension of credit, and be provided a legal bill of sale later."

"Of course, Ross. It'll be a clean deal, trust me."

"Trust *that* bunch?" Ross muttered aloud as he hung up.

4 April 1947
New York City

Ariel wheeled into a parking spot at the rear of the Water Street headquarters. She set the parking brake and smiled—she actually has dimples, Ross noticed for the first time. To him, the old building looked less forbidding in daylight. More activity was noticeable as well. Once inside, Ross heard voices behind closed doors on the first floor; a telephone rang somewhere nearby.

They climbed the worn stairs and entered Mantz's office without knocking. Julius looked up from where he'd been writing and greeted Ross with a warm smile. "Welcome back," he said. "Moshe tells me you have good news for us."

Ross glanced toward where Barnett sat in the same chair he'd used previously. He wore that odd, straight-line smile of his. "Well," Ross said with a sigh, "it's a start, at least."

All three listened closely as Ross rendered a concise report. Barnett leaned back. "And the smaller planes, the ones that can use unprepared strips, aren't available?"

"I couldn't get a lead on any. There weren't that many to begin with, and they were the first ones snapped up for civilian use."

Mantz looked briefly at his notes. "A man from Palestine just arrived yesterday. They urgently need a half-dozen planes of the Piper Cub–Taylorcraft variety. Can you locate any? Buy them new from the factory, if necessary. There is only one stipulation: they must be identical."

Ross pursed his lips. "I'm sure I can. Where do you want them delivered?"

Mantz and Barnett exchanged glances. "Teterboro, for now," Barnett replied.

"Okay," said Ross, "but they must be identical?"

"In all respects."

"Out of curiosity, how will you get them inside the country?" Ross asked. "Aren't light planes on the embargo list?"

"Are you sure you want to know?" Julius gave Ross a direct look.

"Well, it's sort of hard to operate in the dark. I might make a big blunder without knowing it."

"I agree," Mantz replied. "This is the situation. The British permit us to have a flying club. It operates out of Tel Aviv. Virtually all flights are to the various kibbutzim—delivering food, medicine, and such. The flights are strictly regulated.

"The flights also perform—er—certain other services. The need in that area exceeds the number of planes they presently operate. The plan is to acquire six more, never keeping more than one at Tel Aviv. Each of the identical planes will carry the same serial number. The five extra ships can move freely without filing flight plans, because that plane number is on the ground in Tel Aviv."

Ross stared, then chuckled in admiration. "Now *that's* using your head." He quickly sobered. "Why did you tell me that?"

"Because you asked," Mantz responded. "And, perhaps our candor will reassure you with regard to this next matter."

Ross's eyes narrowed. He sipped his coffee and waited.

"Actually it was you who caused us to seriously consider airlifting material instead of attempting to evade the regular sea lanes," Mantz said. "'If you can't go through, go over,' I believe you suggested. I'll let Moshe take it from here."

Barnett hitched his chair closer to Ross and tapped the palm of his left hand with his right forefinger. "Next to the British navy patrols, export permits present our greatest problem. The laws governing exports are actually rather vague. Various departments, and employees, set up their own rules. As usual when this happens, you get inconsistency. Just now, the official position seems to be that anything shipped to Jewish Palestine has the potential to be converted to military use.

"They aren't altogether wrong, of course." He flashed a grin. "We require some location—call it a way station—as a destination not embargoed. This interim holding point—another country—must in turn have export laws that permit the shipment of items of any description, including arms, to any destination."

Moshe observed Ross's wary reaction. "Do you see anything illegal about such a procedure?"

"N-o-o-o," Ross replied. "But I'm not a lawyer. Go ahead."

"Very well. Frankly, we are doing this now with surface ships. Exporting to Nicaragua, thence to Europe. But we come to the matter of airplanes. For reasons I won't go into, we don't trust General Somoza for what we have in mind. The little country of Panama, however, is ideal. It's already a source of convenience flags for ships. Why not airplanes?"

"Airplanes? You mean to set up your own airline?"

"Exactly. Panama recently completed a modern airfield, Tocumen—with U.S. funds, I might add—for which it has little use. We will furnish the Panamanians with their own airline, with an international charter."

"Wait a minute." Ross held up a hand. "International charters are not easy to come by. The company will need landing rights, maintenance facilities . . . there's a whole flock of details."

"That's right. But Allied Air, Incorporated, is already franchised for international operations."

"Are you asking me to let some banana republic use *my* franchise? Forget it. Most of their mechanics couldn't overhaul a bicycle."

"What if this new airline contracted with Allied Air for everything? Leased your airplanes, crews, mechanics—the entire operation, in other words."

"Why—why . . ." Ross sat, at a loss for words. The scope of Barnett's scheme exceeded his imagination. "That would mean me working for some Panamanian, in effect," he said finally. "As contractor, he'd be calling the shots."

"The shots, as you refer to them, will be called right here, in this office." Mantz's voice was flat and positive.

"Who would you pick for the new airline's president?" Barnett's question had the offhand quality of asking about a fourth for bridge. Without waiting for an answer, he asked Ross, "Would you like the job?"

"I—I don't think so. I don't know. This will take some thought."

"Of course." Mantz's tone had regained its previous affability. "Why don't you think about it on your flight to Panama? I'll give you a letter to a Senor Arias. He's a lawyer there, related to Panama's previous president. Get a feel for the route, the political atmosphere, the facilities at Tocumen—you know. How long will it take you by DC-3?"

"Uh, let's see. It's about a three-thousand-mile trip—have to get diplomatic clearance—uh—I guess I could be there three days from now."

"Excellent, that'll be Friday. Why don't you give me a call—say, Saturday night. Let me know the score. Oh, and can you keep someone working on the light-plane business while you're gone?"

Not until they were speeding toward the airport did Ross become reflective. "Jesus Christ, Ariel. Do you know what I just agreed to do?"

Ariel concentrated on the traffic ahead. Watching her profile, Ross saw the corner of her mouth twitch. "Julius can be preemptive," she responded. "Are you having second thoughts?"

"No. It's just that, my God, I'm supposed to go blundering into a foreign country and set up an international airline operation, buy a half-dozen light airplanes and prepare them for shipment, all the while buying and restoring another half-dozen war-weary hulks. And, oh yes, 'call me, say, Saturday, and tell me the score,'" Ross mimicked in a shrill falsetto. "I won't fly down there; hell, I'll just strike out over water and walk."

Ariel swept past a plodding Buick sedan and sped through an intersection as the light turned red. "If the situation weren't so serious, Ross, I'd laugh. Believe me, he's asking no more of you than any of the others. He likes you and has great faith in your ability. If, however, you don't think you can do what he asks, please say so. Now. Too much depends on it."

"I'll do it, by God," Ross flared. "If it can be done, I'll lay those airplanes and that airline charter in Julius Mantz's lap on any schedule he can dream up."

Ariel started to speak, but Ross cut her off. "So, while we're on the subject of tough jobs, how would *you* like to be president of a South American airline, huh? Come on now, *is* the job too tough for you? Consider this a firm offer, because there is going to be an airline."

"I can't think of anything I'd like better, Ross. I'm serious. Julius would never agree to it, though. It would take time for me to learn the job, and time is not something we have to spare. There are other jobs I can do better. By the way, there is really no need for you to take that belligerent attitude with me."

They were entering the Teterboro terminal area. Ariel parked in front of the entrance and waited while Ross extracted his single piece of luggage. He stuck his head inside the driver's side window. "I'll see you in a week or so; I'll be wearing my Superman suit. And I'm sorry I spoke that way to you. I—I have a lot of things on my mind just now."

His sally prompted a brief smile. "I'll look forward to seeing you clear tall buildings in a single bound. Ross, the other night, I—I fear I may have hurt your feelings. I'm sorry if I did. It just caught me by surprise. Someday, perhaps, I'll tell you why I acted as I did. Now, have a safe trip." Quickly she leaned toward him; her lips brushed his cheek like the fleeting passage of a butterfly.

Before a startled Ross could react, she rolled up the window and drove away.

Chapter 11

7 April 1947
Tocumen Field, Panama

Ross let the DC-3 roll to a stop in front of an impressive but virtually deserted terminal building. A sign overhead welcomed them to Tocumen in both Spanish and English. Heat rose from the tarmac and swirled through the open cockpit windows like a damp, stifling cocoon. It carried a smell of rotting vegetation from the nearby jungle. Ross pulled the mixture controls to idle-cutoff and wrinkled his nose. "Don't forget to clear the snow off the wings before we leave, Jake," he quipped.

Their passenger, Eddie Kotch, stuck his head into the cockpit and surveyed the somnolent terminal and parking ramp. "Sweet Jesus, what a depressing dump this is."

Ross regarded the moon-faced Kotch with a lazy grin. "I'd think a native of Miami would be used to this kind of heat."

"To begin with, I'm not a native of Miami." Kotch ran a pudgy hand through his sweat-drenched fringe of reddish brown hair. "I grew up on New York's Lower East Side." He smiled at Jake Trask's sour expression. "And you're going to be stationed here permanently, if all goes well?"

"I have a big mouth," Trask muttered. He looked out his window. "Hope they have cold beer in that terminal. Hey, I do believe we're being met. Let's get out of this sweatbox."

Ross dropped to the sizzling-hot ramp and waited for a slender, olive-complected man to cross to the airplane. "My God, he's wearing a coat and tie," Ross muttered to Jake, who stood alongside.

"Senor Ross Colyer?" the smooth-faced individual queried, looking at each of them in turn.

"That's me." Ross extended his hand.

"Welcome to Panama, senors. I am Juan Arias. Mister Julius Mantz called yesterday and told me to expect you. How may I be of service?"

Ross removed a long-billed fisherman's cap he'd acquired in Miami and wiped sweat from his forehead. "Well," he said with a smile, "high on the list just now is to get us inside a cool building and a cold beer inside us. That's a favor we're asking. Then we'll talk about some service we're willing to pay for. How's that?"

"Eminently satisfactory, Senor Colyer." Arias's white teeth flashed an answering smile. "And a tribute to your good judgment." He turned and waved a languid index finger toward the terminal. A long white Chrysler limousine lurched from a line of parked vehicles and sped toward them.

A white-shirted mestizo youth leaped from the driver's side and raced to open a rear door. Arias waved the three Americans inside. "Garcia will see to your bags," he advised. Following his visitors inside the relatively cooler interior, he opened a small refrigerated cellarette and extracted four long-necked brown bottles that were immediately coated with beads of moisture.

The trio relaxed in the Chrysler's deep leather-upholstered seats and gratefully reached for their drinks. "It is a twenty-mile drive to Panama City," their host explained. "We can enjoy our drinks in comfort as we drive. You have reservations at the Pan American Hotel. After you refresh yourselves, I suggest dinner in discreet surroundings appropriate for discussing business. Is that agreeable?"

Ross hesitated. Kotch's presence bothered him; the man had taken charge in Managua. Okay, he'd had business with the palace there, but his arrogance had rankled. A talk before this evening's meeting was indicated. Ross nodded agreement to Arias and sat forward to observe the passing scene.

The gleaming Chrysler lurched and jolted over a road filled with potholes and an assortment of bicycles, mounted riders, and dilapidated North American–made, prewar vehicles. Arias served as tour guide. "A campesino village," he said, waving at a collection of thatched dwellings built around a grassy square. "Ah, they are building a house."

He pointed to a gathering of men and women erecting a pole frame-
work, lashed together with vines. "The women who appear to be wading
in mud are mixing clay and rice straw. The walls will be plastered
with the mixture, called *quincha.*

"The roof tiles you see stacked there were also made on the spot. The
entire village is involved, and they will be finished by dark. We should
come back then—fiesta starts as soon as they finish the new house."

Ross, preoccupied with the task ahead of him, found it hard to remain
interested. Jake was fascinated, however, and maintained a flow of
questions. Kotch finished his beer and dozed.

Arias escorted them as far as the hotel's front desk, where he was
apparently well known. Assuring them that he'd pick them up for dinner
at seven, the dapper Latin American lawyer strolled to the limo waiting curbside.

Ross longingly eyed the sapphire swimming pool. There was time
enough for a dip and a nap, but the first order of business was a talk
with Eddie Kotch, away from Jake. Ross stated his thoughts bluntly.
"Eddie, before this meeting with Arias, we need to discuss a few things.
I'll order drinks in my room. How about dropping by after you've
settled in?"

Kotch frowned. "Things? What kind of things?"

Ross didn't answer; he just gave the man a level stare.

Eddie shrugged. "Very well, I'll be in shortly."

Minutes later, Kotch appeared, and Ross, stripped to shorts, stretched
on the bed. He propped his back with pillows and sipped his drink.
"Eddie, before we go any farther, I want to know your role in this
business. What is it you intend to do here?"

Kotch bristled slightly. "You'd best ask Julius that. I assumed you
knew; he doesn't want team leaders talking to each other about their
jobs. Security, you know."

"No, I don't know. Tell me."

"My business here . . . well, it isn't any business of yours."

"I won't argue that point. But the policy works both ways. What
I'm getting to: I don't want you along tonight when I talk with Arias."

"Just a damn minute," Kotch protested. "Julius said I was to sit in
on your discussions. Hell, I know why you're here—to set up air transport
for cargoes we can't send by ship."

"Then it appears there's already been a breakdown in security," Ross
said dryly. "I'll ask again: what is your role in tonight's discussion?

Or perhaps I should call Julius before we go. I want the matter of who is to be chief negotiator made perfectly clear."

"Well," Eddie grumbled, then took a long pull from his gin and tonic. "No need to get huffy. My job is to provide transportation for all the stuff Julius's other team leaders acquire. I'm to see how I can best use your arrangements here for airlifting some of it."

Ross nodded. "I see. Very well, it's my party, then. Agreed?"

Kotch nodded sullenly.

"Then I'm amending Julius's instructions slightly. To 'sitting in' I'm adding, 'and let me do the talking.' Clear enough?"

"I don't take orders from you, Colyer," Kotch retorted. "When it comes to shipping arrangements, *I* call the shots. I'll decide what I say—and when. Is that clear to *you?*"

"Perfectly," Ross answered. "But before you start shooting off your mouth . . . Oh, hell, Eddie, we're acting like a couple of kids. I *do* respect your knowledge of shipping arrangements. But—well, you came on pretty strong back there in Managua; it sort of rubbed me the wrong way."

Eddie flashed a lopsided grin. "I'm a natural-born driver, Ross—a butt kicker. Okay, it's your party, like you said; but don't crowd me, hear?"

Ross responded by raising his glass and returning Kotch's grin. "Wouldn't think of it, Eddie."

True to his word, Arias provided a private dining room for their dinner meeting. A forty-minute drive from the hotel through a sordid barrio, the golf and country club was a world apart, offering scant evidence that affluent Panamanians had suffered during the war.

A white-jacketed waiter seated them at a round dining table made of dark Spanish oak, then they proceeded to enjoy a flow of drinks and food produced as if by magic.

After the dinner dishes had been removed, and with brandy, cigars, and coffee before them, Arias smiled and asked, "Was everything to your satisfaction, gentlemen?"

Even the sulky Eddie Kotch was forced to express enthusiastic appreciation. Arias folded his hands on the table. "Very well, to business then. I am at your service."

"We are considering opening an international airline here," Ross told him. "The future of transoceanic travel is mind-boggling. We plan to get in on the ground floor. We'd like to retain you to handle the articles of incorporation, obtain a charter, arrange diplomatic clearances for our proposed overseas operations, and such."

Arias lit a Cuban panatela with deliberate movements. When the cigar glowed to his satisfaction, he asked, "Why here? It would seem to me that opportunity for originating profitable cargoes in the United States is vastly greater than in our little country. After all, our major commodity is bananas. Don't tell me that suddenly the worldwide demand for bananas is such that shipping them by air freight is profitable." The slender lawyer's brown eyes twinkled.

"Frankly, it's a matter of bureaucratic red tape," Ross confessed. "We can buy airframes from war surplus stocks for pennies on the dollar. Bringing them up to our government standards, however, is costly—and unnecessary in many cases."

"You are seeking a flag of convenience." Arias made it a blunt statement, not a question.

"Essentially, yes."

"Is it your intention to base any of your flight operations here in Panama?"

"Well," Ross hedged, "naturally we would maintain offices here, originate certain flights, and offer cargo transshipping services."

"That will help your application, senors. President Jimenez is most desirous of utilizing the fine airport you just left. A Panamanian airline logo will go a long way in smoothing your path. But, you mentioned cargo transshipping. You surely anticipate passenger service as well?"

"Uh, eventually, of course. It will take time to configure surplus airplanes to carry passengers, though," Ross explained.

"Naturally. How soon do you envision opening service?"

"Well, we have options on aircraft we'll pick up as soon as we know about the charter. If possible, I'd like to consummate the arrangement before we leave."

Arias's pencil-thin eyebrows rose slightly. He stroked his chin. "Unusual," he murmured, "but not impossible. I have an idea. Senor Reluz, our minister for industry and commerce, was in the dining room as we entered. If he is still there, would you consider including him in this conversation? It could save several days if we obtained his informal agreement in advance."

Ross concealed a smile. The man was a consummate actor. Not only did he know in advance the reason for their visit, but he had positioned the key government official close at hand. Ross nodded. "How fortunate. Of course. We can perhaps wind up this business by tomorrow night." This is apt to get expensive, he added to himself wryly.

Within minutes Arias had introduced Aristoles Reluz, who promptly seated himself at the table. Arias outlined the Norte Americano's proposition. The minister scowled, pursed already protruding red lips, then raised a hand and scratched under his left armpit. He was a coarse man, Ross decided—beefy, with a round, pockmarked face and a truculent way of speaking.

Reclining in the leather and oak captain's chair, with a leg raised carelessly over the arm and a foot dangling in space, the minister was a stereotype of all corrupt politicians.

Not surprisingly, when the party broke up at midnight, informal agreement for early approval of the application that Senor Arias's staff would complete yet that night was assured—subject to certain considerations, of course. Ross had a Swiss bank account number jotted in his pocket notebook.

Back in his hotel room, Ross decided that, weary as he was, he'd best conduct yet another item of business. He placed a call to Bruce Murtaugh, the disgruntled TWA pilot he'd met in Burbank. While he waited for the call to go through, he sprawled in an armchair, nightcap in hand, and tried to fathom the future. All he could foresee was a long series of twelve-hour days and seven-day weeks. The phone jangled, and he scooped up the receiver.

"Bruce? Ross Colyer here. Sorry to call this late at night, but do you still want a job?"

"If it's along the lines we discussed, Ross—damn right. When do I start?" Murtaugh replied.

Ross chuckled. "As of an hour ago, you're on the payroll. But get your roller skates on, guy. This operation is already traveling in the passing lane. Got a paper and pencil handy?"

"I do."

"Okay. The C-46 we talked about—get a crew on it. I want it ready for a one-time flight to Teterboro ASAP. We'll do the compliance items there. Then, the Connies. At fifteen grand each, buy four. One will have to be certified for passenger service. Again, I need it yesterday.

Looking down the road, we need six C-46s and the four Connies airworthy by October. Can do?"

Murtaugh gave a low whistle. "Shades of the early days of WW Two," he replied. "If it can be done, I can do it, Ross. Start writing your flight schedules—you'll have the airframes."

Ross hung up, tossed back the last of his drink, and undressed. All in all, the evening had gone better than he'd had reason to believe. Among other things, Kotch had sat silent and impassive throughout the negotiations. Why the hell did I blow up at the guy? he wondered. A little voice from his subconscious answered: This business that the CIG agent warned you of is making you edgy, old boy.

He shrugged. Oh well, hang tight, Colyer, this has all the earmarks of a wild ride.

12 April 1947
Teterboro Field

"I just had to come out and meet you," Ariel told Ross. "The message you gave Julius sounded so encouraging that I couldn't wait to hear the details. He won't be back until tomorrow morning, however."

Ross regarded the radiant woman through bleary, red-rimmed eyes. A two-day stubble of blond beard itched like crazy. The foul taste of too much coffee and too many cigarets vied with the beginning of a headache for top discomfort honors. "Thank God for small favors. I'm not sure I'm up to a ride into the city and a debriefing just now. Jake, wait until morning to service the bird. You're out on your feet. Grab a cab. I'll close the flight plan, talk to Ariel for a minute, and join you. We'll get to the hotel and try for twelve hours of sleep."

"Sounds like a long, hard trip," Ariel said, falling in step beside him.

"I had easier missions during the war," Ross replied. "Thunderstorms all the way to Miami; a loud, all-night party in the room next door last night; heavy weather from Atlanta to New York; then, an hour in the goddamn holding pattern. Look, I hate to have you waste the drive out here, but can we please wait until tomorrow to talk? It's good news, but I'm a zombie, really."

"Oh, of course. Call me when you wake up, okay?"

Before Ross could reply, Jake stumbled toward them. "It had to be— it figures. There's not a hotel room closer than New York," he snarled. "The cabbie I flagged spent the entire morning hauling a couple from one place to the next."

Ross slumped onto a nearby bench. "Damnit! Well, I'm going to use the terminal washroom, then crawl into a sleeping bag inside the airplane. It wouldn't be the first night I spent in the Douglas Hilton."

Jake, disgust written on his weary features, stared at the floor. "Ross, I hope you don't mind, but Ben, one of the truck drivers you know, offered more than once to let me bunk down at his place. I think I'll take him up on it. His floor might be a better place to spread your sleeping bag than the bird. You'd have a hot bath as well."

Ross considered the offer, but before he could answer, Ariel cleared her throat. "Ross, I have a daybed. I've made it available several times to people in town without reservations. Hotel rooms are impossible to find most nights. You'll have the place to yourself this afternoon, at least; I must go back to the office. Then I have plans for later."

"Lady, you just got yourself a boarder," Ross replied without hesitation. "Lead me to your car; I'm asleep on my feet." Turning to Trask, he added, "Thanks for the offer, Jake. But I just can't pass up a real bed."

Ariel opened the car vents, and cool air flowed over Ross as he let his head rest on the seat back. Eyes closed, he filled her in on the essentials. "The charter application for Aereas Mundial de Panama is in my briefcase. Jake Trask is president. A signed contract, leasing all aircraft and services from Allied Air, Incorporated, signed by the new president of Panama World Air, is with it. Approval is assured just as soon as fifty grand is transferred to a numbered Swiss bank account. Where operating capital will come from is something Julius will have to work out with Trask." He was asleep before Ariel could reply.

The brief walk from the car to Ariel's apartment revived Ross only slightly. Inside, he listened groggily as Ariel explained the workings of the daybed while she set out clean towels. He waved off her offer to fix a sandwich, but accepted a squat tumbler filled with Scotch over ice. Ariel colored slightly at Ross's raised eyebrows. "There are degrees of conformance with orthodox doctrine," she said stiffly. "I'm not a professed drinker, but neither do I observe total abstinence."

A steamy-hot shower consumed ten minutes; locating his last pair of clean shorts and crawling between cool, crisp sheets consumed two more. He was comatose exactly seventeen minutes after entering Ariel's converted brownstone apartment.

*   *   *

Gray mists of deep sleep grudgingly surrendered to near consciousness. Only the sound of a distant siren disturbed a tomblike silence. Where he was seemed of small concern, but curiosity finally won out over his desire to roll over and go back to sleep. Dimly, Ross recalled Ariel driving him from the airport . . . the bath, and those delicious, clean, cool sheets. Okay, he was in her apartment. He opened his eyes and squinted at his watch's luminous dial; it read nearly one o'clock. The room was in total darkness, so it had to be 1 A.M.

Increasing awareness revealed that the room was not completely dark. Faint illumination filtered from an open door he recalled leading to a kitchenette. He heard the clink of metal on crockery. A match flared and the distinctive scent of cigaret smoke wafted into the dark room. Ariel was home and in the kitchenette, he concluded.

Oh well, he'd turn over and sleep until daylight. Moments later, his stomach reminded him that he had last eaten about noon the previous day—a bologna sandwich and a Hershey bar. Visions of a refrigerator filled with food scuttled any thought of sleep. He sighed and groped for trousers he barely recalled draping over a nearby chair.

Ariel sat on a tall stool at a tiny breakfast bar. Bare feet peeked from beneath a burgundy brocade dressing gown. She turned, swallowing a bite of the sandwich she held in one hand. "Did I wake you? I tried to be quiet, but I was starved. The dinner we had was inedible."

"Not at all," Ross mumbled. "Matter of fact, that's what drove me out of bed. I'm ravenous."

"Of course." Ariel pointed to the remains of her sandwich. "Chicken salad. I imagine you'd like something more substantial, though."

Ross's gaze lingered on his hostess as she spoke—a look of frank admiration. The robe's burgundy red sheen accented her olive complexion and jet black hair. The robe gaped slightly as she turned, exposing a scrap of black lace covering a soft mound of breast. You are one attractive woman, Ariel Shamir, ran through his mind.

"I'd give you my right arm," Ross replied. He looked down at his own half-dressed state. "Look, while you're doing that, I'll shave and put on a shirt."

When he returned, Ariel slid a plate of creamy scrambled eggs, a small breakfast steak, and buttered toast onto the kitchenette's bar. Ross dug into the welcome repast with an ecstatic moan. Ariel returned to her perch alongside and sipped coffee.

Ross didn't speak until his plate was wiped clean with the last bite of toast. He cradled his coffee cup in both hands. "That, my dear, was pure ambrosia—you saved my life."

"I enjoyed watching you eat," Ariel replied. "You do it like you do everything else—directly, forcefully, and with purpose. You are very sure of yourself, aren't you, Ross Colyer?"

"Well—I don't know—I guess I've never thought about it," Ross responded with a self-conscious laugh. "Do you dislike that in a man?"

Ariel threw him an irritated frown and slid from her stool. She lit another cigaret and paced the kitchenette's limited floor space. "I didn't say I disliked it. . . ." Her voice trailed off.

"You don't have a very high opinion of men in general, do you?" Ross asked in thoughtful tones. "The other night when I touched you— you almost jumped out of your skin. Are you *afraid* of us?"

"I am not afraid of any man—*any* man, do you understand?" Ariel flared. "I've yet to meet the male creature I felt inferior to. I killed a man when I was twelve years old. Does that startle you?" She paused in front of Ross and stared, arms folded across her chest, as she drew deeply on her cigaret. Ross didn't respond.

"It happened at the kibbutz. Mother took me there every summer to do volunteer work. My father was a member of the British mandatory government and stayed in Tel Aviv.

"A dozen Arab renegades slipped past the perimeter guard. They shot their way through the compound, stopping to loot as they went. My mother saw one approach the building where we lived; she shoved me beneath the bed. I lay there, hidden, while that animal pinned her to the floor, then humped and grunted like a rutting boar. I could have reached out and touched him. He stank.

"He had propped his rifle against the bed. It was loaded and the safety was off; he'd been shooting just before he broke into our rooms. I pulled it down beside me. He was intent on ravaging my mother and wouldn't have noticed an earthquake. I just shoved the muzzle against his side and yanked the trigger. I remember that I closed my eyes first."

Ariel reached for an ashtray and stubbed out her cigaret with vicious stabbing movements, then resumed her endless circuit of the room. "There was a lot of blood everywhere—all over my mother, the floor. Neighbor ladies came in and carried the body away. They placed him where it would appear he'd been shot while running down the street. Then they scrubbed the floor.

"Mother was hysterical. I don't remember how I felt, other than being astonished, and angry, when I was told that no one, even my father, was to know what had happened.

"They told me that rape makes a Jewish woman unclean—no man will have her. My father, her husband, could legally banish her! I don't know what he would have done—we never told him. But I hated him. I hated my own father for having the *power* to do such a thing."

Ariel leaned back against the kitchen counter, as if exhausted by her outburst. As much as Ross longed to reach out to her, to comfort the distraught woman, he confined his reaction to a muttered, "My God."

"Do I hate all men? I thought so, for a time. There was certainly reason to. Not only had I watched while my mother was raped, but an aunt on my father's side told of her experience in the Nazi camp at Belsen. She was pretty. They placed her in a house reserved for the pleasure of the German guards. The *schwarzenfleisch* girls, the dark meat, were in great demand.

"I became an underground member of the Irgun. I told myself that it was because Menachem Begin, its leader, had the best plan for a Jewish homeland. Offset repression with violence, he preached—against the Arabs, the British, any enemy of the Yishuv. The Haganah, my father's party, advocated a more moderate solution. Later, I realized that my real reason for joining the Irgun was to kill. I dropped out. You told me once that I was driven by hatred. I don't even remember what I said to that."

"Ariel." Ross reached for her clenched hands. They were ice cold. "There are doctors who can help you. Please, you'll destroy yourself if you let this thing eat at you."

Ariel uttered a shrill cackle. "A psychiatrist? A head doctor? A shrink, I think you call them? I went to a clinic in Vienna—one set up to help refugees from the camps. A kindly, older man with a neat little beard listened and stroked my hand. As therapy, he suggested that I let him help me overcome my aversion to sex by going to bed with him."

Ross sat silently, Ariel's limp hands enclosed in his. She resumed speaking in more normal tones. "I knew the first time I saw you that you were dangerous. My life was planned and orderly. I had a purpose for living; men were relegated to the shadows of my existence. The fumbling, sweaty ordeals with boys my own age just left me feeling disgusted. I couldn't believe, after meeting you, that I had fantasies of—of—well, oh, forget it."

She turned toward Ross, her face a pathetic mask in the kitchen's harsh overhead light. "I want so badly to be a real woman. Perhaps that is why I reacted the way I did when you placed your hand on my shoulder; I don't know how to deal with men who make passes." Ross felt her hands trembling. "I know what you're thinking, and the answer is no—not yet, not now."

The telephone's strident clamor woke Ross. He fumbled for the offending instrument and automatically lifted the receiver. About to answer, he paused. Awareness of his surroundings returned with a rush. The thought flashed through his mind that a man's voice answering a telephone in a single woman's apartment might be unwise. He settled for a hoarse, "What number are you calling?"

"Ross?" Ariel's voice was crisp and businesslike. "Did I wake you?"

"Uh—yeah. I was just about to get up anyway," he added lamely.

"Good. I'm calling from the office. Julius would like to meet with you and Jake Trask at eleven. I've already located Trask at Ben's place. He'll be here. Be prepared to have lunch with Julius at his desk; he never goes out to eat. You'll find coffee set out and the makings for breakfast in the refrigerator. Can you manage?"

"Sure."

"Very well. You'll find the number of a local cab company by the phone. I'll see you shortly before eleven then."

"I'll be there," Ross replied. He hung up the phone and turned his thoughts to the previous night's events. Preoccupied with reconstructing the conversation with Ariel, he made coffee, then proceeded to the bathroom for a shower.

He made an egg sandwich and seated himself at the breakfast bar, wolfing down the impromptu meal and allowing strong coffee to drive the cobwebs from his brain. What the hell had he gotten himself into? The woman was crazy. No, not crazy as in demented or deranged. He searched for the right words and settled for mixed up. Intelligent as all hell, dedicated to a cause, victim of some unbelievably sadistic experiences—yeah, mixed up was the right phrase. She also had a body filled with passion that could drive a man to strong drink.

So where does that leave *you*, Ross Colyer? It leaves you with thinking of shacking up with your boss, he conceded ruefully—the greatest mistake, careerwise, a man could make. Well, maybe not your boss, as such,

but damn close to it. He washed his breakfast dishes and stacked them
in the sink to dry.

Searching for clues to the inner, private world where Ariel Shamir
lived, Ross shamelessly prowled the apartment. The three rooms bore
the marks of a transient—much like his own living quarters. Books—
always a clue to personality. A waist-high bookcase displayed a catholic
taste in reading. A couple of best-selling novels, Theodore Dreiser's
An American Tragedy, two heavy tomes with indecipherable Hebrew titles,
and a well-thumbed paperback copy of *Wuthering Heights* were propped
up by a French-English dictionary. A biography of Amelia Earhart
rested alongside a government publication on irrigation. Nothing revealing there.

The apartment's decor. Furniture obviously included in the lease—
little different from a hundred hotel rooms he'd occupied.

He stripped rumpled bedding from the folding daybed and returned
the bed to its sofa configuration. Grinning, he dumped the used linen
in a bathroom hamper and chased the thought from his mind that if
he spent another night here, it sure as hell wouldn't be on the couch.

Feeling like an intruder, he nevertheless allowed curiosity to guide
his footsteps to the apartment's only bedroom. Again, it reminded
him of a modestly priced hotel room. Nothing frilly and feminine was
in evidence.

He opened the sliding door to a clothes closet. A long, ivory satin
dress with a square-cut neckline hung alongside a severely tailored
dark gray wool suit. A tan gabardine raincoat, a half-dozen nearly
identical white blouses, two pairs of slacks—one black, the other blue—
and several pairs of khaki shorts were arranged with military precision. The ornately brocaded dressing gown struck an incongruous note.
Less than half the available space was in use. Four pairs of sensible
shoes, shined and with shoe trees, were lined up alongside one pair
of black pumps with four-inch heels.

Stop it, he told himself. You have no business . . . On his way
out, he paused in front of the dresser. A single photograph in a standard, dime-store frame caught his attention. A girl of ten or twelve
stood between a fierce-looking, bearded man who wore a natty, double-
breasted suit, and a vacuous-looking woman wearing a flowered dress
and wide-brimmed white hat. The girl wore a solemn expression beneath
square-cut black bangs.

Almost of their own volition, his hands eased the top dresser drawer open. Neatly folded flesh-colored panties were stacked alongside an equal number of flesh-colored bras. A folded pair of suntan-colored nylon stockings rested on top of another pair, still in their cellophane wrapper. It occurred to him that the battered suitcase resting on the closet's top shelf would hold the woman's entire wardrobe.

Feeling faintly guilty, he slammed the drawer and stepped into the short hallway leading to the living room. Passing the open bathroom door, he glanced inside. He hadn't before noticed the underwear, matching that which he'd seen in the dresser, drying on a towel bar. Something nagged at his subconscious. He crossed to the clothes hamper and lifted the bedding he'd deposited only minutes before. Filmy, black lace panties and bra lay crumpled on the bottom.

Ross seated himself on the sofa, propped his feet on the coffee table, and lit a cigaret. Ariel hadn't been wearing those scraps of lace when she met him at the airport—he'd bet next month's pay on it. He allowed his mind to develop a scenario. She'd returned to the apartment after her evening out, gone to the bedroom, undressed, and dutifully rinsed out her underwear. Then she'd put on the only bit of frivolous clothing she owned—black lace bra and panties and brocade dressing gown—and gone to the kitchen. Had she deliberately made enough noise to rouse him?

He chuckled out loud. "You're a devious woman, Ariel Shamir," he announced to the empty room. He repacked his carryall and reached for the phone. The card with the cab company's number was tucked beneath the base. He stopped and looked around the room. Why did he have this feeling that something wasn't right? He frowned, then identified the source of his puzzlement.

There was nothing of Ariel in the apartment; it could well be a department store display. Who *was* the person who lived here?

Ross's answer came in fits and starts. He accepted it with reluctance. Saddened by the revelation, he sat and stared at the floor. There was no *person* by the name of Ariel Shamir. That name belonged to an empty shell, a husk with no kernel. The woman for whom he felt an emerging affection, her inner self buried beneath scar tissue, was incapable of expressing such emotions as love, tenderness, and compassion.

What to do? He realized she was, in her own crippled way, begging him for help last night. Goddamnit, he told himself sternly, you have enough problems just now without adopting a stray.

Chapter 12

18 April 1947
New York City
Ross chewed great mouthfuls of a pastrami and Swiss cheese sandwich while Julius talked between bites. Jake sat at the other corner of the walnut-veneered desk. Ariel had left the office soon after exchanging greetings, Ross noticed. He'd tried to catch her eye—make some acknowledgment of the new intimacy they shared. She hadn't evaded him, just busied herself elsewhere. Oh well, he thought, many people were uncomfortable the following morning with the person to whom they had bared their soul in the dark of night.

Julius was saying, "I'm impressed. To put together a new company, acquire the airplanes we need, and set up shop on the West Coast in only two weeks—well, it took some doing. I hate to ask in the face of such accomplishment, but how about the light planes—the Cubs?"

"The West Coast distributor promises delivery of the next four off the line to Allied Air in Ontario, California. That's all he could do right now. The other two will come later, perhaps as long as two months," Ross replied. "We're paying a premium to jump his waiting list," he added dryly. "By the way, the funds that Barnett wired to K.C. have just about evaporated. We'll need at least another hundred thousand when the Connies are ready to be picked up."

"Better than I expected, actually," said Julius. "I'll have Ariel arrange the transfer. Now, the organizational setup. What are your suggestions?"

"Jake, here, is listed as president of Panama World Air. I think he should go back to Panama City and start leasing office space and hiring ground crews. I plan to open a branch of Panama World Air at Teterboro. I'll keep Allied Air headquarters in Kansas City, but I'll use part of PWA's space here.

"Bruce Murtaugh will bring the first C-46 here, and I'll use local help to get it airworthy. As soon as it's CAA certified, we can paint Panamanian registration on it and commence flights to Panama. We'll keep the DC-3 and the Norseman registered in the U.S. for the time being."

Ross glanced at his notes and frowned. "I'm afraid I'll have to hire another crew for the DC-3. I'll be running between here, Kansas City, California, and Panama until the operation is up to speed. Jake has some figures on operating capital for his end. I'll let him talk to you about arrangements, but the fifty thousand—I'll call it bribe money because that's what it is—is due and payable before we get President Jimenez's signature. God, it galls me. That minister Reluz—what a piece of slime."

Mantz nodded. "Galling, but necessary, I fear. We are hardly in a position to protest. But wait until you start dealing in the Middle East. I assure you, public officials there can give your man Reluz lessons in chicanery.

"Very well, I'm sure you have things to see to. I'll go over the funding business with Jake, here, in the morning. But, Ross, you've done a superlative job. I want you to know we appreciate it.

"Back to security," said Mantz. "As spread out as the airplane business is shaping up to be, we'll use code words for all future communications concerning the machines. What are your suggestions?"

Ross thought a moment. "Bird names are sort of obvious; how about fish? The Cubs can be minnows and the C-46s guppies." He looked at Trask. "What shall we call the Connies?"

"Dolphins," Jake replied immediately.

Ross nodded. "Appropriate—they sort of look like them. Okay, Julius?"

"Fine with me," Mantz replied. "How about the fighters and bombers?"

Ross's expression tightened. "What fighters and what bombers? They're impossible to export, even to register with the CAA."

"We need them, Ross. The day will come."

"Very well. If and when, we'll call them sharks and whales."

Julius scribbled the names on a pad. "There is one more thing—
the Piper Cubs. After they're delivered, get in touch with Eddie Kotch.
He'll take care of shipping them."

Ross started to speak, then closed his mouth and nodded. "I understand," he said cryptically. "We'll work it out."

Mantz's expression grew frosty. "Do I detect a reluctance to work
with Eddie?"

"We had words during the trip to Panama. Never mind; like I said,
it's nothing we can't deal with."

"I see." Mantz studied his desktop. "Ross, you know I've tried to
compartmentalize this entire operation. It's the only way to plug leaks.
I will tell you this much, however. Eddie is responsible for moving
critical items through the blockade. He is very good at his job. The
trickle that manages to reach Palestine is due entirely to his efforts.

"The airlift you have so efficiently put together is, in effect, another means at Kotch's disposal. I'm afraid you must work together.
I'll talk to Eddie, but that's the way it is."

Mantz watched the pair leave with a wry smile. He needed strong
men for the seemingly impossible job they faced. He had them. Conflict was unfortunate but inevitable. If it came to a decision, however,
which man would he choose?

18 April 1947
Milan, Italy

Dov Friedman studied the bearded, middle-aged man seated across the
table as he strained to hear the low-pitched voice. Around them, fashionably clad patrons, taking midmorning cappuccino and croissants,
crowded the sidewalk cafe. They chattered gaily of jobs, family, and
vacation plans. The subject under discussion between Dov and the man
from Aliyah Bet's Paris office, however, dictated discretion. Even speaking
Hebrew, they conversed in low voices.

"There are many equally deserving, but the ship will accommodate
no more than four thousand at the most. The longer it takes to outfit
and load her, the greater the chance of British interference. The matter is urgent," the dark-suited man insisted.

"But Mister Bader, I know nothing of ships or the ocean. I'm an
airplane pilot. Why have you come to me?"

"By your own admission, efforts to restore the English Auster to flyable condition are futile," Zvi Bader replied. "You plan to return to Palestine. Why not as a crewman aboard the *President Warfield?*" The man's disconcertingly intense gaze pinned Dov like a hapless butterfly.

"What crew position could I possibly carry out?" Dov countered laughingly. "I'd only be in the way—another refugee."

"You are a leader of men, Dov Friedman. You are a cool thinker, capable of improvising when matters do not go as planned. There is much more to this endeavor than just boarding a ship and sailing to Palestine. Your captain is Ike Aronovitch, a most capable and courageous man. Except for a dozen or so skilled ship's crew, he has untrained volunteers to perform a multitude of tasks. They are young members of the Palmach—brave fighters, but they require direction.

"We obtained the *President Warfield* in the USA. A group of patriots in Baltimore raised the funds. She was a river cruise boat with a hundred and twenty cabins. She must be modified to carry *four thousand five hundred*—in bunks. We must install a kitchen capable of feeding that many, and a dispensary and sanitary facilities. . . ."

Bader ignored Friedman's dazed expression. "Her passengers are now scattered over much of Europe in refugee camps. They must be transported to the port and provided papers—all this with the British watching every step and doing everything in their considerable power to prevent the ship from sailing."

Dov stared blankly at the bearded Aliyah Bet representative for several moments. "It sounds impossible," Dov said weakly.

Bader's expression softened—to a wintry smile—for the first time since their meeting. "Exactly. Everything we do is impossible. Now, the ship is berthed at Portovenere, near La Spezia. Your duty is clear."

Two days later Dov stood on the worn stone quay at Portovenere and gazed up at his new home. Oblivious to the babbling flow of humanity swirling around him, the stench of garbage, the sounds of engines and whining winches associated with dockside commerce, he searched for something reassuring about the *President Warfield*. He could find precious little.

Dov was no judge of seagoing vessels, but this one looked as if she could tip over and sink right there at the dock. Her upper structure was made of wood, he observed with dismay. Even if the impossible happened and she *did* make it to the open sea, one shell from a British destroyer would wreak horrible destruction. He sighed and trudged toward a sagging gangplank leaning dispiritedly against the ship's rusty hull.

A hard-faced young man barred his passage on deck. He eyed Dov's white shirt and freshly ironed khaki shorts. "Only crew members and workers are permitted," he stated in no-nonsense terms.

"Don't make it too easy for me to turn around and leave," Dov responded sourly. "I just might. But it seems the powers that be think I should join your happy little family. I'd like to see the captain. I'm reporting for duty, you see."

"Is the captain expecting you?" the sun-browned deckhand asked suspiciously. Dov glimpsed an illegal British Sten gun poorly concealed beneath a scrap of canvas within the man's easy reach.

"Why don't we go find out?" Dov asked wearily.

"Well, the captain isn't on board. Mister Hilvitz has the watch. Do you want to see him?"

"If that's the procedure for reporting for duty, yes."

"Go up those stairs over there and knock on the first door on your left. I'll be watching you all the way," he cautioned.

Dov followed the sharp-faced youth's instructions. A voice called, "Come in," in response to his knock.

The room—cabin, Dov supposed it was called—was cluttered beyond imagining. Four tables were crowded into floor space measuring barely twelve feet by twelve feet. A man wearing metal-rimmed glasses regarded him from behind one of the tables. "Yes?" the sweating, harassed-looking individual greeted him.

"My name is Dov Friedman. The Paris office of the Aliyah Bet sent me here. If you're Mister Hilvitz, well, then I guess I'm reporting for duty."

"Thank God!" The man stood and extended a hand. "We were sure they would find some reason, in the end, to leave us on our own. The captain will be glad to see you, be sure of that. He's ashore just now trying to wrangle fuel oil. And yes, I'm Avraam Hilvitz, first mate. Here, have a seat." He gathered papers from a straight-backed chair and dumped them on an adjacent table. "Coffee? Tea, maybe?"

Dov sank gratefully into the proffered chair. "Coffee would be fine. Can you tell me, generally, what's going on? Or should I wait for the captain?"

Hilvitz ordered their refreshment by the simple expedient of yelling out an open window, "Herzl, bring coffee." Then he crossed his hands behind his head and leaned back the scant twelve inches separating his chair from the bulkhead. "Oh, I can tell you the overall situation," he said brightly. "It's unbelievably bad. I don't envy you your job. Maybe now I can get back to being a first mate."

"Yes. My job," Dov said. "You see, I don't know just what I'm expected to do. The Aliyah Bet man was a bit vague on that point. Maybe you could enlighten me."

Hilvitz goggled in astonishment. "You *what?* No one told you? . . . Oh, dear." The balding, sandy-haired first officer twiddled a pencil between his forefingers. "Well—you see—" He cleared his throat. "I may be wrong, but I think you're—you know—sort of in charge."

20 April 1947
Jerusalem, Palestine

Sir Donald Ashton-Smythe stood before an office window staring down at a street fronting the stone-block building. The street was filled, sidewalk to sidewalk, with serpentine coils of barbed wire. Concrete tank traps provided random punctuation marks. "So this is what they call Bevingrad?" he asked softly.

"Wha—what's that, now?" the ruddy-faced general asked. "Bevingrad? I don't believe I understand, sir."

"A term coined by the Jews for our headquarters here, no doubt. But the chaps at Whitehall have picked up on it. General Wyckham, my time here is short. Mister Bevin expects my report within forty-eight hours—by wireless. The UN has appointed a commission on Palestine. They will show up here any day now. They'll be poking about, being a complete nuisance, no doubt. What are they going to find, General?"

"I—I'm sorry, sir. Find? What are they looking for?"

"That ill-advised request by the prime minister for a United Nations recommendation on Palestine's future. Already there's talk of partitioning the country—of dividing it between the Jews and the Arabs, each with an independent government. The commission's report can carry great weight." He started to add, "You dolt," but he held his tongue.

"The Foreign Office is most concerned that this recent incident, the public hanging of three Jews, coincides with the commission's appointment. The Jews will undoubtedly drag that out and flaunt it in the commissioners' faces. Is there a trial record?"

"I believe not, sir," the general replied. "There was no question of guilt, you see. We caught them red-handed, and they confessed to looting a police armory. The governor ordered a summary execution."

An aide scuttled in, deposited a tray of tea and biscuits, then fled. Ashton-Smythe walked to the table; deep in thought, he poured for himself. In his late fifties, the man typified British officialdom: aesthetic features, ruddy complexion, aquiline nose, and a prominent jawline. His dress, almost a uniform, featured an oxford gray jacket, striped pants (he wore spats until wartime shortages forced their disappearance), stiff white collar, and regimental tie. The tie reflected a stint between wars in the Queen's Own Rifles, where he served without distinction. His miliary-style brush mustache and hair displayed touches of gray.

"Pity there's no trial record," Ashton-Smythe murmured. Resuming his position before the window, he continued, without facing his host. "Partitioning would never work, you know. Plus, British interests dictate close ties to an Arab-dominated Middle East. After all, the bloody wogs sit directly astride Suez and have all that lovely oil.

"The Jews have had a rum go—shocking treatment at the hand of the Nazis. They truly deserve a place to settle down, I grant that. But they can never succeed here. They have no experience in running a country. And the Arabs are being absolutely churlish about the matter. They refuse even to consider allowing 'infidel curs' to desecrate holy land.

"No, the Jews will just have to accommodate the Arabs. They've survived all these centuries doing that; they'll have to do it again. They will, never fear. But it would actually be a disservice to the poor buggers to help them prepare for war—a war they can only lose." He sighed. "Our strategy, the one I'll present to the minister, will be one of making it impossible for the Jews to form a government. A related measure to guarantee our continued presence here will require placating the Arabs. This influx of refugees and arms past our blockade must be shut down—forcibly and without nonsense."

25 April 1947
Cairo, Egypt

Hafez Kamil crossed his legs and tried to find a more comfortable position. The little velvet upholstered chair wasn't made for his muscular, six-foot frame. The unaccustomed black suit and colorful silk tie made him feel like a fop, but his mother had insisted that his uniform was inappropriate for the occasion. The occasion. He glared toward where she sat, her bulk shrouded in her customary full-length black tunic, benignly chatting with more elegantly attired matrons.

Why was this charade necessary? he wondered. The marriage had been arranged, and he wanted to get on with it. Oma Kamil, a slave to tradition, had decreed otherwise. To dispense with the "display" was unthinkable. He glanced again at his bride to be. She seemed pretty enough. Her red silk dress was cut sufficiently low to give a glimpse of pleasingly full breasts, and high enough to expose trim ankles and calves. Supposedly Hafez and Aziza Daoud were seeing each other for the first time today. That wasn't true, of course. After the marriage was arranged, he'd parked his moss green Alfa Romeo down the street from her house and observed her from a distance. He assumed she'd done something similar; she'd have been a dunce not to.

He sighed unobtrusively and sipped the sickeningly sweet mint tea. He'd prefer a glass of the dry, malty Scotch whiskey he'd acquired a taste for. England was a dreary, chilly island, but the people lived a good life. Even with wartime shortages, the Royal Air Force mess he attended there while taking fighter training never wanted for ample food and drink. Egypt, with its anachronistic ways, seemed dull and backward when he returned—this foolishness that accompanied a marriage ceremony, for example. And the precious supply of liquor he could consume only in secret—utter stupidity.

A dry, papery voice at his elbow interrupted Hafez's dark thoughts. "Do you think there will be war, Squadron Leader?"

Hafez gave the elder seated beside him a startled glance. The man was an ancient reminder of the old ways. Garbed in a striped *gullabiya,* he regarded the young air force officer through rheumy eyes, magnified to resemble withered turtle eggs by thick, horn-rimmed glasses.

"Pray to Allah there won't be, Father—immediately, at any rate," Hafez murmured.

"Pah," the old man spat contemptuously. "Our fine army will sweep the cursed Jews into the sea, like blowing chaff." He stroked his wispy white beard while waiting for Hafez's reassuring confirmation.

"Insh'Allah," Hafez replied vaguely. He had no intention of being drawn into a discussion of Egypt's "fine army"—especially its air arm.

At the desert headquarters, where Hafez was expected to appear the next morning for an important meeting, senior officers complacently disregarded rumors that the Jews were building an underground arsenal at an alarming rate. The officers boasted, "The Jews have no tanks, do they? They have no air force, do they? On the day their British protectors withdraw, forces of the Arab Legion will slaughter those who dare assert their independence."

Hafez wasn't so sure. Jewish farmers, ensconced in fortified kibbutzim, repelled raids by bands of Arab irregulars with distressing regularity. And the Americans—ah, the Americans. There were rumors of a clandestine arm of the Haganah making massive purchases of U.S. guns, arms-producing machinery, and, even more alarming, airplanes. Once acquired, the items disappeared—presumably slipped past the English blockade with surprising ease. If the American government decided to provide military aid to the hated usurpers of Palestine's rightful birthright . . . Hafez had seen what the Yanks, as the British called them, could do. And he had no illusions that Egypt's English allies would have the stomach to offer forceful resistance.

Hafez politely extracted himself from the querulous old man's persistent questions and escaped from the spine-cracking chair—less comfortable even than the cockpit of his beloved Spitfire fighter plane. He strolled to the suite's open French doors and stepped onto the Mena House Hotel's sunny terrace.

In the distance the pyramids of Giza shimmered in building heat waves. Was his country never to be free of foreign invaders? he wondered. With the best of intentions, the English—not to mention the Americans—had despoiled Cairo's beauty. Shepherd's Hotel, once the city's prize edifice, had become an exclusive domain of Egypt's so-called allies until the posturing English were invited to leave Cairo. During those days, Egyptians entered that Western enclave only by invitation.

Hafez's thoughts returned to the present. Aziza was a beautiful woman—she would probably be a delight in bed. But marriage? He could pick and choose beautiful young girls who were *very* good in bed, and with no commitment. His mother was ecstatic, however. The Daoud family was highly regarded in Cairo society's inner circle of landed gentry—another term he'd picked up in England. Aziza was their only child. And the Kamil family fortunes were in decline. What more perfect union could his mother desire?

Well, *he* could think of a better solution. The army—air force to be more specific. Already, at twenty-eight, he was the youngest squadron leader wearing wings. The prospect of war was exciting, but his plans didn't include a wife, an estate to manage, and family obligations. Perhaps if a war did ensue, he could distinguish himself and make a meteoric rise to high rank.

Then they would drive the damned English from the land altogether. The plan was still nebulous, but the Muslim Brethren—loosely organized and underground now—was gaining in number. Members had infiltrated the sole remaining British base at Suez. The weak and corrupt monarchy would one day fall prey to the growing group of dedicated army officers.

Hafez exhaled a gusty sigh and turned to reenter the chattering crowd of well-wishers. He'd procrastinate, plead the injustice of subjecting a new bride to the rigors of impending war. He shrugged—Insh'Allah.

Chapter 13

Colonel Prine had most of the characteristics Ross disliked in a man. He was overweight—grossly so for an army officer. His uniform—olive-drab serge instead of the pink trousers and green tunic favored by most air force officers—strained across his gut, making his florid, jowly face look porcine.

Colonel Deckard crossed his legs. "Colonel Prine thought the detachment commander should be on hand for his exit interview, Ross. We know you have an airline to run, but your annual IG inspection *is* important."

"Of course, Colonel," Ross said smoothly. "I'm just sorry I couldn't be here during the inspection. I'm anxious to hear what Colonel Prine found."

The Fourth Air Force inspector general (IG) spoke in unctuous tones through full red lips. His words did nothing to increase Ross's respect for the man. "Harrumph. This ready reserve business is new to all of us, Major. Frankly, there is a question in many minds that a purely civilian organization can ever instill the discipline and state of readiness that we would require in the event of a sudden outbreak of hostilities."

Ross felt his face flush. "I consider the officers and men of the 7017th to be soldiers not presently on active duty, Colonel, not civilians per se."

Prine's face darkened. He tugged his tunic lower across his sagging stomach. "Be that as it may," he growled, "the concept has yet to be tested. However, we find your records to be in order—and we examined them with the same scrutiny we would those of an active unit. Your supply inventory is up-to-date, and aircraft utilization is, er, well, commendable. My report will state that your unit is capable of performing its assigned wartime mission."

Deckard regarded Ross with a judicious demeanor belied by twinkling eyes. "What he means, Major Colyer, is that you get an 'outstanding' evaluation—a rating, I might add, not given any of the fourteen detachments inspected to date."

Ross stifled his elated response. His reply matched Prine's pompous manner. "I find it most gratifying to have our readiness status verified, Colonel. I ask that if any of the detachment personnel are cited by name in your report, Lieutenant Frazier, here, be commended for the excellent manner in which he has guided us through our formative stages. Also, Master Sergeant Miskowitz, my first sergeant—the state of our records can be directly attributed to his exemplary effort."

"Harrumph. It is so noted, Major. Now, if the rest of you will excuse us, I have another matter to discuss privately with Major Colyer."

Lieutenant Frazier gave Ross a broad wink as he, Deckard, and Prine's team of NCOs filed out. Ross's high spirits were short-lived, however. Prine's piggish eyes took on an icy look. "The reason I insisted on your presence, Major Colyer, has nothing to do with your annual readiness evaluation. I was most pleased to hear your rather pointed observation that you are, after all, a military officer presently not on active duty." His face cracked briefly in a wintry smile. "I have been instructed to examine your fitness to command a unit."

"I beg your pardon?" Ross exclaimed. "My *fitness?* Good God, sir, I commanded a fighter squadron during the war—was ops officer for a bomber outfit. I have decorations to prove it. I—I . . ." He let his voice trail off into bewildered silence.

"An enviable record, Major. I've read it. It's your conduct *after* being released from active duty that raises concern."

"Concern? By whom? About what? What does Colonel Deckard say about this? He's my immediate superior officer."

"Lieutenant Colonel Deckard has *not* been apprised of the circumstances, nor will he be until my investigation is complete. You will not divulge any portion of this interview until my report is rendered to the commanding general, Fourth Air Force. That's an order, Major."

"Sir, I demand to know what I'm being charged with."

"You are not being 'charged' with anything, Colyer. You are not subject to the Articles of War for acts committed while in an inactive status. But I assume you already know *that.*"

"What the—" Ross bit off the expletive. "I just don't understand what this is all about then."

"The FBI has requested that the army cooperate in a much broader investigation. It is alleged that you have—are—violating provisions of Title Ten, United States Code, while a commissioned officer. I remind you that such actions can be the basis for an administrative discharge."

"I've never knowingly violated any law," Ross spat indignantly.

"That is precisely what I have been instructed to determine." Prine's eyes gleamed as he warmed to a task he obviously relished. "I might add that knowingly or unknowingly has nothing to do with the disposition of your case."

"This is asinine. What if I just politely tell you I don't choose to answer your questions?"

·"Then I will note the fact that you refused to cooperate and recommend you be relieved as detachment commander. I will further recommend that you be required to show cause why you shouldn't be discharged."

"But I still don't know what I'm supposed to have done," Ross protested.

"You are president, chairman of the board, and majority stockholder of Allied Air, Incorporated, are you not?"

"Yes, sir."

"It is alleged that your firm has acquired and transported cargoes for a foreign power in violation of Title Ten, United States Code."

"Specifically what, where, and when?" Ross asked sharply.

Prine's huge stomach heaved in a sigh. "Major Colyer, you are not on trial. As I said, there are no charges—at this point. Believe me, the army is no happier than you to have accusations leveled that one of our commissioned officers is engaged in activity inimical to American interests. All that you need do is give me a sworn statement that you have never accepted, and are not presently accepting, compensation from a foreign power."

Ross's mind raced. "Colonel, I'm not sure of what's going on here," he countered. "You say I'm not being charged with anything, but your questions make me wonder. Before I swear to anything, I believe I should consult a lawyer.

"You see, Allied Air has a contract with a not-for-profit organization called the Jewish Relief Foundation. I'm not stupid—the FBI obviously believes that the foundation is illegally smuggling arms to the Jews inside Palestine. Maybe they are; I have no way of knowing—and there is no reason for me to know. I operate my air freight business in accordance with all U.S. laws and regulations I'm aware of. That, I'm afraid, is the extent of any statement I can give you until I talk with the foundation's president—and perhaps an attorney."

Prine glared. He slammed his briefcase closed and stood. "This investigation is far from finished," he snapped. "You will hear from me again, and you are well advised to have that attorney present next time." His waddling attempt to stalk angrily from the room evoked an inner chuckle from Ross, the gravity of his situation notwithstanding.

29 April 1947
New York City

Ross tossed his bag to the motel room floor and flopped across the sagging mattress. The war's over, for Christ's sake, he grumbled to himself. Is it impossible to find a decent room in this town? I suppose I should be grateful that Ariel can find even this much for me. Well, guess I'd better call her and report in—damned if I'm going to do any more today, though. In fact, I'm gonna have a drink before I even unpack.

He struggled to his feet and extracted the bottle of prewar Old Grandad that he'd paid a fortune for during the layover in Kansas City. He returned to the bed with the tepid bourbon and tap water, plumped both limp pillows into a backrest, and resumed the ruminations he'd wrestled with on the long flight home.

What the hell to do? Dropping the relief foundation contract was out of the question. Alex held his note for five thousand, although it was understood that the due date was open. Without this contract, he'd have to struggle for years to put that much aside, not to mention replacing the other DC-3—essential for any decent profit potential.

Active duty? It wasn't out of the question. Deckard had told him that the Fairfax operation was far ahead of any of the other embryonic reserve units. He grinned to himself. It even had an officers' club.

The guys had converted a small office, built a four-stool bar, and had their wives give the place a few festive touches. He'd dropped by his office the night before and found a poker game in progress. He hadn't enjoyed an evening so much since '45.

Although he'd told Wallace, the CIG agent, that he was no longer interested in a military career, that wasn't exactly true. He was a good commander. He'd built the detachment to eleven officers and six enlisted men. They liked and respected him, and damnit, it was a *military* operation. But active duty was still a very iffy proposition—and it didn't put money in the bank.

Face it, though, he told himself—you're getting deeper and deeper into this Palestine business. How far do you dare go? Wallace's words returned: You'll get caught—I can offer you immunity. Damnit, it won't hurt just to *talk* to the guy. He rolled over toward the nightstand and picked up the phone.

"Algonquin Hotel. May I help you?" a pert voice inquired.

Ross hesitated. He'd been told to leave a message with whoever answered. "Yes, do you have a Mister Wallace registered there?"

After a pause, the operator replied, "Yes, sir, but he doesn't answer. May I take a message?"

"Yeah, if you will. Tell him to deal the cards. His man is in room three-eleven at the Traveler's Rest Motel." Ross next dialed the phone at 44 Water Street. Ariel wasn't there. He left a message for her as well, then drained his drink, stretched out, and closed his weary eyes.

Barely enough daylight filtered through the grimy window for Ross to locate the phone after its clamor awakened him. "Colyer," he growled into the mouthpiece.

"I do admire dedicated employees who work after five," quipped a voice he recognized as Hank Wallace's. "I understand you want to draw cards."

"Could be. Depends on the rules," Ross replied.

"Okay. You like movies?"

"I can take 'em or leave 'em."

"I got one I highly recommend. It's showing at a little theater just off Times Square—the Rialto. Go in and find a seat; I'll join you. Last feature starts at ten o'clock."

Ross scowled. "Why all the—" He realized he was talking into a dead phone.

*   *   *

Ross surrendered his ticket to a pimply-faced youth and entered the theater's dark, malodorous interior. As his eyes adjusted to the gloom, he saw fewer than two dozen scattered patrons slumped in seats that had seen better days. His gaze followed the projector's blue-white finger of light probing through a haze of tobacco smoke. The screen showed a robed and turbaned man with a swarthy visage fondling a scantily clad girl. They chattered in a tongue Ross guessed was Arabic.

Sweet Jesus, what's with this guy Wallace? Ross grumbled under his breath. He selected the third row and took a center seat.

Less than five minutes later a shadowy form slid into the seat beside Ross. Wallace's face was a pale blur in the half-light. "I love your idea for an evening out," Ross muttered. "Did you bring popcorn?"

"Ideal place to meet," Wallace said crisply. "Not too many ears, easy to spot a tail, and there's a back way out. We'll not be seen together in public anymore, by the way. Now, have you thought through your decision?"

Ross perceived that their exchanges of bantering innuendo were a thing of the past. "If I hadn't, I wouldn't be here," he replied, his terse answer matching the federal agent's no-nonsense manner.

"What made you decide to call me?"

"Let's just say I'm fed up with the way some assholes are running things," Ross said curtly. "*Somebody* has to do *something* positive."

"You'll have to do something about that flippant attitude if you're going to work for the company, Colyer."

"Sorry, mother. If I take the job, I'll try to do better. Let's talk terms," Ross snapped.

"It's like I told you, give us facts and figures to include in our assessment. We give you five hundred a month plus reasonable expenses— and immunity from prosecution for violating the range of offenses connected with your smuggling operation."

"Keep going," Ross prompted.

"That's it."

"Like hell. What about my regular commission?"

Wallace hesitated. "I can't guarantee that. We'll work on it."

Ross sat silently for a time. "Work hard, Wallace—I mean *really* hard. I now have a new problem. A light colonel from the IG's office, Prine, is on my ass. Says the FBI asked the army to cooperate in that agency's investigation into the Jewish Relief Foundation."

Wallace grunted. "What kind of questions did he ask?"

"He wanted to know if I was aware that my cargoes were destined for illegal shipment to Palestine. Wanted a sworn statement that I didn't know anything."

"And?"

"I stalled. He left, but he'll be back, probably with some charges next time. Now, about this immunity business. I'll grant that you can maybe fix violations of import-export regulations, but does your clout reach inside the army?"

"Our director has access to the president. Does that answer your question?"

"Not really."

"Like I said, we'll work on it."

"Wallace, you start jerking me off, I walk. Is that clear? I'll cancel this damned contract and head for high ground.

"Now, I'll hang in—for a while, at least. I'll take the expense money, but you can keep the five hundred. Double-crossing Julius Mantz is bad enough; taking money for it is out."

Wallace sighed. "Sorry. I can't accept that. You'll be a contract employee and take the money. What you do with it is your business."

"Then donate it to the Jewish Relief Foundation."

"Okay. You'll have to sign for it, though."

Ross gave a mirthless chuckle. "What you're saying is that once you get my signature on a receipt for money, walking might not be easy."

"You didn't hear that from me. Now, we need statistics. How much of what is being shipped is reaching the Palestinian Jews? How big is their war chest? Are the troops at the other end trained to use what they're getting? That sort of thing. I'm giving you a business card from the D & G Novelty and Amusement Company. List everything you can think of and mail it to that post office box. If anyone notices it, you're ordering a gag gift—understand? That will be your only contact with me. If I want to talk to you, I'll make the arrangements."

"You're a real paranoiac, aren't you, Wallace? This sounds like a bad movie."

Wallace sighed. "Colyer, I'm beginning to think I misjudged you. Now, what can you tell me about the Irgun-Haganah situation?"

"They spend damn near as much time fighting each other as they do the English and Arabs," Ross replied. "Menachem Begin and Ben-

Gurion split back in '46. Begin's followers—the Irgun, or IZL—are convinced that the British army can be driven out with guerrilla tactics. They figure the Brits will get tired of being picked off one by one and just go home. They may be right. Anyway, they spend what time they aren't squabbling with the Haganah blowing up British outposts, police stations, and military bases—the King David Hotel, for example.

"Ben-Gurion favors collaborating to a degree with the Brits—gain time to arm against the Arabs. It's as simple as that."

"We know all that," Wallace replied impatiently. "We're looking down the road. Assuming the Palestine Jews succeed in gaining independence, who's going to come out as top dog?"

"Ben-Gurion."

"Why?"

"He has a larger following and more money, and gives the West the feeling he'll make concessions in the name of peace."

"Okay. Will Begin—and the IZL—roll over and play dead? Or are we going to see a civil war? That, Ross, is to be the salient conclusion of our paper to the president."

Ross appeared to study the flickering screen, reading subtitles as the camera zoomed in to show the girl's head hanging upside down over the bed's edge—her lips forming a moue of ecstasy. Finally Ross spoke. "Mantz and Rabinovitch believe that Begin will take a lesser post in any new government—become the leader of an opposition party. I have to agree with them."

"I see. Can you maybe get a letter, memo, or something from Mantz's files that spells out *why* they think that way?"

"Goddamnit, Wallace. I won't—"

"Yes, you will," Wallace interrupted. "You'll at least try. Can't you get it through your thick head that we—including the president—have the interest of the Jewish *people* at heart? We have a history of backing the wrong leaders—Tito instead of Mihajlovic in Yugoslavia, for instance. The president has to make a decision, and soon. Now get cracking."

"I'll try," Ross conceded grudgingly.

"Do that." Wallace's voice was rock hard. "Okay, it's time to break this up. I'll look for your letter—soon." He stood and started to leave, pausing to add, "She sticks a knife in his back in the next scene—I've seen this one before."

Ross didn't wait to see the cruel-faced villain get his due. He strolled around Times Square while he considered his radically altered status. Could he maintain his former friendly demeanor with Mantz while he was pilfering his files? As for Ariel—there's no way she would *ever* condone his actions.

In fact, what would be Colonel Ted's and Janet's reaction? A cold fist closed over his heart as he realized he could no longer confide in the people closest to him. He scanned the closed, purposeful expressions of individuals forming the bustling crowd. What if I stopped one of them and started talking about what just happened? he wondered. He grinned and felt better.

Chapter 14

14 May 1947
Fairfax Field

Ross shook water from his raincoat onto the office floor and tossed his dripping hat onto the coatrack shelf. Jake Trask looked up from the paperback novel he was engrossed in. "You're getting my book all wet," he grumbled. "Go someplace else to do your wet dog act."

"Bite my butt, Trask," Ross replied. "Why aren't you doing something useful, instead of poisoning your already warped mind with that trash?"

Jake chuckled and reached for the coffeepot. "Remember how you used to look forward to days like this in flying school? A whole day of doing nothing?" He sobered. "It wasn't costing us money then."

"So right," Ross agreed. "I just came from the met office. They're saying late afternoon before we're up to minimums. Which means that cargo at Salt Lake City won't move until tomorrow—which in turn means we won't be in Atlanta on the sixteenth, which means . . . Damn, Ariel is going to have a fit."

"And this weather is just the fringe stuff," Trask observed. "The radio says they're expecting another four inches northwest of here. The Missouri is bank full at Leavenworth—only one bridge still open— and the Platte is out of its banks west of Omaha. Nobody knows when the crest will reach us."

"Well, thank God for that twenty-foot dike we cuss every time we land here," Ross muttered.

"Oh, I've just been giving you the good news," Trask added cheerfully. "The old hands tell me the danger isn't from the Missouri; the Kaw River backs up before the Big Muddy reaches flood stage. It comes into the bottomland here from the west."

"Are you trying to say that *Fairfax* may be flooded?"

"Kansas City Southern is getting ready to evacuate their planes."

"Jesus Christ!" Ross exclaimed. "The met types didn't tell me that. Oh, well. We can make a below-minimums takeoff and go to Denver, I guess."

Trask added sugar to his coffee. "What about the air force birds?" he asked. "And the Norseman?"

"Oh, shit." Ross scratched his chin. "I can get a pilot from K.C. Southern to ferry the Norseman. The air force planes will have to be moved to Olathe Naval Air Station—that's our emergency deployment base."

"You maybe plan to tow them there—like gliders?"

"Hell, that's the air force's problem—the planes belong to them. . . ." He paused and scowled.

"Yeah," Trask added. "Seems to me I remember someone saying that *you're* in charge here. Or did I hear wrong?"

"Lieutenant Frazier is responsible for handling official matters. I'll call him and suggest he contact Fourth Air Force HQ at Mitchell— lay it in their laps. But, hell," Ross fumed, "there's nothing they can do. I'd call out our own pilots, but there isn't a green instrument card among them."

"Okay," Ross said after a moment's hesitation. "Here's what we'll do. I'll try to call Frazier at home and bring him up to date. While I'm doing that, you see if the pyramid alert system we drew up really works. Get as many pilots down here as you can. This *would* have to happen on a Saturday—they'll be scattered all over. We can file operational clearances to make it legal for white-card pilots to take off below minimums."

"Gotcha, chief," Jake replied. "I'll go upstairs to the orderly room and make my calls. Oh, one thing, the C-47 we got last week. It hasn't had an acceptance inspection. What will we do with it?"

"The sonofabitch flew in here; it'll fly out," Ross snapped. "If we can round up a crew. None of the reservists are checked out in it except that Braniff pilot, Simms. Pray he's in town. If not, old buddy, one of us will have to put a reserve pilot in the right seat. Let's go. This could get hairy. Those reservists haven't logged so much as ten hours' hood time in the past year. Not only that, half of 'em are ex–fighter pilots who never could fly instruments for sour owl shit when they were on active duty."

"*I* beg your pardon." Trask arched his brows in mock indignation.

Ross grinned. "Don't pull that crap on me, Jake. I'm an old fighter jock myself, remember?"

Frazier swept into what Jake was facetiously terming the command post an hour later. "What's the situation?" he asked Ross.

"Better than you could expect, really. We have six pilots and four mechanics on the way; three more pilots are supposed to call in soon's their families can run them down. Olathe is above minimums, so all we have to do is get the planes airborne out of here. We need authorization from Fourth Air Force at Mitchell to launch on operational clearances, and a waiver to fly the new Gooneybird without an acceptance inspection, and we're gone.

"That's the good news. The bad news is that the Kaw is rising faster than was forecast. They're starting to sandbag the dikes. It's my guess that we'd better be ready to haul ass by noon."

Frazier seated himself behind the first sergeant's desk and started dialing. Ross heard him say, "Let me talk to the duty officer, Sergeant." A pause, then, "I see. Well, call him at his quarters and ask him to call the 7017th. And Sergeant, on the double—we have an emergency down here."

The lieutenant hung up and made a grimace of disgust. "Peacetime army. 'The captain went to his quarters for breakfast, sir. I'll try to reach him,'" he mimicked in a shrill falsetto. "I'd be willing to bet that the bastard is on the golf course—where I would be if not for this damned rain," he added ruefully.

Three flight suit–attired men strode into the command post. "Hey," a chubby, balding lieutenant called, "what's going on? This isn't a drill weekend."

"Hi, there, Jerry," Trask responded. "You guys didn't lose any time. We're getting ready to evacuate the planes to Olathe. The Kaw is rising fast, and this place may shortly be a swimming pool. The weather is forecast to slowly improve, but not to be above minimums before noon. We're standing by for approval for you to take off operational.

"Jerry, you and Kinser will take the AT-6s; Wes, you and the next pilot to show will take one of the AT-11s. You may as well file flight plans now and preflight your birds."

Jerry peered through the rain-smeared window. "Jake, have you been outside? For your elucidation, it's raining—you know, that cold, wet stuff that you can't see through?"

Ross laughed. "Okay, I know it's a nasty day. But we stand to lose every plane we have. Then, Jerry, what will you take to International Falls to go fishing on weekend training cross-country trips? It's strictly a volunteer operation; if you don't think you can hack it—well, we don't want anyone busting their ass."

The phone rang while the three pilots exchanged wary glances. "Looks like our Fourth Air Force duty officer got pulled off the first tee back there where the sun is shining," Frazier muttered as he scooped up the receiver. "Lieutenant Frazier, 7017th Command Post," he barked. "Who? Mister Goodson? Yes, sir, this is the reserve flying detachment. How can I help you?"

Frazier listened intently for several moments, frowning. Finally he rolled his eyes at Ross. "That's sort of outside our line, Mister Goodson. Besides, we're in the process of evacuating our airplanes—Fairfax is threatened by floodwater. I—uh—I don't know what to say. We want to help, but I just don't know how—stand by."

He turned to Ross. "This is a guy with the Red Cross. A dike broke north of Saint Joe. There are two towns and about twenty square miles of farmland cut off. He's desperate for transportation. His national headquarters suggested he call a reserve or National Guard outfit."

Ross stared into space, thinking furiously. "We *can* help, of course. But is it legal? A reserve unit using military planes to support a civilian operation?"

"Damned if I know," Frazier replied. "I don't think it's ever come up."

"Okay, why don't you tell him you'll have to check and call him back. And put a rocket up someone's ass when you get to Fourth Air Force."

Five minutes later, Frazier was connected with the duty officer at Mitchell. "The Red Cross says it's a bad situation, Captain Ord. Two towns with about two thousand people cut off. They've already lost power and fresh water, and the crest hasn't even reached them. There's a hospital there—it's running on an emergency generator—and their only link outside is a ham radio operator with a battery-powered rig.

"Boats? He says there's too much current and debris for fishing boats, and they can't get anything of any size through the break in the dike. Airplanes seem to be the only answer.

"Headquarters USAAF? How long will that take on a weekend? These people will need medical supplies before nightfall. There are sick and injured to evacuate, and we can't get in there after dark. I see . . . hold on a minute, sir." Frazier covered the mouthpiece. "He can't approve the request—it has to go to air force headquarters."

"Oh, shit," Ross snarled. He reached for the extension phone. "Captain, this is Major Colyer, detachment commander. Can you patch me through to Lieutenant Colonel Deckard? Yes, I'm very much aware it's a weekend. Just try, will you? Tell him Ross Colyer says it's urgent. Right, I'll hold."

He looked up at the ring of serious-faced onlookers. "You guys game to give it a try? It's gonna be touch and go, weatherwise."

He grinned at the immediate nods of agreement. "Okay, here we go. Colonel Deckard? Ross here. Did the duty officer fill you in? Good. Can you light a fire under someone up there? If we don't get this show in the air by noon, there's gonna be a real problem up there by tomorrow."

"Ross, this is sort of off the wall, isn't it?" Deckard replied crisply. "I can appreciate your concern, but the army just isn't equipped to handle civilian emergencies. Has anyone checked with the National Guard?"

"National Guard? Yes, sir, there's an air guard squadron at Saint Joe—they have P-51s. There's a Nebraska unit at Lincoln—they have B-26s. The way I see it, we're gonna have to put something on the ground up there. We can air-drop supplies, but they need doctors and nurses, and they have people to evacuate. Either the AT-6 or AT-11 can land on unprepared surfaces."

"Do you have anyone to fly the planes?" asked Deckard.

"Yes, sir, we have crews standing by. We were fixing to get out of here ahead of the floodwater."

Deckard chuckled. "I won't even ask about that operational clearance business, but I take it you're below weather minimums there. Well, short and sweet, Ross—Fourth Air Force can't authorize this diversion. I'll call the USAAF command post in the Pentagon and ask, however."

Ross listened intently. "I appreciate that, sir, but we both know that by the time we get the word—even if it's an approval—it may be too late for some of those people. Colonel, may I tell you something off the record?"

"Something tells me to say no, but go ahead."

"Okay, here's what I'm going to do. I'll close the command post—we're evacuating. You won't be able to contact me, but I'll get back in touch when we're set up again—follow? Then the 7017th is going to have a training weekend—local flights and maybe a cross-country or so."

"Jesus Christ, Ross! You don't have authority to do what I know you're planning."

"Yes, sir, I know that. And I'm sure Colonel Prine, your IG, will take great delight in getting me fired."

"Prine?"

"Yeah. I'll have to tell you about that when we talk next. Anyway, adios, amigo."

Ross cradled the receiver and made a face. "You all heard enough, I guess. There isn't anyone around with authority to approve the mission. Lieutenant Frazier, I suggest you go home and take your phone off the hook. No point in getting your ass in a sling.

"Now, Jake, get in touch with this Red Cross guy. Tell him to have anything they want air-dropped out here—right now. Load it on the C-47 and stand by. I'll take an AT-6 and fly pathfinder. The rest of you stand by until I can locate a decent place to land up there. If the Red Cross can find a doctor and nurse who will fly with you, bring them on the first shuttle. We'll operate from here as long as we can, then move to Olathe. The best you can expect in the way of weather is about five hundred and one—so look sharp."

Ross trotted downstairs to don flying gear. He was filling out a flight plan when Lieutenant Frazier appeared at his elbow, wearing a flight suit. Ross scowled. "I thought you went home."

"Ross, your ass is on the line. If you can stand the heat, so can I. Now, there's another problem. Goodson says they desperately need an iron lung. They have a young girl in a coma and are about to lose her."

"That's peachy. Where are we supposed to get one?"

"Saint Luke's will lend them one. Soon's I call, they can send it over."

"I see. More important, how big is it?"

"He didn't say, but from pictures I've seen, they look about the size of a baby crib."

"It won't go inside an AT-11 then."

"I'd say you're right."

"And we can't plan on landing a Gooneybird up there. Great. Well,

I know we can get it in the Norseman—I'll take it. That old bird will land anywhere an AT-6 can."

As Frazier trotted back up the steps, Ross changed flight plan forms from military to civilian. You dumb ass, he thought. What are you doing? You'll get your head chopped off, clear down to the ankles, for violating air force regs; now you're about to violate a whole bunch of civil air regs. Oh, well. He shrugged and picked up the direct line to the weather office.

The ambulance wheeled up beside the Norseman in a shower of spray. Two men jumped out and opened the rear doors of the vehicle. "Where do you want this thing?" one yelled.

Ross opened the Norseman's surprisingly large cargo door and motioned inside. The other man crossed to join him in the protected area beneath the wing. "I'm Sid Gluckman," the man said, extending his hand. "I'm a doctor. A pediatrician now, but I was an army flight surgeon during the war. I'm going along, if you don't mind. Sounds like that child is in critical condition."

Ross returned the handshake. "It's okay by me. But I guess you know the weather is below minimums and I don't have any idea of where, or even if, we can find a place to land. Believe me, I wouldn't be going if it wasn't an emergency."

"I know all that. Let's go before I lose my nerve."

Fine rain reduced visibility to mere yards even before Ross cleared the field boundary. "It'd be a lot simpler to file IFR, make an instrument approach into Rosecrans at Saint Joe, then feel our way upriver," he yelled to Gluckman. "But I got guys coming behind me who are pretty weak instrument pilots. I'll try to follow the river all the way to see if it can be done. Keep your eyes peeled for bridges, power lines crossing the river, and the like. . . . I told you this wouldn't be a joyride."

The Norseman's sturdy Pratt & Whitney radial engine filled the cockpit with a reassuring drone. Ross dodged in and out of dirty gray wisps of cloud, trying to stay between the bluffs rising sharply on both sides of the river's muddy torrent. Gluckman sat with compressed lips. The automatic direction finder needle marked passage of an unseen radio beacon at Saint Joe. Ross keyed his mike. "Rosecrans Tower, this is Nan Four-Six-One, over."

"Rosecrans Tower here, Four-Six-One, go ahead."

"Roger, request clearance through your control zone at three hundred feet, VFR. We are en route to the flood area on an emergency relief mission, over."

"Roger, Four-Six-One. Rosecrans has no reported traffic. Do you have contact with the disaster area?"

"Negative. The Red Cross there was advised via ham radio to expect us, however."

"Understand. Good luck, Four-Six-One. I understand that's a real mess up there."

"Thanks, Rosecrans. I'll stand by your frequency. If I'm able to land, request you relay message to the 7017th Air Force Reserve Detachment at Fairfax that they can expect ceilings of three hundred feet with one mile visibility on their flight up, over."

Ross replaced the mike and started searching for the first isolated town, Albertville. The floodwater now obscured both riverbanks, only occasional islands of treetops marring the river's ugly brown expanse. A mound of solid ground, no larger than a football field, flashed past. Ross caught a glimpse of perhaps fifty farm animals huddled dejectedly on the sodden turf. A sudden squall further reduced already marginal visibility. "Damn," Ross muttered. "Don't tell me we get all the way up here only to turn around."

Gluckman nodded glumly, then pointed to his right. "There! A water tower. We just passed it."

"All right!" Ross exclaimed. "Let's go have a look." He wrenched the lumbering Norseman into a tight turn and peered into the murk. A cluster of houses and the outline of a town square materialized. His heart sank. Only the business district had dry streets. Roads leading out of town disappeared beneath swirling, silt-laden torrents.

Ross stood the plane on one wing and circled the embattled village, searching for anything resembling a landing area. He made out a group of wildly gesticulating figures. "They're pointing north," he told Gluckman. "Maybe . . ." Ross reversed his turn until the compass read zero degrees.

A break in the ragged ceiling revealed a stretch of blacktop highway perhaps two miles in length. A half-dozen cars and two farm tractors were parked in a meadow bordering the road, blinking their headlights. Ross chopped the power, dumped landing flaps, and let the Norseman settle onto the rain-slicked surface.

They were surrounded by grinning, raincoat-clad figures before the prop wound to a halt. Ross stepped into the excited group. "Which way to the terminal building?" After the laughter died down, he added, "I have an iron lung and a doctor on board. There are three or four planes right behind me with medical supplies and a couple of portable generators."

A leather-faced man detached himself from the group and strode toward the plane. He grasped Ross's hand with both of his. "Mister, that lung is for my daughter. There's gotta be a special place in heaven for the two of you." Rain mingled with tears as he added, "I never thought you'd make it. I do a bit of flying myself—got a Cub and a little grass strip over yonder a ways—underwater now. I know damn well I could never have made that trip."

"Those car lights did the trick," Ross told the grateful father. "That your idea?"

"Yeah, I knew you'd be hard-pressed to find a place to touch down." He chuckled. "There was some hell raised, but I also took my tractor and pulled down those telephone poles. Didn't figure you'd want to drag a wing on one of 'em. Now, if you'll excuse me, I'm gonna load the machine, and that doctor—Lordy, what a blessing he'll be—and get going. But Mister, I'm a-tellin' you: when we get back on our feet, I wanta see you and that whole bunch of yours back in Kansas City come up here. You're gonna get fed fried chicken, corn on the cob, and strawberry shortcake until it's comin' outta your ears."

Ross leaned back in his office chair, propped his feet on the desk, and let his eyes sag closed. He could hear the sounds of the last of the detachment straggling out of the command post. The early-afternoon sun, peeking between broken clouds, cast a golden oblong on the floor. Now you show your face, you fickle bitch, he mused.

Twenty sorties by four airplanes in twenty-four hours. Not bad. Goodson had been effusive in his praise. He'd called at noon. Residents of Albertville had suffered only one casualty since the previous morning's disaster. The Red Cross was now throwing massive assistance into the area, but Saturday afternoon and Sunday morning had been crucial.

It was time to go home and grab a good night's sleep, he decided. They were two days behind schedule, and Ariel would be getting impatient.

He gathered up the Sunday edition of the *Kansas City Star* and was looking at the front-page headline when the phone rang.

"Major Colyer here," he said wearily.

"Well, so you're back to answering the phone," the caller growled.

Ross grinned. "Colonel Deckard. So good of you to call. What can I do for you, sir."

"You can start by telling me how you managed to get your ugly puss on the front page of most of the country's Sunday papers."

"I had nothing to do with that, sir, honest. A local reporter got a call from a national news agency that there might be a story here. He just sort of got carried away."

"He did that. 'Local Air Force Reserve Unit Distinguishes Itself During Mercy Mission.' Detachment commander Major Ross Colyer says . . . blah, blah, blah. What a goddamn ham."

"Like I said, sir, he just sort of—"

Deckard interrupted with a brusque, "Colyer, you probably don't know what you managed to do. General Swinton wants to meet you—to kiss your feet, if you ask him to."

"Wha-a-a-t?"

"I said he wants to kiss your ugly feet. Ross, the old man is waving that paper around like a captured battle flag. It proves the worth of a ready reserve, according to him. A *reserve* unit, mind you, mobilizes and reacts *twenty-four* hours before the regulars can get their act together." Deckard chuckled. "That term you threw out, 'modern-day Minutemen,' he uses it every other sentence."

"Maybe someone will break down and authorize pay for us poor, starving volunteers," Ross suggested. "Anyway, are you telling me I can stop waiting for the roof to fall in?"

"What do you mean?"

"I—uh—sort of cut a few corners yesterday, Colonel."

"I have no idea what you're talking about, Major. I couldn't get through to you yesterday, I'm sorry. But it's the general feeling here that you reacted in the finest tradition of the army—immediately and decisively—and demonstrated superior leadership, et cetera, et cetera."

"And the duty officer, Captain Ord. What's he saying?"

"The last I heard, Captain Ord is claiming credit for suggesting the impromptu weekend drill to anyone who'll listen."

"I see. Well, sir, I'm glad it turned out okay. I was sure I'd be hearing from Colonel Prine."

"You mentioned him yesterday. Now what's this all about?"

"I'm under orders not to discuss a conversation we had during the IG inspection, but I'm on his watch list."

"Bullshit. That guy is a pompous prick. Pay no attention to him. After today, General Swinton will flat chase anyone off the reservation who raises a finger against you."

"That's good to hear," said Ross. "And thanks for covering for me; I owe you another barbecued rib dinner. I'll even throw in some trombone lessons."

Ross endured Deckard's good-natured abuse and hung up wearing a skeptical expression. Prine might be a pompous prick, as the colonel said, but he was also a *mean* pompous prick. You could see it in his eyes. And the man had a long memory.

Chapter 15

10 June 1947
Paris, France
With thinly cloaked disgust, Dov Friedman eyed the beaming, ebony features of the white linen–clad individual sitting across from him.

"Perfectly legal, sah, I assure you," the man said. "A visa from the Republic of Liberia, bearing the great seal and my signature, will make the French port authorities very much pleased." Round brown eyes, peering through glasses with pink lenses, oozed deep sincerity. Assam Triozu, ambassador to France for the destitute African country, was proud of his sovereign nation's sole, hard currency–producing export—paper. Not that more than a few francs would ever reach the nation's treasury, Dov thought.

Liberian passports were gaudy works of art. End user certificates for arms were flawlessly worded in six languages. The visas Dov wanted were the least costly of Triozu's inventory of sought-after items in the postwar world, but the minister smelled a sale of significant proportions. He arranged his perspiring features in a benign expression, settled his two-hundred-pound bulk into the barely adequate cafe chair, and awaited his customer's reaction.

Dov signaled a waiter for more coffee while he considered the proposition: one hundred Swiss francs for a visa stamped on identification papers of extremely dubious origin. But the French official he'd contacted at Zvi Bader's recommendation had seemed unconcerned. Obliquely he'd told Dov that the French were very much in sympathy

164

with the Jewish refugees from Europe's death camps. Yes, the English were constantly complaining of complicity and covert support of efforts to thwart their blockade. But—a Gallic shrug—the English are always complaining of something.

"There may be several," Dov told the minister carefully. "I'm not sure we can pay that much; our funds are not unlimited."

"How many?" Triozu dropped all pretense of diplomatic negotiation.

"Perhaps as many as three thousand," Dov replied.

The portly black man sat upright. Even in his wildest speculation, he hadn't dreamed of numbers like that. The tip of a pink tongue flicked across his full lips. "A sizable group," he agreed. "I am a man sympathetic to your cause, sah. Eighty francs."

"Fifty," Dov responded, his face twisted with agony, his tone mournful. "These people are very poor. Even at this generous price, not all will be able to escape the hell they live in."

Triozu's bloodshot eyes narrowed with suspicion. Distorted by his thick glasses, they reminded Dov of squashed insects. The minister pretended to consider Dov's counteroffer with dismay. He knew full well where money for the transaction would come from. But to queer this deal could possibly mean the loss of future transactions—passports, for example, at a thousand francs per copy. He turned both hands palm up and shrugged.

"I am a generous and sympathetic man. The Liberian people wish to be fast friends with those needing a helping hand. Fifty francs it is. When can you provide the identity documents?"

"Soon. Perhaps two weeks. Your"—Dov searched for a tactful term for the minister's shabby, one-man office—"chancery?"

Triozu frowned. It would take hours to stamp that many documents. He brightened. "I wouldn't think of causing you that inconvenience," he said. Reaching into a fat briefcase, he extracted a rubber stamp and waved it at Dov. "I will deputize you as a senior immigration clerk. You may apply the stamps yourself—as soon, of course, as the fee is paid."

23 June 1947
Armitage, France

Dov slumped in the Renault's seat and watched a convoy of buses of mixed manufacture roll to a stop at the German-French border town of Armitage. Drawn, anxious faces stared from open windows. My God,

Dov thought, when this is over, I'm going on the biggest howling drunk
Tel Aviv has ever seen. Exposure to hardship is one thing, but more
than a month of trying to soothe shattered minds and bodies drove one
to unbelievable depths of depression. Their tearful reaction to his promise
of delivery to their homeland was frightening. The thought of failure
haunted him.

Dov swung tired, stiffened legs to the ground and approached the
barrier. The German and French border guards met him there. "This
is the first group," he told the pair. He saw Greta, the Aliyah Bet
representative, dismount from the lead bus, and he waited for her to
join them. "Congratulations," he told the dour-faced woman warmly.
"You've done an amazing job. How many in this group?"

"Four hundred eighty-six," Greta announced in tones that defied anyone
to question her accuracy. "Another six hundred arrived at the Oberschlagen
bahnhoff as we were leaving. After these people cross over and board
the train for Marseilles, I will return for the others."

"Excellent," Dov enthused. He turned to the sharp-faced French official.
"We shall have the remainder of the thirteen hundred authorized by
this document across by nightfall." Dov produced a legal-sized sheet
of heavy paper bearing the seal and signature of France's interior
minister. Its formal language authorized the movement of thirteen
hundred stateless individuals across France for the purpose of em-
barking for onward travel.

The Frenchman nodded, barely looking at the document; Dov had
produced it and explained the project to the man earlier. "*Oui,*" the
Frenchman responded. "We will board the buses now and examine identity
papers. Two doctors and members of the Red Cross will accompany
us. Do any of the passengers require medical treatment? Are any known
to carry communicable diseases?"

"*Nein,*" Greta replied shortly. "Unless you count the aftereffects of
malnutrition, broken bones badly set, mental anxiety, and assorted internal
disorders. None pose a threat to the general public's health."

Dov took Greta's elbow and steered her toward the Renault. "Come.
Sit and talk a bit while these worthies do what they must. If I remember,
I have a flask of old cognac in the glove compartment."

He grinned as the chronically dyspeptic–appearing woman flashed
him a barely recognizable look of gratitude. She promptly tipped the
flask and consumed enough of the fiery brandy to floor a dockhand.
More and more Dov was coming to appreciate Greta's administrative
and executive abilities.

"How did the identity papers turn out?" he asked.

Greta made a sour face. "They would fool nobody but a blind, imbecilic ape," she grunted. "Don't be surprised if you hear uncontrollable laughter from those guards. The photographer hadn't the supplies to take original photos of everyone. He brought a box of his file pictures and matched them, as best he could, with his subjects. Children of ten or twelve have beards and bald heads. Women of sixty have the svelte lines and wrinkle-free faces of a movie actress."

Dov chuckled. "And the other group?"

"I confirmed by telephone that the first convoy would arrive at Brugge simultaneously with this one. One can only hope, and expect the worst."

Dov nodded. It had been Greta's idea to duplicate the original document authorizing passage of the thirteen hundred reluctantly agreed to by the interior minister. The resident Aliyah Bet forger prepared an exact replica. Greta explained that until border officials stamped the original and returned it to the ministry, there was nothing to prevent coincident crossing of a second shipment at another crossing point. The temporary holding camps established outside Marseilles would thus receive an influx of twenty-six hundred refugees under an authorization for half that number.

Dov patted the woman's arm. "I see the inspection party has finished. I'll walk you back." He extended the depleted flask. "Will you take this? You face a long ride."

He was favored with a rare smile. "Badly as I'd like to, save it for our arrival. And thank you, but I can negotiate the twenty-meter walk by myself."

"Very well. I'll expect to see you Sunday. I insist on treating you to the best seafood dinner in all of southern France." He watched the hard-faced woman stalk toward the line of buses, their engines already rumbling to life, with the autocratic aplomb of a duchess reviewing her palace guard.

Adolf, he muttered to himself, you never stood a chance. And neither, Mister Bevin, do you.

24 June 1947
Municipal Airport, Burbank

Ross sat at Bruce Murtaugh's makeshift desk and shouted over an erratic long-distance phone connection to Miami. "Kotch? We just caught two minnows. What shall I do with them?"

Kotch's reply was immediate. The circuit cleared momentarily and his voice boomed above the clatter raised by Bruce Murtaugh's C-46 overhaul crew. "Cut them into pieces and put them in boxes."

"What?"

"You heard me. Boxes. I'll send you a destination later."

Ross slammed down the phone. "This stupid code word business," he snarled to Murtaugh. "What the hell is he talking about? Put two airplanes in *boxes?*"

The ex-TWA captain pursed his lips and nodded. "It figures," the tall, middle-aged pilot observed. He arranged his sinewy figure in a creaking swivel chair with a broken spring. "Trying to ferry a Cub to the East Coast VFR could take a month. He probably aims to ship them by rail."

"The man is a total jackass," Ross grumbled. "Where the hell am I going to find boxes big enough to hold two Piper Cubs? Besides, this is his end of the business. I buy and fly airplanes—period."

"It might be easier than you think," Murtaugh replied. There's a packing and crating outfit across the field. Give them the dimensions of a disassembled Cub, and I'll bet they can come up with a crate in a day or less. How's your C-46 checkout coming, by the way?"

Ross's foul mood worsened. "That bastard of an instructor should be banned from the skies. He's a menace. How he keeps those two clapped-out planes flying, I'll never know.

"I tell him I'm pressed for time. I figure I need about ten hours and a checkride. I memorize the pilot's operating handbook overnight, and he puts me in the left seat the next morning. We fire up, taxi out, and line up for takeoff. 'The recommended technique for takeoff is to set the brakes, run the engines to full power, and get the tail up as soon as you can,' he says.

"Well, I damn near ran off the runway before we'd rolled a hundred feet. I was all over the place—jerking back throttles, pumping rudder pedals. . . . And you know what? The stupid son of a bitch just sat there *laughing*. He wears this damn straw cowboy hat, and he was slapping his leg with it and whooping and hollering, tears rolling down his cheeks. I'll never know how I got that ungainly crate airborne."

Murtaugh wiped the beginning of a grin from his face at Ross's ferocious glare. "Anyway, after we get settled down and out of the pattern, he tells me, 'Y'see, the engines sit close to the fuselage on this bird. She's a bitch to handle on the ground. On takeoff, y'got to walk the throttles forward until y'get rudder control. It's hard as hell even to taxi in a strong crosswind. We sometimes had to tow 'em to takeoff position when I flew the Hump out of Burma. I always let a green pilot learn this the hard way—keeps 'em from forgetting.'

"I told him in no uncertain terms that, by God, I wasn't exactly a green pilot, and to save his games for someone else. So, if I can tolerate those god-awful cigars he smokes, I should be checked out by the end of the week."

Murtaugh made no further effort to suppress his laughter. Ross was forced to break into a sheepish grin. "Okay, enough of that," Ross said. "Will this one be ready to fly to Teterboro by Monday?"

"We'll run up the engines this afternoon. If they check out, I'll say yes. For a one-time, daylight, VFR flight, that is. There's still a lot of rewiring to do—half the instruments don't work. We're finding more corrosion than I figured. There's a bad hydraulic leak, but the new fittings you brought from Oke City will take care of that. You want me to go with you, or will you take one of the new guys?"

"I'd sure like to have an old hand in the right seat, but you need to get to work on that first Connie. Jake Trask is in Panama City right now, but he'll be here next week. As soon as this plane will fly, give him a good checkout. He'll take it to Tocumen when it's finished. It'll be Panama World Air's flagship, configured to carry passengers. They mousetrapped us on this first one; the other planes will be strictly cargo carriers. President Jimenez is all excited about his country having an international airline. He's already planning a champagne flight for the company's first scheduled trip."

"Gotcha. Well, while you're circling and bouncing with your friend this afternoon," Bruce chuckled, "I'll see what I can do about getting some shipping crates put together for those two Pipers. See you in the bar tonight. Can't wait to hear the next installment of 'Hot Wings.'"

Ross glared at Murtaugh's departing back, then strolled across the hangar to watch a pair of sweating mechanics wrestle with a new tire and wheel on Allied Air's most recent addition to its fleet. She didn't look like much, Ross was privately forced to admit. With inspection plates removed, wires and tubing dangling here and there, and a weatherbeaten coat of drab camouflage paint, she was hard to envision in her prime. But after only four hours' flying time, the C-46 had impressed Ross with her cargo-hauling potential.

A squawking voice over a nearby loudspeaker interrupted Ross's musing. "Mister Colyer, you have a long-distance telephone call."

Ross returned to Murtaugh's office cubicle and picked up the desk phone. "Colyer here," he barked.

"Ross, this is Ariel."

"Ariel." Ross suddenly felt like a schoolboy talking to the girl he'd made out with at the high school prom the night before. "Uh—I started to call you three times this week. But I'm coming back there in a few days. I'd like to tell you what I have to say in person, if you know what I mean."

"I'm not sure I do. Listen closely, this is urgent. I talked with Eddie Kotch a few minutes ago—"

"I'm not impressed," snapped Ross, cutting her off.

"Please don't interrupt. Those two minnows—have you arranged to have them crated?"

"I'm working on it."

"Very well. It's imperative they reach here no later than Thursday next."

"How do you propose to arrange that?"

"We want you to load the crates on the C-46 you're bringing back here."

"That's out of the question."

"Ross, those Piper Cubs are more important than you know. That fleet of light airplanes represents lifeblood to the kibbutzim. The crates are part of a shipment for which Eddie already has export permits. The ship sails on Saturday."

Ross sighed. "Ariel, I can't help what they represent. I'm bringing that C-46 back under a waiver granted by the CAA for a one-time flight to an overhaul facility. It is not certified to carry passengers or cargo. A violation could cost me my license. Hell, it could cost Allied Air its charter."

"We're all running risks. We're talking survival now, perhaps the survival of a nation. Julius considers this to be a crucial matter."

"Ariel, I've been in the position of weighing risks against the consequences of failure before—with lives involved. Now, you ask Julius if those two Piper Cubs are worth the possible loss of the entire airlift project. At the same time, I'll talk with Murtaugh; it may be possible to work something out. I'll do my best, but don't expect miracles."

After a static-filled pause, Ariel continued. "Ross, why must you be so difficult? I wish I could convince you that this request is most urgent."

"*I'm* being difficult?" Ross retorted. "When Kotch sets up an operation, it's 'This is Eddie's show. We must do what he says.' And you tell me *I'm* the one being difficult? Well, it's my airline that's at stake. If Kotch is so damn capable, let *him* figure another way. Like I said, I'll do everything in my power to get that cargo to the East Coast in time, but I'm *not* bringing it on board under that one-time flight waiver. I'll call you when I find a way."

"Ross . . ."

"I'm sorry I yelled at you, Ariel." Ross's voice softened. "But I know what I'm talking about. Trust me."

"I—I do. Julius also has faith in your judgment. It's just all so damn frustrating."

"I'll see you in a few days. Now, I'd best get to work lining up a way to get those Cubs headed east." He hung up, a rueful smile on his face. Wallace would blow a fuse if I got myself fired, he thought. But damnit, these people are obtuse. Or am I maybe equally difficult to get along with? I'd give anything to sit down with Janet, Colonel Wilson, even Colonel Deckard, and talk about this screwed-up life I'm living.

Ross swirled the ice cubes in his drink. "So, Bruce, I may not be your boss much longer. But shit, those people know absolutely nothing about the flying business. Pile a load of cargo on an unlicensed plane barely out of the mothball fleet? I so much as scrape a wingtip and my ass is sucking wind."

"So what are you going to do?" Murtaugh's usual jovial air was subdued.

"Damned if I know." Ross signaled for refills to a shorts-clad waitress across the bar's press of five o'clock patrons. "I'm into this business, Bruce. I feel like I'm doing something important—like I felt when I was flying combat missions. But this contract, while a lifesaver, won't last forever. I can't put my only livelihood at risk on a whim. Can't the damn fools see they risk losing the whole ball game if I'm caught?"

Bruce accepted his drink from the waitress and chose his words carefully. "From what I see, they need you a helluva lot more than you need them, Ross. I don't know what you're mixed up in—it's none of my business. But I'm not totally stupid. If my guess is right about your involvement, I may have an idea."

"I'm listening."

"Okay, *if,* as I believe, those airplanes are headed for Jewish Palestine . . ." He paused and gave Ross a level look. When Ross didn't respond, he continued. "I'd guess they want them on the East Coast to load on board a ship."

"I'm still listening," Ross responded.

"That C-46 in the hangar is an unusually good airplane. We couldn't get the maintenance history, but the Form One for its last flight was filed with the local army ops here. It shows that the engines and airframe had only three hundred sixty hours logged when the army parked it out there. Sure, there are bugs—corroded electrical contacts, dry seals, inoperative instruments. . . . But give me a week with that crew, and I wouldn't be afraid to load 'er up and *fly* that cargo anywhere you want to name."

"Without an airworthiness certificate and CAA registration? Without an export permit?" Ross scoffed.

"Look, have Jake Trask apply for a one-time flight to Panama World Air's maintenance facility at Tocumen. Throw those crates on board at night and get the hell out. Your first refueling stop could be in Mexico, and they can't even *read* the documentation—especially if there's a twenty-dollar bill folded inside. Get your export permit in Panama and put those crates on a fast ship to Haifa."

A bemused grin creased Ross's features. "Not bad," he said. "Not bad at all. I like this."

"Ariel? This is Ross." He spoke from his favorite position: stripped to his shorts, stretched on the bed, his back propped with pillows.

"Yes?" Her voice was cold.

"Ariel, I feel bad about . . . this afternoon. I want to apologize."

Ariel hesitated briefly. "I accept the apology, Ross. But I don't know what Julius is going to say."

Blood pounded in Ross's temples. Using every ounce of self-control he could summon, he kept his voice even. "That's for him to decide, of course. But I have an alternative to what I think would be a possibly devastating mistake. Will you consider it?"

"Yes."

"Very well." Ross explained his scheme with brief, concise sentences.

Ariel remained silent for several moments after he finished. "I'll tell him. Thank you for calling. I'll get back to you after I talk with Julius."

Ross slammed the receiver onto its cradle. Glaring at the empty room, he snarled, "Damn that woman. Why do I let her get under my skin this way?"

Chapter 16

2 July 1947
Burbank

Eddie Kotch leaned across the battered desk in Bruce Murtaugh's cluttered office, his round, flushed face only inches from Ross's. "Don't try to tell me my fucking business, Colyer," he snarled. "I've been running stuff past the Brits for almost a year now. I know what will work and what won't. I don't know how you talked Julius into this crazy scheme. I had export permits and space in a freighter that could have tied up in Haifa without causing a second look."

"Maybe Julius agreed because he has good sense, Eddie," Ross replied wearily. "The chances of that airplane reaching Teterboro, with a refueling stop en route and without the CAA boys sticking their noses in, were virtually zero. The feds have been watching me ever since they shook us down last spring."

Kotch waved a beefy hand in disgust and turned to pace the tiny office floor, his jowly face quivering with rage. "Okay, okay," he muttered. "We're too late to make that ship, so at least let me tell you how to get those airplanes into the right hands. We'll use the same permit, just change the carrier. I'll contact a shipping office in Panama. See that those crates are labeled 'Prefabricated Storage Buildings.' They'll sail right through customs. I've used the Consolidated Manufacturing label before."

"Okay, then," Ross said. "Clean hands all around—well, almost. I'm putting my license at risk by violating CAA regs when I head for

Mexico instead of New Jersey. If Ariel can sweet-talk someone into closing that one-time flight plan at Teterboro, we may just slip one past them."

"Well, I wash my hands of the whole stupid idea," Eddie snorted.

"Good thinking," Ross said. "I'm not sure what prompted you to fly out here in the first place." Remembering his promise to Mantz, he added, "Damnit, Eddie, we're on the same side. I know you have a tough job, and I don't want to make it worse. When we're set up, this airlift can be the most secure route we have, and I promise to cooperate to the fullest.

"There are other reasons I want to take this run, however. I want to check out facilities at the refueling stops at Parimaribo and Natal, maybe grease a few palms to make subsequent trips smoother. We'll need other airfields with maintenance facilities."

Ross paused. Damn this double—no, *triple*—life he was leading. He didn't dare let Kotch, of all people, know that he had been promised a protective cover from prosecution. He added, "The final reason, though, is that I refuse to knowingly break U.S. laws. What we're doing now is contrary to *rules,* but you won't get hit with a federal indictment for bending rules. Smuggling contraband with false documentation is a whole different ball game."

Kotch snorted and turned toward the door. "Okay, have it your way this time. I gotta admit shipping through Panama is smart—we'll probably do it again. But stop crowding me." He brushed past Jake Trask and Bruce Murtaugh, who were just entering, and stalked across the hangar floor.

"Wow," Jake exclaimed, "what the hell did you do to *him?*"

"I just maybe killed whatever chance I had of smoothing things over with Mister Kotch, I'm afraid," Ross replied slowly. "And I have a feeling that Eddie does not forgive and forget easily. Oh, well," he added with a shrug, "how goes the preflight?"

"We're rolling her out of the hangar now for fueling," Bruce replied. "If you're ready for a test hop, we'll have time to clear any write-ups before dark. We'll load the crates inside the hangar tonight. She'll be ready for takeoff by midnight."

"Good work," Ross told the pair. "We'll plan for gear-up at first light. No need to get the tower controllers all in a lather by jumping the gun on a daylight-VFR flight. You have your charts, flight plan, and such put together, Jake?"

"Two days ago, Ross. I cozied up to one of the weather types at a bar the other afternoon. He has a night shift. After I bought him a few drinks, he agreed to give us a weather briefing for Mexico and points south without asking questions. I'm ready."

Before we go any farther," interjected Murtaugh, "I have something to talk over with you." Murtaugh cleared his throat. "I may be imagining things, Ross, but I think we have a snoop keeping track of our overhaul work," he said, frowning.

"Oh?"

"Yeah, I wouldn't even mention it except for this business we discussed the other day. The guy claims to be a student, going to UCLA under the GI Bill. Says he's always been a flying buff—hangs out at airports in his spare time just to pick up tips."

"But you don't believe it."

"Something about him doesn't add up. He asks the wrong questions for one thing; he seems more interested in what we have in those crates than the airplane itself."

"Well," Ross said thoughtfully, "I'm not surprised, in a way. Several people seem to be taking a lot of interest in Allied Air of late. If he comes around asking questions after we leave, just plead total ignorance. You were hired to prepare the plane for a one-time flight— you have no idea where we took it. In the meantime, we have a test hop to do. I'm on my way to file with the tower. See you shortly."

"Ross? It's Bruce. Hate to wake you, but I think we got a problem."

Ross shifted the telephone to his right ear and regarded the bedside clock through bleary eyes. Midnight. He'd been asleep less than two hours. "Wha'sh up?" he mumbled.

"Johnson, one of the loading crew," Murtaugh replied in cryptic tones. "He went across the street to the diner after we got the plane buttoned up. Says he heard some local cops—three of 'em—grumbling about being kept up all night. They mentioned an airplane and a search warrant. They were bitching because customs had just called and set the operation back to four in the morning."

Ross became instantly alert. "Customs?"

"That's what he said."

"Our plane, you think?"

"Figure it out."

"Why the hell is *customs* interested in cargo on what, for all they know, is a domestic flight? I smell something I don't like." Ross was reaching for a shirt. "Where you calling from?"

"The all-night service station next to the diner."

"Swing by and pick me up, will you? I'll be in front in five minutes. Oh, and give Jake Trask a call. We may want to get that bird out of here on short notice."

"Wilco, I'm on my way."

The airfield was silent and deserted as Bruce killed the car's headlights and drifted to a stop alongside the hangar door. Ross surveyed the absence of activity and cursed under his breath. "Can you see the ramp from that diner?" he asked Johnson, the shop foreman.

"Not from the lighted interior, no. Only from the diner's parking lot, and the street, of course."

"We need an hour, at least. What are the chances of them staying put for the next hour or two?"

"It's hard to say. They're bored as hell. They might just up and leave to be doing something."

"Maybe we'd better give them something to do—away from here. Any ideas?"

"I heard one of them call their dispatcher. They told him they were holed up waiting for the guy to show up with the search warrant."

Ross nodded. "What would happen if they got a call—big robbery in L.A.—get the hell out to the bridge and watch for a green Ford sedan."

Johnson's grin was barely visible in the darkness. He tossed the stub of a dead cigar from the window. "Gotcha. I'll call from the office."

The trio entered the unlighted hangar and waited for their eyes to adjust. "Jake, if you'll locate the tug and tow bar while Johnson makes his call, I'll start rolling the doors back. No lights. And try not to make too much noise."

Ross applied his weight to one of the massive sliding doors. He heard Jake muttering obscenities as he attempted to wrestle the hundred-pound tow bar onto the C-46's tail wheel. Stepping outside, Ross cocked his head to listen for signs that their movement was drawing attention. A heavy mist rolling in from the ocean muffled traffic sounds from the nearby boulevard. The airport's rotating beacon silently probed the mist with a long white finger. Its reflected light was replaced regularly by an eerie, double green flash from the beacon's rear side.

Suddenly a siren moaned to life. Ross mentally congratulated Johnson on what must have been a very good acting job. He trotted inside. "Okay, we can have lights. Get the tug started and hooked up. I'll tell the tower what we're doing—that ought to keep them from getting excited."

Quickly dialing a number scrawled beside the phone, Ross drawled, "This is the crew chief in hangar twelve, Tower. We're fixing to roll out a plane and park it down by Bascom Flying Service. Then we'll tow one of his back to the hangar. We'll be showing navigation lights. Okay?"

"Roger," the sleepy tower operator replied. "Don't reckon you'll have a lot of traffic to contend with. Gettin' real soupy out there, ain't it?"

"Yeah, looks to be well above minimums, though. You have any kind of forecast that it might sock in by daylight?"

"Naw. Not supposed to get below a thousand and three." Ross released pent-up breath. That's all we need, he muttered to himself. Caught red-handed because of goddamn fog.

Hearing the tug rumble to life, Ross stepped aside to guide Johnson as the bulky airplane commenced moving toward the open hangar doors. To Ross, the journey to where Bascom's two identical C-46s crouched in the gloom seemed to take forever.

Only the mutter of the little tow vehicle's exhaust disturbed the dank stillness. The airplane's twenty-ton bulk ghosted through the night, navigation lights casting faint red and green halos. An occasional crunch as a wheel encountered a stray pebble marked its passage. Ross almost stumbled and fell as he craned his neck to watch for the patrol car's premature return.

At last they were even with Bascom's two rows of parked airplanes. Short hairs prickled on the back of Ross's neck. If they got caught making the switch, it would be impossible to explain. After five silent, tension-laden minutes, their own plane—someone had already dubbed her *Beulah*—squatted alongside Bascom's number one C-46. His number two was rolling toward Murtaugh's hangar, and relative safety.

Ross sagged with relief as the hangar doors clanged shut. Grinning, he turned to Jake. "I'd give anything to see Bascom's face in the morning when he finds one of his airplanes missing. Maybe make up for the ordeal of that checkout he put me through. Johnson will have the fun of explaining how some cretin made a mistake and towed the wrong airplane to this hangar. I figure we have a good hour to get our bags packed and on board the *Beulah*. I'm tempted to stay here and play watchman when that crew busts in here with a search warrant. But I think we'd better spend the rest of the night on the airplane. We'll file with the tower by radio and start our takeoff roll at official sunrise."

Ross relaxed fully for the first time in twenty-four hours as the thunder of *Beulah*'s engines echoed off the thirteen-thousand-foot peaks of the Sierra Nevada sitting off their left wing. The plane was above the layer of morning mist, and pink light suffused the cockpit. Ross clutched in the autopilot, lit a cigaret, and turned to look at Jake Trask in the copilot's seat. "That was a near thing back there," he observed.

"Tell me." Trask sighed. "I was sure those bastards were going to search the flight line after they came up empty-handed."

"There was that possibility," Ross conceded. "I gambled that whoever asked for the search warrant described the premises only. They didn't have a serial number for the plane and wouldn't know one C-46 from another. The thing that has me wondering, though, is why they would use a search warrant in the first place. Those crated airplanes are legally ours, as is the C-46. What the hell were they looking for?"

"Good question," Jake responded. "What could they have done?"

"The fact that we had cargo loaded on a plane prefiled under a waiver for one-time flight would have been enough to keep us on the ground for a while," Ross said. "Other than that . . . I can't help but wonder if the customs people are actually behind this. I have a hunch someone knew we had those two Cubs on board and wanted to examine them—maybe take serial numbers and track where they ended up.

"Anyway, I'll bet they're taking Bascom's plane apart piece by piece right now." He chuckled. "Luke isn't apt to get it back and restored to flyable condition for a week. Well," he asked, changing the subject, "what do you think of this bird?"

"I'm impressed, actually," Jake replied. "The cockpit is a helluva lot more comfortable than the DC-3's. And even grossed out and cubed out, she's still climbing at eight hundred feet per minute. That twenty-eight hundred is some engine. Same one I flew on the Corsair, you know."

"A big plus," Ross agreed. "Replacement engines and parts are everywhere. It's a workhorse all right. Now, we have a ten-hour flight ahead of us. I'm heading straight for Tucson and direct from there to

Mexico City. I'd rather not crew rest there, so it looks like about another eight hours to Panama City. We may as well start sleeping in shifts. You want the cot first?"

"I'm too worked up to sleep right now. Why don't you let me get the feel of this crate while we have plenty of daylight?"

"Have at it." Ross unbuckled his seat belt and stood. "A word of caution, however. The props are in manual mode. Bruce advised against using the autofeather feature until we have a good electrical overhaul. I'll see you in about four hours."

Ross stretched and entered the cargo compartment. The GI folding cot beckoned. Eyes closed, lulled by the engines' hypnotic drone, he mulled over the near miss back at Burbank. Exactly who was behind it and why? He'd tell Wallace, but the agent had made it clear that Ross was on his own when dealing with the authorities. The agency would step in only as a last resort.

Sleep not far away, Ross's last thoughts were of his conversation with Ariel. Why couldn't he just put the exasperating woman out of his mind? What she really needs is to be turned over my knee and spanked like a spoiled child. His lips curled slightly as he tried to envision her reaction.

9 July 1947
Toronto

Eddie Kotch stood in Acme Metal Fabrication's goods yard, his face wreathed in a smile. He watched the motorized crane lower a twelve-foot-high electrical transformer in place alongside an identical pair. "There you are, m'boy, room to pack your entire arms factory," he told Clifford. "Strip the copper innards from those babies—you should turn a profit from that, by the way—and you have shipping containers. By the time you get your machines torn down, and the parts numbered and packed inside those things, I'll have shipping documents. We'll load them on the *Pole Star,* scheduled to sail in two weeks, and set them on the dock in Haifa right under the ruddy Brits' noses.

"The blueprints are already on microfilm—two sets. One will go over stitched inside the brassiere of a deep-chested friend of mine; hell, she could put plans for the *Queen Mary* in there. The other set will go by way of—well, let's just say we have a backup route. When you get all the machines torn down and numbered, we'll send the reassembly instructions the same way."

Clifford, displaying his normal ebullience, slapped Kotch on the shoulder. "You're a damn genius, Eddie," he crowed. "How on earth did you come up with this idea?"

"I spotted those transformers in a storage yard the first day we were up here last December," Kotch replied smugly. "In my business, you keep an eye out constantly for unusual shipping containers. We once bought a scrap boiler, gutted it, and replaced the tubing with lengths of four-inch seamless steel. Sent over enough to make twenty mortar tubes." He gave a wicked chuckle and added, "You will maybe have enough room to pack your favorite employee inside."

Clifford's good humor soured. "That crazy bastard," he growled. "I always knew inventors were nuts, but Sweitzer has me tearing out my hair. He refuses to let well enough alone. He wanted to reduce the bore to seven millimeters—increase the rate of fire, he said. He's redesigned the recoil mechanism four times. Substituting a folding tubular stock for his original had him in tears. No, I'd sure as hell *like* to ship him inside, but I'll settle for your just getting him out of Canada."

"Well, about that now," Kotch responded mildly. "We got this problem, see. Moshe is convinced that the guy will create nothing but chaos in Palestine. He'll blow the entire operation. We sort of hoped you could fit him into one of your existing plants."

"Uh-uh, never," Clifford exploded. "I've done my bit for the cause. What you're asking is above and beyond the call of duty. On top of everything else, the guy is a solitary drinker. About once a week he shuts himself inside his room and goes on a two-day binge. No, he's all yours, Eddie."

Kotch sighed. "I sympathize, Clyde, I really do. But Julius asked—insisted, actually—that you keep him."

Clifford's apoplectic response was cut short by a man who stuck his head out the factory's rear door. "Telephone call, Mister Clifford. The man says it's urgent."

Kotch strolled over to have a closer look at his prize shipping containers, glad to have time to rehearse his response to Clifford's adamant objection. He was spared the ordeal. Clifford burst from the factory door cursing like a wild drunk. "Get in my car, Kotch," he snarled. "You're in this too, after all."

Eddie slid into the Cadillac's front seat. "What's up?"

"Sweitzer—the son of a bitch is in jail. We have to get him out."

"*What?*"

"The bastard got drunk and ran his goddamn car into a storefront."
Kotch rode in silence as Clifford whipped the big car through swirling midmorning traffic. Suddenly Kotch chuckled. The chuckle grew
to a belly laugh. Clifford glared at him as if he had lost his mind. "What's
so goddamn funny?" Clifford rasped.

"Sweitzer. If he's in jail, he can't go to Palestine."

"Forget it. I'll spring the stupid bastard if I have to mortgage my
wife and kids."

Kotch was still chuckling when Clifford slid to a stop at the curb
in front of the police station. He was in a no-parking zone, Eddie observed.
The angry, rotund Canadian stalked through the entrance and approached
a uniformed constable sitting behind a chest-high counter. "You got
a Sweitzer here, in the drunk tank," Clifford snapped. "I'm here to
get him out."

The overly polite young officer consulted a file folder. "Ah, yes.
Mister Sweitzer. Yes, sir, he is here, but I'm afraid his release may
present some difficulty. Would you have a seat over there, sir? I'll
call the inspector—he'll explain the situation."

"*Now* what the hell's wrong?" Clifford growled as he and Kotch
settled onto a wooden bench, its back and seat polished to a gleaming finish over the years by several hundred nervous bottoms.

Five minutes later a lean-faced, mournful-looking man, appearing
much like an undertaker in his black suit, returned with the constable.
"Inspector Bilkerson, sirs," he introduced himself. "Understand you
chaps are here on behalf of our Mister Sweitzer."

"That's right, Inspector," Clifford responded briskly. "Sweitzer's
an employee of mine. It sounds as if he had a drop too much. I'm quite
prepared to post bond—to include any damages he may be responsible for."

"Ah, yes. Mister Sweitzer is fortunate to have such an understanding employer." The inspector removed a stubby pipe from a jacket pocket
and slowly tamped the bowl full of coarse, vile-looking tobacco. Kotch
found his patience growing thin as the man lit the pipe and puffed
deliberately until it was drawing to his satisfaction. Finally, he continued. "I guess you'd say he is a trusted employee, then?"

"Why, yes. Absolutely trustworthy. Why do you ask?"

"It's his passport. He's a Swiss national—no resident visa. He couldn't
have worked for you long, I'd say."

"Well, no." Clifford grew cautious. "He came highly recommended, though."

"You aren't missing anything of value from your plant then." It was a statement rather than a question.

"Not that I know of. Again, why do you ask?"

The inspector's doleful expression lengthened. "We found some items in his car that he refuses to explain. Rather curious. I'm not sure I know what they are, but they look valuable. I thought perhaps he'd nipped them from your shop. Would you care to have a look?"

"Of course," Clifford replied. "What sort of 'items'?"

"Come along, if you will. They're in the evidence room."

Kotch felt his stomach lurch as Bilkerson placed a flat wooden box on the table. He saw Clifford's lips tighten to a thin line. The opened lid exposed a half-dozen oddly shaped pieces of highly polished steel. Dies! Kotch screamed silently.

Clifford retained his composure, however. As the inspector watched his reaction with hawkish alertness, the industrialist shrugged. "Can't say that I recognize the things. I'm no machinist, though. I'd like to have my plant superintendent take a look, if you don't mind. But first, could we talk with Sweitzer? Perhaps he'll explain things to me."

"That will be arranged. And we would rather like to speak with your superintendent, too. Today yet, do you think?"

"Well, this being Saturday, I'd have to run him down. Monday would be better, I'm sure."

"I'd really appreciate your trying, if you would. I'll tell you what, if you'll give me your superintendent's name and address, I'll just have a patrol car drop over and try to locate him. It is rather important that we see him today. A chap from the Mounties is interested in the contents of this box, I understand. Now, if you'll just step into this room, I'll have Sweitzer brought in."

Sweitzer sported a bandage above his right eye, and his spectacles dangled awkwardly as he faced Clifford and Eddie's thundercloud-like expressions. "Sorry to have put you out this way," he muttered finally.

"What the fuck have you done?" Clifford hissed. "What were you doing with those dies in your car?"

The battered-looking little Swiss assumed a defiant air. "They're my property. I'll do with them what I please."

"They are *not* your property." Clifford showed signs of losing his composure. "Those dies have been bought and paid for. But answer my question: what were they doing in your car? They're supposed to be in the vault in the drafting room."

"I've decided not to continue with the project," Sweitzer replied sullenly. "I'm going home to Switzerland. I'll find another buyer for my gun. I've been listening to stories about Palestine; I don't think I want to work there. Besides, you've changed my gun into a piece of cheap junk."

Clifford sat speechless. Eddie couldn't contain his outburst. "You ass. You were running away, weren't you?"

The little Swiss inventor nodded.

"I can't believe it. You were going to board a ship, enter France, then Switzerland, carrying parts of a machine gun on your person."

"They've never searched my luggage before."

Kotch threw both hands above his head. "Mother of God," he implored. "You really must have to work at being as stupid as you are, Sweitzer. Look, you're in deep shit. Just possession of those dies can get you put away for maybe ten years—if they're properly identified. And they will be—just as soon as that guy from the Royal Canadian Mounted Police gets a look at them. This inspector is suspicious, but he doesn't know for certain what he has. The only smart thing you've done so far is to keep your mouth shut.

"Now you listen to me, and you listen good. If you screw this up, you'll have me to answer to. Then you'll wish you *had* been thrown in jail. You'll need more than Band-Aids, that I guarantee. I'll break both your goddamn knees with a baseball bat—understand?"

Sweitzer's eyes grew round, and the blood drained from his face. He nodded.

"Okay. Now," Kotch continued, "you're going in there and tell that inspector that those dies belong to you. You're an inventor trying to sell a new kind of gearbox for farm tractors. You're afraid someone will steal it before you get a patent for it; that's why you were so secretive. Be convincing; God help you if he doesn't believe your story.

"Clyde will post bond for you. You come straight to my hotel room— seven-fourteen at the Savoy—directly from here, understand? Don't go to your apartment or back to your car. Don't even stop to take a piss. I'll see to getting both you and your dies out of the country. We'll straighten things out between us later, back in the U.S. Now, I'm leaving. I don't want to seem to have anything to do with you from here on."

*   *   *

Kotch leaned back in his chair and placed both feet on the hotel bed. He picked up the phone and took a healthy slug of Scotch while he waited for the switchboard operator to place his call. "Ariel?" he barked. "Tell Julius it looks like rain up here. Oh, yeah—y'better have Colyer stand by with one of his flying machines."

Chapter 17

10 July 1947
Sète, France

Dov Friedman leaned from an open window on the *President Warfield*'s bridge and watched straining dockhands loop wrist-sized hempen hawsers around bollards set into the stone quay. Behind him he heard Captain Aronovitch move the engine room telegraph to ALL STOP–FINISHED WITH ENGINES.

The captain joined Dov at his window vantage point. "Well," Aronovitch said, lighting his pipe, "next stop, Palestine."

"Or a Cypriot detention camp. Look," Dov replied sourly, pointing to a rakish vessel silhouetted against the hazy Mediterranean horizon. "The Brits are waiting."

"Getting out of the harbor will be our greatest obstacle," Aronovitch responded. "Once at sea, even the damned British wouldn't dare open fire on a ship crowded with innocent old men, women, and children."

"Be sure the destroyer captain knows that," Dov answered grimly.

The watch bos'n struck two bells. Dov, coffee cup in hand, watched the serpentine line of blurred figures shuffle forward. Sickly yellow light from a naked overhead bulb at the foot of the gangplank briefly illuminated the passengers as they passed underneath. The line coiled upward, along the narrow deck, and disappeared into the black maw of the aft hatchway—all in eerie silence. Somewhere he heard a child whimper; it was immediately shushed with a sharp admonition.

186

Dov was struck by the analogy of Noah overseeing the loading of his ark. Not entirely incongruous, he thought bitterly. Was he not a spectator to the salvation of what remained of Europe's displaced Jews? Was it up to this pathetic collection of weakened and ill to perpetuate God's chosen children? There must be some special corner in hell for the men who conceived and carried out the prelude to this gut-wrenching scene.

Dov stifled an urge to seek out the cognac bottle, and turned instead to the blue-granite pitcher of rancid, hours-old coffee. Aronovitch joined him. Dov turned, a wry smile curving his lips. "Depressing, isn't it?"

Aronovitch gazed morosely at the scene below. "There's worse to come," he said.

"Really?" Dov raised his eyebrows.

The dim light cast by a single bulb above the chart table emphasized deep lines in Aronovitch's face. "I just finished speaking with the harbormaster by ship-to-shore phone. The French governor has issued a restraining order. We're not to leave port."

Dov turned to take one last look at the row of trucks, stretching out of sight in the gloom of a starless night. They disgorged a slow but steady stream of human flotsam into the bowels of the darkened ship. He compressed his lips and threw the dregs of his coffee overboard. He turned to the captain and asked, "Is this the coup de grâce?"

Aronovitch stroked his chin. "Perhaps, but if we wait, the noose will only be drawn tighter. We sail at high tide—oh-one-twenty."

The first mate, Hilvitz, joined them in time to hear the captain's pronouncement. "The navigator hasn't reported yet, Captain."

"Then we'll sail without one, Mister Hilvitz. I bought drinks for a trawler captain this afternoon; I was beginning to get a feeling something like this was afoot. He told me that as soon as we were abeam Andora Light, to turn hard to port. Now, pass the word, quietly—and don't alarm the passengers. This place is crawling with British agents."

Darkness produced a cooling sea breeze. Volunteers passed among the crowded passengers, dispensing fresh water, bread, tinned beef, and cheese—and words of encouragement. The waterfront drifted into its usual nighttime routine. Fishermen scrubbed down their boats and retired to the taverns before catching a few hours' sleep. They would be under way long before dawn. Prostitutes timed their workday accordingly, and soon the sounds of revelry filled the narrow streets.

On the *Warfield*'s bridge, Hilvitz coached Dov on the use of a pelorus. "I'll compute the correct bearing to the light from our heading," he explained. "When you can look through this peephole and see the light through this slotted piece up front, sing out. That's our turning point."

Dov nodded. The atmosphere on the bridge crackled with tension. Aronovitch was on the speaker tube to the engine room, giving precise instructions. Hilvitz, who would serve as navigator, plotted and replotted their departure route a dozen times. The helmsman, a laconic oldster, was the only one seemingly unperturbed. He had departed tight anchorages before.

The dimly lit ship's clock read 0115 when Aronovitch walked to the portside window and turned his flashlight toward the bow. He flashed it three times—the signal to slip the bow lines. "Engine ahead one-third," he called in even tones. As the nine-foot propeller sent a slight shudder through the ship, crew members slipped previously loosened pins free of the gangplank. It fell to the dock with a resounding clatter.

The ship's forward motion tightened the single remaining stern line. The twelve-inch wooden bollard to which it was attached groaned, but asymmetrical thrust swung the *President Warfield*'s bow into open water. Aronovitch aimed four quick flashes astern. An ax flashed in the dim light, and the ship's last connection to land splashed into the roiled, oily water below. "All ahead, slow," the captain ordered. He turned to Hilvitz. "You have the con."

On deck the Palmach members wormed their way through suddenly aroused passengers. "Quickly, everyone, go below—*now*. You must; it's imperative to clear the deck. Hurry, now," they urged. "There may be trouble; you *must* get below."

An alert passenger noticed objects ashore sliding past. "We're moving!" he shouted. "We're moving—we're on our way." Despite the crew's efforts to silence the passengers, cheers, ragged at first, then swelling to a crescendo, filled the harbor.

Ashore, the sound of the refugees' jubilation penetrated even the noisy taverns. Patrons streamed into the streets, pointing toward the dark hulk ghosting toward the outer harbor. "The Jews are making a run for it," an amused sailor called. "Bully for them!" British agents made themselves immediately known by their horrified expressions. Two recovered from their astonished consternation and raced for telephone kiosks, followed by derisive chants.

Dov, oblivious to the uproar, crouched behind the portside pelorus. The unaccustomed tremor beneath his feet felt good. By God, they were *doing* something for a change. He wiped sweat from his brow and concentrated on a slowly flashing light approaching on his left. They were almost even with it. He squinted into the eyepiece—there, the front and rear apertures were perfectly aligned. "Andora Light abeam," he called.

"Full port rudder, Helmsman! All ahead two-thirds!" Aronovitch shouted.

Dov straightened and felt the increased engine speed provide a surge of forward progress. He grinned hugely—they'd made it. His elation was short-lived. First the barest change in the easy roll set up by the approaching open sea. Then a slight hesitation. He heard the captain snap, "All ahead full; rudder amidships. We're in shoal water, Mister Hilvitz. Call the engine room. Tell them to make a full head of steam and turn max revs until ordered otherwise."

The next hesitation was more pronounced. The bridge crew had to grab supports to stay on their feet. Dov heard the engines race as the screw cavitated briefly. There was no reassuring surge this time. Even a landlubber like Dov could tell that they were hard aground.

Aronovitch, his face set and white in light reflected from the binnacle, faced straight ahead. The engine responded gallantly. Black smoke poured from the ship's single stack; the blast of her compound exhaust thundered into the night. She moved—an almost imperceptible quiver—advancing a few inches, a foot; then she shuddered to a full stop once more. Aronovitch never changed expression, allowing the engine to howl its defiance.

A trawler captain, drink in hand, stood among the crowd of well-wishers ashore and chortled, "Show the buggers, Captain, show the buggers." Then he sobered and muttered, "No, no you fool, not to *port*. Oh, Mother of God. She's aground on Andora Bar."

Aboard the *President Warfield,* gloom settled like a dark cloud. Only Captain Aronovitch remained at his station with no sign of defeat. Hilvitz moved to his side. "Can we reverse off the bar?" he inquired.

"Unlikely," the captain replied calmly. "The moment we come to full stop, silt will fill the void around the propellers. No, she's a riverboat, made for riding over bars. We have better conditions than we will enjoy for the next twenty-four hours—high tide, just turning, and momentum. She'll claw her way out, I feel it."

Just then the deck lurched beneath them. A hesitation as she bottomed again, another, then a swell lifted her bow. The propellers, biting into deep water, changed their protesting whine to a subdued rumble. "Make a course south by southeast, Mister Hilvitz. All engines ahead full," Aronovitch said without turning.

Almost a thousand miles to the north, Sir Donald Ashton-Smythe, clad in a burgundy smoking jacket and with a crystal balloon glass of Portuguese brandy in one hand, clutched the telephone in the other with a white-knuckled grip. "They *what?* With a regiment of your men present and the entire French harbor patrol watching, they up and sailed away?"

The senior civil service officer's normally ruddy features darkened further. The delicate brandy snifter shattered in his grasp. He glanced at blood welling from a tiny cut, the brandy stain spreading on the Persian carpet, and cursed under his breath.

Aloud, his notorious aplomb in shreds, he screamed, "Well, stop them, damnit! Signal the *Ajax*. Crowd the *Warfield* into shallow water; hole her below the waterline. *Sink* her, do you hear?"

He strummed the rosewood desktop with impatient fingers as he listened. "Blast the French. You heard me. Ram the ship if necessary. She must not leave French territorial waters."

The furious crown emissary slammed the phone to its cradle. Lady Ashton-Smythe laid her book aside. "Whatever? . . ."

"The bloody Jews," her husband raged. "I sometimes think we should have allowed Chancellor Hitler to finish what he started."

"Donald!"

"I'm sorry, my dear, but those arrogant people have defied a duly issued order from the French government. Well," he said from between clenched teeth, "let them learn what it means to defy an order issued by His Majesty, the King of England."

11 July 1947
Egyptian Army Desert Headquarters

Hafez Kamil swung the green Alfa Romeo two-seater alongside a desert tan army staff car, wincing as the plume of dust he'd stirred settled around him. He guessed that he was early for the meeting; only a half-dozen cars occupied the parking area.

Wiping dust from the bill of his service cap, Hafez strode toward one of a clutch of sagging, bedraggled tents that served to camouflage the army's underground field headquarters. He was surprised to find two armed guards inside. They carefully examined his ID card and checked it against a list of names before waving him toward a flight of concrete steps. What in Allah's name? Hafez wondered as he descended into a spacious underground chamber. Guards? *Armed* guards? Perhaps this *was* to be an important meeting.

He joined a group of perhaps a dozen officers chatting and sipping coffee. Recognizing a classmate from the military academy, he wandered toward the group, after pouring himself a cup of coffee. Nodding to the others, he said, "Hello, Hassan. What's with the guards?"

His friend, a heavyset lieutenant, gave Hafez a sharp glance. "You weren't told?"

Hafez shrugged. "Only to be here."

"Then you'll have to wait. The meeting will start as soon as Colonel Nasser gets here."

"Nasser?"

"Right. He's a headquarters officer, stationed in Cairo, I believe. I don't know exactly what his job is—" Their conversation ended abruptly as three grim-faced officers entered, bringing the group to rigid attention.

"Find seats, gentlemen," ordered a tall, stern-visaged officer wearing the flashes of a lieutenant colonel of infantry. He scanned the array of attentive, serious faces, pausing to give Hafez more than a cursory look. "We have grave matters to discuss this morning," he continued. "Our source within the United Nations advises that a resolution to partition Palestine into separate Arab and Jewish states is destined to pass."

He paused until the import of his words was digested. "If it does, Egypt will share its northern border with an independent Jewish state by this time next year. Thousands of Palestinian Arabs will either be driven from their homes, their land—or be subjected to Jewish rule. The situation is unthinkable. Already, King Farouk and leaders of Syria, Transjordan, and Lebanon have issued a message to the world that we will not abide by such a decision. If this comes to pass, the combined forces of Palestine's neighbors will restore Arab rule to the entire territory."

There was a rustling sough of indrawn breaths. A bald-headed infantry officer asked, "Pardon me, sir, but what will the British say about an invasion?"

"The British will have nothing to say about the actions of sovereign nations coming to the aid of a neighbor," Nasser flared. "After they abandon the Palestinian Arabs, *we* shall maintain order."

"But—but if the United Nations declares that part of the country belongs to the Jews, won't they resist?" the bald-headed officer persisted.

"Oh, come now, Sidky," said a voice from the rear. "The Jews have nothing to resist *with*. Those foolish enough to make the attempt will be dealt with in short order."

Colonel Nasser continued. "Battle plans are being drawn up even as we speak. The army will drive north across the Sinai and occupy Tel Aviv—the Jews' principal headquarters. At the same time, forces from Syria, Transjordan, and Lebanon will attack from the north and east."

Hafez shifted uneasily. This man made the incursion sound like a casual walk along the beach. The young officer had observed Egyptian troops maneuvering close to the airfield at Huskstep. Most were dregs rounded up from the cities' slums, incapable of following orders. He'd seen tanks whose engines chronically overheated and whose guns wouldn't fire. He found himself on his feet.

"Squadron Leader Kamil, sir—"

"Yes, Squadron Leader, I recognize you. Do you have a question?" Nasser asked impatiently.

"Yes, sir. What will our role be?"

"You fighter pilots will make reconnaissance flights in advance of the armored column. Your transports will bring high-priority parts and supplies to forward positions, and evacuate any wounded. In the event a target worthy of their attention is observed, the transports may double as bombers."

"Yes, sir." Hafez took his seat, too astonished to say more. Wrapped in his own thoughts, he took no part in the increasingly spirited discussion. The air force was to have no meaningful part in the upcoming fray. His aspirations to use combat as a means to promotion appeared dashed. As soon as Nasser declared the meeting over, Hafez headed for the exit.

"Squadron Leader Kamil, one moment."

Hafez turned to see Nasser's beckoning finger. He retraced his steps. "Yes, sir?"

"I'd like a word with you after the others leave," the staff colonel said in a low voice.

Hafez helped himself to another cup of coffee and chose a seat removed from where the others were discussing "the war" in excited voices. Finally the room was empty except for him and the suddenly weary-looking staff officer.

"Squadron Leader Kamil, nothing of what I'm about to say is to be repeated. Is that clear?"

"Ye—yes, sir."

"Your actions have been observed by people I trust. They tell me you are intelligent, possibly our best pilot, and a competent leader."

Hafez blinked but didn't interrupt.

"Tell me, Kamil, what is your opinion of our King Farouk? Please," Nasser raised a hand at Hafez's wary look, "when I told you nothing said in this room would be repeated, I included myself."

"Well—well, sir, it is said that he spends a great deal of time entertaining on the royal yacht; he frequents fashionable resorts—"

"That he's a playboy, a drunk, and a womanizer," interjected Nasser.

"I've heard those terms used—yes, sir."

"Do you think him—or his handpicked Wafd—capable of directing an aggressive military campaign?"

"I—I really can't say, sir. It is also said that he favors an accommodation with the English, that he is opposed to using force."

"Exactly!" Nasser slammed a fist into his open palm. "That is why, Squadron Leader, he is unaware of the plan I described—and will remain that way until the time comes to carry it out. The English would convince him that it's unwise."

Hafez gaped. "But, sir . . ." He let his voice trail off.

"I detected a questioning look on your face during the briefing. You have reservations?"

"Sir, the army cannot carry out a sustained drive against determined opposition. And I believe that the Jews *will* put up a stiff defense. They've been arming and training in secret."

"I see. And your own air arm?"

Hafez gulped. "Not much better, I fear," he replied in abject tones. "My fighter pilots are largely sons of prominent families, commissioned by the king. The RAF pilots assigned to help train them did their best, but they still are far from being ready to enter combat. Rarely are more than half of the Spitfires the English left us in flyable condition."

"I applaud your candor, Kamil. Now, do you know of an organization called the Free Officers?"

"I have heard the term," Hafez replied cautiously.

"And the Muslim Brethren?"

Hafez felt his stomach knot. Dare he disclose his ties with the Brethren? "Yes, sir," he replied warily.

"We must dispense with the monarchy, Kamil." Nasser pinned Hafez with a steely gaze. "Our present profligate sovereign can be disposed of, but another of his ilk will follow; such is Egypt's history. The British will be banished from Egyptian soil. We must follow the Western example of democracy. The Free Officers is a group dedicated to bringing that about."

"But how? Would you assassinate the king?"

"Only in a dire emergency. But, to the immediate future. Now is not the time to throw the country into turmoil. We face the possibility of confronting a dangerous enemy on our northern border. And you are quite right about our army's state of preparedness. Do whatever you must to prepare your men to mount air attacks outside our borders. As for the organization I mentioned, you will be contacted and asked to declare yourself. Good day, Squadron Leader Kamil. Think deeply and well before you decide."

Hafez held the speedy Alfa in check as he followed the main road back to his base at Huskstep. His mind whirled with the implications of Colonel Nasser's words. *Was* the Free Officers' organization in a position to carry out a coup? Where did that leave the Brethren? More important—where did that leave Hafez Kamil and his lofty aspirations?

Chapter 18

12 July 1947
New York City
Ross consulted his notes as he briefed Julius. "The first Connie will be ready for CAA inspection by the end of the month. Murtaugh has a full crew on it and is working on two more of the six Commandos we bought. I estimate a full fleet by November, Julius."

"None too soon." Mantz's voice sagged with fatigue. "The English added another thirty thousand troops in Palestine. They're getting worried. Bevin didn't really believe that the UN would terminate their mandate. But rumor has it that the UN Special Commission report will recommend partitioning. The British plan is believed to be one of keeping the Yishuv too weak to form a government. They're doing a good job of it," he added grimly.

"Jake is well along with the base at Tocumen," Ross told his weary leader. "He has the C-46 we flew out of Burbank; we can't bring it back here for certification, of course, but it's usable."

"Which brings me to my next proposal. We need bases in Europe. As soon as the Connie is ready, I'd like to look for some alternatives and try to line up a source for combat airplanes. There's no way we'll ever get fighters and bombers out of the U.S., but there are surplus Norsemen available from the U.S. Army in Europe. The English have Austers and Beaufighters for sale in England. The Czechs are selling surplus Me 109s left by the Germans like they were so many sports cars."

"Benes would never sell arms to the Jews," Mantz observed dispiritedly.

"I'm not so sure about that," said Ross. "According to what I hear, President Benes is on shaky ground. The Communists claim they'll be in control before year's end. Some of your people have already negotiated for small arms from the Skoda works. Delivery will be a problem, but that's something we can let the Connies do. They can haul ten tons from Zatec, in Czechoslovakia, to Greece, Italy, even Tel Aviv, without refueling."

"Interesting," Mantz responded with a noticeable lack of enthusiasm.

Ross frowned. "Julius, excuse me if I'm out of line, but you seem really down. Something big going wrong?"

Mantz stared back dully for several moments, then blurted, "Ross, can you get a visa for Palestine?"

"Why, I suppose so," Ross replied, his eyebrows arched with surprise. "I'm in the air charter business; I have a franchise for worldwide operation. I don't see how an application could be turned down."

"It can be, believe me," Julius replied dryly. "But since you're not Jewish, perhaps the Palestine mandatory government will grant one. Try it. It would tie in nicely with your idea to tour Europe on a shopping trip."

"Julius, I have to know: what will I be carrying when I land in Palestine?"

"Get that visa—then we'll talk," Mantz said. "As for my sour disposition, yes, I've received disturbing news. Ariel's father—he was a member of the mandatory Palestinian government."

"She told me as much," Ross responded.

"Morris was a moderate, able to deal with both Arab and British members."

"Was?"

"I'm afraid Morris Shamir was arrested; then he disappeared. But we have reason to believe he is alive—probably held in a British detention camp. Ariel is terribly worried."

"She didn't tell me." Ross's voice carried an angry overtone. "I talked with her only this morning."

"Ariel does not confide her inner feelings easily."

Ross bit back an impulsive hearty concurrence. Instead, he asked, "Why was her father arrested?"

"He made a public announcement condemning the Irgun for blowing up a British police barracks—pleaded with the Jewish people for moderation in these troubled times. Then the Brits found evidence that pointed to Morris as a collaborator. We believe the Irgun planted the evidence, but the British arrested him anyway."

"My God," Ross muttered. "What can be done?"

"Very little, I fear. Ben-Gurion filed a protest with the British Foreign Office asking for an investigation. But"—Julius shrugged—"it will no doubt join the hundreds of other still-unresolved complaints. Worst of all, Ariel blames herself. She feels her actions here resulted in recrimination against her father."

"Nonsense," Ross snorted.

"Possibly not. Ariel has been called to the local FBI office twice this week for questioning."

"What? They can't be serious. It's just more harassment. Did they tell her what she's suspected of doing?"

"No charges have been mentioned, but the questions have to do with her speeches before fund-raising rallies. It's pretty clear that they're trying to uncover a reason to revoke her resident visa."

Ross scowled. "Damn her closed mouth—sometimes I feel like shaking that woman."

A hint of a smile flickered as Julius asked, "Is there something between you and Ariel that I don't know about?"

"She's attractive and I'm fond of her, yes. I don't think the feeling is mutual, though," Ross answered shortly.

"Don't be too sure of that," Julius said, the faint smile still in place.

Ross stepped back and admired dark blue and gold lettering on the glass-paneled door, stating that ALLIED AIR, INC., operated alongside Aereas Mundial de Panama. Ross turned to Ariel. "My new office—how do you like it? I don't want to give up my address in Kansas City, but I seem to be spending more and more time here."

Ariel gave him the briefest of smiles and strode through the open doorway. She paused and surveyed the spartan layout, then seated herself in one of the two straight-backed chairs facing the office's army-surplus desk. "Ross, you've flown fishing charters to Canada, haven't you?" she asked without preamble.

Ross didn't respond to the question. Walking behind Ariel, he placed his hands on her shoulders. "I don't understand you. Why didn't you tell me about your father?"

He felt her stiffen. She shrugged his hands from her shoulders. "It is not a matter you need be concerned with."

"But it is," Ross scolded. "Look, you've treated me like a leper since that night in your apartment. Why? Ariel, if you keep all that hate and thirst for revenge bottled up inside, you'll end up in a straitjacket. Show some human emotion, for Christ's sake—like you started to do that night. Tell me—have you ever, in your entire life, bawled like a baby? Let someone who is very fond of you help? . . . Talk to me, damnit!"

Ariel sat rigidly erect, staring straight ahead, for several minutes. Finally she replied, "Some people can't do that. Some people dare not become fond of other people—misfortune always follows. Will you send the Norseman to Canada?"

Ross raised his hands in a gesture of surrender. "Okay," he said. "So it's business as usual. Sure, just tell me where, when, and who."

"The party will leave Cleveland on Friday. The airplane will return the same day, then go back to pick them up on Sunday. One of the men has been there before; he'll guide your pilot."

Ross concealed his seething anger at Ariel's curt refusal to respond to his overture. He found himself actually reaching for her folded arms; he would shake some sense into the contrary damned woman. Hastily, he withdrew and glared at the ramrod-straight figure. Her words, "Some people dare not become fond of other people . . . ," had shaken him more than any combat mission he had ever flown.

"I'll do it, Ariel," he said quietly. "And I won't send another pilot. I'll go myself."

14 July 1947
Cleveland, Ohio

Ross braved a chilly, early-morning wind blowing off the lake as he made a thorough preflight of the Norduyn Norseman. It was not a pretty airplane—squat, fabric-covered fuselage, the front end blunted by a single radial engine. Fixed landing gear added yet another awkward-looking appendage. Slow, capable of only 100 miles per hour at cruise power, the Norseman carried an amazing two-thousand-pound payload. It had become the favorite of Canadian bush pilots from the very beginning.

Ross saw four men emerging from the door used by nonscheduled airline passengers. They turned in his direction. Ross made a final check of the plane's landing gear, tires, and struts, then stood to greet the men. As a group, the four were so typical in their fishing getups as to be suspicious, he thought. They wore identical canvas pants and jackets, red-plaid billed caps, and midcalf lace-up boots; they even seemed about the same age.

He exchanged nods and smiles with three. He reserved a cool, impersonal gaze for Eddie Kotch. Ariel had stipulated that he and Eddie weren't to reveal the fact they knew each other. Ross had filed four names on the manifest for Canadian clearance, but he didn't have the vaguest idea who the other three were—nor did he want to know.

Ross showed them where to stow their bags and the ostentatious tubes containing fishing rods. "I have maps," he commented, "but I'm told that one of you has made this trip before. If so, I'd like him in the right seat, okay?"

A florid-faced man nodded. "Yeah. I've fished the lake before. I can show you the landing strip; it's only about a quarter mile from the lodge."

"Good. You'll be copilot then. You ever been at the controls of an airplane?"

"I have some Cub time." The man didn't elaborate.

Ross grinned to himself. This was not going to be a trip filled with scintillating conversation, he thought. He helped the others strap into the Norseman's wicker seats, then he slid into the pilot's seat.

"I don't anticipate needing you," Ross told the expressionless occupant of the right seat. "But, just in case, this bird flies pretty much like any other. Throttle, prop, and mixture controls are mounted on this center quadrant. We both have rudder pedals, but the elevator and aileron controls are in this single stick-wheel arrangement. See, the wheel is mounted on the stub that angles toward me from the centrally located stick. If you're going to fly from the right side, we just pass the wheel across. Neat, huh?"

The ruddy-complected man gave the faintest of smiles. "Well, I'll be damned. That is cute. If you don't mind, I'd like to try it when we get airborne."

Ross nodded and gave the engine primer pump four short, sharp strokes. The engine's stuttering roar filled both cabin and cockpit, effectively shutting off further conversation.

The copilot's stubby forefinger pointed toward their two o'clock position. "There, see that point of land with the boat docks?" he yelled above the engine noise. "That's Kate's resort. Beaver Lodge is five miles north on the far shoreline. The strip is on top of the ridge. You'll see it after we cross this arm of the lake."

"Okay." Ross reduced power and set up a gentle glide while he spoke. "I'll just stop long enough to refuel, then return Sunday, late, and pick you up."

"That's the plan," his copilot said with a nod.

The grass strip proved to be more than ample for the Norseman. Minutes later Ross switched off the engine and watched his passengers clamber to the turf. They played their roles well, he observed. If it wasn't for Eddie Kotch's presence, he would almost believe they were here for nothing more than a weekend of fishing. They joked in loud tones and acted as if they were having the time of their lives.

A pickup truck arrived with four fifty-five-gallon drums of fuel and a portable pump. Ross helped the taciturn driver top off the Norseman's tank while the "fishermen" disappeared into an aging Buick sedan.

Ross had filed a round-trip flight plan at Cleveland, so, refueling complete, he paid the truck driver and settled himself in the left seat for the solo trip back. Priming the still-warm engine with only two strokes, he depressed the starter switch. Silence. Disgusted, he flipped the switch up and down several times. Nothing. "Shit!" he exclaimed aloud to the empty airplane. Turning off the ignition and master switches, he leaned back and considered what to do.

The nearest aircraft mechanic would be a half-day's drive away. A new starter? A full day would be optimistic—he was in the Canadian bush. He didn't recall seeing a town for the last fifty miles. Very well, he'd "propped" an airplane before. A light plane, such as the J-3, didn't even have an electric starter. It worked best with two people— one in the cockpit to operate the controls, the other to pull the prop through. He eyed the quarter mile or so to the main building. He'd try it single-handedly.

His four passengers were gathered in one corner of the lobby when he stalked through the door. Eddie Kotch turned as the screen door slammed behind Ross. Kotch's face lit up with a relieved expression.

"Thank God you haven't left yet," he muttered. "Let's step outside."

The worried looks on his passengers' faces gave Ross cause for concern. He followed Eddie onto the rustic veranda and waited silently.

"I don't know how much you've been told about this trip," Eddie began anxiously, "but we have a problem."

"Oh?" Ross replied cautiously.

"Look, we were supposed to meet a man here. One of us was to change places with him and he was supposed to go back with you on Sunday."

"Yes?"

"Well . . ." Eddie hesitated, then jerked his head in the direction of a parked truck. The Royal Canadian Mounted Police emblem was emblazoned on the driver's door, and the truck sported a pair of blue spotlights. "This friend of ours has had some trouble with the Mounties. We have to get him away from here before they find him."

Ross surveyed the white Land Rover. Preoccupied with his own problems, he hadn't even noticed it. "You're confusing me," he said. "What kind of trouble is your friend in? Where is he, and what do you expect me to do about it?"

Kotch looked thoughtfully at Ross. "I have a hunch you know more about all this than you're letting on," he said. "But here's the situation: this man hasn't robbed or killed someone—it's more like a political thing. Right now, he's in a fishing boat tied up out of sight in a little cove not far from here. The Mountie is quizzing the owner of this place in the office. We need to get our friend on board the airplane and the hell out of here—quickly."

"Sounds like a good plan," Ross said dryly. "But I see a couple of problems. One: I'm being asked to conspire to smuggle a fugitive into the United States—that's a felony. Problem number two, and it's a big one, the airplane is broke. It needs a new starter. I tried to prop it, but it locked up."

Eddie's jaw dropped. *"What?"* His voice rose. "The goddamn airplane is *broke?"* His shoulders slumped. "What a fucked-up mess," he muttered. He straightened. "Okay, how long to fix it?"

"Well, I can remove the starter and start the engine manually. If I had tools and a little help, maybe sometime this afternoon."

Kotch stroked his chin. "This guy rents boats and motors—he must have some tools around here. I've worked on cars—I'd like to give it a go."

"That's my problem, Eddie. Yours is something else. You see, I'm not hiding your man on board when I leave."

Kotch's face turned crimson. "I tried to tell Julius to dump you. Whenever things get tight, you try to chicken out."

"Watch your mouth, Eddie. You keep up that shit and you'll be shopping for some new teeth—not to mention another airplane driver."

Kotch bit back his retort and allowed his balled fists to relax. "This is big, Colyer. The stuff this guy has with him is critical. Okay, so we need you and your airplane. I—I'm sorry I lost my temper, but will you at least consider hearing me out?"

"I'm listening," Ross responded coldly. "But make it good. And don't leave anything out; I don't like surprises. What has this man done to make the Mounties so interested in him?"

"Well, really, they just want to question him," Eddie replied grudgingly. "You see, he has something in his baggage that's critical to a project we have under way. We've bought and paid for it, but he refuses to turn it over until we get him out of Canada."

"Contraband, in other words."

"Not by itself, but it could lead to something we'd rather not go public with. Anyway—damnit, Colyer, if he *does* get stopped with it, you aren't responsible for what your passengers have in their baggage."

Ross shook his head. "Don't try to tell me my business, Eddie. Give."

"Okay. The guy has a box of dies . . . you know what dies are?"

"I do."

"Well, these are dies to make parts for an automatic weapon—fully automatic." Eddie peered at Ross and waited.

"An illegal machine gun, in other words. I'm not totally stupid, Eddie. Go on."

"They need these dies over there—you know—in the worst way," Kotch finished in a rush.

Ross gnawed his lower lip. "And when I get this man—and his baggage—to Cleveland?" he asked pointedly.

Kotch grunted. "Just outside Cleveland there's a little town, Elkland, with a private airfield. They close at dark. I can arrange by phone to have some lights for you if you'll touch down, drop your passenger, then land in Cleveland." His raised eyebrows asked a question.

"Shit." Ross spread his hands. "You want to make me a candidate for the ten-most-wanted list? No, thank you."

Kotch's eyes grew cold. "Okay, Colyer, you're in the driver's seat. Play it safe."

Ross bit off an angry retort. His jaws snapped closed. "See if you can get those damn tools," he said abruptly.

Ross hunkered on his heels and glared at the offending starter. It lay on a scrap of old tarp borrowed from the dock operator. "We'll have to somehow drive that pin out of the Bendix gear, remove it and the spring, then replace the casing to close the opening in the flywheel housing," he told Kotch. It would be dark in about an hour, Ross judged.

The sound of an automobile engine groaning in low gear made Ross look toward the lodge. The Royal Canadian Mounted Police Land Rover was jouncing across the open field toward them. "Just what we need," Ross grumbled.

The white vehicle stopped twenty feet away. A lithely built man emerged, dressed in blue breeches and a red jacket. After setting a broad-brimmed campaign hat squarely atop his head, he strolled toward the airplane. Halting within arm's reach, he stood, hands clasped behind his back, and studied the work in progress through deceptively mild blue eyes. "A bit of a bother, I take it," he said.

"You might say that," Ross growled ungraciously.

"Will you be staying the night? Or do you hope to have the old girl flying by dark?" the Mountie inquired.

"With any luck, I'll have the engine working within an hour," Ross replied. "If so, I'll be on my way. My friend"—he jerked a greasy thumb at Kotch—"will be staying on. Try to catch up on the fishing he missed this afternoon."

"Ah, yes. I saw the others in the boat. I'm afraid old Luther, at the dock, steered them toward the poorest fishing in the entire lake. I expect they'll be coming in empty-handed before long. Makes one wonder why they would make an expensive trip up here without a guide."

"Some of us can't afford guides when we get a fishing vacation," Kotch growled. "Speaking of messing around in the dark, what brings you to this godforsaken outpost?"

"Ah, just a bit of routine nosing about. A fellow we'd like very much to talk with is reported to be in these parts. Thought I'd wait until your friends come in from fishing—ask if they've seen anything suspicious. Don't suppose either of you noticed a furtive figure slinking about."

"Not likely," Ross answered shortly. "We've had our noses stuck inside this damned engine, mostly."

"I can see that," the Mountie said. "And a right dirty job it must be. Ross noticed that the uniformed officer's aimless strolling had taken him to where he had an unobstructed view of the Norseman's interior. "I must tell you," the Mountie continued, "that the man we're looking for is a dangerous criminal." He looked straight at Ross. "I'd not be taking any hitchhikers along when you leave. A lot of people I know would be terribly upset if you did."

"I'm sure they would," Ross replied impatiently. "Now, if you'll excuse us, we do have an hour's work ahead of us."

The Mountie smiled and apologized. Ross and Eddie watched the Land Rover bounce back toward the lodge. "He smells a rat," Kotch mused. "This may be more tricky than I first thought."

Full dark was less than thirty minutes away when Ross taxied toward the distant stand of trees marking the field's takeoff point. The engine, as if in apology for its cantankerous behavior, idled with a happy burble. He turned into the wind for an engine run-up and searched the field's perimeter. The deepening shadows revealed no sign of life. Ross switched on the navigation lights.

Within minutes of the agreed-upon all-clear signal, he felt and heard the passenger door open, then slam closed. He started to advance the throttle for a mag check, then tensed. A pair of automobile headlamps blazed from across the field. Flashing blue warning lights marked the vehicle's progress.

Ross never slowed the throttle's advance. The empty Norseman picked up speed; it would be a near thing to avoid a collision with the speeding Land Rover. Would the Mountie shoot? Ross wondered. No matter—he was committed. He hauled back on the wheel, hanging the Norseman by its prop. The brilliant lights of the police car dropped from view.

15 July 1947
New York City

Ross paid the cabbie in front of 44 Water Street and stalked through the double glass-paneled doors with determined strides. He went straight to the second floor and without knocking entered the little cubicle Ariel reserved for herself.

She looked up from a sheaf of papers, and returned Ross's grim expression with a tentative smile. "Hello, Ross, I'm so glad you're back safe and sound. Uh—someone called. We heard about your problem."

Ross halted in front of the desk and glared. "Problem?" he grated. "I now have problems that have little problems. The only reason I'm not in handcuffs right now is because officials are no doubt still looking up charges to slap me with—in two countries."

Ariel's face and tone reflected abjection. "Ross, your actions are beyond what we had any right to expect. Everything humanly possible will be done to keep you from being charged with anything. My people are in your debt."

"You know, I asked myself in the cab coming over here. Colyer, you idiot, *why* did you do that? Running from the police, for Christ's sake. And you know what I finally figured out?"

"No," Ariel replied unnecessarily, her voice small.

"At first, I told myself it was because those Jews stranded in Europe are getting a rotten deal, and I want to help. Then I discovered that wasn't the reason at all. The reason is that you have the ability to twist me around your finger. Every time I've taken risks in this business, it's been after a long talk with you.

"I want the entire story, every word of it. I don't want to blunder around with my eyes closed anymore. Now, tell me about this so-called fishing trip."

Ariel's eyes glinted dangerously as she nibbled her lower lip. "Very well," she said with a sigh. "The Haganah has operated underground arms factories for the past year. The manufacture of guns requires very specialized machinery. Two men in Canada worked for months to develop a simple, dependable, rapid-fire weapon similar to the British Sten gun. They've finished and shipped major parts of the machinery needed for its manufacture disguised as used agricultural machines."

Ross listened closely, his eyes narrowed with suspicion.

"The Canadians discovered the plant and issued a warrant for the arrest of the inventor. We planned for four of our people to enter Canada with forged driver's licenses—the only identification required for border crossing. One was to change places with the man seeking to leave Canada, who would return on your airplane with your party. The fourth fisherman would come back by train, showing his rightful identification at the border."

The pair stared at each other silently. Ariel finally lowered her eyes. "You've said all along you didn't want to know what the foundation does. I—I feel so strongly about what we are doing, so afraid that we may fail. I apologize. But I *am* grateful. What will you do now?"

"Well, I'm going to assume—stupidly, probably—that I've gotten away with breaking the laws of both the U.S. and Canada. I'm going ahead like nothing happened. After I get back from Kansas City this weekend, I'll find a place to live close to my new office."

"I see. Do you have any idea where?"

"No, I'd like someplace near the airport, but it won't be easy. I may go to Long Island. My air force boss is stationed at Mitchell Field; maybe he can help. Don't worry, I'll do the job I signed on to do." He turned abruptly and strode out the door, leaving a pensive-looking Ariel staring at her desktop.

Chapter 19

16 July 1947
Aboard the *President Warfield*

Dov Friedman watched lifeless dawn light penetrate the driving rain. It battered the wheelhouse roof like an insane drummer. Visibility gradually improved to reveal angry, white-fanged waves, burying the ship's bow beneath tons of gray water. Dov rubbed his aching, bloodshot eyes. There had been no sleep for the forty-five hundred passengers and crew after the storm hit early the previous evening.

Dov was no deepwater sailor, but the riverboat's constant wallowing, corkscrew motion didn't inspire overwhelming confidence with respect to the vessel's seaworthiness in a storm. Whereas years spent in the cockpit of an airplane had inured him to the miseries of motion sickness, most of the passengers were less fortunate.

Jacob Zakia, the Palmach leader, had considered it his duty to visit belowdecks on a confidence-building tour at the height of the storm. He'd returned white-faced and shaking his head. "Bad—unbelievably bad," he'd muttered in response to Dov's inquiring look. Hilvitz's concern regarding a deck top-heavy with passengers wasn't a factor in this weather, but at least a hundred wretched creatures, unable to tolerate the conditions in their stinking, congested quarters, lined the rails. Braving the wind-driven sheets of rain mixed with spray from monster waves, they clung to stanchions, lines—anything offering protection against being swept overboard. Dov took grim satisfaction in knowing that crews of the British destroyers endured even worse conditions aboard their narrower, faster-moving craft.

None of the half-dozen lean gray silhouettes were visible just now, but they remained out there, Dov knew. The destroyers' radar would be tracking the refugee ship like wolves relentlessly pursuing a tiring stag. Far from instilling a feeling of apprehension among the refugees, however, they served to heighten their determination. One ship, which Hilvitz identified as a cruiser, sailed close enough the day before to use its loud-hailer. "Are you carrying illegal immigrants?" a tinny voice had asked across the then gentle swells. Aronovitch hadn't responded. The question was followed by, "If so, you are acting illegally and will be imprisoned upon reaching Palestine's territorial waters."

Despite the captain's orders not to provoke the warships, several passengers gathered to point to the new sign, boldly displayed on both sides. Hastily painted letters read "Haganah Ship *Exodus* 1947." The Aliyah Bet's Paris office had provided the name via wireless, and it set off wild cheering when it appeared.

Dov turned as Captain Aronovitch, Hilvitz, and Jacob Zakia entered the cluttered cubicle that served as their office.

"The storm will abate by midmorning," Aronovitch announced. "I know the passengers are cold, wet, and seasick, but we must resume our defensive preparations. I talked last night with Palmach headquarters in Tel Aviv. The plan they advocate calls for continued sailing at a reduced speed of twelve knots. Off the shore of Gaza, after dark, we will reverse engines. Our escorts will overrun us. When they do, we will turn directly toward the open beach, making our maximum speed of eighteen knots. Our shallow draft will allow us to get at least a hundred yards beyond the destroyers before they run aground. Palmach troops will seal off that stretch of beach, meet us with trucks, and transport the passengers to populated areas. Not all will escape, of course, but many will."

The sober-faced mate asked, "Then why the extensive defensive measures?"

Aronovitch sighed. "The plan is a good one, but it presumes that the British navy will wait until we are inside territorial waters to make its move. Zvi Bader tells me the English are furious; this ship seems to have upset them more than any of our previous efforts. My gut reaction is that they will try to board us."

Hilvitz frowned. "In international waters? Deliberately violate maritime law? Fire on us perhaps?"

The captain shrugged. "They control the sea lanes. Who is to prevent them? Or to testify as to our *exact* position? As for using their ship's guns, I doubt it. World opinion would never condone firing on an unarmed vessel carrying innocent civilians, irrespective of position. I anticipate them using boarding parties. Here is my defense plan. . . ."

The sky had cleared by noon. Dov stood, head bowed, as the rabbi consigned Simia Kaplanski's flag-wrapped body to the still-unsettled sea. The woman's distraught young husband slumped despondently, tears streaming from his eyes. An elderly matron stood beside him, holding his hours-old son, closely wrapped against the wind still gusting across the fantail.

This was their first fatality—surprising in itself, Dov observed, considering the deplorable state of the refugees' health, and the fact that several were of advanced age. Perhaps the mother could have been saved, given a modern hospital, and without the stress of living like a fugitive. Another score to settle with the damned British, he thought bitterly.

The mourners dispersed in somber-faced groups. Dov heard a white-bearded patriarch, yarmulke balanced precariously atop his bald skull, mutter, "God willing, the child will know freedom—the only legacy his mother can bestow." I wish I could feel as confident of that as you, old man, the blond pilot cum sailor said to himself.

Dov returned to his task of overseeing the erection of barriers across each and every passageway. The convoy of sinister gunboats prowling their flanks lent a sense of grim urgency to their efforts. Jacob, surrounded by the younger, stronger women as well as men, issued instructions regarding the most efficient use of short clubs, lengths of pipe, even spare engine parts and tools from the engine room. "You aren't serving a tennis ball," Dov heard him say. "Keep your weapon low. Jab—don't take roundhouse swings. There'll be no lethal knives or firearms now. We're outgunned, so don't give them an excuse to use theirs."

Aronovitch toured the ship after the evening meal, inspecting the handiwork. Rolls of barbed wire provided additional defense for the bridge; the captain had deemed the ship's nerve center a priority target of boarding parties. Mounds of foodstuffs, not only canned goods but even potatoes, lined the rails, ready to be thrown at the British. Hilvitz spent the afternoon rigging an emergency ship's wheel below deck near the engine room.

Two former railroad engineers among the passengers had showed
the engine room crew how to rig a steam line along the upper deck.
Pierced with small holes at two-foot intervals, it would engulf a boarding
party in scalding steam. The hoses used to fuel the ship in Sète were
attached to fuel pumps and aimed overboard. They should provide a
devastating rain of slick, noxious oil onto exposed decks, the proud
designers explained.

If the experienced Palmach naval officer shared Dov's somber
evaluation of the outcome of their pathetic armament facing a seasoned,
well-armed military force, he concealed it well.

Back in the wheelhouse, Aronovitch and Hilvitz checked and double-
checked the ship's position. "Come to a heading of zero-one-five,"
the captain ordered. "We are abeam Palestinian territory, gentlemen.
We will maintain a course at least ten miles outside territorial waters
throughout the night and make our move just before dawn."

Dov, standing at a starboard window, watched the bow swing to
port and settle on their new course. He tensed. The British destroyer
that had held station all day a mile off their stern quarter was increasing
speed, racing to a position slightly ahead of and between the *Exodus*
and the still-invisible shoreline. At the same time, he saw signal lamps
blinking furiously from each of the warships in sight.

"Something's up, Skipper," Dov called over his shoulder. "They're
closing in."

Both Aronovitch and Hilvitz rushed to his side. "They've made up
their minds," the captain muttered harshly. "Mister Hilvitz, go on the
wireless—the broadcast band. Announce to the world what is happening.
Let the bastards mull *that* over before they blow us out of the water.
Then send a coded signal to Palmach headquarters. Tell them that attack
is imminent. Shift the rendezvous point south of Gaza." His terse orders
complete, the captain stepped to the voice tube. "Engine room, this is
the captain. Build a full head of steam and stand by for maximum revs."

Dov lowered powerful binoculars and announced, "The crews are
doing something on the side away from us, Skipper. It's getting too
dark to see properly, but they appear to be building something."

"Boarding platforms," said Aronovitch. "Built to ride over our upper
decks. Well, we shall give them a warm welcome, Mister Friedman.
Tell Zakia to prepare to repel boarders." He chuckled. "Shades of the
days of the Barbary pirates. In all my years at sea, I've never heard
that order issued seriously."

Dov remained at his window, scanning the threatening warships through glasses. Full darkness arrived with startling swiftness. High clouds, remnants of the previous day's storm, raced across the sky, obscuring even reflected starlight. Only phosphorescent wakes generated by churning screws identified the darkened vessels' positions.

The attack opened with stunning swiftness. A powerful searchlight stabbed the gloom with a brilliant white finger. The probing shaft swept the length of *Exodus*'s hull and settled on the bridge. Dov ducked and closed his eyes. A voice, seeming to emanate from the blinding luminescence itself, boomed, "You have entered territorial waters! Stop the ship. You are under arrest."

Dov moved aft of the blinding orb and peered into the darkness. He sensed, as much as observed, the lead destroyer drop back and close with the *Exodus*. Aronovitch's response to the order to halt was an ear-shattering *whoop-whoop-whoop* of the ship's siren. The deck trembled beneath Dov as two thousand pairs of feet raced toward battle stations.

He felt a shuddering jar on the port side. An instant later the destroyer closing from starboard made contact. Terrified screams punctuated the grinding, screeching sound of railings and lifeboat stanchions being ripped from their mounts. The *Exodus*'s wooden upper structure opened with a sound resembling the crushing of orange crates.

Aronovitch's voice rose only to the extent necessary to carry above the nerve-shattering din. "Full speed ahead," he ordered. "Standard starboard rudder. Mister Friedman, get me a damage assessment."

For a moment they were free. The unexpected surge of power and the turn into the attacking destroyer placed them a ship's length ahead. Dov raced outside. The boat deck had escaped serious damage, from what he could see by reflected light from the following searchlights. In two bounds he descended the ladder leading to the main deck. Losing his balance, he stumbled and fell.

The sprawl saved Dov's life. The stuttering bark of heavy machine guns shattered the sudden stillness. A hail of steel-jacketed slugs raked the fleeing refugee vessel, passing inches above his head. "Oh, my God!" Dov moaned. "No! Oh, you bastards. You miserable, bloody bastards." He scrambled to his feet and, jaws clenched, surveyed the chaos on the main deck.

As far as he could see, the scene was a jumbled mass of boards mixed with struggling bodies. The extent of the havoc wreaked by the ramming could be measured by screams and wails from the injured. Jacob

Zakia and his men were already struggling to free several trapped passengers caught racing to their battle stations along the rail.

Dov saw them examine one man, his beardless cheeks testifying to his youth, lying partially beneath a collapsed section of outer wall. Zakia shook his head and indicated that the victim was beyond help. The crew pressed on. Dov saw a length of two-inch pipe, with an improvised grip of black electrician's tape, still clenched in one fist. Death relaxed the man's grip; his now useless weapon rolled in the scuppers as the *Exodus* dodged and weaved to evade her relentless pursuers.

The wounded were in capable hands, Dov observed, so he shouldered his way into the crush of humanity below decks. He was immediately struck by the calm, orderly demeanor exhibited by the tightly packed refugees. Wide eyes reflected fear and apprehension in the dim, flickering light, but there was no hint of hysteria. He noticed a mother holding a girl of about six. The child's arms circled the woman's neck like steel cables, her brown eyes round and staring. No sound escaped her quivering lips.

This was the first deck sheathed by the steel hull. Other than a smashed porthole, it remained intact. Dov shook his head as he visualized what it must have been like: imprisoned, without being able to see, they had been pummeled by not one but two bone-jarring collisions. He raised his arms to attract attention, feeling the urge to reassure, to encourage his audience. Words wouldn't come. What could he say? An elderly woman, her silver hair coiled into a neat bun, seemed to read his thoughts. She patted his arm. "Don't worry about us, my son. We will persevere—we have faith in you and the captain."

Dov worked his way aft to where a tight-lipped Hilvitz stood by the emergency steering wheel. "It isn't good," Dov advised in tones too low to be overheard. "We've shaken them off for the time being, but they'll hit again, and soon. I'd say there's a good chance you'll be able to try out your handiwork."

The mate nodded his understanding, and Dov returned to the bridge. "I estimate at least twenty injured, some fatally," he told Aronovitch. "There's extensive damage to the main deck, but none below the hull line. The passengers—hell," his voice cracked, "I've seen combat troops show more panic. We can't, simply can't, let those rotten bastards stop us."

The captain relaxed his vigil long enough to light his pipe. "Those were boarding platforms you saw, all right. Three of them are being maneuvered into position now. They've put the big cruiser between us and the shore. I can bounce those tin cans around a bit, but not that one."

Dov saw a dim glow on the horizon. "There," he said excitedly, "the shoreline. How much longer?"

"Left alone, about thirty minutes," Aronovitch replied laconically. "But we're going to have some distractions along the way—visitors on board, I'd guess. Is everyone ready?"

"As ready as they'll ever be. But, machine guns! My God, can we subject these helpless people to *that?* It will be a slaughter."

Aronovitch's eyes reflected the dim light like a burnished brown gun barrel. "Go ask them," he ordered with stony composure. "Look at those tattoo marks; look at them closely. I will subject these people to the depths of hell, if necessary, to free even a fraction of their number. They know that—it's my obligation."

Dov averted his gaze, the captain's words a cold flame in his mind. His eyes bulged: a dark mass loomed in the port window. He could make out men with Bren guns held at port arms; they were less than a stone's throw away.

Aronovitch's terse, "Full port rudder," came seconds too late. The contact was gentler than the first time but long enough for the destroyer's crew to toss grappling irons.

Dov raced for the wheelhouse's aft door. He realized he was unarmed. Grabbing a stool from in front of the chart table, he emerged on deck to join the surge of defenders rushing to meet khaki-clad troops wearing dark berets and carrying police batons and sidearms. They dropped onto the shattered boat deck from the devilishly clever boarding platform, constructed to override the *Exodus*'s upper decks.

The boarding party encountered a solid wall of defenders, standing shoulder to shoulder and three deep. Marines aboard the destroyer stood helplessly by, unable to add covering fire with their automatic weapons. The struggle aboard the *Exodus* was a primitive match of brawn against brawn, marked only by grunts and muttered curses.

Then Dov saw a uniformed attacker detach a grenade from his belt and toss it into the midst of the massed Palmach troops. A warning yell died in his throat as the muffled detonation released a cloud of pungent tear gas. The boarding party quickly disengaged for the time it took to don gas masks. Other grenades followed.

A few members of the defensive wall collapsed, blinded and moaning with pain. They were immediately replaced by others. Dov rushed to help a man locked in a struggle with two masked attackers. Between them they wrestled the pair to the deck. From the corner of his eye Dov glimpsed a cudgel rise, then heard it impact with a sickening thud. A cluster of three grenades dangled from the man's belt. Dov grabbed them all, pulled the pins, and heaved them overboard. The result was impressive. Massed troops aboard the British gunboat stumbled blindly in choking clouds of white smoke.

In the wheelhouse, Aronovitch abruptly threw both engines into reverse and ordered full starboard rudder. Grappling lines parted with a singing *twang.* The *Exodus,* freed of her unwelcome parasite, shifted to full ahead and was soon separated from her attacker by a hundred yards of open sea.

Their respite was brief. Excited yells from starboard announced the approach of a second destroyer, its boarding platform filled with crouched marines. Aronovitch timed his next maneuver to a split second. He slowed again, then as the closing warship slid alongside—too fast to secure with grappling irons—he swung sharply into her side. The impact was the strongest thus far. Even the combatants on the port side were thrown into tangled confusion. The *Exodus* surged past the surprised attacker, carrying away most of the wooden boarding platform. Dov saw at least two dozen figures tumble overboard.

Danger loomed immediately from the same quarter, however. A third ship, hard on the heels of the one sent reeling into the darkness, closed and secured itself to the elusive refugee ship. Zakia, directing defense of the starboard decks, ordered all his men to stand clear of the high-pressure steam line. He waited, face stretched with grim satisfaction, for the unwary troops to spill on board.

Zakia dropped his raised arm—the signal for crewmen aft to open the steam valve. The defenders waited for the ten-foot lances of superheated steam they'd observed during practice to emerge. The designers had failed to take into account the demands of the *Exodus*'s racing engines, however. Only disappointing plumes spurted weakly toward the invaders.

Too late, the Palmach rushed to form their human barrier around the wheelhouse. The British cut a path through the barbed wire and formed a defensive semicircle, their backs to the bridge. Without fear of hitting their comrades, they drew pistols and fired into the crush of defenders. The advancing line reeled, but then surged forward over a half dozen of their fallen numbers. Again it was savage, hand-to-hand engagement. But this time the attackers held the high ground. They were at the wheelhouse entrance when Dov saw Jacob stumble and fall, blood streaming from a head wound.

Dov fought his way to his friend's side. Before he could render aid, however, he saw khaki-clad figures pour into the wheelhouse. Captain Aronovitch succumbed to a rain of blows. The portside boarding crew, half their number showing bloody badges of the engagement, breached the port bridge entrance. The *Exodus*'s nerve center was now in enemy hands.

Dov raced to the emergency steering station below decks. "Take the con!" he yelled at a grimly alert Hilvitz. "The bridge has been captured—the captain as well. Disable the main steering engine and tell the engine room to ignore the telegraph."

The mate grasped the wheel. "Take a man topside. Relay the situation by voice. I have a line to the engine room. This standby compass is barely adequate. What is our position?"

"About ten miles off the Gaza beaches," Dov panted. "Their cruiser is between us and the shoreline. I'll try and steer you east every chance we get. The captain said the water gets quite shallow along this stretch. If we can crowd the cruiser just a few miles closer, she'll have to break off."

Hilvitz nodded and gave Dov a quick thumbs-up. Dov and a helmsman from the second watch clambered to a vantage point on the aft topside cabins. The thunder of the engine exhaust driving a plume of black smoke up the single stack in front of Dov made conversation difficult. Toward the bow, Dov could see that the destroyer had failed to follow up the first boarding party. A stream of black viscous liquid from the fuel oil hose drove massed troops from the destroyer's open deck.

As Dov watched, two figures flung seaboots stuffed with burning rags into the melee below in a vain attempt to ignite the pools of oil. Recalling Aronovitch's successful maneuver to break free, Dov relayed instructions to Hilvitz to reverse and swerve. His eyes adjusted quickly to the darkness. The glow of lights from shore seemed closer, but the cruiser's forbidding hulk still held station off the starboard beam.

The ship's sudden, violent change of course and speed almost threw Dov to the deck. Regaining his balance, he loosed a mighty yell— they were free once more. "Get forward and see what the situation is there," he called to the helmsman. "Try to find out if the captain is still able to command."

As the young man scrambled into the gloom, Dov searched for signs of the destroyers. My God, he realized with a start, I'm in *command*. Dov Friedman, you're in charge of an oceangoing vessel—something you know nothing about—and worse, four thousand plus passengers! He briefly considered changing places with Hilvitz. No, he decided, the mate was better equipped to handle things from his emergency steering station. He eyed the distant shoreline, then relayed a command to come ten degrees right—starboard, damnit, he corrected himself. He'd get the hang of this sailing business yet.

The young crewman—Herzl, Dov recalled his name—scuttled into view. "The British are prisoners," he yelled delightedly. "They're in the bridge but they can't get out—we have them surrounded. We have control of the wireless shack, and Sparks has contact with Tel Aviv. Any messages?"

Dov grinned into the darkness. They had a chance. They'd stood off the entire British Palestine squadron! He was about to dictate a message to the Palmach when eye-searing white light drenched the ship. The cruiser had edged closer and bathed the battered *Exodus* with the merciless glare of her spotlights. The fight isn't over, he told himself wearily. They're lighting us up to make it easier for the destroyers.

Dov could only guess at the time. His eyes were swollen nearly shut from the oily smoke that poured from the stack. He could taste the foul stuff, knew he must be black from head to toe. His throat was dry, and the orders he shouted to Hilvitz below were little more than hoarse croaks. He'd lost count of the times the destroyers had sped alongside and attempted to board. The macabre game of bumper cars continued without letup.

The defenders had relentlessly dumped their stores of prosaic am-munition—potatoes, tinned food, screws, bolts—on their foes. Two men had rigged axes on the end of lines, hurling them at the board-ing crews, then retrieving them. But despite their heroic stand, time was on the navy's side. Plus, an ominous footnote: the *Exodus* was taking water—lots of it. Repeated pounding by the more sturdily constructed naval vessels had opened a seam. When pumps failed to contain the flood, a bucket brigade was formed to dump the water overboard.

They were no closer to shore. The cruiser blocked Dov's every attempt to slip past into shallower water. They still held the ship, but Aronovitch was in there with the British troops, his condition unknown. It was only a matter of time, Dov conceded. He tried to see a bright side. At least they would send the passengers to internment camps in Cyprus. Eventually they would reach their goal. For him and the crew—prison. A victory for the Yishuv, but not without a price.

Dulled by fatigue and depression, Dov failed to notice the two destroyers closing from both sides at flank speed. Suddenly they were there. Their captains, with skill more appropriate for speedboats, reversed and skidded alongside. The *Exodus* was pinned.

Dov joined the weary defenders in a last-ditch stand. Wielding a steel crowbar, he rushed a trio of marines stepping across the rail. One looked toward Dov and raised his pistol. He was a mere youngster, Dov noticed, his face strained and pale. "Don't," the youth croaked hoarsely, "please don't. Don't fight anymore, I beg you. It's so hopeless. It wasn't supposed to be like this."

Dov glanced around the deck. It was, as the young man said, hopeless. Dov slumped and let the crowbar fall from nerveless fingers.

He saw Captain Aronovitch being helped from the bridge. The grizzled officer wore a bloodstained bandage on his forehead and had to be supported. But he regained his feet and walked with firm steps to where a British officer waited. "I ask that you leave my ship, sir. Our destination is Haifa. Upon arrival, I will submit to boarding by proper port authorities of the mandatory government. But I will never surrender during an act of piracy on the high seas."

The British navy commander studied the battered but still-defiant Aronovitch with something approaching admiration. "We will withdraw and break off our engagement, Captain," he stated crisply. "Our ships will escort you to port. I offer to remove your wounded for proper medical treatment."

The *Exodus*'s commander considered the offer briefly, then snapped, "My ship's doctor will see to our wounded. Mister Hilvitz?"

Avraam appeared at his side. "Yes, sir?"

"Set a course for Haifa. Make twelve knots. Signal the port authorities that we carry sick and wounded."

17 July 1947
London, England
Sir Donald Ashton-Smythe read the typewritten radio transmission twice
over, his eyes lighting up with an expression of grim pleasure. He
handed the sheet of pink paper back to his secretary. "Take a message to the commander of the Palestine Squadron: 'Make prison ships
presently anchored off Cyprus ready to remove illegal immigrants
arriving Haifa on Haganah ship *Exodus*. Destination, Hamburg.' Then
send another signal to the commander of displaced persons' camps in
Hamburg: 'Prepare to receive forty-five hundred displaced persons
from Palestine.'"

Chapter 20

13 September 1947
Thirty Miles Northwest of Teterboro Field
Ross felt the Connie slew to the right. A swift scan of the instrument panel's array showed a drop on number three's brake horsepower indicator. It read 105 BHP. His headset crackled; he heard, "Engineer to pilot. We're losing number three."

"Roger, Engineer," Ross snapped. "Simulate feathering number three. Set METO power on one and two. Run your engine failure checklist." He hit the rudder trim to compensate for asymmetrical power—number four prop was already spinning uselessly—and watched the airspeed indicator stabilize at 140 miles per hour. Glaring at Bruce Murtaugh, slouched in the copilot's seat, a broad smirk on his face, Ross growled, "Bastard. Give me seventeen inches on number three to simulate feathering. Call the tower and request a practice two-engine landing."

"Roger, Mister Pilot, sir," Murtaugh replied cheerfully. "I'll tell them this one will be a full-stop landing. If you can manage to set 'er down with number three and four inop, your checkride is finished."

Ross's intended sarcastic response was sidetracked by the flight engineer's expressionless drone. "Engineer to pilot. Simulated engine shutdown complete. Fuel tank selectors—number three and four, simulated OFF. One and two, tank to engine. Prop deicers and nonessential electrical systems, OFF. Cabin pressurization, OFF. Engine fire extinguisher, set number three."

"Thank you, Engineer," Ross responded. "I suggest you prepare for emergency landing gear extension. We seem to have a sadistic gremlin aboard."

Murtaugh whooped with laughter. "Naw, I've had enough fun for one day." He sobered and added, "You're a cool hand at the controls, Ross. I can't remember flying a checkride with a better pilot."

"Thanks." Ross grinned. "Can I count on having all four engines for reversing on touchdown?"

"Sure. No point in burning up expensive brakes just to prove a point. Are you figuring to take the first trip in her to Palestine?"

"I plan to." Ross took time to maneuver the sluggish plane on an extended straight-in approach. "Call the tower, and give me fifteen degrees of flaps. As for Palestine," he continued, "we have sixty-some passengers who were able to get visas. Plus, I have a shopping list for European markets—stuff we can't get export permits for here."

Bruce fell into step with Ross as they strolled from the parked airplane toward the Allied Air office. "I'm sorry as hell about the other three Connies. We're going balls to the wall on the C-46s, but paperwork on the four-engine stuff seems to be perpetually lost, misrouted, wrong forms—you name it."

"Yeah, we were lucky to slip this one past the pencil pushers before they discovered who was really buying the planes. How's the pilot-training program coming?"

"So-so. Not a lot to work with. Not enough pay to attract the older heads. The kids willing to stick it out need lots of work. Luther Bascom is getting rich running the checkout program. We'll miss your October target date for sure."

"Well," Ross shrugged as they paused in front of the office, "it can't be helped. I know you're trying. Are you free to have dinner with Ariel and me this evening?"

"I wouldn't miss it." The big Connie pilot grinned. "I want to see close up if you've managed to tame that one."

Ross's smile was wry. "Tamed is a mite optimistic, I'd say. Reaching an accommodation would be a better description. She's been through some pretty rocky stuff; maybe I'll tell you sometime. Don't be late tonight." He turned and fumbled for the office door key.

*   *   *

Ross emerged from the subway terminal and threaded his way through the noisy, crowded street leading to Ariel's apartment. The arrangement to take his meals with Ariel had happened suddenly, and—so like her—without explanation. Colonel Deckard had found him a place on Long Island, but commuting by train to Teterboro was an ordeal. He'd finally located a sleeping room in Newark.

Ariel had driven him there with the meager possessions he'd brought from Kansas City. Taking one look at the place, she announced, "You will eat at my apartment when you're in town." She left no room for argument. Not that Ross objected to the idea of home-cooked meals, but he found her arbitrary way—hardly an invitation—amusing.

Still deep in thought, he turned to mount the flight of concrete steps leading to the brownstone's entry. Suddenly he stopped and snapped his fingers. Damnit. He'd gotten into the habit of bringing a little something when he came. A bunch of flowers from the vendor by the subway, some candy—Ariel loved black licorice—a pair of scarce nylon stockings if he happened to see them in a department store window. The gifts were never much, but they always elicited a smile.

Ross considered returning to the candy store, but he was late already. Resuming his climb, he wondered what surprise she might have in store for him. Ariel was so unpredictable. It was like trying to befriend a skittish colt—one minute nuzzling his pocket for a sugar lump, the next, turning to kick at him and gallop off, then standing alone sulking and unresponsive. He found his own emotions riding a roller coaster as well. One minute he would be overwhelmed with desire, long to hold her; the next minute he'd feel like spanking her for a display of obstinate temper.

Entering the apartment, he received no response to his cheery, "Hi, it's me." The living room and kitchenette were empty, but the bedroom door stood ajar. He peeked inside. Ariel lay across the bed, staring out the window. Red puffy cheeks and eyes told of recent tears. She ignored him.

Ross crossed the room and sat beside her, resisting the urge to stroke the disheveled cap of raven-black hair. "Hey, now, it can't be all that bad," he murmured.

"Go away." Ariel's voice was flat and without emotion. She didn't turn from contemplating the dreary view of a brick storefront.

"All right, now. What's happened?"

"I have to go back. I have fourteen days."

"You aren't making sense, Ariel. Back where? Fourteen days to do what?"

"Palestine. The State Department is revoking my visa. I have two weeks to leave."

Ross sighed. "Oh, for God's sake. What reason do they give?"

"Engaging in activity detrimental to the interests of the United States."

Ross felt an icy hand clamp his heart. Julius had warned him. . . . "Okay," he said briskly. "Screw 'em. We'll outsmart them all. We'll go down tomorrow and apply for a license—take our blood tests. Three days later, you are Mrs. Ross Colyer. Just let them try and deport the wife of a natural-born citizen."

Ariel jerked upright. Seeing her mouth open, he hurriedly added, "Now before you say no, hear me out. I'm not forcing myself on you; we wouldn't live together. We can have the marriage annulled as soon as it looks safe to do so. It's just I hate to see . . . damnit, I *am* fond of you. You do know that, I hope."

Ariel slumped back to the bed and somberly regarded Ross's worried countenance. She shook her head. "No," she responded dejectedly. "It's no use. Something else, probably worse, would happen. It was never intended that I . . . oh, never mind. I'll go back. I'm sure I can rejoin the Irgun. I'll find out who in the organization betrayed my father. Then I'll kill him."

14 September 1947
New York City
Ross faced Julius Mantz across the leader's oversized walnut desk. "Why, Julius? Why have they waited this long to deport her? They don't have a shred of proof."

Mantz rubbed his haggard features with one hand. "Unfortunately, Ross, they do—at least of sorts. You see, revoking a visa is an administrative action; the forensic evidence required for deportation isn't necessary. I talked with an undersecretary who is privately in sympathy with our efforts. But Ariel spoke at two rallies recently. This time she did more than ask for donations; she also instructed young men wishing to join the Haganah in Palestine on how to evade U.S. laws. A couple of FBI agents heard her. That was all they needed."

Mantz chewed his lower lip and drew aimless circles on the yellow pad before him. Ross watched silently. Finally, Mantz looked up. "There's nothing that can be done. I want you to take Ariel with you on the flight to Haifa. We can't afford to fight the revocation in court. Too many other things could emerge."

"I asked the stubborn damn woman to marry me—strictly a marriage of convenience," Ross said savagely. "That would put an end to the whole stupid business."

"Ariel is an extremely complex person, Ross," Mantz said gently.

"You know what she plans to do if she goes back?" Ross asked harshly.

"I do."

"She's making progress here, Julius. She even laughs occasionally. Even if she isn't thrown into prison back there, or even killed, this bitter hatred she carries will consume her."

Mantz nodded and sat silently for a moment. "Hatred is a curse we Jews must contend with. It . . ." Without finishing the sentence, he shook off his somber air and spoke briskly. "But, to business. I've asked David Ginsberg to meet with us here. He should arrive momentarily. Before you go, I'd like you to meet him. He's in charge of the recruiting end of our project. Ariel was helping him."

"Meet him?" Ross asked with a puzzled frown. "What has happened to your strict need-to-know policy?"

"I'll answer that after you meet him," Julius replied enigmatically. He ceased talking as the office door opened.

Ross turned to face a belligerent-looking young man of about his own age. Ginsberg's stocky frame strained the fabric of a crewneck sailor's jersey and blue denim pants. The unannounced visitor was speaking even before he closed the door. "What's this about Ariel?" he barked. "Why are those sneaky fuckers deporting *her?* Why not me? *I'm* the one who set up those meetings."

"Simmer down, David," Mantz responded soothingly. "First, Ariel is not being deported; the State Department is revoking her visa. She hasn't been charged with a crime. We'll work on trying to get her another entry permit after things cool down a bit.

"Now, I want you to meet Ross Colyer. Ross is running the flying part of our operation. Tell him what your problems are and see if we can work around them by flying our people to staging camps instead of sending your recruits directly to Palestine by ship."

Ginsberg barely glanced at Ross, ignoring the outstretched hand. "Aren't we going to fight this? Goddamnit, they can't treat people like the Nazis did. I'll talk about the flying business *after* we settle this deportation thing."

"The deportation *thing,* as you insist on calling it, is settled, David," Julius said sharply. "I want you to give Ross numbers, projections, needs, and the like. Between the two of you, work out a way to circumvent that blockade. We need soldiers—even those with minimum training—and we need them soon. The number of Arab raids is growing every day."

Ginsberg acknowledged Ross's presence with a surly nod. "Nothing much to tell," he grumbled. "We look for ex-servicemen, preferably Jewish, and induce them to volunteer to work in the kibbutzim. We have a list of Jewish employers in Palestine who provide letters offering employment. Another list provides hypothetical relatives our men can visit.

"It worked well—until recently. The State Department is getting nosy as hell when anyone with a Jewish-sounding name applies for a passport, especially when they list the purpose as visiting or taking employment in Palestine."

"Do you have any suggestions?" Ross asked coolly. He didn't care for the dark-haired man's prickly attitude, and let it be known.

Ginsberg's truculence lessened. "Yeah, a couple," he replied. "First, there's no trouble getting a passport to visit any other country in Europe. If we could establish temporary camps someplace, ideally ones where we could provide training, we could use small boats to evade the British patrols. Also, there's a crying need for former officers, especially ones with experience commanding large numbers of men.

"My own case is an example. I escaped from Poland and joined the British army to fight Nazis. The Brits were thinking even back then. They could see that someday they might face a Jewish problem. So, Jews weren't given combat training. The Brits were right, damn their black hearts; now we are without experienced officers and NCOs."

Close to an hour later, Ginsberg departed in better spirits. Ross walked to the door with him, assuring the recruiter that he would attempt to arrange for staging camps in Europe. Corsica had distinct possibilities. After one parting shot, expressing his displeasure with Ariel's plight, Ginsberg stalked down the steps.

Ross also prepared to make his exit but was restrained by Mantz. "Sit down a minute, Ross. I promised to answer a question you posed earlier: why I wanted you to meet David Ginsberg."

"Yes," Ross responded. "I'm curious."

"Here's the situation. With Ariel leaving, the operational end of this effort is beyond my ability. I can't both manage it and perform my main task in the diplomatic and financial areas. I am asking you to become my deputy for operations."

Mantz held up a hand, palm out, as Ross gaped in astonishment. "Don't give me an answer now. Think about it, then give me your answer before you leave for Tel Aviv. Your job will commence after your return, if you accept it. It will entail overseeing the entire range of procurement and transportation of men and materiel. It's a demanding job, Ross, but one for which you are uniquely qualified. You have natural leadership abilities, which the cause needs desperately.

"Now, go. Talk it over with Ariel, if you like. I'm fully aware of the painful decision you face. I could never fault you for refusing, but the fate of our people may hang in the balance. They need you."

18 September 1947
Chicago
Janet Templeton flung herself into a deeply upholstered chair, kicked off low-heeled pumps, and ran fingers through her tousled mahogany-hued hair. "Ross, in the future, don't *ever* ask me to go for a walk with you. And I hope never to see that damn waterfront park again. My feet and legs will ache for a week; I may have permanent damage."

Ross crossed to the apartment's little corner bar and poured generous portions of Scotch over ice. He added a splash of water to each, then handed one to Janet, quipping, "Doctor Colyer's magic elixir. One of these will cure anything that ails you. And don't blame me if your soft life behind a desk has made a physical wreck of you."

Janet accepted her glass and hoped her inner feelings weren't obvious. She'd had mixed emotions at Ross's unannounced appearance. Was there a tiny feeling of guilt, possibly? True, she'd told him that she was working on an in-depth profile of Senator Templeton, but would he approve of the direction the thing was taking? She wished for more time to organize her thoughts.

The conversation she'd had with her editor, Max Foley, the day before flashed across her mind.

The sharp-featured newsman let out an exasperated sigh and looked up from the rough copy he'd been reading.

"Janet," Foley barked, "this isn't the article we discussed when I gave you the go-ahead."

"I—I guess maybe I didn't foresee the direction it seems to have taken," Janet murmured. "But I've read everything the senator has ever written, including transcripts of his speeches. Every word obtained during interviews has been confirmed by at least two sources."

Foley snorted. "I'm not worried about libel, damnit, although I must confess I'd have thought his daughter-in-law would have been a bit less critical. But I'm asking myself, 'Is it news?' It smacks of anti-Semitic propaganda. Mister Green won't stand for that, Templeton."

Janet felt spots of crimson form in her cheeks. "But sir, the senator has come down squarely opposed to Mister Truman's support for a United Nations negotiated settlement in Palestine. Most Jews favor the president's position. Why would the publisher think that attacking the senator's stance is anti-Semitic?"

Foley regarded her with an icy stare, then tried a different tack. "The real problem is that you've wandered into the international political arena. The way you've written it, the entire piece may even be detrimental to U.S. interests. I can't approve this on my own."

"So it won't run," Janet said, controlling her anger with difficulty.

"Look, I'm putting it on the spike for now. At the right time I'll run it past the entire editorial board. Fair enough?"

By the time Janet slammed the door to her apartment behind her that evening, she'd built up a full head of steam. After mixing a drink, she looked up Clayton Henderson's number at the San Francisco office of the International News Service (INS). She consumed half her drink before her old boss came on the line. Bypassing banal greetings, she barked, "Mister Henderson, this is Janet Templeton. I'm job hunting. Do you have any openings?"

"Whoa there, Redhead." Henderson paused to laugh. "I detect that temper I recall so vividly working overtime. Now slow down and tell me what has you in such a tizzy. And I'm fine, thank you. How the hell are you?"

"I'm sorry, sir," Janet replied with a rueful chuckle. "It's just that I finally got a shot at a feature article and that bastard editor of mine put it on the spike. It's a good story and, damnit, he's not running it for personal reasons."

"Tsk, tsk," the INS bureau chief teased. "I don't recall *ever* hearing of an editor using such poor judgment. Spiked a big story? Unbelievable."

"All right, all right, you unsympathetic clod. So I'm overreacting. Seriously, I'm fed up. First he said the article puts the Jews in a bad light. But it doesn't, and when I pointed that out to Foley, he accused me of writing a piece detrimental to American interests—and he *still* spiked it."

"Hmmm. So what do you plan to do now?"

"Oh, hell, I don't know," Janet lamented. "But it *is* a big story—one I'll bet *you* would run."

"Don't bet on it. And don't try to soft-soap me. What's it about?"

"I really don't think I'd better go into that on the phone. Look, the reason I called is to ask if you know of any openings with INS. I'm serious."

Henderson didn't reply immediately. "Janet, I have to be in D.C. soon. If you can make it there, get in touch. I'll be glad to talk to you; we're always in the market for people with your qualifications."

"I'll be there, if I have to walk," she replied grimly.

Janet pushed the conversation from her mind and took an appreciative sip of her drink. "Well, what momentous decision did you reach during that marathon?" she asked.

Ross shot her a sharp look. "Decision? A momentous decision?"

"Ross Colyer, I'm Janet, remember? The gal who can read little boys' minds. You blow into town, looking like you've lost the old homestead in a poker game, paying not the slightest bit of attention to anything I say. Then you want to take a walk—on a chilly evening in Chicago. Now give, before I fall into an exhaustion-induced coma."

"I'd forgotten what a nagging, nosy broad you can be," Ross grumbled good-naturedly. "Okay, if you must know, I didn't reach a decision."

"I'm listening," Janet said. "And for Christ's sake, stop that pacing back and forth. I'm too tired to watch."

Ross took the chair facing hers and cradled his drink. "Janet, Julius Mantz wants me to be deputy for operations for the Jewish Relief Foundation."

Janet closed her eyes. "Oh, dear God," she muttered wearily. "And I suppose you're seriously considering it."

"Well, yes," Ross answered defensively. "I have to . . . consider it at least. It's the thing I'm doing for a living now."

"I thought you were running an airline—keeping your nose clean."

"And a few other things. I told you about buying the airplanes, damnit."

"So, not content with just bending the rules a bit, you are thinking of becoming an outlaw—helping *run* an illegal operation."

"It's all so crazy, Janet—what the U.S. is doing. Plus, at this point I'm not sure—and you can't be either—that what I'm doing *is* illegal. Okay, I took on this charter contract to save my company, neither understanding nor caring a lot about what was at stake. Later, I told myself there are people in government who favor openly helping the Jews, and I'd go along until their view prevailed. I told you I'd bail out at the first hint of anything that violated the law, remember?"

"So what made you change your mind?"

Ross leaned forward, and his tone grew harsh. "I *haven't* decided, damnit. But Janet, those people don't have a prayer. The bureaucrats won't change things. By the time they act, the Jews will be behind barbed wire again."

"So, Sir Don Quixote, you have decided to single-handedly become their salvation." Janet's tone was scathing. Look, those 'other people in government' you refer to don't have at stake what you do."

"And *none* of us have at stake what the Jewish people have," Ross said softly. "I'm going to be free, no matter what happens. Oh, I may be arrested, fined, even do a stint in prison. I may lose my chance to ever return to active duty. But in the end, I'll be a free man."

"Ross! You don't owe those people that much. You—" Janet bit her lip, hesitated, then continued. "I'm sorry, you're right, of course. They *have* received atrocious treatment. I *do* feel sorry for them. It's just that"—Janet swallowed audibly—"I've watched you from those days at Hickam. You were so dedicated, so in love with flying. The army was your life. I admired your single-minded, forceful approach to adversity—so different from the man I married. It tears me apart to see you risk throwing that away.

"And—I have to say this—I can't help but feel you're being manipulated by that crew, especially by that Shamir woman. Maybe Alex Taylor had the right instincts."

"Alex was a damned bigot," Ross snapped. "And Ariel Shamir has nothing to do with my decision about the job—one way or another. Anyway, the State Department pulled her visa last week; she has to go back. . . . I won't pretend I'm not angry."

Janet sat erect and squared her shoulders. "I know. Oh, I'm making a mess of things—forgive me. I'm afraid I'm not myself this evening. I had a really bad day."

"That's okay, and I'm sorry I yelled at you. What happened?"

"You remember the article I told you about—a profile of my father-in-law? The one you didn't want me to do?"

"I remember."

"It was a good piece. I spent most of the summer researching it. I
kept my personal feelings to myself; the article is objective and factual but, as you might expect, it isn't highly flattering. My damned
editor spiked it. You want to know why?" Without giving Ross time
to reply, she rushed on, telling him about her confrontation with Foley.

"It figures," Ross mused aloud when she'd finished. "That Templeton
would be a bigot as well as a lot of other undesirable things doesn't
surprise me. Well, I guess not running the story solves your problem.
You didn't put your job on the line by refusing to write the article,
but you still didn't endorse the man. You'll have other opportunities
to do a feature."

"That isn't the point at all!" Janet blazed. Foley killed a *news* story
for personal reasons."

Ross frowned.

"Look, Ross," Janet continued, "the people have a right to read the
facts I presented. Every word of it is *true,* and to have it killed because it doesn't agree with some editor's or publisher's personal bias
is *wrong.*"

"Well," Ross said with a dry chuckle, "it is, after all, *Green's* newspaper."

"It's petty," Janet flared. "Foley is flat wrong, Ross; the article *isn't*
anti-Semitic. I quote Senator Templeton as saying, 'Truman should
keep his hands out of Mideast politics. We won our freedom with our
own bare hands—let the Jews do likewise.' Foley had circled that passage
in red. Why? They may be the words of an isolationist, but don't they
support the Zionist movement in principle?"

Ross shook his head. "I can't ever remember us shouting at each
other. I guess dropping by unannounced was a mistake." He stood.
"As for your problem, it's all above my head. But I admire your determination—you're a damn good reporter. I hope you get things straightened out. Don't let just one defeat get you down." He turned to leave.

Janet scrambled to her feet. "Goddamnit, Ross Colyer, come back
here."

Ross turned. Seeing tears welling up in her eyes, he wordlessly handed
her his handkerchief.

Janet barked a short, bitter laugh. "Fine friend I am. You came to me for help, and I act like a bitch. Not only that, but I dump my own problems in your lap. I know *you'll* make the right decision—you've always had that knack. As for myself," her jaw took on a pugnacious set, "well, I haven't lost this one—not yet. And, in spite of my yelling at you, I'll always be here when you need someone to talk with. Remember that, please."

Janet tilted her face upward, and he bent over and kissed her lightly. "I know that," he responded, his voice husky. "Your honesty is the one thing I can count on in this crazy world."

Janet watched the apartment door close behind him. She regarded the empty glass in her hand, then flung it the length of the room, where it shattered against the oak-paneled door.

"You dumb broad!" she raged. "You did it. Oh, that was a *brilliant* performance, Janet Templeton. Why can't you just admit to yourself that you've fallen in love with a man who only wants to be your brother?"

Chapter 21

25 September 1947
New York City

"I'll take the job, Julius," Ross said, returning Mantz's level stare as he spoke. "I'll make this run to Haifa, go on to Europe, do some shopping, then come back and go to work."

Mantz nodded. "Good. I'll create space for you. Is Ariel's office adequate?"

"Of course," Ross replied. "There are a couple of things, though. . . ."

"Yes?"

"You know about my membership in the air force reserve, of course. If I move permanently to New York, well, I'd have to give up my slot in Kansas City. It's important to me to keep it."

"I understand. You'll be on the move much of the time anyway. The second item?"

"Is it necessary to call me 'deputy'? I think I'd be more comfortable with a title like 'coordinator.'"

Mantz shook his head with a faint smile. "You know otherwise, Ross. You're a seasoned military officer; you've commanded a combat unit. Authority and responsibility go hand in hand. Some tough decisions have to be made behind this desk. They can't often be made through gentle persuasion."

Ross sighed. "I know. It's just that—"

"You feel Eddie, David, and Moshe Barnett will resist taking orders from you," Mantz said, finishing the thought for him.

"That *had* occurred to me, yes."

"Do you think you can handle it?"

"Of course," Ross retorted brusquely.

"Good. I'll see you when you return. Now, there's one other thing." Mantz extracted an envelope from his desk drawer and regarded it at length. "This is a very personal letter from me to David Ben-Gurion. Please do not deliver it to anyone else."

Ross accepted the missive and nodded. "How do I get in touch with the man?"

"Ariel will make the arrangements. How did she react to your promotion, by the way?"

Ross flashed a rueful grin. "I was listening closely. I believe it was a grunt."

"As you said, Ariel has to do a great deal of sorting out of her emotions, Ross. Her job here is her therapy, actually. This business with her father, and losing her visa . . . well, it's upset her terribly." Julius stood, signifying the end of the meeting. He gripped Ross's right hand with both of his own. "Go with God, Ross. This mission is of extreme importance."

Ross returned the warm pressure of the handshake and turned toward the door. What is so earthshakingly important about transporting sixty-five people to Tel Aviv? he wondered.

1600 Hours, 26 September 1947
Teterboro Field

Ross sat at the rear of the hangar, behind sixty-five young men standing in a semicircle around Ariel. Her intense voice echoed in the steel building. "Boarding will be at eight o'clock tonight. I have your passports, but expect sharp questions from the customs and immigration people as you pass through the loading gate. Remember your reason for going to Palestine. To accept employment? With whom? Visiting relatives? Their names? Their house number? Above all, be courteous; do *not* make jokes or wisecracks."

Ariel reached behind her and picked up a sheaf of papers. "I have here a—" She stopped in midsentence as David Ginsberg stepped through the hangar door and wigwagged with urgent gestures. She continued smoothly, "Let's take a smoke break now. When we come back, I'll cover your arrival in Tel Aviv." She smiled sweetly and strode to where Ross had joined David. "What's up?" she demanded.

David's jaw was set. "Trouble. Let's go into Ross's office."

Ross and Ariel took the only two chairs; David paced as he talked. "I just got a cable from a group of recruits we put on a ship bound for Athens this morning. They couldn't get passports and visas for Palestine, so we sent them the roundabout route. The group leader told me that just as they were boarding, some clown from the State Department showed up and stamped all their passports, NOT VALID FOR PALESTINE."

Ross broke the stunned silence. "What the hell? They can't do that."

Ginsberg sighed. "My lawyer says they can. It's an obscure emergency provision that was passed during the war: the secretary of state can restrict travel to countries experiencing riots, civil wars, and the like. It's still on the books. The State Department contends that allowing persons with Jewish surnames to travel to Palestine at this time foments unrest."

"What you're saying, of course, is that they're waiting in there for me to present this bundle of passports," Ariel said calmly. "At which time they will promptly invalidate them, for this trip at least."

"But your group on board the ship—hell, they were going to *Greece,* a peaceful neutral," Ross blazed.

"As my lawyer said, 'You want to take them to court?'" Ginsberg replied.

Ross pounded the desk. "Okay, we won't depart for overseas from here. We'll refile for Miami—won't even show those passports. Maybe it's only the locals who dreamed up this illegal gimmick. We'll refuel and head east from there."

"That might work, but I doubt it," Ginsberg reasoned. "They'll have thought of that. A better way might be to put the group on a bus, send them to Toronto, and pick them up there. Their unstamped passports won't cause any questions in Canada, and they can use a driver's license for border crossing."

"Whatever we do, we must do it by noon tomorrow," Ross said. "Ariel's visa expires then." He brightened. "Ariel, do you know which agent is waiting to process the boarding?"

"I certainly do. He's a smirking little bastard named Hoskins. We've had words before."

"I'll bet he's the only one who's privy to this stunt." Ross stroked his chin. "Send the boys back to a motel—no, wait. I'm going to take the engineer out to the bird. We'll rearrange some spark plug leads

on number three engine, then run 'er up. They'll be able to hear the
missing and backfiring all the way inside the terminal.

"We'll cancel the flight and casually mention that we're resched-
uling for twenty hundred hours tomorrow. Put the passengers on a bus,
take them for dinner, a late-night movie, whatever. The State Department guy will have to go home sometime. So, at about oh one hundred, we fix the engine and make a hurry-up call for customs and immigration. If we're lucky, we'll draw a half-asleep dodo. If not, we'll
switch to David's plan. Let's go."

The jovial, middle-aged flight service clerk rubbed his bald head
and scanned Ross's flight plan with a faint smile. "Got her fixed sooner
than y'figured, huh, Cap'n Colyer?"

"Yeah, it turned out to be nothing more than a faulty magneto lead,"
Ross grunted. "As soon as our passengers show up and the customs
and immigration people clear us, we'll have wheels in the well and
be outta here."

The clerk made notations on the flight plan, then looked up at Ross.
"Hoskins hung around 'til about eleven, then went home. I figured
he wouldn't want to be disturbed again tonight, so I called a new boy—
he should be along any minute."

"That's mighty considerate of you," Ross said, equally deadpan. He
looked at the clerk's name tag. "Ben," he added.

"Stands for Benjamin. Benjamin Goldberg, Cap'n Colyer. Have a
good flight, now."

Two hours later, Ross keyed his mike and drawled, "Saint John's
Radio, this is PAL Baker King, over point Indigo. Switching now to
Gander Oceanic Control, frequency thirty-six-fifty. Over."

"Roger, Baker King, Saint John's Radio here. Good-night, and have
a safe trip."

Ross switched to intercom. "Pilot to crew. We just passed into international airspace."

Ragged cheers filled the Connie's flight deck. "We did it, by God!"
copilot Chris Wofford chortled. "I wasn't sure there for a while. Even
the goddamn tower operator must have been in on it. The bastard did
everything he could to screw up our takeoff clearance."

Cal Thornton, a flight engineer who followed Murtaugh from TWA, chimed in, "There were two beady-eyed characters hanging around all afternoon. They tried to pump me about our trouble with number three. I told 'em it looked like an engine change to me, and they disappeared."

Ross heard, "Navigator to pilot. Hold your altitude, heading, and airspeed constant for two minutes, if you will. I'm taking my first celestial fix." Andy was all business. A safe arrival at Santa Maria, the Azores, was now his responsibility.

"I'm going to stretch my legs, have a cup of coffee, and check on our passengers, Chris," Ross said. "I'll relieve you in a couple of hours, okay?"

"Fair enough, Skipper." Chris patted the autopilot control. "Me and old George will make out just fine." The cocky young pilot slouched comfortably and gave Ross a wide grin.

Ross drew a cup of steaming coffee, paused to glance at the navigator's array of charts and manuals, then went aft into the passenger compartment. Dim blue lights revealed a jumble of snoring bodies, except for Ariel and a lad wearing dark trousers and a tan poplin jacket. As Ross paused beside them, the youngster jumped up. "You like to sit here, sir? I'll find a seat farther back."

Ross thanked him and slid into the seat alongside Ariel. She continued gazing out the tiny window without speaking. Ross sipped coffee and followed her preoccupied stare. A quarter moon, sinking from sight through broken high clouds, turned the top of a lower deck into burnished silver. Combined with the muted drone of the four big radial engines, the effect was hypnotic.

"I passed this way four years ago," Ross said softly. "The circumstances were a helluva lot different. I was in a drafty, noisy B-24 bomber with a crew of kids, half of whom didn't shave. We were on our way to save the world from a madman."

"Would you do it again?" Ariel murmured. "Knowing then what you know now?"

"Sure," Ross replied. "In a manner of speaking, I *am* doing it again."

Ariel laid one warm, blunt-fingered hand atop his free one. "We haven't talked much lately," she said.

"No."

"You think I'm being stubborn and bitchy about the whole thing, don't you?"

"Ariel!"

"Your proposal wasn't serious, I know. I appreciate your trying to help me, but I felt like I was forsaking my country, becoming a guest in a foreign land—abandoning my father. Things have probably turned out for the best."

Ross moved his hand to capture hers. "Perhaps. It's just that I hate leaving you in that place alone, believe me." They sat silently until Ross's eyelids drooped. Ariel reached across and retrieved his empty coffee cup. She left her other hand in his, however.

29 September 1947
Haifa Airfield, Palestine
Ross straightened the Connie's nosewheel and set the parking brakes, calling, "You can shut down all four, Cal." He scanned that portion of the airfield visible from the cockpit as the big Pratt & Whitneys ground to a stop. "Christ, things look warlike here," Ross muttered to his copilot.

Chris Wofford craned his neck and peered out the copilot's window. The darkly handsome youngster from Atlanta chuckled. "They do at that, Captain. I don't recall ever seeing so much armament on an airfield, even when I was flying Gooneybirds into Algiers. And them mothers were real nervous Nellies."

The place did resemble an armed camp, Ross noticed. Coils of barbed wire outlined the field boundaries and sensitive areas such as the fuel storage compound and a row of parked Spitfires. Guards with automatic weapons slung from their shoulders roamed the parking ramp, hangars, and terminal entrance.

Four desert-camouflaged Land Rovers, two with mounted Vickers machine guns, took up positions just off the Connie's left wing.

By the time the crew ran their final checklists, a khaki-uniformed official with a ginger mustache and wearing a red beret appeared in the cockpit entryway. "Your paperwork," he demanded imperiously. "Crew list and passports, landing permit, manifests, and declaration of any prohibited items."

Ross concealed his irritation by storing flight manuals and other assorted papers in his briefcase. "Yes, we did have a pleasant flight," he said, snapping shut the briefcase. "Thank you for asking."

The man's ruddy complexion took on a deeper hue. "Cheeky, are we? Captain, you are in a potentially hostile area, not some sleepy South American backwater." His red-rimmed eyes narrowed. "But then, you're a Yank, what? With a Panamanian flag of convenience. Interesting." He held out his hand.

Ross sighed. "Look, it's sort of congested in here. Don't you have an office for these formalities?"

"Nobody and no article leaves this aircraft until you've been cleared. I have two arrivals twenty minutes behind you, Captain. Unless you want to wait here until I clear them, I'll take those papers, please."

Ross shrugged. Opening his briefcase, he handed over the sheaf of required papers without further comment. Through the open door he saw two eagle-eyed noncoms moving slowly down the center aisle subjecting his passengers' passports to lengthy examination. Meanwhile, the officer gazed about the cockpit, impatiently slapping his leg with a well-worn swagger stick.

"Look, Major," Ross said after glancing at the man's shoulder pips, "I'm sorry to have wised off just now. It's just that—well—I flew bombers out of England during the war. I guess I'm accustomed to the English being a more friendly type of people. Everyone I see here has a ferocious scowl and packs more armament than a Wild West cowboy."

The British major stared down his nose at Ross for a moment, then his expression softened. "Eighth Air Force, I take it. My brother flew Lancasters. This is a different war, Captain? . . ."

"Colyer. Ross Colyer. A different war you say? Who is the enemy this time?"

"Well, anytime both sides are having people killed, it's a war—that's my feeling. The night before last, the Jews murdered two of our blokes—hanged them. The troops are a bit worked up just now, you see."

An NCO checked his list against the Connie's manifest, then handed the stack of papers back to Ross. "Everything seems to be in order, sir. You can arrange for refueling and overnight parking inside. If you will have your crew baggage set aside, I will check it for you—save standing in the queue inside. It's a bit slow there, I'm afraid."

The major extended his hand and growled, "I say, I'm sorry if I came on a bit testy just now. Trying times, you know. Would you be free for a drink in our mess this evening? Allow me to make up for being something of a boor to a fellow officer."

Ross hesitated, then, on impulse, shook the man's hand. "I'd be most happy to, Major? . . ."

"Wooster. Say eightish? Tell the cabbie to take you to the Victoria

Hotel. Our mess is in the basement there. Nothing elaborate, you know, but the food and drink are rather decent. Tell the man at the door that Major Wooster is expecting you. Cheerio."

Ross collected Ariel as she emerged from the customs area. "You say you know of a hotel?" he asked.

"Right. It's been some time, but I'm assuming it's still there—and open. It's small, but they know me. Look, I realize you and the rest of the crew are tired, but I would like to stay here until all our passengers clear."

"Very well, I'll send the others ahead and stay with you." Ross caught a fleeting look of gratitude as he led her to a row of hard benches in the waiting room. After giving Chris directions to the hotel, he returned to sit beside Ariel. "Hey," he said, "why the grim face? Aren't you happy to be home?"

"Oh, Ross, it's terrible. I can remember when this was a cheerful, pleasant place. Families with children on holiday, young lovers, stuffy-looking businessmen bustling about. Now look at it. Armed guards. I just saw a man being hustled off by the police. Everyone talks in hushed tones. It's even worse than when I was last here. I'm *glad* I was forced to come back."

Ross sighed. "Ariel, an old CO of mine once told me, 'Ross, anger is an emotion you can't afford in combat—it'll get you killed. Fight with your head, not your heart.' Right now you're thinking of going back to the Irgun: kill people, avenge my father—I can see it in your face.

"I can't tell you how to live your life. But stop and think, damnit, before you go charging into the fray with a gun in each hand and a knife in your teeth. Take some advice from a guy who's been there."

Without giving Ariel time to protest, he continued. "Perhaps I can give you some idea of how things are shaping up tomorrow. You see, I've accepted that British customs officer's invitation for a drink at his mess this evening. The conversation there could be enlightening."

"Ross!"

"Now, now. Wait before you start accusing me of consorting with the enemy. In situations like this, information can be more valuable than gold. Think about what I just told you—think hard. I won't be late. Will you be all right?" Ross gave her a level look.

"Yes," Ariel replied, sounding unconvinced.

Ross grasped both her hands. "Like I said, I won't be late. Shall I check in with you?"

Ariel shook her head. "I might not be there. I plan to contact someone I know here—maybe get some word of my father."

Ross closed his eyes briefly and shook his head. "You didn't hear a word I said, did you?" he asked in disbelief.

"I did," Ariel replied indignantly. "I know you're interested and concerned, but I can't just sit and do nothing when so much needs to be done."

"Listen, the British secret service has this town covered like a blanket— you know that. Your old contacts are probably under surveillance, even house arrest. Don't do anything stupid!"

Ariel's eyes blazed, then quickly dulled. "You're probably right," she said dejectedly. "Very well, I'll stay in my room until you come back."

"Okay. Another thing—I'll be here in Haifa only about two days. I'm to arrange a meeting with a Haganah contact in case we find some airplanes for sale on the Continent. Be thinking of a safe place to live."

"I'd rather find out what's happened to my father," Ariel replied in a small voice.

It was eight o'clock when Ross's cab deposited him at a break in the coils of barbed wire and tank traps surrounding the Victoria Hotel. The man at the door stood at parade rest with a Bren gun slung from his shoulder.

Major Wooster, apparently oblivious to the fortresslike surroundings, greeted Ross warmly and ushered him inside with a cheerful, "So good of you to show up. I've been telling the chaps we're to be honored with a former Yank bomber pilot."

Ross looked around the room. The British always manage to re-create a little bit of England anyplace they happen to be, he observed with concealed amusement. The hotel's basement bore little resemblance to the building's otherwise contemporary decor. Heavy oaken beams on the ceiling, dark-paneled walls, and an authentic-looking English pub bar and beer pump made one instinctively listen for the sonorous toll of Big Ben.

The atmosphere Ross recalled from the officers' messes he'd visited during the war was noticeably absent, however. The booming laughter, crude jokes, and general bonhomie were replaced with subdued, almost somber demeanor. Wooster seemed the only happy man among the dozen or so patrons, who nursed their pints in relative silence.

Ross raised his mug of warm beer in a silent toast. "All the trappings outside—I wasn't sure I had come to the right place."

"Ah, the wire and all," Wooster replied. He sobered. "Not a pleasant outlook here, I'm afraid. What with the Jews potting Arabs, the Arabs potting Jews, the Jews—the Irgun and Haganah—potting each other, and both sides potting us, one is well advised to keep one's head down. I don't recommend riding the buses, by the way. They make tempting targets."

"Why do you stay?" Ross asked casually. "Why not simply say 'have at it,' and go home?"

"Oh, really, now," Wooster replied in astonishment, wiping beer from his ginger mustache, "quite out of the question, that—you know. We have an obligation to sort things out down here—the UN mandate and all."

"This 'sorting out—'" Ross stopped in midsentence as the unmistakable sound of automatic-weapons fire filtered through the heavy door behind them.

The bar's occupants jerked to startled attention and turned toward the entrance. Ross heard a muttered, "Oh, I say now—" Then he saw the door bulge inward. The blast, when it reached them, had been dampened by the three-inch-thick barrier. Nevertheless, the explosion retained enough force to hurl tables, chairs, and random bric-a-brac in a deadly hail. Only the bartender, hunkered behind his sturdy partition, escaped injury. Ross's last conscious recollection was surprise at seeing his drinking companion's ruddy features, pale blue eyes bulging in surprise, dissolve into a reddish, shapeless blur.

Ross became aware of dim light. The sharp, astringent odor of alcohol assailed his nostrils. His head pounded with a sickening rhythm; he was suddenly overcome with nausea. A vague shape materialized and guided his head over a cold metallic container. He wretched and felt stabs of pain. Settling back with a groan, he struggled to orient himself. Where was he? What the hell had happened?

Memory returned with a rush. The bar. The explosion. He blinked rapidly and tried to focus on blurred shapes moving nearby. The effort was too much. He drifted into a gray, pain-filled void. Two warm hands enveloped one of his own. Somehow they felt familiar.

When next he awoke, Ross realized he was in a white-walled room bright with filtered sunlight. He detected movement; before he could turn his head he dimly heard a voice call, "Nurse."

A buxom woman dressed in white swam into his range of vision. "Well, now. It's awake, we are. That's good. Can we speak?"

How the hell can I? he thought irritably. You just stuck something in my mouth. He felt cool, firm fingers at his wrist. Turning his head hurt, so he rolled his eyes in the other direction. Ariel. Her face was pale and drawn—she looked like hell. He grinned and saw her face light up. Then the as yet faceless figure removed the thermometer from his dry, cracked lips and boomed, "Everything seems nicely normal. Doctor will be around any minute now. You just lie back and rest a bit."

"Hi," Ross tried to say to Ariel. A strangled croak emerged instead.

"Oh, Ross." Ariel grasped his hand. "My God, you gave us a scare. You're going to be all right, they say. Just a mild concussion and assorted scrapes and bruises."

"What happened," he mouthed.

"It was a bomb. Some terrorists drove a Land Rover right up the steps of the hotel. Four of them jumped out and started shooting. They rolled a drum of explosive down the steps leading to the officers' mess. Only one of them escaped."

"Who did it?"

Ariel's expression tightened. "Jews, the ones who were killed. They were Irgun."

Ross signaled toward the water pitcher. Ariel fed him a half glassful, and he cleared his throat. "Major Wooster?" he asked.

"The British officer who invited you? He's dead, Ross. Three others were killed, too, I'm afraid."

Ross, still in hospital pajamas, sat in a lounge chair placed in sunlight streaming through the windows of the patients' lounge. Ariel, looking unexpectedly demure, sat to one side.

One of the two men facing Ross—a policeman—was speaking. He was a big fellow, dressed in a paramilitary khaki getup consisting of a short-sleeved shirt with epaulets, matching shorts, and tan knee-length stockings. He appeared to be at least a size too large for his clothes, making him look as if he was about to explode out of them— an impression heightened by his rosy cheeks and nose. "Terribly sorry that this had to happen to a guest in our country, of course. This violence must end. Now, about your future plans. The doctor tells me you'll be discharged tomorrow. Light duty until that head is clear again, I understand. Will you be bringing in a new pilot to fly your plane out?"

Ariel interrupted with a flat, "Captain Colyer will stay with me until he's cleared to fly again—possibly in a week." Ross glanced in her direction, concealing his surprise.

"Harrumph." The other man, a British army colonel, cleared his throat. "Terribly inconvenient, you know, leaving your ship parked at the airdrome that long. Never know what can happen. You saw what those fellows are capable of doing."

Ross studied the beefy, autocratic figure and decided he didn't like the bastard. "I'm not actually wild about the idea myself, Colonel," he replied. "But, then, I'm not particularly wild about being nearly blown to bits while a guest of His Majesty's Finest. I can only hope your airport security is better than what you provide for your men."

"Now look here." The man's face flushed in anger. "We didn't ask you to bring your cargo of unwanted visitors to this country. You did that for profit, I assume—knowing the unstable political situation in advance. As a matter of fact, your sixty-odd passengers add a potential for violence. Despite the transparent reasons they gave for visiting Palestine just now, their similarity in age, background, and the like stretches credibility. A month from now it could be one of *them* who tosses a bomb into the officers' mess. One would hope you were unaware of that potential."

Ross stood, masking the pain and effort it cost. His voice was an icy lash. "I find your remarks personally offensive, sir. I can only suggest you take up any complaints you may have with the United States and Panamanian governments. Good-day."

Back in his room, Ross sank gratefully onto the bed. He turned to a grim-faced Ariel. "Now, what's all this about you nursing me back to health?"

"You told me to find a safe place to live. So, I'm taking you to the kibbutz—the one where I spent most of my summers as a girl. It will be good for you."

Chapter 22

2 October 1947
Haifa Airfield

Ross refused Ariel's help as he eased himself out of the sedan's rear seat. Unaided he walked the short distance to a battered Taylorcraft, but the show of physical normality was not without extreme effort. Ariel, wearing a disgusted look, followed, carrying their meager baggage. Ross eyed a dirty Piper J-3 Cub parked nearby. Turning to Ariel, he raised an eyebrow and asked, "Could that possibly be—"

Ariel nodded. "I don't know for sure, but it easily could be. Now that you've displayed your machismo to all and sundry, let me help you into your seat."

As she turned, a compactly built man—Ross judged him to be in his thirties—hurried across the ramp from a building displaying a sign for a flying club, written in both Hebrew and English. In addition to the customary khaki shorts and white open-necked shirt, he wore a broad grin and dark aviator glasses, and was clean shaven.

"Hi," Ariel said. "I assume you're our pilot. I'm Ariel Shamir. I don't remember you, but I used to fly from here frequently a couple of years ago."

"But I remember you, Miss Shamir," the pilot replied. "I was a mechanic then. My name is Ehud Appel. Welcome back."

The Taylorcraft skimmed the flat, sandy shoreline at an altitude of barely five hundred feet. Despite a nagging headache, Ross eyed the passing scene with interest. Dun-colored terrain, slightly rolling and checkerboarded with green squares of irrigated fields, stretched toward a distant range of purple-hazed mountains. The history of this scene of ancient struggle, the cradle of Christianity, was sobering.

Ross turned to Ariel. "Will you stay on after I leave?" he yelled above the engine noise.

Ariel hesitated. "It depends," she replied. "They may have another assignment for me. If not . . ." She shrugged.

"Ariel," Ross's voice had sharpened. "Have you given up that crazy threat you made back in New York?"

"It wasn't a crazy threat." Ariel's voice was also sharp. "Ross, you're going to see the Jewish struggle at its roots. In a way, I'm glad to have the chance to show you life in the shadow of unrelenting threat. It's a harsh, savage existence. Life is cheap. The old 'eye for an eye and tooth for a tooth' is not an empty adage. I won't discuss it further—you must see the situation for yourself."

She leaned forward, pointing to their two o'clock position. "The kibbutz!" she cried. "There it is, Ross. Oh, it's changed—it's so much larger, and with so many buildings." She talked nonstop while their pilot lined up with a cleared swath parallel to the inevitable roll of barbed wire outlining the pathetic-looking cluster of buildings. "There, that two-story concrete building—that's where mother and I stayed. In all the years we came here, it was never finished. Our room had no door; the building was without electricity, floor tiles, or plaster on the walls—just gaping holes for windows. But mother and I had iron bedsteads with palliasses."

"Is that where? . . ." Ross let the question hang.

"Yes," Ariel replied without elaborating. She fell silent as the little plane touched down, bounced, and rolled to a stop near an ancient Land Rover.

The dust-caked vehicle had been converted into a truck by hacking away its rear bodywork. A bearded man wearing black trousers and a tan work shirt straightened from where he leaned on a battered fender. "Shalom, Ariel. How good to see you back," he called.

Ariel flew into the oldster's outstretched arms. "Amos, what a welcome sight you are. Oh, I've missed you all so. How is Sarah? The young ones . . ." She chattered on as Amos shifted their bags from the Taylorcraft to the truck. Ross had only a glimpse of the small wooden box, about the size of a liquor case, that Amos removed last. Judging from the man's expression, the box must have weighed a hundred pounds. He and the pilot exchanged almost imperceptible nods.

Ariel finally noticed Ross standing to one side and gasped. "Oh, how could I? I almost forgot to introduce your guest for the next few days, Amos."

Ross endured the jouncing ride to the built-up area with a faint smile on his face. Ariel had come home. He recalled asking her what would make her happy. His answer was in her beaming features and the lilting laughter he'd so seldom heard.

Ross turned his attention to the layout of the fortified outpost. It was hard to visualize a serious threat, but he accepted the fact that one existed. A figure lounging atop a thirty-foot-high water tower, which dominated the scene, confirmed that the residents certainly thought there was a threat. Ross surveyed the barren stretches of surrounding land, the unpainted wooden buildings, the outer barricade constructed of two plank walls with a gap in between filled with dirt. Hell, it's Fort Apache all over again, he mused.

He noticed that Amos and Ariel were talking in lowered voices, their faces unsmiling. He saw Ariel turn and shoot a quick glance at him. Faintly annoyed at his obvious treatment as an outsider, Ross vowed to confront Ariel at the first opportunity.

It came after the evening meal. Ariel led him to a bench outside her quarters. Sitting with arms locked around her knees, she told him of the good times she remembered—singing atop the water tower after the day's work ended, dancing the hora by moonlight in the central clearing. He waited until she paused, then asked, "What were you and Amos discussing that you didn't want me to hear?"

Ariel sighed. "Damn," she muttered. "I thought you noticed. We came at a bad time, Ross. Amos wants you to return to Haifa—for your own safety."

"Isn't that thoughtful of him," Ross replied sarcastically. "What grave danger does he foresee? An Indian attack, maybe?"

"Worse, perhaps," Ariel said. "I'm inclined to agree. As soon as you feel up to it, I suggest we leave. I'm sorry—it's my fault for bringing you here. I thought a few days of sunshine and light exercise would help."

"Look, damnit, I'm not exactly a lowly spear carrier in this operation. I'm entitled to an explanation," Ross said irritably.

"Then talk to Amos," Ariel answered shortly. "He's the man in charge here. His word is final." They parted in chilly silence.

Two days later, Ross observed a flurry of activity from the bench where he rested after a long walk around the compound. He felt stronger, he had to admit. The headaches were gone, and battered, bruised muscles no longer screamed in protest at the slightest exertion.

The past two days had been both interesting and puzzling. Everyone worked, he noticed. Trucks rumbled through the wood-framed, barbed-wire gate each morning headed for the citrus groves and vegetable plots. A Palmach member, carrying a rifle, sat in the rear of each vehicle. Boys too young to be field hands took turns climbing the water tower for sentry duty. Most of the women and older men disappeared after breakfast. Where did they disappear *to?* he wondered.

The people were friendly, but their reserve was embarrassingly evident. Ross's attempts to talk with the busy, harassed Amos proved fruitless. After his angry exchange with Ariel that first evening, Ross chose not to seek answers from her.

Ariel was excited but uncommunicative during the evening meal; she disappeared immediately thereafter. Ross assumed she was among the select few asked to meet with the obviously distinguished visitor who had been a passenger on the afternoon plane. She came for Ross just as he was preparing for bed.

"Ross, David Ben-Gurion is here," she said. "He wants to talk about the airlift you've put together. I'll take you to his hotel."

Ross's pique at being kept in the dark disappeared as Ariel introduced him to the Yishuv leader, then left them. The man radiated energy. The hour was late, and Ross knew that Ben-Gurion had had a grueling day, yet the man appeared alert and fresh for battle.

Ben-Gurion didn't offer to shake hands. Instead, he barked, "I'm happy to meet you, Colyer. I've heard what you're doing for us in the United States. I'm impressed, *and* grateful. Do you think you can really break this accursed blockade with airplanes?"

"Given secure airfields, yes, sir," Ross replied. "The term 'secure' presumes fighter cover, however. But by the end of this year we'll be capable of delivering fifty tons of cargo per day, from both the Western Hemisphere and Europe."

The pink-scalped leader blinked. "A bold statement, Colyer. My people estimate only a trickle."

"Your people don't know what I know about aerial transport operations, sir."

"Is this Julius Mantz's estimate? How is Julius, by the way?"

"It's my estimate, but Julius accepts it. He's showing the effects of fourteen-hour days and seven-day workweeks, though. By the way, he asked me to hand-deliver this letter to you."

The weary-faced Ben-Gurion accepted the envelope and nodded. "As are we all. Ariel tells me you are recovering from an unfortunate accident. How do you feel?"

"It was no accident," said Ross. "But I'll be able to fly in a couple of days."

"Good. I'm much encouraged by what you tell me. Tell Julius I send my warmest regards."

Ross stood and thanked Ben-Gurion, then went outside.

Ariel waited for him in the gloom surrounding an outdoor bench. "How did it go?" she asked softly.

Ross slumped beside her. "An amazing man," he replied thoughtfully. "Anyway, I'm ready to go back. When do you think you can arrange a ride for me?"

"Tomorrow night, I believe. But you need more rest."

"I'm not comfortable here. I feel like I'm in the way."

Ariel sat silently for a moment. "Amos be damned. You were right; you *are* entitled to know what's going on here. Ross, we're sitting on top of the Haganah's largest underground arms factory."

"*What?*"

"I didn't know. It was built after I left. Furthermore, they're using the very machine parts you helped deliver."

"*I* helped deliver?"

"That trip to Canada. The man you brought back was the inventor."

"I'll be damned. Is he here?"

Ariel shook her head. "No, he was angry that they didn't follow his design. Eddie told me it was a beautiful piece of work, but it required too much precision handwork for our primitive factory. What we're producing here uses his principle but is somewhat crude, compared to his standards. The man was paid and left in a huff. Eddie believes he went to South Africa."

Ross laughed. "So, an arms factory. That accounts for where the people in this kibbutz go every morning—as well as the cold shoulder I sense."

"Yes, and that's the reason I think you should leave. The British raid everyplace they suspect of manufacturing illicit arms. If you were to be arrested here, well—"

"It'd be a real mess," Ross finished for her. "I see what you mean. Okay, I'll leave tomorrow. What about you?"

"I can't." Ariel's voice was a barely audible whisper. "My place is here. I've come home."

5 October 1947
Haifa

Chris Wofford and Cal Thornton met Ross at the flying club. The cab ride to their hotel was mercifully short. Other than to assure the pair that he was okay, and to ask how they'd fared during the past few days, Ross didn't join in their desultory chatter. This damn curfew was going to be a royal pain in the ass, he told himself. Two more days was about all he could reasonably stretch a crew rest. During that time he had to make contact with the man whose name Julius had given him. All he had was the phone number for an underground member of Ben-Gurion's Yishuv staff.

"Join us in my room for a drink?" Wofford asked after Ross checked in.

"I think I'll pass, Chris," Ross answered vaguely. "I may look up a guy I know here—newspaper reporter. I'll maybe join him for a drink and dinner."

Ross used a pay phone in the lobby. The number Mantz had given him was answered after the third ring. *"European News,"* said a cheery voice.

"Hi, my name is Ross Colyer. I was told that an old friend of mine was assigned to your office—Andy Crutchfield. Is he around?"

"One moment, please," the voice advised. Ross could hear the hum of the hold key. Then, "Ross! You old rascal. What brings you to these parts?"

"Just passing through. I wondered if we might have dinner."

"Sure thing. Look, I'm chasing a deadline. How about dropping by the office—say sevenish? I'll be wrapped up by then; we'll do the town."

"Is that wise?" Ross asked. "I understand people here are sort of upset. And what about the curfew?"

"Aw, don't worry about that. News reporters have passes, and I know a place to eat that's guarded like Fort Knox. Just tell the cabdriver to take you to the *European News* office. I'll see you then, okay?"

Ross hung up and smiled wryly. Okay, if you say so, he grumbled to himself. The last time I had dinner in this town, the place was guarded by the entire fucking British army. And look what happened.

A sour-faced receptionist ushered Ross past a bank of clattering teletypes and shirt-sleeved individuals yelling into telephones. His guide stopped before a cluttered cubicle in a relatively quiet zone. A balding, middle-aged man with granny glasses perched on a thin, red-veined nose looked up. "Colyer?" he asked.

"Right. You must be Andy Crutchfield."

"Yep. Got any ID?"

Ross produced an Allied Air business card with a note on the back signed with an indecipherable scrawl.

"Okay," the man grunted. "We can talk here. We'll do business before we go to dinner. Now, what do you need?"

"Do you know why I'm here?" Ross asked.

"I do. I also know why you're late checking with me."

"Very well. I want to contact a man named Dov Friedman. He's a pilot—flies with the Jewish Flying Club."

Crutchfield leaned back and steepled his fingers. "I know Dov. No problem—he's here in Haifa right now, in fact. He's at large, but I don't think you should be seen together. I'll set up a meeting in the men's room at the restaurant. Can you finish what you have to say in ten to fifteen minutes?"

"I think so."

Ross backed away from the urinal, zipped up his pants, and turned to see two grinning faces at his elbow. One belonged to a short-haired blond, the other to a slight, balding man with a pockmarked face. The blond extended a hand. "Dov Friedman," he said. "The ugly runt here is Larry Perlberg. You must be the American deliveryman we were told to expect."

Ross smiled and shook the proffered hand. "How are the Cubs holding up?" he asked.

"Famously, thanks to you. Ariel told us you were responsible for getting them out of the U.S. Andy said you had business to discuss. We can't be in here too long."

"Right. We understand from your Paris office that Messerschmitts and other arms are available in Czechoslovakia. I'm headed there. What do you need?"

Dov whistled softly. "Wow. Yeah, we've put out feelers from here. Skoda is willing to do business, and the airplanes are available. But how do you plan to get the stuff from there to here?"

"I have a Lockheed Constellation—ten tons, two thousand miles."

Ross saw both sets of eyes light up. "Just what we need," Dov breathed. "But you aren't going to just casually breeze in here, land something the size of a Connie, unload ten tons of illegal arms, and take off into the blue again. We've already talked about trying to bring in the fighters, but we can't get permission to land and refuel anyplace in the Balkans."

Ross nodded. "I realize that. One of Mantz's men was on the Continent last month. He put feelers out in both Italy and France. Two airfields, one in Corsica and one in Italy, will look the other way while we unload. We'll take the wings off the fighters, load them on the Connie, then reassemble them there."

"Hallelujah!" both men exclaimed at once. "We can slip the guns in by boat—we're pretty good at that—and have the fighters within striking distance."

"Italy is damn near two thousand miles away, Dov," Ross observed.

"Yeah, but when the Brits pull out—and they will, if partitioning is rammed down their throats—a lot of attitudes in the Med are going to change. Take Greece and Turkey, for example."

"If you say so." Ross sighed. "Anyway, I'm taking off for Prague tomorrow or the next day. Can either or both of you come along? My American passport won't make me too popular in Czechoslovakia right now. The Czech government is miffed because we suspended forty million in foreign aid."

Friedman and Perlberg looked at each other. "One way or another, I'm going," Dov replied. "This is too good to pass up. Let old Andy out there earn his pay. Hopefully, he can produce some high-class paper and we'll both be aboard. I'll leave a message at your hotel."

Chapter 23

Ross clutched in the autopilot and watched the coast of Palestine drift behind. "Set climb power, Engineer. Your engines," he called to Cal Thornton. Dov had come forward and stood between the pilots' seats. Ross waved toward the copilot's position. "Chris, why don't you let Dov get a feel for a four-engine job?"

Dov strapped himself in and flashed a grin at Ross. "I'm impressed. You four-engine chaps have it easy. I was watching the flight engineer on engine run-up and takeoff. My old aunt could do your job; the engineer was doing all the important things. By the way, what is that little screen with the green squiggles he was playing with?"

Ross chuckled. "That's the engine analyzer. It gives you a picture of the ignition system primarily—much more accurate than watching the rpm needle for a mag drop. Now, Andy told me you were on board that ship, the *Exodus*. What the hell happened?"

Dov sobered. "That was as close to hell as I want to get. Forty-five hundred innocent refugees, most of them taken out of the Nazi death camps. The Brits fired on us—with *heavy* machine guns—and in international waters. They damn near sank us by ramming and trying to board. We finally had to give up. I swear they would have kept at it until they killed half our passengers.

"We made it to port, and the passengers were hustled off to detention camps. The Brits arrested the crew." Dov grinned. "In the confusion, this guy in a British uniform grabbed me, yanked me out of the line, called me all sorts of vile names, and hustled me into a truck. It was old Larry back there, all dressed up in a soldier suit. So the authorities didn't get my name. I'm back doing business at the same old stand."

Ross made a minor course adjustment and silently considered Friedman's bizarre tale. So, it had come down to open warfare. Firing on an unarmed vessel in international waters amounted to nothing less. The day is coming, Ross Colyer, when you're going to have to declare yourself, he mused. Someone—British, Arab, or whoever—is going to take a shot at you. Will you shoot back?

During the war, things had been simple, clear-cut. Ross's country was in danger. The enemy wore a distinctive uniform. If you saw one, you shot him. No decision to make, no questions asked. It was a duty; they gave out medals for it.

Take those British sailors. Did they see that unarmed ship as an enemy vessel? What would I do if I were one of those destroyer captains? Were they, right now, congratulating themselves for doing their duty?

More to the point, what would I have done if I'd been a passenger aboard the *Exodus?* Would I have shot back? Damn right!

Ross turned to Dov. "Okay, what do you suggest when we get to Zatec? I have the name of a man, Zlotky, in their ministry of trade. Should we see him first?"

"Well"—Friedman stroked his chin—"not right off, I think. The Communists are shaking the tree—Benes may lose his perch. If he does, Zlotky will go down with him. The government has been slow to get into the arms trade. The industrialists, on the other hand, are eager to get their hands on some hard currency, and the Communists are cheering them on. If they throw out the conservatives, they'll need cash—lots of it.

"Let's talk to the folks at the Skoda works first—see what the arms situation is. Then let's find out who can authorize the sale of some of those fighters. They're not the same Messerschmitts you saw during the war, by the way. The Diamler-Benz engine works was a war casualty. The Czechs put another engine in the Me 109 and named it the Avia S-199. It's a good airplane, I understand, but a real bitch to fly. The new engine is heavier and upsets the aerodynamics. In a nutshell, she's as unstable as a whore with a hangover."

Ross nodded, and the pair lapsed into silence.

*   *   *

"Field in sight," Chris announced. "You want to continue an instrument approach, or cancel and land VFR?"

Ross stretched weary shoulder muscles. "I'm pooped. Let's make a visual, okay? Give me the before-landing checklist. You copy, Engineer?"

"Roger," Cal answered crisply. "I make our landing weight a hundred twenty-two thousand. One-thirty-five approach speed; touchdown, one-oh-four."

Chris checked that Ross's comm selector was on VHF, then drawled, "Zatec Tower, this is Easy X-ray George, ten miles south, field in sight. Canceling IFR, request landing, over."

"Roger, Easy X-ray George. Zatec weather is one thousand five hundred meters, broken, visibility fifteen kilometers. Winds, light and variable. You are cleared to land runway three-two. Call tower on final approach, over." Ross nodded understanding. "Give me sixty degrees flaps. Gear down."

"Roger, flaps set, gear coming down," Chris responded. About to call, Landing checklist complete, he paused in midsentence. "We have an unsafe nose gear indication, Ross."

"Oh, shit!" Ross exclaimed disgustedly. "Cal, can you see any problems back there?"

"Negative, Captain," Thornton replied. "Hydraulic pressure is up and steady—no electrical malfunction that I can see. Are you going to recycle? It may be a sticking relay."

"No, one thing I learned in B-24s: don't retract what you have down and locked in a case like this. Too many pilots have ended up not being able to get *anything* extended again. Chris, call the tower. Request a flyby for a visual check. The damn thing may be down and locked with a faulty indicator."

Fifteen minutes later the tower operator confirmed that the nose gear doors remained closed. "Okay," Ross sighed, "tell them we'll orbit west of the field and attempt a manual extension. Go to it, Cal—see if you can get that stubborn bitch down by hand." Ross eased the power back to hold airspeed at 145 miles per hour and entered a lazy, oblong pattern, adding, "Get your manual out, Chris. Let's go over emergency landing procedures."

Cal finally entered the cockpit, wiping sweat from his dirt-grimed forehead. Ross took one look at the engineer's expression and made a wry grimace. "No joy, I take it?" he asked.

"Not a prayer. Best I can tell, the uplock linkage fractured. The emergency release doesn't have any resistance. If that's the situation, it would take a sledgehammer to release that uplock. First of all, I don't have a sledgehammer. Second, I can't get to the damn thing if I had one."

"Whooo-boy," Ross said with a gusty sigh. "Guess it's down to nut-cuttin' time, troops. I'll try one pass bouncing the main gear on the runway. They say that'll sometimes jar a sticky gear loose. I've never heard of it actually working, but who knows? Guys *have* been known to fill inside straights."

Ross crossed the airport boundary low and hot. The cockpit crew's bleak expressions reflected collectively held breath. Ross leveled off inches above the runway and allowed his airspeed to bleed off to 110 miles per hour. Feeling the plane sink slightly, he jammed the wheel forward. The Connie's main gear impacted with a jar that rattled loose equipment and caused the crew's heads to jerk forward. Ross immediately jammed all four throttles to their stops and eased back on the wheel.

The big, triple-tailed craft skimmed over the runway's far end, climbing rapidly. All eyes zeroed in on the offending nose gear position indicator. The red and white barber pole stared back.

"That's it," Ross muttered. He pressed his mike switch. "Zatec Tower, Easy X-ray George here. We'll have to land with a retracted nose gear. Request emergency equipment to stand by on the runway, over."

"Understand, Easy X-ray George. Alerting emergency crew now. How many souls aboard, over?"

"Five, over."

"Roger. Your remaining fuel?"

"Six thousand pounds—all in internal wing tanks."

"Roger. Will you be touching down on the runway or alongside, over?"

Ross hesitated. Landing gear-up on turf reduced the danger of fire from sparks. However, it was impossible to detect hidden obstacles, ditches, and the like from the air. They could turn a successful landing into a disaster. "On the runway, Tower," he replied.

"Understand. Be advised that we have diverted all traffic from the immediate area. You are cleared to land at pilot's discretion, over."

"Many thanks for your assistance, Tower," Ross replied. "See you on the ground in about, oh, four minutes, over." He switched to intercom. "Pilot to crew," he called. "I'll make one long orbit before turning final. Cal, are you all clear on your emergency procedures?"

"Roger. I'll jettison the overhead escape hatch on final. When do you want me to cut the switches?"

"Wait until the nose touches down. I want control boost right up 'til then. Now, go to the rear and see that everything loose is secured. Tell our passengers to come forward."

Dov and Larry entered the cockpit almost immediately. "Well, guys, your first landing in a big airplane is going to be one to remember." Ross smiled reassuringly. "Other than grinding a few inches off the nose, it shouldn't be too bad. I suggest you take seats by the rear cargo door. You know what to expect. Put a jacket or something on your knees and bury your face in it. When we come to a stop, jettison the cargo door and slide down that big rope stowed just aft of the red handle. You'll be damn near twenty feet off the ground, so don't jump."

Dov slapped Ross on the shoulder. "Piece of cake, old boy. First round will be on me tonight."

With her engines muttering softly, the Connie settled toward terra firma. As they swooped over the boundary fence, Chris called the airspeed: "One-fifteen . . . one-ten." Out of the corner of his eye, Ross saw the rotating red and blue lights of fire trucks and ambulances flash past. He rolled in trim to hold a nose-up attitude, then felt the controls grow mushy as Chris called, "One-oh-five, touchdown coming up."

Ross felt the main gear kiss the runway with that prolonged squeaking of a "paint job." The spinning wheels set up a rumbling vibration as more of the Connie's sixty tons of weight settled. With the control wheel sucked into his gut, he saw the nose start to settle. It passed the normal landing attitude and continued downward.

The nose touchdown was deceptively gentle. Although Ross knew that outside the scene would be one of screeching metal with a train of sparks spitting toward the rear, inside the cockpit it could just as well have been a normal landing. Try to keep her straight with the brakes, he muttered to himself; don't let her slew sideways. He saw the instrument panel turn dark as Cal cut the master switch. Engine noise faded to a dull whistle. Cal was right on the ball, Ross found time to observe.

Christ! Won't she ever slow down? he wondered. Everything seemed to be happening in slow motion. Then he saw the nose drifting left. He tromped on the right brake pedal but was powerless to stop the turn. They went off the runway with a gentle bump and began bouncing across green turf. "Settle down, baby," Ross murmured—then thought, don't collapse a main gear now!

He felt himself thrown against his restraining harness as the plane finally came to rest. The alarm bell clamored. Ross released his seat belt and scrambled up the sharply inclined flight deck toward the gaping escape hatch. He heard the dying wail of the emergency vehicles stop as they caught up with the crippled aircraft. It was a fitting epitaph not only to an airplane, but to their mission as well, he observed glumly.

Ross stretched on the hotel room's single bed and cradled the phone on his shoulder. "Jake?" he asked. "Yeah, I know what time it is there. Listen, we pranged the Connie landing here at Zatec." Ross listened briefly, then said, "Nope, no injuries, but the bird is a wipeout. Goddamn nose gear wouldn't extend. Thornton is out there now, helping get the plane moved off the field. I'll know more when he gets back, but I'm not optimistic. We'll come back by commercial air.

"Listen, call New York, tell them what happened, then call Murtaugh in Burbank. Tell him to light a fire under the War Assets people and break at least one of the other Connies loose. Put every man he has on it. We have to have one of the four-engine jobs flying, no matter what, understand?"

Ross replaced the phone and confronted his companions' long faces. Dov, Larry, and Chris were slumped in chairs, drinks in hand. "Well, troops, looks as if the show got canceled before the damn curtain even went up." Ross slammed the mattress with his fist. "Of all the rotten, miserable luck."

Dov cleared his throat. "Things like this happen, Ross," he said. "First of all, thanks to a masterful job on your part, we're all sitting here nursing our wounds with booze instead of being fed through a tube in some hospital room, or worse." He raised his glass.

"Yeah, there is something to be said for that," Ross said with a rueful grin. "I guess we may as well make our rounds while we're here. It sure screws up my swing through Europe, though. We can use the C-46s to carry guns, but we need a place to take them *to*. The fighters"—he shrugged—"will have to wait until we can put another Connie into service. *If* we can buy any of their damn fighters, that is. Well, let's get a good night's sleep—see how things look in daylight."

24 November 1947
New York City

Julius Mantz regarded his assembled project directors with a bemused smile. He'd outfitted his office with a long golden-oak table, its top scratched and marked with cigaret burns. He sat at its head. Ross occupied a seat at the opposite end. The team members regarded each other across the scuffed surface, exchanging uneasy looks and guarded comments. Why call a general meeting? It was a first—Julius had been adamant about not sharing information. Eddie Kotch, who hadn't spoken to Ross since their trip to Canada, sat contemplating the ceiling. Barnett and Ginsberg chain-smoked, drank coffee, and waited.

Mantz finally opened the meeting. "Slightly more than a year ago I met with each of you, individually, in this office. At that time the foundation had nothing more than a lease on this building, a few dollars in the bank, and a goal.

"It's a different picture today, eh? I won't render an accounting, but each of you has earned the undying gratitude of the Jewish people. Thanks to you, an impossible-looking dream is now within reach. Although much remains to be done, sources in the UN assure us that the resolution to partition will pass—by at least a sixty-forty margin."

Julius waited while grinning team members exchanged muttered exclamations of delight. The easing of tension was palpable. "When that happens," Mantz continued, "two significant changes will occur. One, the British will become our protectors so long as they remain in Palestine. Two, the Arab Legion will become our greatest threat. Our strategy must be changed accordingly."

"Talk about the lambs snuggling up to the lions," Moshe Barnett muttered. "The British will *have* to call off the blockade. They can't let a new nation be formed without the means to protect itself."

"Don't count on it," Ginsberg interjected. "If the Yishuv can't form a government, the British will have to stay. You'd better believe they're counting on that."

"A good observation, David," Julius said. "One that the foundation committee agrees with, I might add—and one of the reasons for this gathering. Ben-Gurion radioed a coded dispatch last night containing the current Palmach preparedness status. It's a frightening picture. The Palmach has only two to three thousand regular soldiers. Not all of the reserves have rifles, and those who do have only a handful of cartridges. Without tanks and armored cars, artillery, and combat aircraft, we face quick annihilation by a well-armed Arab force of superior numbers."

Mantz scanned the serious expressions his comments evoked. "British troops are seizing the product of our underground arms factories with ever-increasing frequency. The dismal picture I just gave you may have already worsened," he added somberly.

"The answer, gentlemen, lies in a massive airlift. Stockpile in friendly nations, then, on withdrawal of British troops, deliver those stores in one colossal effort."

Ginsberg broke the ensuing silence. "Manpower," he muttered dejectedly. "Of what use is a mountain of weapons if we have no one trained in their use?"

"Very little," Julius answered quickly. "Which brings me to the second reason I called you together. Ross Colyer just returned from a train trip through Europe. He made some very interesting discoveries. But before he relates the results of his trip, I have an announcement. I made the decision earlier, but I wanted to wait until Ross returned to tell you about it.

"Air transport and an airborne combat capability are essential. Because Ross is experienced in both, and because he has commanded military forces in the field, I'm naming him my deputy for operations. In the future, he will assume overall direction of both procurement and transportation. It's a big job. In fact, it has grown beyond my ability to directly oversee all of your projects and continue my role as diplomat and fund-raiser. I'm sure I can count on you all to give Ross the same wholehearted support you've given me."

Ross attempted to make eye contact with each of the shocked team leaders. Only Eddie Kotch met his gaze, and that look was hardly promising. Mantz waited a few moments, then spoke into the hostile silence. "Ross, you have the floor."

Mantz's new deputy crossed his arms on the table and leaned forward. "Julius tells me you are all tops in your field. From the little I've seen, I agree. I have no intention of telling you how to conduct your specific tasks. But the situation just changed this morning with our agreement that a new Jewish state depends on arms. Undeclared war exists, and we must place ourselves on a wartime footing.

"We're now an army. An army can function only with a free exchange of information. My first move, therefore, is to rescind the com-

partmentalization concept. I've discussed it with Julius, and he agrees."
Ross noticed three sets of eyes turn to Julius, who nodded.

"Every government agency you can name now has a file on the foundation and each of us," Mantz interjected. "Better we watch each other's back than to work in a vacuum."

"Look, I'm no mind reader," Ross continued, "but I think I can guess what you're thinking." He grinned. "I'm here to stay. Now, if any of you feel you can't work under this new arrangement, please advise Julius by noon tomorrow. The loss of any of you at this juncture would be a blow, but to stay on and let emotions interfere with duty could lead to a major disaster."

After a pause, during which no one spoke, Ross went on. "David, your concern is with the manpower levels and state of training. After we wrecked the Connie, I traveled Europe by rail. I found two locations that lend themselves to training camps. Ajaccio, on Corsica, and an airfield in Italy—Castiglione del Lago. Both have aircraft overhaul facilities—an ideal combination.

"You know," Ross leaned forward again and confided, "we have a stronger support base in Europe than we'd thought. Everywhere I went, France and Italy in particular, I had offers of under-the-table help. England, despite the shattered condition of her postwar empire, clings to her previous colonial mentality. Europeans resent that. So long as we don't flaunt our activities before the world and embarrass their governments, official heads will turn the other way.

"Moshe, there's a good chance we can obtain all the arms and airplanes we want in Czechoslovakia. Their Skoda arms works escaped the war virtually intact. They have surplus Me 109s coming out of their ears—at least their version, the Avia S-199. Transportation poses a headache but not an insurmountable obstacle. I think you and I should make a trip there.

"Now, I'll meet with each of you individually, to catch up on current projects. But I think this is a good time for a general rundown before the entire staff. Moshe?"

Barnett looked confused. "Well, Ross, uh . . ."

Moshe stumbled to a halt as Eddie Kotch rose. Kotch's jaw was set, his face a mottled pink. Ignoring Ross, he faced Julius. "I must have time to think about this new setup. I'll see you in the morning." Kotch stalked toward the door.

"Eddie," Ross called softly.

Kotch halted short of the door. Without turning, he uttered, "Yeah?"

"Eddie, I saw two of the Piper Cubs we got through the blockade—talked to a couple of the pilots. They keep a half-dozen kibbutzim open with those planes—kibbutzim the Arab guerrillas would have wiped out. I visited the underground arms factory where they're using the machine tools you and Moshe got to them around the clock. They send their thanks."

Kotch stood still for a moment, then left without speaking.

Ginsberg broke the embarrassed silence that followed. "How about Ariel, and her father?" he asked.

"Ariel stayed at the kibbutz," Ross replied slowly. "Ben-Gurion either gave her a new assignment or permission to do something stupid; she didn't say which. Her father is being held by the British in an old coastal fort at Atlit. He was able to get a message out—he's being treated well and is in good health."

David frowned. "You said something about her doing something stupid. What did you mean?"

Ross glanced at Julius. The older man sighed and answered for Ross. "An angry Irgun member falsely betrayed Ariel's father. She wants revenge."

Ginsberg's eyes widened. "Oh, my God," he muttered. "I'd hate to be in that guy's shoes if she ever catches him."

The next morning, Ross finished stacking his files in a cardboard carton and took a last look around his Allied Air office. He was searching a mental list for the name of someone to take it over when the phone set up a jangling echo in the empty room. He scooped up the receiver on the second ring.

"Ross? Bruce Murtaugh here. I have good news."

"I could use some, Bruce. What'cha got?"

"The Connies are flyable and four C-46s are ready for certification."

"Great!" Ross enthused. "Look, I was going to call you later this morning. There's been some changes at this end. Julius wants me to be sort of an overall coordinator; so I'm changing offices. Do you have someone there to leave in charge?"

"Yeah. You remember Johnson?"

"The one who helped us get that C-46 out ahead of the feds?"

"Right."

"He'll do. I want you to come back here and run Allied Air from this office. Bring the Connies on a one-time flight, and we'll do the mods here at Teterboro. The C-46s can operate out of Burbank for the time being. Jake Trask has the uncertified one at Tocumen, but we need to feed stuff to him faster than we've been able to with the DC-3. Got it?"

"Roger, roger, old buddy. I don't look forward to moving to New Jersey in the winter, but I'm on my way."

Ross carried the box of files into his new office and raised his eyebrows in surprise. Eddie Kotch occupied a chair facing Ross's desk. "'Morning, Eddie," Ross said evenly. "What can I do for you?" He took his seat behind the desk and waited.

"Ross," Kotch responded with a grim look, "I won't pretend to like this arrangement, but for Julius's sake I'll stay."

"I'm glad to hear it, Eddie. We're going to need your talents more than ever with partitioning upon us. This Friedman fellow I met in Palestine says the Arabs won't wait for the British to withdraw. They have an advantage now, and they'll start a war before the boundaries are even drawn."

"Yeah, that's the way I see it," Eddie mumbled ungraciously. "Anyway, I'm here to bring you up to date on the shipping business."

"Good. I'm anxious to hear how things stand."

"First off, I have a solution to most of our problems getting stuff into Palestine when the Brits decide to give us some room."

"Go ahead."

"I've bought an aircraft carrier," Eddie announced calmly.

"You've *what?*"

"You heard me. They call it a baby flattop. It's tied up at Norfolk, Virginia, waiting to be cut up for scrap. We formed a dummy company and told War Assets that we were bidding for a contract to haul lend-lease locomotives to Turkey."

"I'm almost afraid to ask how much you paid for it," Ross said with a sigh.

"Scrap prices—hundred and twenty-five thousand. "There'll be a cost to demilitarize it. The flight-deck overhangs have to be removed, the gun turrets immobilized—you know, things like that."

"And just what the hell do you intend to do with it after all that?"

"Think about it." Eddie's eyes sparkled as he warmed to his story. "We load it up with troops, tanks, artillery—whatever—and fill the deck with fighter planes. Then we sail it right into Haifa harbor. We can use the fighters to keep the Egyptian planes away; they're the only Arabs with any sort of air force. The planes can land at airfields we'll control by then. In one fell swoop, we will have armed the Haganah."

Ross gulped. "Eddie, you'll never in hell even get out of U.S. territorial waters with that kind of rig."

"Right," Eddie responded smugly. "We leave Norfolk empty, sail to Mexico, and load there. They have fighter planes for sale, and guns running out their ears. We can send the troops down there by train."

"What kind of fighter planes are we talking about?"

"P-40s."

"Off a *carrier?* Eddie, flying—catapulting—a loaded P-40 off a carrier, a baby flattop at that, takes skill and training—lot's of it."

"They did it during the invasion of North Africa," Eddie shot back. "They were army pilots. And how about Doolittle's raid on Tokyo? Hell, they flew B-25 *bombers* off a carrier."

"So that's what gave you the idea," Ross mused aloud. "Eddie, listen. The men who flew those P-40s were experienced fighter pilots; they had several hundred hours in the airplane. Ditto the B-25 pilots. They spent weeks practicing short-field takeoffs in Doolittle's case—even painted lines on a runway to replicate a flight deck. Those airplanes were fine-tuned to absolute max performance. Factory engineers computed exact fuel and ordnance loads.

"No problem, Ross. Now, you propose to round up a dozen or so pilots and mechanics off the street—some of whom haven't even *seen* a P-40—sail into some harbor in Mexico, and take on a load of airplanes that have been parked outside for months—flat tires and engines that won't start and all. Then you intend for this mixed bag to carry out a flawless mission? Really now."

"No Problem, Ross. We put the maintenance crews and spares on board and work on 'em at sea. We can find enough out-of-work ex—fighter pilots who can study the airplane en route."

"Eddie, Eddie," Ross moaned. "I accept the fact you're a genius at smuggling stuff past the British, but you know absolutely nothing about airplanes and the logistics of supporting combat troops and machines. Even if those crates can be made flyable, they'll need spare parts and maintenance crews at the other end. The idea is crazy."

"I knew you'd be against it," Kotch said sullenly, "just because it was my idea. But it can work, damnit. I'll go to Julius if you don't want to go along with it."

"You will *not* go to Julius—with this or anything else, Eddie." Ross's voice was harsh. "You heard the rules. I'm the boss when it comes to operations. You knew that when you agreed to stay. I'm not saying abandon the scheme—it's bold and imaginative. But I *am* going to think about it. Okay, what other little surprises do you have for me?"

Eddie glared. "We're shipping out ten tons of TNT today."

Ross could only gape. Kotch went on, "Not the pure stuff, actually. Demolition blocks. It'll be used to make mines, blow up buildings—you can even make crude hand grenades with it, I'm told."

"How and from where?" Ross asked quietly.

"New Jersey—by ship. It's due to be loaded this afternoon. I'm going down to keep an eye on things. Want to come along?" He cocked a derisive eye.

Ross hesitated only fractionally. "I'll get my coat."

Ross turned his back to the icy November wind slicing across the exposed pier. He and Eddie moved through the cavernous shed's open doorway and watched as longshoremen, collars turned up and knit stocking caps pulled over their ears, manhandled a telephone booth–sized crate alongside a rusting freighter. The container was boldly stenciled: USED INDUSTRIAL EQUIPMENT. Fifty to sixty other similarly labeled crates were scattered on the shed's asphalt floor. Just beneath the label, they bore an identical destination: PALESTINE.

The clamor of dockside activity prevented Ross from hearing what was said, but he saw a plume of vapor emerge from the mouth of a checker as he called something to the crew attaching a sling to one of the crates. The checker made an upward, spiraling motion to the crane operator. Steel cables tightened, and the crate began to rise.

Ross watched a wind gust catch the laden sling, turning it into a huge pendulum. As the crate neared the freighter's deck, eighteen to twenty feet in the air, a poorly nailed board yielded to the strain. Ross watched it pop loose. Then the next board gave way. A black box about the size of a footlocker slid through the opening. Their eyes wide with dismay, Ross and Eddie watched the box tumble to the pier, where it landed with an audible crunch. Ross saw beads of moisture gather on Eddie's upper lip.

An angry dock foreman signaled for the crane operator to lower the damaged container back to the pier, then trotted to where a group of men warmed their hands over a fire of scrap wood blazing in an empty oil drum. One of the men nodded, picked up a toolbox, and trudged toward the splintered black box. He surveyed a half-dozen square metal cans and started placing them back in the box. He stared, then jerked upright. A spurt of vapor was the only sign he'd yelled for help.

Even from where Ross stood, he could read the letters TNT, followed by Corps of Engineers, U.S. Army. Eddie Kotch rolled his eyes upward, grasped Ross's elbow, and urged him toward a door opening onto the street behind them. Back in the car, Ross asked, "What now? Jesus Christ, what a disaster. What if that stuff had gone off?"

"It takes more than just a fall to set off those demolition blocks," Kotch answered morosely. "If something had blown, however, there was enough of the fucking stuff to give Jersey City a new deepwater port. Twenty-five crates of TNT. As if that isn't enough, the other thirty crates hold parts of a machine used to manufacture ammunition. The explosion is going to come when that dock foreman gets around to calling the FBI."

"Are we in trouble?" Ross asked.

"Not likely. They can only trace the shipment to a freight-forwarding warehouse in Trenton—a dummy company. The signatures on the paperwork covering the purchase belong to men a thousand miles from here. But the FBI will come calling on us, never fear. We'll have to make some changes in the future."

11 December 1947
Cairo
Hafez, wrinkling his nose at the odor of rotting garbage and slops, guided the Alfa Romeo down a dark, littered alley between the great walled mosque and an abandoned, dilapidated warehouse. He paused at a pair of sagging, rusty, wrought-iron gates and, as instructed, flashed his high beams. An ancient, skinny servant, his white robe and turbaned head a pale blur in the gloom, rushed to unlock and open the barrier. After parking alongside a dust-coated Land Rover, Hafez tugged at a tasseled bell pull dangling beside a heavy wooden door.

The man who responded was obese. He wore a short-sleeved white shirt that strained across his massive paunch, and black trousers that could have housed camels. A broad smile was barely visible beneath a luxuriant black mustache. Dark eyes twinkled from pouches of fat as he greeted Hafez. "*Ahlan wusahlan!*" he boomed. "Enter this humble dwelling and be comfortable."

A half-dozen men lounged on cushions scattered along the walls.

One wore a white *gullabiya* and the pleated skullcap, resembling a baker's hat, of a sheik; the others wore Western dress. Colonel Nasser waved a languid hand without speaking. Hafez chose a seat as a stooped, black tunic–draped woman scuttled into the room with mint tea and sticky date confections.

Nasser started speaking as the servant left the room. "Conditions worsen. Prime Minister Nuqrashi openly favors a negotiated settlement in Palestine. He sits idly by while Jews smuggle huge amounts of gold and weapons from our country, all the while 'guaranteeing' Egyptian Jews his full protection. His nickname, 'the timid sphinx,' is most apt. The army is without direction and ill prepared to fulfill its role if an incursion into Jewish Palestine becomes necessary." Nasser paused and sighed deeply before continuing.

"Alas, our Arab brothers are far from acting from purely altruistic motives either. Britain's puppet, King Abdullah, aspires to join Palestine with Transjordan and rule the whole. Since a partitioned Palestine—separate Jewish and Arab independent states—is intolerable, Egypt must dominate the territory south of the Sea of Galilee. And without a British presence!

"Even now, certain steps are being taken. The Muslim Brotherhood is openly recruiting volunteers to aid the Palestinian Arabs. The brigade they infiltrated earlier to foment terrorism and train saboteurs inside Palestine has been a proven success; witness the King David Hotel incident last year. The Jewish Irgun took credit without knowing that Egyptian explosives and know-how were responsible.

"Here at home, demonstrations against the British and destruction of their facilities will be stepped up tenfold. Tomorrow, the Grand Ulema of al-Azhar University will declare a jihad against the Zionists. During an Arab League meeting last week, a secret agreement was reached to provide the league's military committee with ten thousand rifles and one million pounds sterling for the defense of Palestine. In return, Syria will permit passage of three thousand volunteers—the Muslim Brethren—into Palestine."

Hafez sat transfixed, drinking in every word. War is inevitable! he exulted silently. The time had come to show his mettle. But—a big but—how? Unless the regular army was to be involved, he and his fighter squadron would be relegated to the sidelines. Join the volunteer army? His talents as a commander of ground troops were nonexistent. Nasser's next words cheered him.

"The time for bold, decisive action is upon us, gentlemen. The volunteer army, no matter how dedicated, how well trained and armed, cannot carry out an attack without tanks and airplanes. If the government refuses to act to protect our interests in Palestine, the Free Officers, in conjunction with the Muslim Brethren, are prepared to assume control of the country."

A hiss of collective indrawn breaths preceded a period of absolute silence. After a dozen heartbeats, the stern-faced Nasser turned to a saturnine-looking figure and asked, "General Roushdi, are you prepared to stand for the Brotherhood and lead your tanks in support of an incursion?"

After a slight hesitation, the general replied, "If the king fails to recognize Egypt's destiny, I will act."

Nasser nodded as if he already knew the answer and stared at Hafez. "Squadron Leader Kamil, how do you stand?"

Hafez's mind raced. What the man spoke of was nothing short of treason. If the coup failed, its ringleaders could expect to lose their heads or, at best, be expelled from the army in disgrace. However, if the conquest of Palestine was successful, and the English were driven from Arab land, he—Hafez—would easily become a general, commander of the entire air arm!

Nasser appeared to be growing impatient. Hafez gulped as unobtrusively as possible. Forcing his voice to be firm and even, he said, "I stand with General Roushdi, Colonel Nasser."

Chapter 24

17 December 1947
Washington, D.C.

Janet paused in the doorway of the Willard's sumptuous dining room and scanned the seated patrons. A haughty maître d' materialized at her elbow. "Good-afternoon. Does madam have a reservation?"

"Uh—no. I'm to join a Mister Henderson."

"Yes, ma'am. Mister Henderson is expecting you. Follow me, please."

Janet trailed in the stiff-backed man's wake, conscious of admiring glances. By God, I *should* attract some attention, she thought. I spent enough time deciding what to wear. She'd ended up selecting an oxford gray suit with a faintly mannish cut. A high-necked white blouse with a touch of lace at the throat and plain black pumps with three-inch heels added a feminine touch. She spotted Clayton Henderson's six-foot three-inch frame slouched before a linen-draped table, and discreetly waved glove-clad fingers.

She saw her ex-boss's eyes light up behind thick glasses as he unfolded his lanky frame and greeted her with open arms. "Janet, what a treat. My God, you look as ravishing as ever."

Janet accepted a bear hug, then stepped back and quipped, "You don't look so bad yourself—for an older man."

"Watch that," Henderson shot back with mock severity. "I may be forced to strip right here in public and display my youthful figure."

Janet responded with a tinkling laugh as Henderson continued. "I'd like you to meet Ed Adair, Janet; he's the INS honcho here in

Washington. Ed, this is the gal I was telling you about—an old friend
and a helluva news hawk."

Adair gave her a warm smile and extended his hand. "Clayton didn't
do you justice, Mrs. Templeton. He's usually more effusive when
describing beautiful women."

Janet returned the firm handshake and made a quick assessment. A
handsome man, she decided. He had a friendly, suntanned face, dark
hair with a hint of gray, and a compact, athletic build. Those widely
spaced gray eyes missed very little, she surmised. She took an instant
liking to him.

Henderson seated her and ordered martinis without asking. She saw
him glance at the slim leather portfolio she placed on the floor beside her chair. "Well, I suppose you heard the news this morning. Your
esteemed father-in-law formally announced what most people were
predicting. He'll oppose Truman at the Democratic convention. What's
your reaction?"

Janet made a sour face. "A national disaster," she responded, "if it
comes about."

"*If?*" Henderson asked.

"If. But more—much more about that later."

"Well, bring me up to date, my dear," her old boss said briskly.
"What have you been up to?"

Janet gave Henderson a carefully edited version of her work with
the *Globe.* Lunch was consumed between exchanges of anecdotes and
casual observations about current events.

After they were down to coffee, Henderson turned to business. "Janet,
I've known Ed for a long time; I've told him what little I know about
the article you're upset about and your wanting to make a move. You
can speak freely. Now, what's your problem?"

"Last spring, my editor—"

"Max Foley," Henderson interrupted. Adair nodded understanding.

"He gave me a chance to try my hand at a feature article," Janet
continued. "Rumors were circulating even then that Senator Templeton
would make a run for the presidency and Foley thought it was a good
story for me to tackle.

"I didn't know what to do. You see, Foley wasn't aware that I hated
the man. If I turned down the chance to show what I could do, I'd
probably not get a second chance. I talked it over with a friend and
decided to go ahead; I'd make it factual—not a spite piece—but neither would it be a glowing eulogy."

Henderson nodded silently.

"Anyway," Janet continued, "when Foley saw my first draft, he rejected it. Not because it wasn't highly laudatory, but because he claimed it showed Templeton to be anti-Semitic. I couldn't believe it—the piece isn't anti-Semitic at all; it hardly mentions the senator's position on the Palestine question. But Foley still spiked it, said he'd run it by the editorial board when he thought the time was right."

Henderson chuckled. "But *you* think it's a burial, not a delay."

"I do. I believe he's afraid of Nate Green's reaction, and I can't understand why. But it doesn't matter, personal bias isn't a reason to suppress information the public is entitled to know."

Henderson pursed his lips and concentrated on stirring his coffee. "I'd almost bet you have the draft in that portfolio," he said finally.

"Yes, I do. I wish you'd read it."

"I'd dearly love to read it, Janet, but I'm not going to," Henderson said after some thought. "And I doubt that Ed will either." He glanced at Adair, who remained expressionless. "Let me tell you why. You were on the *Globe*'s payroll when you wrote the piece. It's still their property, to do with as they please. Furthermore, while Foley may have been excited about your relationship to the senator, I'm not. It makes you a biased reporter."

Henderson gave Janet time to absorb his words, then continued. "For another publisher to even print paraphrased extracts of an original work without permission is a violation of ethics, and possibly the law.

"But INS will be looking into the good senator's background, now that he's announced. When we do, I don't want to be influenced by words I have no right to use—especially words written by a biased reporter."

Janet seethed inwardly but forced herself to speak without undue emotion. "I know that, Clay, and I understand your position. Look, Foley or Green can say anything they damn well please in their editorials, but the fact remains that they're using their personal subjectivity to censor news. I don't want to work for them anymore."

Both men nodded. "I can understand your frustration, Mrs. Templeton—Janet," Adair said. "But Clayton is right. Still, he speaks very highly of you. If you are determined to leave the *Globe,* I may be able to offer you something."

"That's great news, Mister Adair. I'm most interested, but I've saved the best for last."

"Aha," Henderson chortled. "You learn fast. We're all ears."

"When Foley spiked my story, I had already arranged an interview with a source who claimed to have some really sensational information. I kept the appointment."

"And?"

"This person told me about an unrecorded cash contribution to Senator Templeton's campaign—fifty thousand dollars."

"Yes?" Henderson looked puzzled.

"Yes. The money was from a wealthy New York Jew."

Henderson and Adair exchanged questioning looks. "Wait a minute," Henderson mused aloud. "Templeton has been most vocal in opposing Truman's insistence on higher immigration quotas for Jews waiting to enter Palestine, halting arms sales to all Middle East countries, and the UN partitioning resolution. Now you're saying that the man is getting backing from the Jews? That doesn't make sense!"

"Clayton, my father-in-law—I prefer to think of him as my *ex*–father-in-law—learned the fine art of bribery and executing the double-cross on the elementary-school playground. He boasted that he never lost a game of blindman's buff. But you can bet the old homestead that he's made a promise of *some* kind that the Zionists believe is worth fifty thousand dollars."

Adair gave a soft whistle. "How do you suppose he plans to do a switcheroo, providing he intends to play straight with this anonymous contributor after he's elected?"

"I suggest you don't even try to guess," Janet said dryly. "I saw him change sides three times on use of the B-17 bomber during the war. Each time he had the most plausible-sounding reasons on earth."

Adair drummed the tabletop with manicured fingernails. "Your source?"

"I'm sorry, sir."

The bureau chief grinned. "Just checking. Is he reliable?"

"I didn't say it was a 'he,' Mister Adair. But yes, I consider the source to be gilt edged."

"Verification with a second source?"

"Not yet—and frankly that may prove difficult."

"Very well. But first, let's talk about your employment situation. Just now, we're getting our news from Palestine via a stringer in Tel Aviv. He's prolific, and he's sending good stuff. But we're having a problem developing our own editorial policy. The reading public is divided on the Palestine issue, and our subscribers are sensitive to any hint of bias in what we put on the wire. We can use another rewrite specialist. Plus, the research you've obviously put in on your article will be invaluable background. I can only offer you a temporary job, but with the way things are going, I think we'll soon have need for a separate Palestine desk."

"I see." A puzzled frown creased Janet's forehead. "And the Templeton piece?"

Adair sighed. "Mrs. Templeton, haven't you heard a thing we've been saying? Your relationship to the senator forces me to pull you off that story."

Adair tried to read Janet's reaction. "I'm sorry, I know how you must feel, but let me continue. I can bring in a freelancer—I know two who'll do handsprings to get this story. And instead of bringing you in to do rewrite, I'll hire you as an associate editor; the freelancer will be assigned to you. You'll be in charge, but the story won't carry your byline. If it's as hot as it appears to be, then of course there'll be a bonus. That's the best I can do, Janet."

"Clayton?" Janet gave Henderson an anguished look.

Henderson shook his head. "Look, I've done all I can. I won't advise you, Janet. If you decide to take Ed's offer—it's more than fair in my opinion—I think you'll like being in Washington again. But before I shove off and let you two haggle over terms, I'd like to give you both some food for thought—okay, Ed?"

"You're the old master, Clay," Adair replied with a wide grin.

"Very well. Janet, what you've told us doesn't add up. I know Nate Green. He's a Democrat who hates Truman. I'm sure you've detected this in the *Globe*'s editorial policy." He made his deceptively benign look a question.

"Yes," Janet replied. "I assumed that's why Foley wanted a pro-Templeton piece."

"Right. But Green *is* a staunch Zionist. I'm suggesting that Templeton having taken a contribution from a supposedly Jewish source isn't earthshaking. Sorry, Janet, but politicians are free to accept contributions from anyone foolish enough to make them. The story is in *who* laid out that kind of money and *why*. Now, when I start collecting facts that don't add up, I run for the old spade. Need I say more, Ed?"

"You're coming through loud and clear, Clay." Adair's expression resembled a hungry shark's. "And I know exactly where to start digging. There's an organization that calls itself the Jewish Relief Foundation. They've been buying stuff from the War Assets Administration like there was no tomorrow—embargoed war materiel they're smuggling to the Palestinian Jews. This is going to be fun."

Neither man noticed Janet's stricken look as she turned her face up for Henderson's farewell peck on the cheek. "You're a prince, Clay," she murmured. "I don't forget people who do favors for me—and I have a long memory."

She turned toward Adair. "I—I'm sorry. May I take time to think things over? This is all more complicated than I'd anticipated. You see, there's another aspect—a personal one—I have to consider."

"Of course. I'm glad to see you look before you leap. This can be a dynamite story. Imagine having the issue of the presidency in your hands; it scares even me. Take your time, but I need an answer by February."

30 January 1948
Alexandria, Virginia

Doris Wilson flung both arms around Janet. "What a pleasant surprise! Oh, I'm glad to see you." Doris backed away. "And you look like a million dollars. How do you do it?" She surveyed her own full figure and added ruefully, "Every time I see you, I vow to lose ten pounds."

Janet chuckled. "Stop that. You have the sexiest figure in Washington."

"That's kind of you," Doris replied. "I keep telling Ted that, but I really don't believe it. Hey, let's not stand outside all day. Come on in. I have chicken salad for lunch, and the sherry bottle is where it's always been."

"Oh, no you don't," Janet said, laughing, as she followed her friend into the den. "I recall the last time you fed me wine all afternoon. I vowed to avoid you forevermore. Well—maybe one glass for old time's sake."

Doris gave her a wicked grin. "And another one to celebrate your new job—right here in D.C. I can't wait to hear about it."

Janet bit her lip. "There may not *be* a new job. As I told you on the phone, I have an offer, but . . . that's what I wanted to talk with you about."

"Oh?"

"Doris, you once gave me the best advice I've ever had—that time you told me to strike out and make my own life after BT was killed. I'm back now for a second helping."

"Goodness. This sounds grim. Maybe I should make yours a *big* glass."

Janet's chuckle was without mirth this time. "I only wish that's all there was to it. I've gotten myself in one big mess."

Doris poured, handed Janet her glass, and joined her on the sofa. "Okay, what's bothering you?"

"I want the job with INS, but there are conditions. They gave me time to make up my mind, only my time is up and I'm still undecided. Ross is involved, Doris."

"My favorite guy," Doris replied promptly. "What's he done now? Has that rascal tried to ravish you? If so, did you do the sensible thing and submit?"

"*Doris.*" Janet felt her cheeks flush. "I refuse to discuss my personal relationship with Ross just now. And, besides, it's none of your damn business."

Doris whooped with laughter. "I'm sorry," she said, wiping her eyes. "I'll find out one way or the other. Go on."

"Doris, please. This is serious. Do you know about a contract Ross has with an outfit called the Jewish Relief Foundation?"

"Yeah, he told Ted it saved his company."

"Well, it may also land him in prison."

Doris sobered. "How so?"

"That so-called foundation is a front organization to buy arms for the Jews and smuggle them into Palestine. We're talking millions of dollars worth of stuff. Ross is right in the middle of things—he's become their director of operations."

"That doesn't sound like Ross," Doris mused aloud. "I assume you've talked about it with him."

"Not really—not in depth, anyway. And therein lies my problem. You see, my editor spiked the story I did on Senator Templeton. That's why I went to INS looking for a job.

"But there's more. INS offered me a position because I dug up an under-the-table contribution to Templeton's campaign fund from an anonymous Jewish source in New York. This all came to light *after* the *Globe* killed my profile of the senator.

"My new boss doesn't want me to write the story—says I'm too close to the senator. He plans to bring in a freelancer. I'm to be this person's editor because I've done the preliminary background, but I won't have control of the new research."

"I'm sorry, Janet. I'm not following you. What does all this have to do with Ross?" inquired Doris, her brow wrinkled.

"Listen to this. Ed Adair, INS's Washington bureau chief, thinks that the Jewish Relief Foundation is the most logical source for the mysterious campaign contribution. He sees a bigger story in that than in their arms-smuggling operation, especially if you tie the two together."

"Oh, m'God. When the story breaks, then Ross—"

"Exactly. I *must* get word to him. Doris, I'm blabbing my head off telling you something I shouldn't be breathing a word about, but I'm at my wit's end. Please, don't repeat any of this—even to Colonel Ted—please?"

"My lips are sealed, gal. Trust me. But I—I don't know what to tell you. I'm sorry. Christ, what a mess."

Janet heard the mantle clock chime twice. "Oh, I have to get back to the city. I'm supposed to give Ed Adair my answer by five o'clock."

Doris crossed to the little corner bar and refilled their glasses. "Are you maybe taking this reporting job a bit too seriously?" she asked.

"In this business, you're either a professional or a hack. I aim to be a professional—and I'll be damned if I'm going to see Broderick Templeton in the White House."

Doris released a gusty sigh. "There's a time to be guided by your heart and a time to be guided by your head," she said slowly. "There's also a time to do something and a time to do nothing. You're afraid of losing Ross, aren't you? You want him, but you're afraid that if you follow through with this story business, he'll walk."

Janet didn't respond. Her face was pale and her jaw set.

"Are you two sleeping together?" Doris asked relentlessly.

Janet glared at her friend. In a barely audible voice she said, "We tried."

"*Tried?* Jesus Christ, Janet, you're a widow. Do you maybe need more training?"

"That's enough, Doris."

"Okay, okay. Well, it's a decision only you can make. But if it were me, *I'd* get that guy into bed and try to talk some sense into him. I have faith in Ross doing the right thing—don't you?"

Janet's lips twisted. "That's what I like about you. You're so delicately subtle and tactful." She stood and retrieved her purse. "You also have a way of putting things into perspective—like, just how much is a free lunch worth? I have some more thinking to do, I guess."

Doris followed Janet to the door, one hand on her shoulder. Giving her pensive guest a squeeze, she murmured, "I also have faith in *you* doing the right thing, Redhead."

Tears filmed Janet's eyes and she stumbled, almost missing the front step.

*   *   *

The apartment management had thoughtfully installed room phones with extra-long cords. Janet carried the telephone in one hand as she paced. "Ross, thank God I tracked you down."

"Hey, you sound like the world is coming to an end," Ross said. "Trouble?"

"Make that plural. Do you remember that night in Chicago—I told you I was working on an article on Senator Templeton?"

"Yeah. You were afraid it would be killed."

"It was, but it led to something else."

Ross chuckled. "You do get around, don't you? What are you into now?"

"You realize that I'm violating professional ethics by just discussing work in progress with you, don't you?"

"I'm not unaccustomed to dealing with classified information, Janet," Ross replied dryly.

"Your Jewish Relief Foundation is under investigation. Did you know that?"

"Now, first off, it isn't *my* Jewish Relief Foundation. And it doesn't surprise me to hear they're under investigation, but by whom?"

"Half the agencies in the U.S. government, that's who. You have to bail out of that contract you have with them—and stop having anything to do with the organization, like buying airplanes—do you understand?"

"Janet, slow down. What does this have to do with your article on our mutual friend?"

"I can't discuss the connection, even with you, Ross. But that isn't the point. The investigation will go on regardless of what I write. Do you know *everything* that outfit is up to?"

"Probably not, but please listen closely. You say you can't discuss your story; well, I can't discuss the foundation. But I'm doing what I believe is right, *and*"—he slowed his speech and emphasized each word—"I'm keeping my options open, *every* option. Does that ease your mind?"

Janet heaved a deep sigh. "I don't know why it should," she replied crossly. "Ross, damnit, I wish you would talk with me about this."

"I can't. I'll explain it all someday; that's the best I can promise." His voice softened. "You're putting your neck on the block by telling me this much, aren't you?"

"Maybe, but I have something else we *can* discuss. I suppose you heard that Templeton formally announced he's going to run against Truman."

"I heard."

"You know he opposes help for the Palestine Jews."

"I know."

"What would you say if I told you he recently accepted a fifty thousand dollar contribution from a Jewish source? We need second source verification, but it happened, believe me."

Following a protracted silence, Ross said, "That's surprising, to say the least. You obviously think it's from the Jewish Relief Foundation. Is this the subject of the project you can't discuss?"

"Ross, please don't ask questions. Just get out of that mess. Now, I have one other thing to tell you—something I haven't even told INS about."

"You're developing into a real Mata Hari, aren't you? I'm listening."

"When I was packing to move, I came across the box of BT's personal possessions they shipped back after he was killed. I'd never looked closely at the stuff before, but I found a letter to BT from his father that I'd like you to see. It concerns something I heard during the Ploesti hearings. They talked of an overnight change in mission leaders."

"That happened, all right."

"Ross, I can't be sure, but I think from something in this letter that the senator had a hand in the change."

"*What?*"

"It's sort of obscure, but was General Sprague given the lead position at the last minute?"

"Yes, he replaced White One as lead only shortly before takeoff. That's when I was pulled from my briefed slot to fly his plane."

Janet sighed. "I think you'd better read this. I'll mail it tonight."

"Please do. My God, this is unbelievable. Janet, I know this call took a lot of soul-searching—I'm touched. I—I . . . may I make a suggestion?"

"By all means. As you can tell, I'm concerned."

"Okay. Don't worry about me. Dig hard and deep on that contribution. Put all the details you can reveal in that letter and send it along with Templeton's by air-mail special delivery. I just may be able to find that second source verification you need."

"You *what?*"

"Trust me, and hang in there. You're one in a million, gal."

Chapter 25

7 February 1948
Rialto Theater, New York City
Ross made his way through the theater's fetid gloom to a center seat near the back. He waited for his eyes to adjust to the semidarkness, then looked around for Hank Wallace's distinctive profile. The place doesn't look any different than last time, thought Ross. Christ, is that the same drunk snoring two rows up? Ross glanced at the screen. At least the feature had changed—a moonlit tropical-island beach this time. As he watched, a dusky, nubile girl emerged from the surf and shook seawater from her waist-length tresses. Her wet sarong emphasized melon-sized breasts with prominent nipples.

Ross shook his head, then saw Wallace take an adjoining seat. "How many times have you sat through this one?" Ross's barely visible companion asked.

"You're late," Ross growled.

"Never. Your letter—you sounded upset."

"Damn right. Ariel Shamir was sent home. I thought your people were going to take care of the situation?"

"We didn't see that it mattered—not enough to call in a chit anyway."

"*Didn't matter?*" She'll get herself killed over there. That doesn't *matter* to you?"

"She's an enterprising young woman—a survivor. We don't think she's apt to get in over her head."

Ross clenched his fists and sat silently, not trusting himself to speak. Finally he asked, "What have you done to verify that business of a Jewish contribution to Senator Templeton's campaign?"

"We're working on it."

"Oh, great. I feel much better. It could be the lever to get that flag pulled from my personnel records, you know."

"It'll help." Wallace chuckled. "You might be surprised to learn that the publicity you got during that mercy mission last fall is a better lever. Templeton will be hard-pressed to go public with his objection to your appointment. Plus, there's been a big shake-up in the Pentagon. The air force finally gained its independence from the army last summer and started wearing blue suits—but hell, you know that. More importantly, they've streamlined my outfit. We're now the Central Intelligence Agency. Someone decided CIA sounds better than CIG. But with the name change came a big personnel shuffle. It'll be a while before things settle down after they sort out who won the game of musical chairs."

"Just so you deliver," Ross grumbled. "I have something else I didn't put in the letter."

"Oh?"

"Yeah. Something I didn't trust to whatever roundabout system you use for getting messages."

"Oh, shit."

"Don't give me that. This is an original and I decided to hand-deliver it."

"Well, now that you've dragged me down here when I could be home watching my new television set, let's have it."

"It's a letter," Ross said as he handed over a square envelope of heavy, expensive stationery. "I think you'll find it interesting."

"I can't wait. But you know it's too dark to read it in here—what does it say?"

"What I *think* it says is that during the war, our illustrious servant of the public, Senator Broderick Templeton, tampered with the low-level raid on Ploesti. A lot of men may have needlessly died as a result."

Even the phlegmatic Wallace couldn't restrain a sharply indrawn breath. "You *think?*" he asked impatiently.

"That part of the letter is worded in a cryptic, obscure manner. You see, there was an overnight change in mission commanders: General Brereton, who had planned the raid, was replaced by General Flynt, who had barely been in on the planning. Brigadier General Sprague was moved into a high-profile slot, leading the second wave. Templeton's son, BT, was Sprague's aide."

"And you flew left seat for Sprague," Wallace said softly.

"You've done your homework."

"What do you think happened?"

"I think Sprague planted a seed with Templeton that Brereton was in possession of plans for the invasion of Italy—that was one explanation given later—and couldn't run the risk of being captured. During the shuffle that followed, Sprague manipulated himself into a glory-grabbing position."

"Why would the senator go along with a stupid thing like that?"

"He cut a deal. He would help Sprague reap a bunch of publicity, and certain promotion. Sprague, in turn, would swing the military vote when our upstanding example of political integrity ran for president. Oh, yes, according to Janet, he had aspirations way back then."

"Does the letter spell that out?"

"Not in clear language. One sentence reads, 'Tell S it's a deal. B will not be a player, nor will some others.'"

"Not exactly what you'd call the bloodstained blunt instrument," Wallace observed. "What am I supposed to do with this?"

"Get hold of the transcript of an army board of inquiry convened in late '45 to determine why our losses were so high at Ploesti. If there is no clear explanation, it might prove interesting to hear the senator's version—in public."

"Hmm. Like I told you, we'll work on it." Wallace stood and patted Ross's shoulder. "Just play your cards as they come up, guy; you're doing great. Now, I got a report to deliver. Somehow, I think the chief is gonna enjoy this."

Ross watched the agent amble through the doorway. Minutes later he realized that he hadn't gotten around to asking Wallace how far his so-called immunity from prosecution *did* extend.

4 March 1948
44 Water Street
Ross finished reading the tenth, and last, page of Dov Friedman's letter. Hand-carried by a messenger aboard the previous day's Pan American arrival from Portugal, the missive was laden with bad news. Ross commenced rereading portions:

Ariel is living in the kibbutz she took you to last fall. I
don't know how long they can hold on. The Arabs are wild.
They refuse to accept partitioning and are bent on wiping
out all Jewish settlements. Ramat Hakovish is subjected
to raids at least once a week. I've been there twice trying
to help. Ross, it's pitiful. Our air support consists of the
light planes the British allow the flying club to use.
We've removed the doors and put a man in the backseat
with all the hand grenades and homemade bombs we
can carry.

It's a matter of trying to find a concentration of Arab men
and vehicles, then hoping the "bomb chucker" can hit them by
throwing grenades. How primitive can you get! Just now, the
British have started pulling out of their peripheral outposts—
anticipating the 15 May date when their mandate expires. The
Arabs are right on their heels, occupying every fortified town
or base vacated. The Arabs have declared a general strike. The
Brits don't lift a finger to keep them from killing and looting.

I think more and more of those fighters parked in Czechoslovakia. We've had arms buyers looking at them; the guns
and planes are there for the taking. We just can't transport
them here. The blockade is every bit as tight as before, maybe
more so. We were able to get one shipment of small arms
smuggled across Romania, and we salvaged a cargo of stuff
bound for Syria aboard a ship we sank, but we're in a bad
way. 15 May is looking more and more like the end instead of
a beginning. Ross, we need an airlift. Can you possibly help?

Ross snapped on the overhead lights as Bruce Murtaugh, Eddie Kotch,
and Moshe Barnett seated themselves around his desk. Returning to
his chair, Ross rubbed red-rimmed, burning eyes. "Things are getting
steadily worse over there." After reading them portions of Friedman's
letter, he asked, "Eddie, what's the status of the carrier?"

Kotch shifted in his chair. "Progress is slow, Ross. In fact, the con-
tractors are threatening to file a lien if we can't make payment. The
bills total something like fifty thousand."

"Surely we can come up with that much."

"Well, it isn't as simple as that. You see, so far the FBI hasn't linked
me to the front company that bought the carrier. If I get involved down

there—bingo. They're keeping a close eye on me. If they connect the demolition block business, the carrier, and me, we're dead in the water."

Ross snorted. "Oh, for Christ's sake. The thing can't possibly be ready in time. Junk the project, Eddie."

"Ross!"

"I said junk it, damnit. It's a liability we can't afford. Now, Bruce, what about the Connies?"

"A month away, Ross. It's like trying to swim in quicksand. The inspector decided that the seats, toilets, and galleys we've installed don't meet airliner standards. 'Rip 'em out and start over,' he says. It's getting expensive, Ross."

"I know it. But we have two C-46s certified in Burbank, right?"

"Yeah, but they're just sitting there. We can't even get export permits for Panama since the December presidential order banning export of military items to the Middle East."

"Okay," Ross's tone was brisk. "I talked with Julius this afternoon. Here's what we'll do. Keep on with the Connie mods. Sooner or later they'll have to certify them, and we *must* have four-engine transports. In the meantime we'll head for Tocumen with empty C-46s, land in Mexico and take on a load of small arms, then head for Palestine. Friedman will have a field ready for us. The Commandos will at least give Dov a way to get small stuff from Czechoslovakia."

Ross slumped deeper into his chair as he watched the subdued team managers shuffle out. Another report to Wallace was due. This one would be easier, but he still felt like Benedict Arnold. *Was* his information to be used to the Jews' advantage? Wallace was a trained liar; he wouldn't hesitate to use Ross—or anyone else—if his precious "company" ordered him to. And, Ross glanced at his calendar, it had been almost a month since he'd given the closemouthed agent Templeton's letter and asked him to dig up verification of Janet's story. Was Wallace making *any* effort? Ross shrugged off his self-doubt and reached for a pad of paper. The news he had to pass on sure as hell should jar *someone* into action.

14 March 1948
Burbank
Ross watched the loadmaster strap the crew's luggage to rings in the empty C-46's cargo compartment. Ross checked the hastily installed

fuselage fuel tank, then trudged forward to the flight deck. Settling
into the left seat, he turned to the darkly handsome young man he knew
only as Denny. "Cashman's plane will be ready in about another thirty
minutes. There's time for a stretch and a smoke, if you like."

"That's all right, sir," the youngster replied. "I'll just go over our
flight plan again."

Ross nodded. Denny had less than four hundred total flying hours
and only fifty in the C-46. Ross had selected the man to fly right seat
only because he had grown up in northern Palestine and knew the terrain.
They'd be going into an unprepared field, after dark, and without radio
navigation aids. Besides, Denny spoke Hebrew. According to Murtaugh,
Cashman was a good pilot, but he too was a recent graduate of Bascom's
C-46 flying school.

Not the finest pilots to have along on this kind of mission, Ross
complained to himself, but they were the best available. Two other
depressing events served to darken his mood. Janet had called him one
afternoon the previous week.

"Hi," she'd chirped gaily. "I'm here in the big city—all alone—
looking for someone I can buy dinner for. My treat; I'm on my expense account."

Ross had hesitated. There's so damned much I can't tell her, he mused.
And she'll have a million questions. He forced pleased surprise. "Deal.
My place or yours?"

"Could you meet me at a restaurant called Luigi's on Broadway?
It's not far from my hotel."

The evening went almost as badly as he'd feared. After eating, and
with coffee and brandy served, he asked, "Okay, I'm dying to know
about your Senator Templeton story. Are you coming up with anything?"

Janet's expression had become guarded. "I was rather hoping you
wouldn't bring up that subject. You see—well, I've sort of been taken
out of the investigative part."

"How come?"

"Well, Os—the freelancer—tells me he's about to give up. He can't
come up with so much as a whisper that the Jewish Relief Foundation gave anyone a dime. Maybe I was being an alarmist when I called
you, but Adair seemed so sure.

"Anyway, the freelancer—well, he started developing a related story.
That's when Adair told me he thought it best if I distance myself even
farther from the project.

"Oh . . . By the way, what did you do—you know—about providing a second source verification?"

"I just passed the word along to a friend of a friend. I haven't heard back, but I hadn't expected to." In truth, Ross had fumed inwardly at Wallace's apparent indifference.

"You didn't call back about the letter to BT," continued Janet. "Could you make sense of it?"

Feeling very much like a louse, Ross shrugged. "Pretty vague. I *think* the 'S' and 'B' he mentioned were Generals Sprague and Brereton— but again, there's no verification."

"Damn. Can *nothing* be done to expose that man?"

"He'll trip up," Ross said with confidence he didn't feel. "Once he starts to campaign, someone's going to find that closet where the skeletons are hidden."

"I wish I could be as sure," Janet replied. "Ross," she said, her eyes glinting dangerously, "the real reason I wanted to have dinner with you is to ask if you're still working for the JRF. You haven't mentioned it, so I have to assume you are."

"Yes, I still have my contract to fulfill."

"You didn't believe a word I said. Do you think I imagined all that? I just made it up out of thin air? Maybe that campaign contribution didn't originate there, but the investigation I mentioned is very real."

"I—I—this is all mixed up, Janet. Please, please, don't ask me to discuss the subject. I know the risk you took to warn me. I'm touched, deeply, but I'm not—just now at any rate—in danger of being charged with a crime. Can you trust me on that?"

Janet's face was a furious mask as she stood and retrieved her purse. "I'm sorry I tried to meddle in your precious private life. I will never make that mistake again—ever. Good-night." She stalked from the table with brimming eyes.

Then, just a couple of hours later, Bruce called from New York. A CAA inspector, not bothering to conceal his glee, had advised Murtaugh that the Connie engines would have to be equipped with the new fuel injection system before they could be licensed. Everyone knew that the Connie engines were prone to overheat, especially on takeoff. You just flew in a way to reduce the risk. Newer models eliminated the problem by replacing carburetors with fuel injectors. The conversion job would add thousands of dollars to modification costs already straining the foundation's coffers. The money notwithstanding, Ross was running out of time.

He told Bruce to get the goddamn airplanes out of the United States before they were grounded. Take them to Panama and figure out the next step from there. It had come down to this. From grandiose plans for a fleet of first-line airplanes, flown by professional crews, the end result was two marginally certified twin-engine jobs, a third one unable to enter the United States, and crews barely able to find their way out of the traffic pattern.

He'd failed. Unless—unless, damnit, he and these untrained airmen could pull off the miracle of transporting enough guns and airplanes to the beleaguered Jewish Defense Forces to turn the tide. Ross lowered the back of his seat, rested his head, and closed his eyes.

14 March 1948
Mazatlán, Mexico
Ross hadn't been expecting a replica of L.A. Municipal Airport, but he gulped as the single, blacktop runway materialized through mist left by a late-afternoon rain shower. Oriented north and south between the Pacific Ocean on the west and jagged peaks of the Sierra Madre mountains to the east, the field exuded neglect and disrepair even at a distance of ten miles.

Upon landing, Ross saw a pair of fat-bodied transports dwarfing the half-dozen light aircraft squatting off his left wing on the rain-puddled parking ramp. He leaped to the ground from the plane's rear entrance and gathered Denny, Flight Engineer Masters, and the pink-cheeked young loadmaster, Alec, in a huddle with Cashman and his crew. "Okay, when you refuel, be sure to drain the fuel tank sumps at least twice. I suspect there'll be enough water in the gas here to float a rowboat.

"And be damn sure you fill to the top. It's two thousand miles to Panama; I want a full fourteen hundred gallons in the mains. If you stop at the filler neck, we'll be two hundred shy. Cashman and I will close our flight plans, clear customs, and meet you in the lobby."

Ross was about to enter the whitewashed adobe terminal when he paused and turned to look once more at the cracked and uneven runway. "If that damn thing is five thousand feet long, I'm a goat's asshole," he announced to Cashman. "While I'm looking up this contact of Eddie Kotch's, why don't you try to get an accurate measurement—borrow a car and measure it on the odometer if necessary. With the runway located like it is, the wind is going to be from the east or west, so it's certain we'll have a crosswind takeoff. Whatever you do, don't let your loadmaster overgross us. Load by the book."

Eddie Kotch's man found the crews as they were finishing a meager meal at the shabby hotel outside the airfield. Ross had been adamant regarding the menu. "Look, you clowns," he had told the crews, "you're not back at Paco's Taco Palace in L.A. Don't order a meat dish, don't eat any fresh vegetables, and drink beer instead of water. We have a long trip ahead of us, and you can pick up bugs down here that will lay you low for a week."

Ross looked up to see a potbellied man wearing black trousers and a gaudily embroidered vest over a white shirt, and carrying a broad-brimmed sombrero in one hand. His swarthy, mustachioed face was wreathed in a wide grin that exposed most of his startlingly white teeth.

"*Buenos noches,* senors," he said. "I am Carlos, at your disposal, sirs. Do I have the pleasure of addressing Senor Colyer?"

"That's me," Ross replied, grinning.

"*Bueno, bueno,*" Carlos responded, nodding vigorously. "Only two days ago I speak with Senor Kotch on the *teléfono.* He arranges with me to see to moving items from the fine boat in the harbor to your magnificent aircraft."

"Great," Ross replied. "How soon can you get us loaded?"

"Ah, yet tonight, senor. I have the big truck waiting outside. It will be done pronto."

"Very good, very good. See me here tomorrow morning. I'll pay you then," Ross said.

"Ah, senor." Carlos's smile crumpled. "I visit Senor Smith on the fine boat only today. There are many items, very heavy." He spread pudgy hands. "Carlos cannot move them alone."

"Oh? Well, can't you hire someone to help?"

"But, senor." Carlos lowered his voice to a conspiratorial level. "Senor Kotch, he say items are, what you say, secret? Only the Norte Americanos and Carlos"—he stopped and beamed with pride—"are to see them."

Ross felt his jaw sag. "Are you telling me, Carlos, that Kotch expects the plane's crews to unload the damn boat and transfer the cargo to the airplanes?"

Carlos rotated the brim of his sombrero with nervous gestures. "I believe that is what Senor Kotch desired. The crew from the fine boat have all gone back to los Estados Unidos. Senor Smith is much angry."

Ross groaned. "Oh, Christ. Okay, troops, up and at 'em. Let's get down to this 'fine boat' and see what's to be done."

The group piled onto the bed of Carlos's "big truck," a noisy 1934 Ford. After a short, jouncing ride through the humid night, Carlos screeched to a stop on an aging, splintered pier. Ross searched the area lighted by a single, low-wattage bulb. All that was visible was the upper mast of some type of sailing vessel. It was low tide, and the deck appeared to be six feet or more below pier level.

Carlos motioned for Ross to follow as he strode to the dock's edge. "Senor Smith," he called. "I have come for the cargo."

Ross joined the Mexican and peered down to the deck of an eighty-foot motor sailer. No judge of boats, Ross could nevertheless see that she was a luxury yacht. Gleaming brass and chrome, unblemished white paint, and brightwork spelled money. An unshaven, tousle-haired man appeared from an open hatchway. "About time," his disgruntled voice rumbled. "Come on down and get to work."

With a wheezing Carlos leading the way, Ross descended a narrow wood ladder nailed to one of the dock's supports. Stepping onto the spotless deck, he crossed to the slouching, shorts-clad man and extended his hand. "Ross Colyer," he said. "You must be Mister—Captain?—Smith."

"Yeah, I'm Smith. You the one who flew in here this afternoon in those two transport planes?"

"Right."

"Well, I'll sure as hell be glad when you get this junk off-loaded and I can get the hell out of this place. What a goddamn screwed-up operation."

"How's that?"

"Well, I got talked into bringing the guns down here from L.A. by this friend of mine. A pleasure cruise, he says. All expenses paid plus ten grand. And it's all to help the Jews over in Palestine. So I borrowed this boat from a friend who's in Europe. If you ask me, the damn guns are hotter than a mink in heat. My friend just laughed when I asked for some kind of bill of lading in case I got stopped.

"He lines up this crew who he says are experienced sailors and will load and unload. I don't think any of the dumb shits had ever been out of Long Beach harbor. Anyway they start carrying stuff on board and first thing I know, we've got it crammed into every square inch of the boat. We're riding low in the water, and I can't get 'em to stop.

"Second day out we run into a storm. The load shifts, busts up a lot of paneling, the crew gets seasick, can't handle the sails—I end up bringing the boat here all by myself, using the diesel. This friend is going to have a shit fit when he sees what I've done to his boat."

"I see," Ross was finally able to say. "Best I have a look. Where's the cargo stowed?"

"Where?" Smith brayed with laughter. "Just step inside. It's every-goddamn-where."

Ross entered the main saloon and blinked. Smith was right. Burlap-wrapped bundles were stacked and jammed into every available space. An eighteen-inch path provided passage fore and aft.

"How much does all this weigh?" Ross asked.

"Ten—twelve tons, I'd guess. All I know is we're riding so low in the water that the decks are awash more than half the time."

Ross hefted one of the bundles, then walked on deck and called to his loadmaster. "Take this bundle someplace and weigh it. The rest of you, come on down and start getting this stuff onto the truck."

Ross's watch read two o'clock when he called a break, sank to a recently cleared seat, and wiped sweat from his face. His clothing, and everyone else's except Smith's and Carlos's, was saturated. The truck, groaning under its excess load, had made four trips to the airstrip. The yacht's surly skipper, his mood improving as bundle after bundle of burlap-wrapped machine guns disappeared from his craft, grudgingly opened his icebox and offered them each a cold beer.

Ross sipped his and turned to Carlos. "Jefe," he asked, "do big airplanes use this airfield?"

"Si, senor. Mazatlán has fine airport. Many big planes take off and land here."

"Planes as big as ours?"

"Oh, no, senor. Your planes very big—biggest yet to land here."

"I sort of thought as much," Ross muttered.

Alec reported that the bundle Ross had handed him weighed forty kilograms—roughly eighty pounds. By Ross's count they had wrestled an even hundred bundles from the narrow confines of the yacht's interior and manhandled them up the ladder leading to the dock. Ross turned to Cashman. "I figure another fifty bundles will give us six thousand pounds each. With a full fuselage tank, that'll gross us out for take-off. I'll have Carlos stash what we can't take in a warehouse and send Jake Trask up here with the other bird to pick up a load.

"Okay, everybody, stand to. We have barely enough time to finish by daylight. We'll sleep all day and head for Panama just before dark."

Masters was still struggling with a persistent hydraulic leak when the sun—a bloated, reddish orange ball—sagged low in the hazy western sky. Darkness fell with startling swiftness in these latitudes, Ross knew. He'd much prefer that the relatively inexperienced Cashman make his max-performance takeoff during daylight. Ross pressed the VHF transmit button. "Easy Two, this is One. Do you read?"

"Roger, One. Two is standing by, ready to roll."

"Okay, Masters wants another thirty minutes with this hydraulic leak. Why don't you go ahead?"

"Roger, roger—understand. I'm turning number one."

Ross watched the fully loaded transport lumber toward the runway's north end and swing into takeoff position. He mentally repeated his last-minute coaching to Cashman. Okay, check those damn engines. If you can't turn 2,700 rpm and pull forty-seven inches of manifold pressure, don't go.

Ross cocked a critical ear as the C-46's radial engines filled the evening with mind-numbing thunder. They sounded good. Easy Two lurched forward, accelerating with agonizing slowness. He and Cashman had gone beyond a spot two-thirds of the way down the runway—refusal point. Anything less than sixty miles per hour at that point was an automatic abort. Ross saw takeoff flaps extend—signaling the all-important refusal speed—and breathed easier.

Seconds later, Ross heard the pounding roar of engines change abruptly. He watched, horrified, as the big plane swerved, straightened, then, out of runway, staggered into the air. "Sweet Jesus Christ, he's lost an engine," Ross moaned aloud. He saw the left prop snap to the full-feathered position. Milk those flaps up a few degrees at a time, he urged silently. Keep her at exactly ninety—she'll climb out if you do everything by the book. The faltering aircraft sank out of sight below the horizon. Ross waited with bated breath for the heartbreaking boom and mushroom of flame and smoke. He resisted the urge to get on the radio and give advice. The crew had their hands full—it was no time to be talking.

He and Denny saw it at the same time: Easy Two, one wing low, was clawing for altitude over the placid waters of the harbor. They could hear her remaining engine now, howling at full power. Ross realized he had loosed a hoarse, strangled yell of triumph.

His radio came to life. "One, this is Two. We're over the bay with number one feathered." Cashman's voice sounded strained.

Ross forced a calm, reassuring reply. "Roger. We noticed that. You did a terrific job, guy. Perfect in every way. What the hell happened?"

"Fucking number one just quit cold at liftoff," Cashman grated. "I can't hold number two at emergency power much longer; the cylinder head temp is already over the redline. I have her up to two hundred feet and am circling to land."

"Negative, Two," Ross snapped. "You're way over max safe landing weight. You'll never get stopped on the runway; blow a tire and that's all she wrote." Ross thought furiously. "You're going to have to jettison your cargo. Get some of that power off—give up a few feet of altitude if you have to—and get the crew busy dumping those fucking guns into the bay."

After a protracted silence, Ross heard Cashman's reluctant, "Roger, One. We'll try."

Ross yelled out his window to the crew members, who by now were standing on the ramp urging the crippled C-46 to stay airborne. A group of chattering Mexican airport employees joined them. "Masters, it'll be dark in about fifteen minutes. Get those guys to take every car that's around and park alongside the runway with their lights on. Give Cashman something to line up with."

Cashman came on the radio after fifteen harrowing, nail-biting minutes. His voice sounded firmer and more or less relaxed. "One, this is Two. Things are looking better up here. The engineer says we'll have all the cargo thrown out shortly. I'm at eight hundred feet and able to maintain altitude with number two at climb settings. I can see the car lights, so if everything goes well, I'll be on the ground in about ten more minutes."

"Sounds great," Ross replied. "We'll be waiting for you. We're beginning to get an offshore breeze, by the way. I estimate you'll have about a ten-knot crosswind from your left on landing. Give me a call on final, over." Neither pilot mentioned that a crosswind from the same side as a dead engine made an already tricky landing a *very* tricky landing.

Cashman made a perfect touchdown with a screech of burning rubber. Ross kept mental fingers crossed as the big plane rumbled toward the headlights marking the far end of the runway. Hoping against hope, Ross saw the landing lights start an inevitable swerve to the left as the aircraft slowed. The crosswind, aided by thrust from the idling right engine, turned the ship into a gigantic weather vane that no amount of right brake could control. Ross winced as he watched the left landing gear leave the crumbling edge of the blacktop runway.

It looked to Ross as though Easy Two's pilot would have salvaged the landing, if not for a steeply sided drainage ditch. The left wheel dipped. Momentum provided by twenty tons of airplane applied a twisting motion beyond the gear's design limitations. Easy Two settled to a halt, its landing lights beaming skyward at a drunken angle.

Ross, his thoughts a mixture of relief and dismay, spoke into the darkness. "Congratulations, Carlos. The owners of your fine airport now have a permanent monument to boast about."

21 March 1948
Abeam Amapá, Brazil

"Belém! Belém! Belém!" Jake Trask screamed into the microphone. "Easy X-ray One, calling Belém. Come in, Belém."

Trask grinned at Ross's questioning look. "Something a Panagra pilot told me at Tocumen," he explained. "The Brazilians don't really like North Americans. They like even less the fact that English is the official international language for air traffic control. They don't speak it well. When you make your first call-up in English, if they don't feel like talking, they just ignore you.

"This pilot said the secret is to yell and sound mad as hell. The controllers are afraid not to answer—they might get into trouble. Pretty screwy, huh?"

Ross stared into the sheets of rain bucketing past while Jake yelled their position report to the truculent air traffic controller. The C-46's wingtips weren't even visible; Ross marveled that the damn engines even ran, given the amount of water they must be sucking into the carburetors.

Jake hung up his mike and shook his head. "Did you ever in your life see such rain?" he asked in awed tones.

"Never," Ross replied. "I'd heard about the ITCZ, but I never dreamed it would be like this." He stuffed a towel under a leak above the instrument panel.

Jake finished his entries on the flight plan. "I'm still not clear as to why there's so little turbulence. Can you imagine plowing through a Kansas thunderstorm that looked like these clouds?"

Ross chuckled. "No, thank you. A weatherman explained that prevailing easterly winds along the equator brush against the prevailing westerlies, hence the name inter tropical confluence zone. That movement sets up the clouds, but you don't get the lifting effect that causes those god-awful updrafts you get in a Midwest thunder-bumper."

"Well, I'll be glad to get out of this crap. I'd like to see Cashman's face when he blunders into it."

"After the job that kid did back there at Mazatlán, nothing should faze him," Ross said. "You ought to be in the left seat on Number Two, but I didn't have the heart to bump Cashman. Besides"—he gave Jake a sly grin—"it'll be nice to have you in the lead airplane for that run from Natal to Dakar without a qualified navigator."

"That must have been a hairy ride," Jake said soberly. "I got a good look when I went back to pick up the rest of those guns. That's one sick-looking bird you left there. I just wish we'd had room to bring back some more spare parts from it." He ceased talking as they broke into blinding sunlight. Relief at putting the blue-black line of storms behind them prompted conversation in a lighter vein.

Chapter 26

28 March 1948
Catania, Sicily

Ross, Jake, and Denny watched the harassed-looking Haganah representative trace an imaginary line on the map with a grimy forefinger. Ross noted with dismay that the map spread on the littered tabletop appeared to be a page from a student's geography book—written in Hebrew.

"After you pass Crete, here, your main concern is to stay well south of Cyprus," advised the Haganah representative. "It's not so much a danger of being shot at, although they do have a cruiser in the area. If they detect a sizable transport headed east, you may have a greeting party at Darass.

"There's an all-night radio station in Damascus that you should be able to get a bearing on. There's also a low-powered station in Tel Aviv you can use as a cross-check with your ADF set. It goes off the air at midnight, though. You should make landfall between Haifa and Tel Aviv. It'll be strictly pilotage from there on in."

Ross looked at Denny. "You following all this?"

"Yeah," the young man said, nodding. "If you can get close enough to Tel Aviv to see the lights, I can find the place." Denny turned to the Haganah man. "Do you have a weather forecast for the area? They get some pretty frequent rain showers this time of year."

"I talked with the field last night by radio. They had some rain earlier, but they think it should be clear for the next day or two," the Haganah man replied.

"What about the winds aloft?" asked Ross. "An altimeter setting for the area? Do they have runway lights?" He fired his questions in quick succession.

"You can talk with the Italians over in the airport building," the Haganah representative replied. "They told me an hour ago that you can expect winds generally from the southeast, shifting to the north after passing Crete. An altimeter setting? Nothing you can count on; just set in twenty-nine ninety-two and watch out for the hills east of Darass. They don't have runway lights—wouldn't dare use 'em if they did. The Brits have pulled out, but the Arabs are all around the place. The Palmach troops there will light flare pots when they hear you overhead."

Ross crossed to a window and gazed into the setting sun. Finally he turned. "Look, our man got these guns out of the States one step ahead of the law. Then—after losing one airplane and damned near its crew—we blundered our way across the South Atlantic and the North African desert without a navigator.

"Now you're asking me to take an airplane across the Med without anything more than a low-frequency radio to navigate by, without a weather forecast, hoping to hit a one-hundred-mile stretch of hostile beach, locate an unlighted field in the dark—very possibly obscured by rain showers—using a map I can't read, and land by flare pots at max gross landing weight. If you really need this cargo, why not transfer it to small boats and run it onto the beaches a bit at a time? You're risking the entire load in one damn risky shot."

"Because, Mister Colyer, we needed those guns and ammo yesterday—last week. The Arabs are determined to defy borders set up by the UN, and to occupy every square foot of land they can before the British leave for good in May. Meanwhile, the Brits simply stand by and watch," the Haganah representative added on a dispirited note.

"I read you loud and clear," said Ross. He gathered up the meager bits of paperwork he'd prepared. "Let's get airborne, troops. We have a long night ahead of us. Jake, I'd like you to ride in the jump seat; you'll be going with Cashman on the next run. I'm putting Denny in the right seat, since he can read the damned map and maybe spot landmarks."

Jake examined the terrain contours on the map illuminated by a carefully shielded flashlight. "I hope to hell that *is* a Damascus radio station," he said, his worried, darkly handsome features thrown into cameo relief by the dim light. "Denny, why don't you try that Tel Aviv station one more time? If our ADF bearing to Damascus is correct, we're getting awfully close to Syrian territory."

"I've been trying, Jake," the young copilot said. "More than likely it's been knocked off the air; that happens a lot. Do you think we should reverse course, Ross? I can make out some pretty good-sized hills below."

Ross responded by swinging the plane to a heading of 180 degrees. "Where in the hell is Tel Aviv?" he muttered. "We should be able to spot lights from a city that size from fifty miles."

Denny pointed out the window to where tongues of lightning flickered off a mound of clouds. "I'd guess it's beneath that rain cloud. If so, we're about thirty miles north of the field."

"Guesses I don't need, Denny," Ross retorted. "I'm sorry," he added quickly. "This insanity is getting to me. I'll set up a square search pattern—ten-minute legs, then eight minute, and so forth. In the meantime, we're eating up fuel and time. We have to unload and get the hell out of there before daylight, you know."

Thirty minutes later, Jake yelled, "Over there—eleven o'clock—lights!" Three sets of aching eyeballs peered into the darkness. "Looks like Tel Aviv," Denny breathed.

"Yeah," Jake agreed, "if it isn't a camp full of Arabs fixing shish kebab. Nope, those fires are lined up in a straight line. Field in sight, old buddy." He slapped Ross's shoulder.

0032 Hours, 29 March 1948
Tel Aviv

As the plane eased to a stop, Ross could see shadowy figures extinguishing the flare pots. Two trucks, their headlights turned off, ghosted to a halt alongside. After shutting down, Ross leaped to the ground and was immediately approached by a half-dozen yelling, backslapping men. "Oh man, what a sight for these tired old eyes you are," one of them said, grabbing Ross's hand. The speaker peered closer in the dim light. "Ross Colyer! My God, I should have known it'd be you."

Ross recognized the jubilant voice immediately. "Dov Friedman," he cried. "What brings you to these hills—away from those sinful fleshpots in the city?"

Dov chuckled. "Jealous husbands. It's safer up here letting the Arabs plink at me; they're lousy shots." He sobered. "You have machine guns on board?"

"Mister Browning's finest—fifty caliber, with ammo to match."

"Thank God," Friedman said. "I guarantee they'll see action by sunup." Dov paused and looked at the horizon. "Abdul, my friend, you are in for one big surprise tomorrow," he added grimly, then gazed back at Ross. "Why don't you come over to my tent? We'll have a cup of coffee and a bite to eat. You'll be unloaded and on your way in less than thirty minutes. We don't want to leave this big, fat, tempting target out in the open very long. The bastards have mortars out there."

Ross sipped scalding coffee and asked his beaming host, "What do you hear from Ariel?"

"I think she's back at the kibbutz," Dov said vaguely. "They have their hands full; they don't even try to work the fields these days."

"Is she still obsessed with finding the man who betrayed her father?"

"I'm sure of it. Listen, do you have your Connies over here yet?"

"I'm afraid not, Dov. The FBI has put every government agency to work trying to keep us from flying those birds."

"Damn." Dov pounded the rickety table with his fist. "We have stuff backed up at Zatec—small arms, machine guns, mortars, and grenades— that we simply *must* have."

"Jake will have our other C-46 here two nights from now with another load of machine guns. After that we can set up a shuttle to Zatec. That's the best I can do."

"It will have to do," Dov muttered. "I'd like to go back up there on your first run."

"No problem. Hop on Jake's plane. We'll set it up from Catania. Can we count on having this field to use for unloading?"

"If we have to use every gun you brought tonight—Darass is ours. Where will you refuel for the trip back?"

Ross chuckled. "Adana. The Turks think their lend-lease aid might stop if they refuse. Little do they know: if they checked with our embassy there, they might discover I'm a wanted man in their country. I left without their permission a few years ago. Well"—he drained his coffee mug—"guess I'd better get in the air. It'll be daylight soon."

Jake Trask flew left seat on the return trip to Catania while Ross caught up on several hours of lost sleep. As Jake wheeled the empty transport into the parking slot they'd vacated thirty-six hours earlier, Ross, feeling refreshed but looking forward to shaving and bathing, stood between the pilots' seats. "Where the hell is Easy Two?" Ross muttered to Jake. "Don't tell me Cashman took off on his own."

"No," Jake replied. "That's him in that truck driving up."

Ross leaped to the ground to greet a grim-faced Cashman. "Where's the bird?" he asked.

"There's all hell to pay, Ross," came the tight-lipped reply. "The Italians have impounded the damn thing. It's in that hangar over there with guards all around it."

"Oh, shit. How did that happen?"

"Beats me. I don't speak the lingo. Some guy wearing a uniform, a badge, and a big pistol showed up at our room this morning. He hustled me down to the main building, where a scrawny little man who spoke a few words of English told me we were under arrest for smuggling. I managed to talk him out of throwing us in jail until you got back."

"What a bastard," Ross retorted. "That scrawny little man is the airport manager. He was 'greased' to ignore our activity here as long as we didn't draw attention. Okay, the rest of you go hit the sack; I'll see what this is all about."

Ross stomped up the steps leading to the terminal building's second floor and stopped in front of a frosted glass–paneled door. He knocked once, then entered unbidden. The slightly built man seated behind an oversized desk looked up in annoyance. Ross assumed an angry expression and barked, "I understand there is a problem with our second plane, Signor Ligorna."

"Ah, Signor Colyer," the diminutive airport boss responded in chilly tones. He slid rimless half glasses down his beak of a nose. "You misled me, signor. When we made our—ah—agreement, you assured me you would not violate our import laws."

"And I didn't," Ross responded. "Our cargoes were sealed for transit; nothing was off-loaded. I paid in advance for landing fees, tie-down fees, ground-handling fees, and other 'incidental costs that might arise.' I demand that you release my airplane."

"One does not 'demand' that a government official do anything, Signor Colyer. Now, come with me, please."

Ross deliberately took long strides, forcing the short-legged official to trot in a most undignified manner as they crossed to a nearby hangar. "What the hell have you done?" Ross exploded as they entered the building's gloomy interior. Burlap-wrapped bundles littered half the hangar floor.

"Contraband, Signor Colyer. Arms. Their importation is expressly forbidden without a special permit." Ligorna, his lips compressed in a prissy smirk, gave Ross a severe look.

"My God, I told you we landed here merely to refuel and take crew rest. We are *not* importing this stuff."

"No matter. It is here. You do not have the proper permit." Ligorna crossed his arms and rested his case.

"Okay," Ross said resignedly. "This 'special permit'—it costs money, I assume."

"Most certainly."

"How much?"

The little man's pinched features took on a sly expression. "I will have to consult my book of regulations, signor. You see, different arms require different fees."

"I'm sure they do. Very well, give me the amount. I will call our office in Paris and have them transfer the funds to Italian authorities there," Ross said in disgust.

"Ah, I'm afraid that's not possible. You see, in situations such as this, where we have impounded cargo, the payment must be made here—in cash."

"Of course. How stupid of me not to know that," Ross said with mock seriousness. "But I assume again that because cash payment is required, it would be substantially less than the published rate."

Ligorna glared. "That is possible, yes," he muttered.

Ross hammered on Jake's door and yelled. "Everybody up. Take-off in one hour."

Trask, unshaven and bleary-eyed, opened his door and growled, "What the hell? I just got to sleep."

"We're getting out of here before that thieving son of a bitch thinks up some new scam."

"Scam?"

"You know it. After seeing what we were hauling, he upped the ante. As soon as we can get those guns reloaded, we're hauling ass."

"Where to?"

"Corsica. When I was in Europe before, I laid the groundwork for an aircraft maintenance and troop training operation there. It adds about three hours to our flying time to Palestine, but we can't afford to screw around with this outfit anymore. C'mon, let's get those crates in the air."

3 May 1948
Zatec, Czechoslovakia
Ross stepped from the shower and dried himself with a thick towel warmed on a special rack in the spacious bathroom. This is living, he thought. Best hotel in town—too bad I get an opportunity to use it only about once a week.

The shuttle schedule to Darass was a killer. It called for taking on a mixed cargo of small arms and ammo in Zatec, then making a four-hour flight over the Alps to Corsica. After landing at Ajaccio, they waited until takeoff would establish an after-dark arrival at Darass. Ten hours en route was a one-hour turnaround, then an immediate return via the same route. Both C-46s were in the air every hour they could be kept in commission. Crew members slept en route, after a fashion, on folding army cots tucked into any space not filled with cargo.

Ross had hired a former French air force pilot, Paul Delcour, in Corsica to serve as Jake Trask's copilot. Even with three crews, however, all the men were exhausted after a month of the grueling pace.

Ross tied the towel around his waist, then opened a bottle of golden Czechoslovakian pilsner and slumped into a chair to read Murtaugh's six-page letter. Bruce had posted it from Panama two weeks earlier.

Dear Ross,

I'm sure the situation will be changed by the time you get this, but I'll assume you're not getting newpapers from the States, and at least bring you up to where we are at this point.

The International News Service released a story this morning that is going to cause problems. It provides names, dates, and places involved in smuggling arms to the Haganah. You aren't mentioned by name, but the writer states that, "A private air freight carrier is alleged to be involved and is the subject of investigation by federal agents." I'll get a cable off to you as soon as I get more dope.

I now have all your airplanes here at Tocumen—the three Connies, the other three C-46s, even your DC-3 and Norseman. It's just as well that I got them out of the States when I did. On 15 April they slapped an embargo on shipping *any* airplane, combat or transport, to a foreign country. We managed to get out of Burbank with a good supply of spares and six of the best mechanics, however. Sure wish I had Cal back here, though. He has a way of getting things done with damn few resources.

Speaking of Thornton, I hope he can get that Connie you wiped out at Zatec flyable. You want to hear the latest? A guy from the attorney general's office is saying that you turned a military airplane over to the Communists in Czechoslovakia!

The Connies will be ready to put into service as soon as you give me the word. I talked with Julius before I left. He keeps in touch over there via shortwave and tells me you and Jake are flying your butts off hauling stuff from Czechoslovakia. Too bad you don't have a field inside Palestine that will handle the Connies yet. What's with the Brits? Hell, they have a pullout date, but Mantz says they're hanging tough, at least where the Jews are concerned. Kotch adds that the sea blockade is as tight as ever—maybe worse.

Eddie was able to get us loads for the three C-46s, but another problem has bared its ass. We went to get export permits and were turned down. The Jimenez government is receiving all kinds of pressure from Uncle Sugar to stop exports of anything that may end up in Palestine. We can maybe do an end run and get the C-46s to Corsica for you, but we'll be finished here in Panama.

Of course, we're all but finished anyway. When I talked with Julius, he told me that everyone in New York is facing indictment. He's closing the operation on Water Street. It won't matter too much for the Jewish nationals; they already have bolt-holes waiting. But he thinks Eddie and you may be hauled before a grand jury.

Now comes the teaser: Julius will sign over that C-46 we failed to get certified in the U.S. to Panama World Air. The Jimenez crowd really wants an airline down here. Jake is still president. How about if you, Jake, Eddie, and I set up the operation for them? I can see plenty of business going begging. Think about it—Eddie says he's on his way. He was singing your praises the other night, by the way. Glad to see you two talking at long last.

Ross stood and slammed the letter onto the bed. Goddamn! When are those assholes going to wake up as to what's going on outside of

Foggy Bottom? If Wallace's boss had the clout the agent was boasting of, he was sure as hell stingy with it. Hearing a knock on the door, Ross wheeled and snarled, "Whaddya want?"

Dov Friedman thrust a cautious head inside. "Hey, didn't anyone give you your ration of red meat today? I'm not sure it's safe in here."

"Oh, hell, come on in. I'm just letting off steam." Ross waved toward the offending letter. "All hell has broken loose back home. Julius's operation is described in detail in a nationwide news release. Forty-four Water Street is finished. Not all is lost yet, but Bruce says all the airplanes, especially the Connies, are bogged down at Tocumen."

"Oh, no." Dov sagged onto the bed. "Ross, we simply *have* to have them. The deal with Avia is red hot: a dozen of those converted Messerschmitts, signed, sealed, and ready to ship—complete with mechanics to reassemble them at the other end. Four pilots are to receive ten hours of instruction, gratis.

"Damnit, the Arab Legion has Syrian, Jordanian, and Egyptian troops, backed up by tanks, lined up on every border, just waiting for May 15. We have some Beaufighter and Mosquito bombers sitting in France, but by the time the Brits finally leave so they can land, it'll all be over. We have to find a way to smuggle in some of these fighters and at least slow down the Arabs until we can get some firepower into the country."

"I know," Ross answered dully. "The night before last, at Darass, they told me a pair of Egyptian Spitfires looked the place over that afternoon. You can bet they have every target pinpointed."

"Anyway," Dov said, brightening, "the reason I dropped by is to tell you I had my first flight in one of our new airplanes today."

"The hell you say. How did it go?"

Dov responded with a rueful shake of his head. "They're a handful. The hottest thing I'd ever flown was my fabric-covered fighter in Poland. I damned near lost this thing on takeoff. Torque? You need a wooden leg to hold the thing straight on the runway. That Junkers Jumo engine makes her nose heavy as hell. You hit the brakes at slow taxi and she'll nose over, so the instructor said. Look, you're an old fighter pilot. Why don't you take one up? There's no problem. The contract with Avia calls for ten hours of instruction, but they're loose. Their attitude is, they're your airplanes—do anything you like with them."

"By God, I believe I will," Ross replied. "Maybe wringing out a fighter again is just what I need."

Ross poured another beer after Dov left and, cheered by the prospect of flying a Messerschmitt the next morning, returned to Bruce's gloom-filled letter. The last paragraph caught his eye.

By the way, if Julius hasn't been in touch, he asked me to tell you that Janet Templeton is trying to contact you. She insisted it was important, but Julius—cagey person that he is—wouldn't tell her where you are. You might want to write to her—see what's so urgent.

Ross thought about the message as he dressed for dinner. If Janet said that something was important, it probably was. Damn all this secret hocus-pocus. Suddenly he wanted more than anything in the world to have one of those soul-baring sessions they used to have. Despite his close friendship with Ariel, he'd always had trouble revealing his innermost thoughts to her. If he wasn't behind—probably illegally—that "iron curtain," as Winston Churchill referred to it, he'd call Janet this minute. At the same time, he wondered just what the hell he'd tell her—that he was a spy?

A slight chill tickled Ross's spine as he approached the sleek fighter plane the next morning. The sensation was not entirely attributable to the brisk wind, he realized. The aircraft looked different without the mottled green and gray paint job he recalled seeing on German fighters during the war. Still, the plane projected a sinister air. Unlike the Mustang, with its businesslike, functional lines, the vaunted German machine displayed more deadly qualities.

Ross realized with a start that the English-speaking Czech instructor pilot walking alongside was already giving him lessons. "Don't let the right wing get down at low airspeeds; you'll never get it up again without sacrificing altitude," the fast-talking young man was saying. "Same thing if you feel a stall coming on. Ease the nose down before you add power. Otherwise, with this heavy engine, you'll end up in a power-on spin that takes about a thousand meters to recover from."

Ross dumped his seat-pack chute into the metal bucket seat and lowered himself inside the cockpit. Its cramped interior surprised him. Christ, it was even a tighter fit than the Mustang.

"A bit close, you'll notice," the instructor said cheerfully. "The Jumo engine is six inches longer than the Daimler-Benz—it sort of compressed the cockpit layout.

"The mixture of languages, the metric instrumentation, and the like will take some getting used to. Watch your red, green, and yellow limits. Here, I've given you the takeoff and landing speeds and some power settings in English." He handed Ross a card. "As soon as you get the feel of her, I have a mechanic standing by to start the engine; just give him the signal. Have a good flight, now." The young man leaped nimbly to the ground.

Ross saw a man dressed in white coveralls standing beside the left wing; he held a two-handed crank. My God, thought Ross—a manual starter. The Germans sure didn't believe in fancy frills, such as electric starters. Ross chuckled to himself. He hadn't seen one of those hand devices since his days flying Stearmans at Thunderbird Field.

Scanning the card the instructor had given him, Ross commenced running a before-starting-engine checklist. Fuel selector open; throttle one-third open; prime five strokes with the instrument panel–mounted plunger. He gave the mechanic a twirling motion to start winding up the starter's heavy inertial wheel. Water cooling closed; prop in automatic; master ignition switch on BOTH. He heard the shrill whine of the starter wheel as it reached max revolutions per minute. The mechanic called, "Free!" and stepped back. Ross pulled the red-painted T-shaped handle and heard the big twelve-cylinder Jumo bark to life.

Even before he lined up for takeoff, Ross decided he didn't like the airplane. It just didn't *feel* like a fighter plane should, even on the ground. He applied power and released the brakes, and soon saw what Dov had meant by torque: the thing immediately swerved toward the runway's right-hand edge. Ross finally reverted to a technique he'd heard a P-47 pilot advocate. He just jammed the left rudder pedal to the floor and held the plane straight down the runway by adding power until the lumbering machine reached flying speed.

Dov, the instructor pilot, and a man Ross recognized as Cal Thornton leaned against the hangar wall, wide grins on their faces, as Ross parked the Messerschmitt and leaped to the ground. "How'd it go?" Dov called. "You look a bit pale around the gills."

Ross regarded the trio soberly. "Dov, that machine is a goddamn menace. It'll kill more of your pilots than the Arabs will. I tried a steep turn to the left and promptly pulled it into a high-speed stall. She flipped to the right, and the first thing I knew, I was looking at the ground coming up. I had to use throttle on the landing roll to pull her out of a ground loop—and there's virtually no crosswind." Ross glared at the happy-looking Czech instructor pilot.

The man spread his hands. "She's a tricky beast, all right. You can't relax for a minute."

"I'd recommend canceling your order, Dov," Ross stated bluntly.

Dov looked unhappy. "They're our only salvation, Ross. We have to have fighters, if for no other reason than just to make the damn Arabs keep their heads down."

"The planes will maybe do that," Ross retorted. "The Arabs will be terrified that one is going to spin, crash, and burn right on top of them." Ross turned to greet Thornton. "Good to see you, Cal. I've been intending to drop by and find out how your repair job is going."

The chronically dour flight engineer's features assumed a smug look. "Step around the corner and see for yourself."

The four men moved to where they could see the hangar that Avia had made available. There, parked just outside the hangar doors, sat Panama World Air's flagship—all three landing gear on the ground, the triple tail with its gaudy Panamanian flag gleaming proudly in the morning sun. Ross's eyes widened. "Amazing, absolutely, goddamn amazing," he breathed. "Dov, there's your answer. How soon before we can put her in the air, Cal?"

"Well, it isn't as great as it looks. We had to weld the nose gear in place. It won't retract. The nosewheel steering is disconnected, and I don't know how many landings it will hold up under. But you can safely make a one-time flight to a major overhaul facility where I can get all the parts I'll need—Rome, Paris maybe."

"Still, it's a miracle," Ross said, his disappointment barely discernible. "Funny," he added wryly, "but if we can get that bird out of Communist territory, you may have just kept me out of jail.

"Now, new subject, which I got to thinking about last night. Can you and that crew of Czech magicians possibly cut an Avia into enough pieces to cram inside the '46s in a way that they can be reassembled on the other end?"

Cal turned and thoughtfully surveyed the parked fighter. "It's possible," he said slowly. "Put the wings and fuselage in one plane, the engine and prop in the other—yeah, it can be done."

"Okay." Ross's face split into a wolfish grin. "Dov, your four pilots are going to have airplanes to fly by the fifteenth—in Palestine. Get moving, Cal."

Chapter 27

4 May 1948
Zatec

Loading the disassembled fighter proved to be more difficult than Cal had estimated. Dangling from a motorized crane, the Avia's fuselage could not be inserted through the transport's side cargo door. Cal finally approached Ross. "I give up. It's just a matter of six inches, but that damn tail assembly won't clear. We've tried everything."

"Can we enlarge the door?" Ross asked.

Cal shook his head. "That doorframe is an integral structural member."

"Okay, how about just removing the fighter's tail section?"

Again, a doleful shaking of the head. In the end it was the crane operator who came up with the solution. Insert the fuselage tail first, he advised. The rudder's trailing edge could protrude past the fuselage tank and into the passageway leading to the flight deck. The nose cowling would then have room to pass the doorframe.

Once more, Cal vetoed the suggestion. "Ross, your center of gravity is going to be out of limits aft. Besides making for longer takeoff and landing rolls, she'll drag her tail all the way to Darass. Your indicated airspeed will be about five to ten knots low, and fuel consumption will be off the curve."

"I have to try it, Cal," Ross insisted. "News from Palestine gets grimmer by the day. The Arabs machine-gunned a busload of women and children in Tel Aviv today. A squad of British soldiers stood by and did nothing. They've cut off all roads from Tel Aviv to Jerusalem. Jews there are huddled in the old city without enough to eat.

"When I come back, we'll get that Connie to an overhaul base. You did an unbelievable job. It may well mean getting enough guns to the Haganah so they can hold out."

With the Austrian Alps a formidable barrier ahead, Ross forced the struggling plane toward their minimum en route altitude of fifteen thousand feet. The ADF needle, now pointing steadily toward the Linz radio beacon, would be Ross's sole navigation aid across the still-snow-covered, windswept mountains.

It was beginning to look as if they would make it, Ross mused. Dov had succeeded in chartering a Yugoslavian C-54. The big four-engine transport could carry an entire disassembled fighter in one trip. That boost to their airlift notwithstanding, the C-46s would still have to make at least two trips, but the goal of having four of the Avias flyable by the fifteenth was in sight.

Ross turned to Paul Delcour, his copilot for this run. "Well, she seems to be behaving," Ross observed. "A bit tail heavy on liftoff, but better than I expected, really." Ross pressed the intercom. "Pilot to loadmaster, tell our passengers we'll be above fifteen thousand for almost an hour. They'll feel the shortage of oxygen, but if they stay seated and don't smoke, they'll be okay. Just watch them. Use that emergency oxygen bottle if you have to."

Ross had barely leveled off at fifteen thousand feet when the first gust of turbulent air shook the plane like a playful giant. A white-capped mountain peak, wind whipping a long plume of snow from its jagged apex, towered above and just off their left wing.

"This is going to be a rough one," Delcour observed from the right seat. "Look at that damn wind—fifty knots at least. I hope those Czech mechanics in back have strong stomachs and solid eyeteeth. They're going to get both jolted loose shortly."

"Yeah," Ross agreed. "I'd feel better if they were in regular seats with safety belts. Just hope that damn cargo stays strapped down. Any more weight shifting to the rear and this thing will be impossible to control when we get deeper into these mountains.

"That landscape ahead looks just like the goddamn Himalayas. I knew those guys in the CBI flying the Hump had rough duty, but I'm just beginning to appreciate *how* rough they had it. I can't help but wonder, did this old bird maybe make that run as well?"

Ross's last words ended with a grunt as the aircraft seemingly entered an express elevator—going down. Vertical air currents, set up when the shrieking wind spilled over alpine ridges, effortlessly tossed the forty-ton airplane like a child's balsa-wood model.

Delcour helped Ross wrestle with the controls to keep the wallowing aircraft in level flight. When the placid blue waters of the Adriatic Sea inched into view, both men were drenched with sweat and trembling from exertion in the oxygen-starved atmosphere. Ross gratefully rolled in nose-down trim as the wild, hostile terrain slid behind them.

An hour later, Ross shut down the engines and turned to Delcour. "Okay, Paul, I'm looking to you to keep your ears open for what the French are saying about the Palestine situation. That's the reason I wanted you along on this trip. England is applying pressure all over the Med; I want to be sure that the people we're dealing with here aren't caving in.

"We'll 'cock' the airplane for immediate takeoff and sleep on those cots in the cargo compartment. This load must get through. It's been easy for them to ignore those crates marked pottery, used machinery, and so forth that we've been carrying, but one peek at a goddamn fighter plane, and they may balk. I'll fire up and take off right down that damn taxiway, if necessary."

"It's that bad?" Delcour asked, his dark, Gallic features seriously intent.

"If what Friedman hears is right, it's that bad," Ross replied.

5 May 1948
Darass, Palestine
Ross almost felt as though he was returning home as he lined up with the recently restored runway lights of Darass. He grinned. Damned if they even put a traffic control radio on the air. The place was definitely going uptown. Ross sobered as they rolled past coils of barbed wire and heavy machine-gun emplacements on landing rollout. The runway lights died before he reached the parking ramp. The threat was as genuine as ever, he realized.

Ross plodded into the sandbagged operations building and dumped his gear wearily onto the floor. "Two halves of a Messerschmitt airplane, Hodi," he called to the sad-faced Palmach duty officer. "Cashman is right behind me with the engine and prop, along with the rest of a crew of Czech mechanics to put the thing together. You, my friend, have the beginnings of a combat air force."

Hodi nodded enthusiastically, then bobbed his head to where another man stood, khaki shorts–clad legs slightly apart and bulldog jaw out-thrust above the collar of his white shirt. "That's great," Hodi responded. "Uh, this is Elihu Cohen, Ross. I think he wants to talk with you."

"Sure." Ross approached the stiffly formal man with his hand extended. "I'm Ross Colyer, Mister Cohen. What can I do for you?"

"I'm the newly appointed commander of the eastern frontier, Colyer," the man replied as he gave Ross a brief but firm handshake. "I'm told we have you to thank for our air force."

"Don't be too quick to give me credit, sir. Only four of these are en route—hardly enough to call an air force. It'll be a miracle if they can be assembled, test flown, and put to use by the fifteenth."

"They will be, never fear," Cohen stated. "Now, you look asleep on your feet. Hodi will show you to a tent. I just wanted you to know we're in your debt."

Ross awakened shortly before noon. After splashing his bearded, grimy face with cold water, he stumbled to the mess tent and helped himself to coffee. A familiar voice interrupted his brooding introspection. "Ross? I didn't want to wake you."

"Ariel!" Ross turned toward the serious-faced young woman standing beside him. "Hey, you look great." He immediately recalled the last time he'd seen her, and searched for something appropriate to say. He settled for an inane, "Sit down. What on earth are you doing here?"

Ariel poured coffee for herself and regarded Ross over the china mug's thick brim. "You look terrible," she observed. "Do you ever get any rest?"

Ross was relieved at Ariel's impersonal demeanor. "I'm still a bit fuzzy around the edges after a ten-hour flight from Ajaccio. But if you don't have something to put up against Egyptian bombers next week, this embryonic Israel, as they're calling it, is going to be stillborn."

"And *are* we going to have fighter planes?"

"The first one is out there beneath some camouflage netting right now. The second one will be in tonight. There should be four ready to put in the air by the time the fireworks start."

Ariel's eyes glowed. "Oh, Ross. It's more than any of us dared dream of."

"They're not enough, but their surprise effect should give Ben-Gurion time to get the materiel waiting in Europe in place.

"There won't be much more coming from the United States, however. The foundation got blown out of the water by a newspaper article. Julius, Moshe, Eddie—they're on the run."

"I know," Ariel said, her features pinched and worried. "We've been keeping up by shortwave radio. Will you be in trouble when you get home?"

"Maybe—who knows?" Ross replied briefly, not wanting to discuss it. "Ariel, to change the subject for a moment, are you still searching for your father's betrayer?"

"Yes."

"I see. Any luck?"

"Some," Ariel said without elaborating. "Ross, when will Dov be here?"

"He should be someplace en route right now. I left him and his pilots up there at Zatec trying to learn how to take off and land that miserable airplane without killing themselves. They'll come back with the fourth airplane."

"I see."

Ross saw disappointment written on her face. He gave her an amused smile. "Ariel, is there something between you and Dov? He dropped a couple of remarks that made me wonder."

"My, but we're direct today," Ariel said. "Would you be terribly upset if there was? I admire and respect Dov Friedman very much; we share a dream. We've faced danger together. There's a bond, yes. Does that answer your question?"

"Have you slept with him?"

"That, Ross Colyer, is none of your damn business," the dark-haired woman flared. "You have no reason—no right—to even ask a question like that."

"Take it easy, Ariel. I don't want to see you get hurt, that's all."

Ariel chose her words carefully. "I'm sorry I snapped at you like that. I—I have trouble confiding details of my personal life to *anyone*, Ross; forgive me. Besides, I don't know Dov very well—and the answer to your prying is, no.

"Back to your first question, however. I'm here because I've learned that the British transferred my father to a detention camp located at Dar Eskrim. It's in what is destined to be Arab territory after partitioning. The British plan to release all of *their* prisoners when they withdraw. That means my father and about a hundred others in the camp will be turned over to the Arabs. None of them will survive. I've joined a rescue mission. We leave tomorrow morning. I'm a Palmach soldier, Ross; please remember that."

Ross opened his mouth to protest, then closed it. Ariel's expression told him that any effort to dissuade her would be futile. He covered both her hands with his. "I think I understand. I don't agree with it, but . . . I only wish I could help."

"You already have, Ross—my country and, yes, me as well. Now, your job here will end within days. Go back—your future is there. Surely that silly investigation will be dropped after America recognizes us as an independent nation. Get back to building your airline, and to the Janet you talked about in your sleep in the hospital." Ariel's lips curved. "I'm afraid I listened, shamelessly. She's very much on your mind, and in your heart." Ariel stood and extended her hand. "Remember me once in a while."

Ross watched the trim, shorts-clad figure walk away. He finished his coffee, trying to assess his feelings. She was right, he conceded. He didn't belong here.

7 May 1948
Darass

Ross squatted to one side and watched the Avia fighter tremble as the Jumo engine bellowed at full power. Only one sour-expressioned face marred the grinning circle of Czech mechanics. Its owner, his head down, walked toward Ross as the engine's roar subsided.

"I don't know what else to do," the mechanic said. "The guns will synchronize to fire between the prop blades at about 1,800 rpm, but anything over that and she'll shoot the prop off. We've had problems with the system. It's a modification of the one used by the original Diamler-Benz engine. I don't know what to suggest, other than wait for a new synchronizer."

"That's not a solution," Ross said curtly. "Trask just relayed a message that a big storm front has him grounded at Ajaccio. He has the last Avia and the pilots aboard. Stop work on this one and get the other one flyable. Two will have to do the work of four until we can come up with a fix."

Ross scowled at the desolate, wind-scoured landscape. These people were counting on four fighters to turn back an armada of Egyptian bombers—escorted by Spitfires, no less. They had no concept of aerial warfare. Even if flown by experienced fighter pilots, those underpowered, temperamental Messerschmitt crossbreeds wouldn't last through the first dogfight with the vaunted Spitfires. Cohen was convinced that the enemy would be cleared from the skies within the first week; he'd issued orders to that effect.

Ross watched two dirty, oil-streaked Piper Cubs lurch into the dusty haze. Both had their side doors removed. He glimpsed grim-faced bomb chuckers in the rear seat surrounded by hand grenades and as many obsolete forty-pound bombs as they could crowd aboard from a dwindling supply. He knew they were headed for Latrun, where the Arabs held a Palmach column pinned to the rocky, barren ground. It was the Cubs' fourth sortie of the day, without appreciable damage inflicted on the enemy.

This is a hopeless cause, Ross told himself. Why the hell don't I just up and go home? He immediately answered his own question: you're just too damn stubborn to give up. Those last few days of futile resistance in East China flashed before him. And admit it, he added, you're worried about that stupid woman. Ariel is determined to get herself killed. He stood and turned toward the main terminal building. Maybe there was word on that mysterious mission to storm the detention camp.

Ross found Hodi in a spirited discussion with Elihu Cohen. Hodi turned to Ross. "Those Cubs that just reloaded and took off—they spotted the column trying to liberate Dar Eskrim. They're in a bad way. A party of Arabs with two armored cars has them trapped in a blind wadi about a mile from the detention camp."

"Oh, my God!" Ross exclaimed. "Have you sent a relief force?"

"Every resource we have is tied down trying to break through that pass at Latrun," Cohen replied. "The relief of Jerusalem is paramount."

Ross ignored the man. "How soon are those Cubs due back?" he asked Hodi.

Again Cohen preempted the Palmach officer. "Perhaps you didn't hear me, Colyer. I said that nothing in the way of firepower will be diverted from the Latrun Pass. Besides, it will be nearly dark when they return."

"I'll take the Messerschmitt then," Ross replied. "It still has some problems, but it's just a matter of keeping the rpms below eighteen hundred when you fire the guns. Some low passes over the Arab's heads can divert them long enough for that Palmach column to break out."

"Absolutely not," Cohen replied, sadly but firmly. "Those fighters are reserved to engage Egyptian bombers. The gyppos must not know we have them."

Ross strolled to the quarters he shared with Delcour, deep in thought. The Frenchman sat up and swung bare legs over the cot's side. "From your expression, I'd guess the guns don't work."

"Anything over 1,800 rpm and they'll shoot the prop off," Ross said absently. "Let's just hope the others don't have that problem. Paul, you told me you flew in Algiers—Beaufighters, I believe you said."

"That's right."

"How are you at tossing bombs from the backseat of a Piper Cub?"

The Frenchman flashed white teeth in a wicked grin. "I thought we were headed back to Zatec as soon as it gets dark."

"Weather," Ross replied with a look that defied argument.

"Well, I sure don't want to fly in clouds," Delcour said, deadpan. "Anyway, I've sat on the sidelines long enough. Let's go."

Hodi paced Ross's and Delcour's quarters, chewing his lower lip. "I'm going to dinner," Hodi said finally. "You heard the commander. You're not to take the Cubs. Besides, it will be dark in a half hour."

"I know those planes have only basic needle, ball, and airspeed for instruments," said Ross, "but I've flown a B-24 with nothing more. I'll get there and back."

"Like I said, I'm headed for the mess hall," repeated Hodi. "If you're going to ignore Cohen's order, I don't want to know."

Ross watched the unhappy Palmach officer stride through the doorway, then he turned to Paul. "Let's get a load of hand grenades and bombs on board one of those crates—Cohen be damned."

Racing against the rapidly setting sun, Ross and Paul threw an assortment of bombs and grenades inside the little fabric-covered observation plane. "Look at this," Paul commented. "The crew left two Bren guns with full magazines."

Ross clambered into the front seat. "Switch on." Delcour swung the wooden prop and stepped back as the spunky little four-cylinder Lycoming engine sputtered to life. Ross was taxiing even before his bomb chucker had his seat belt fastened.

"I'm going west of the site and drop down into that wadi," Ross yelled. "This little bug won't stand a chance unless we can surprise them. Just pray that the light holds. That gully probably isn't wide enough to negotiate in the dark."

Without doors, the engine and wind noise made conversation impossible inside the Cub as Ross followed the faint track north. He spotted the deep slash in the desert's flat surface just as a haze-filtered sun touched the horizon. Rolling into a gliding turn, he leveled the overloaded little craft just beneath the wadi's dusk-blurred rim. He felt Paul tap his shoulder, then saw him point ahead to a faint, flickering light. The arrogant bastards had even lit a cooking fire.

Ross throttled back to reduce engine noise and closed on the Arab camp, clearing the dry streambed by scant feet. He was too low and too busy to keep the glow of the enemy campfire in sight. Again Paul tapped his shoulder. This time he pointed directly to their left. Ross added full throttle, hauled back on the stick, then rolled left as the Cub popped above the desert floor.

Paul heaved two bombs into a huddle of startled Arabs even before Ross could set up a dive into their midst. Ross felt, more than heard, two substantial explosions. At least the bombs worked, by God!

Ross flipped into a steeply banked turn and started a return pass. Dark shapes scrambled toward the armored cars. Roaring directly over their heads, he heard another bomb detonate. This pass took him across the rapidly darkening wadi. He spotted movement. Tiny figures clambered toward the gully's rim—great! The Palmach still had fight left in them. He swiveled his head and glimpsed Paul hurling grenades. Two blue-white flashes indicated that the lethal little homemade missiles had spat bits of their cast-iron casings amongst the confused enemy.

Ross withdrew to the west, keeping the waning orange sun behind him. He'd seen the reddish sparks of tracers on that last pass. Was it time to withdraw? The slow-moving plane offered a juicy target to the now alerted Arabs. Turning to discuss the situation with Paul, Ross saw muzzle flashes flickering along the rim of the dry wash. The Palmach troops were counterattacking; he abandoned any idea of withdrawal.

Too late he saw a figure crouched over the 7mm machine gun mounted atop an armored car. It seemed to Ross that he was watching a slow-motion movie. The man turned to face him. The little Cub was laboring as if through molasses. He wrenched the stick down and to the right. The now visible gun muzzle tracked him effortlessly. "Throw a grenade," Ross heard himself yell. Seemingly a year later, he saw the tiny spheroid arc lazily forward, falling short by several yards.

He remembered the Bren gun tucked alongside his seat. Yanking it free, he released the controls long enough to work the slide. Mashing the left rudder, he made a skidding turn that placed him broadside to the menacing gunner. He shoved the Bren awkwardly in the armored car's general direction and fired a long burst. The shots went wild without disrupting the gunner's concentration.

With the Lycoming screaming under full power, Ross turned his tail to the scene. Taking violent evasive action, he darted away like a frightened dove—to no avail. Tracers drifted lazily past his left window. They edged closer; then, despite a desperate effort to evade the relentless orange sparks, he felt them enter the wooden propeller's arc.

Ross jerked the throttle to idle as the unbalanced prop threatened to tear the engine from its mounts. He searched the gathering gloom for a level place to set down the crippled plane. The thought that they were still within range of that damn machine gun flashed through his mind. Using the last of his airspeed to gain a few feet of precious altitude, he discovered the thirty-foot-deep wadi yawning a scant fifty yards away.

Riding the feathered edge of a stall, Ross allowed the Cub to settle into the wadi's dark interior. He snapped on the single low-powered landing light. Its feeble illumination would at least let him avoid brushing one of the walls rushing past the wingtips. Touchdown wouldn't require a major decision, he told himself: with both altitude and flying speed running out, impact in the next few seconds was inevitable. He cut the switches and held her off as long as possible.

Landing gear kissed the dry streambed with a deceptively gentle bump. As more weight settled on the small tires, the loose, shifting sand gripped them like a vise. Ross found himself flung forward against his seat belt. Momentum carried the nose and its still-windmilling prop forward and down; one blade buried itself in the sand. The valiant little craft, her last mission completed, stood on her nose, tail section thrust ignominiously into the night.

Ross could hear Paul swearing softly behind him as he released his taut seat belt. Tumbling to the dry streambed, Ross saw his bomb chucker scramble out the gaping doorway, apparently without injury. Four figures trotted from the gloom. He heard an anxious, "Are you all right?"

"I am," Ross replied. "Paul?"

Ross grinned with relief as the Frenchman grumbled, "As well as could be expected after such a rotten landing." Without the engine noise, Ross could hear the rattle of small-arms fire from the rock-strewn slope behind him. "What's the situation?" he asked.

"We have them pinned down, but they're dug in. The damn gun on top of that armored car keeps us from rushing them. We could pull out now, but with those two cars, they'll find us again as soon as the sun comes up. And then we wouldn't have cover of any kind. We have to take them out, no question about it."

Before Ross could respond, Paul appeared at his side, carrying the two Bren guns and a bulky sack. "Here." The Frenchman thrust a gun toward Ross. "Grenades," he added, seeing inquiring looks cast at his burden.

"*Grenades?*" Ross heard one of the Palmach yelp. "Oh, what a godsend. Just what we need. C'mon, we'll give that bunch a bit of their own medicine."

"Hold on," another shadowy figure advised. "Before we go wasting any of those things, we have to think of a way to disable those armored cars. They're manning the gun on just one of them, but it's too far away to lob a grenade in the open hatch."

"Do you happen to have any glass bottles?" Delcour inquired.

"Glass? No, I don't think so. Too heavy to carry in a pack. Wait a minute—would one of those Arab water jars do?"

"I believe it would," Paul replied, "if it isn't too big. We still have gasoline in the Cub's tank. If we can concoct a good old-fashioned Molotov cocktail—well, good-bye armored car."

As Delcour and one of the Palmach members hurriedly set about filling the three-liter jar with avgas, Ross turned to the third man. "Is Ariel Shamir up there?" he asked.

After a short laugh, the man answered, "Oh, yes. She was one of the first to scramble up there after you started the fireworks. You know her?"

"Yeah, I know her, all right," Ross said softly.

Delcour huddled with two Palmach troops at the top of the wadi, discussing possible ways to deliver the firebomb. Ross crawled along the line of prone figures. He heard Ariel's voice before he identified her crouched form, rifle thrust over a mound of sand. "How many rounds do you have left?" she was asking the man on her left.

"Ariel," Ross said as he settled beside her, "it's me, Ross. How are things going?"

"Ross! My God, so it was *you* flying that plane. What on earth? . . ."

"It's a long story. Your leader thinks the grenades we have left will do the trick. We should have you out of here in no time."

They both ducked as the machine gunner raked the wadi's rim with a random burst. "He has more ammunition to waste than we do," Ariel muttered. "We're each down to only a handful of cartridges for the Lee Enfields."

Ross felt a hand shaking his foot. A voice hissed, "Lay down some covering fire when I give the word. Aya is working his way around that armored car with the gun mounted on top. He'll be exposed when he lights the wick. I know we're short on ammo, so make every shot count. Here are two grenades each. If he torches the car, throw these, then rush their position."

Ross wriggled to the top of the slope and thrust his Bren gun over a hummock of sand. Too far from Ariel to talk, he searched the darkness for signs of enemy activity. He could hear low voices and shovels hurriedly deepening foxholes, but there was no visible target on which to concentrate. Minutes dragged by. Ross wished he was closer to the armored car; his automatic weapon was better suited than the bolt-action Lee Enfield rifles for keeping the machine gunner's head down. About to change his position, he heard the attack commence.

Coming after protracted silence, the sudden outbreak of gunfire was deafening. Ross glimpsed a burst of flame to his left. It spread instantly, lighting up the camouflaged side of the Arab armored car. A hit! He heard yells on both sides and saw men scrambling onto the desert floor. The nerve-shattering concussion of grenades filled the night. He leaped to his feet, seeking a target, and loosed a short burst toward movement that he glimpsed just to his right. He thought he heard a scream.

Muzzle flashes from dug-in defenders identified enemy positions. Ross crouched and selected one to attack. He felt and heard Ariel pound past, firing from the hip.

The attack was over as suddenly as it had started. A handful of Arab survivors huddled, hands in the air, in flickering light cast by the blazing vehicle. Ross worked his way through the milling, jubilant Palmach, searching for Ariel. He frowned and retraced his steps.

Ross knew it was Ariel even before he dropped to his knees beside the inert bundle of khaki. "Oh, my God, *no*. Ariel . . ." He gently slid a hand beneath her and eased her to her side. He felt a warm, sticky substance on his hand. "Is there a medic here?" he yelled. "Ariel is injured. Anyone with a medical kit, get over here!"

Moments later, a man was examining the unconscious woman by the light of two flashlights. "Chest wound," he stated tersely. "Clean, but a bad one. Help me get a compress on this open bullet hole. She's sucking air through it—can't breathe. It may not be fatal, but she needs a surgeon and hospitalization—soon."

"Paul?" Ross called.

"Yeah, Ross, right here."

"That other armored car. Would you check it out? Will it run?"

After what seemed like an eternity, Ross heard an engine cough, splutter, then settle into an even drone. "Okay," he told the man who seemed to be the expedition leader, "we'll put her in that car and at least get her back to Darass. There's another Cub there that can take her to Tel Aviv."

"No, Ross." He turned in surprise. The whisper had come from Ariel. Her eyes still closed, she had regained consciousness. "They'll need the car to free my father and the others."

The faceless leader held up a hand as Ross opened his mouth to protest. "No, Ariel, we won't need it. We couldn't hope to overpower the British who are still in charge there. We'll wait for them to leave, then be on hand to escort the prisoners back to Jewish territory."

Ross gathered Ariel into his arms and walked to where Paul waited in the idling vehicle. After gently laying her inside the back he returned to the Palmach officer and muttered, "You're lying, but thanks. This one deserves saving first."

Chapter 28

19 May 1948
Tel Aviv

Ross rubbed his bloodshot eyes and blinked rapidly to stay awake. Ariel, her hospital bed cranked to a semisitting position, regarded him with an anxious look. "Please, Ross—I'm touched that you took time to come see me, but you're exhausted. Get some sleep; we can visit later. I'm doing fine, really. The bullet missed my vital organs; I'll be on my feet in no time."

"I'll have plenty of time for sleep now," Ross mumbled. "I just made my last trip to Zatec."

"And time enough, I'd say. You've been in a cockpit for more than a week without a break. Is the Czechoslovakian arrangement finished?"

"No." Ross smiled wryly. "I'm out of business. Tomorrow I turn over all the planes Allied Air bought with foundation money to the new Israeli Air Transport Command. And a good thing, too. You see, President Truman announced recognition of the Israeli government the day after Ben-Gurion declared independence. That clearly puts me in the position of not only accepting pay from a foreign government, but taking part in hostilities against a nation *not* at war with the U.S."

Ariel frowned. "I'm told there are hundreds of Americans serving as volunteers."

"They don't hold a commission in the U.S. Air Force ready reserve," Ross replied grimly. "No, Jake and I need to get home and put Allied Air back together as a business. Thanks to the contract with the foundation, we have a healthy balance sheet."

"I see. I'll miss you, Ross. It's, well . . ."

"I know," Ross replied briskly. "But, why I really came to see you is to pass on something that—although you'll know eventually—I wanted to tell you first." He paused to draw a deep breath. "Ariel, Dov was shot down this morning. I learned of it when I landed. They think he's okay," he added, seeing Ariel's stricken look. "His wingman saw him bail out, and he circled until he saw Dov on his feet after landing. He's pretty deep in the desert, however, and it will take some time to get him out."

"How did it happen?" Ariel whispered.

"The Egyptians launched an armored column along the coast toward Tel Aviv the morning of the sixteenth. The Palmach did a magnificent job. They slowed the attack, then blew the bridge at Ashdod. That halted the Egyptian advance. General Cohen decided to counterattack while they were stalled. Dov and three pilots who checked out at Zatec took the four flyable Avias and caught the armored column by surprise. I'm afraid they lost three of the fighters, but the Arabs seem to be in total disarray; they're dug in and showing no sign of moving north."

"And you think Dov is safe?"

"Reasonably certain. Now, I'm going to get some sleep. I'll check back tomorrow and let you know where Dov is." Ross paused a moment, then continued. "And Ariel, you've won your private war. Turn in your uniform and start thinking of your future as a wife and mother. The man who betrayed your father, for instance. Let someone else deal with him. There'll be duly constituted judges and juries to decide the fate of his ilk."

Ariel's eyes flashed briefly. "I tell myself that, Ross. And I'll give the system a chance. At the same time, a tigress may give the appearance of being domesticated, but the claws are only sheathed, not pulled." Her demeanor softened and her voice grew husky with emotion. "I always seem to be thanking you. If I live to be a hundred, I'll never be able to repay you."

Ross brushed her cheek with his lips and forced his weary features into a broad smile. "Just name that first boy after me," he said.

0900 Hours, 20 May 1948
Tel Aviv

"I can't spare a mechanic to change that starter, Colyer," a harassed maintenance superintendent told Ross. "Even using every man I can lay my hands on, we won't have those shot-up airplanes flyable by tomorrow morning. Some of the men have already worked all night. And we gotta have the planes fit to at least disperse to other strips. They're sitting ducks out there. Only their Allah knows how the gyppos missed blowing up the whole place yesterday afternoon."

Two hours later, Ross slowly stood erect on the blistering-hot engine stand and rubbed his aching back muscles. Even twelve hours' sleep couldn't erase the effects of the grueling pace he'd kept up for the past several days. He wiped sweat from his face with a grimy forearm and regarded the C-46's starter, now resting at his feet. He'd taken the easier task of removing the inoperative part while Masters was laboring to salvage one from the '46 that crashed while trying to land in heavy fog three nights before.

Ross leaped to the ground and walked a safe distance before lighting a cigaret. "C'mon, Masters," he muttered. "Get lucky. Let one of those damn starters be where you can get to it—and undamaged. I want to be outta here by tomorrow morning." A ride on the crippled airplane with an Israeli crew to Ajaccio would get him on his way home.

Unable to stand around in the growing heat doing nothing, Ross decided to walk across to operations and check on the effort to rescue Dov Friedman. Making his way past a Beaufighter undergoing emergency repairs to a bullet-riddled wing panel, Ross shook his head in disbelief. How in the hell could he have slept through an air raid that had lasted more than an hour the previous afternoon?

The command post was crowded, hot, and smoke-filled. Ross elbowed his way toward General Cohen's corner office, but he stopped when he saw several worried-looking men huddled around a long table. Just outside, a line shuffled impatiently, waiting for an audience. Ross shrugged; word from the horse's mouth would have to wait. He buttonholed a dispatcher as the young man emerged from behind the ops counter. "What do you hear from the group trying to rescue Dov Friedman?" he shouted above the bedlam.

The bleary-eyed clerk stared at Ross blankly for a moment. "Friedman. Oh, yeah. I hear they located a piece of desert that looks like it will take a Cub. A Harvard trainer is capping the site—keeping an eye on a column of Arabs headed toward him." The man jerked a thumb toward the command post. "You'll have to ask someone in there how it's going; they're in radio contact with the Harvard."

Ross turned to leave, then stopped in his tracks. Across the room a half-dozen men with press cards in their hatbands had the harassed-looking ops officer surrounded, firing questions at him. One of the reporters looked familiar. The seersucker suit and dark glasses couldn't disguise Hank Wallace. Ross worked his way to the congregation's fringe and studied the man's profile. Wallace seemed to sense Ross's presence. He turned and whipped off the dark glasses. Favoring Ross with a direct glare, he shook his head unobtrusively.

Ross sauntered past him, muttering, "I'm available for an interview— an *exclusive* interview. I'll be working on a C-46 across from that bombed hangar."

Ross returned to the disabled airplane with a hundred questions churning in his mind. What the hell was the CIA man doing in Tel Aviv? He was undercover, that was for sure. Well, I'd like some answers myself, Ross mused. And where the hell was Masters and that starter? He sought a shady spot beside the hangar, slumped to a sitting position, and lit a cigaret.

1100 Hours
Huskstep Airfield, Egypt

Hafez Kamil dutifully forced himself to listen to the intelligence officer's unemotional drone. We know what the situation is, damnit, Hafez fumed inwardly. The army is bunched like a herd of goats south of Ashdod. After taking two days to subdue two miserable kibbutzim defended by farmers, four brigades of infantry, reinforced by a tank brigade, had stumbled to a halt well short of their objective—Tel Aviv. Then, following a brief sweep by only four enemy fighter planes, they dug in.

It could all have been avoided if only the fools had listened to him! "Send my fighters ahead," he'd urged. "Strafe the damn Jews' defensive positions. I studied the tactics the English used during the war; you must first clear the way for our ground forces."

"That will hardly be necessary, Squadron Leader Kamil," was the lofty response. So his planes had been diverted to overfly isolated Israeli outposts on fruitless reconnaissance missions. Now he sat grinding his teeth in frustrated rage. He wished that the king and prime minister hadn't changed their minds at the last minute and directed the army to attack. That stupid Abdullah of Transjordan had been the cause. The posturing fool had announced publicly that following the withdrawal of British troops, he would send his Arab Legion into Palestine.

Even the wishy-washy Farouk couldn't stomach that. Egypt would become an impotent bystander in future Middle East politics. He'd countered with a bold statement that Egypt would enter the conflict, and "liberate" the Palestinians, and return the land to "its own inhabitants"—the Palestinian Arabs. The result? A humiliating debacle.

The coup would have succeeded, Hafez believed. With the Muslim Brethren in control of the army, his views would have prevailed. Egyptian troops would be celebrating in Tel Aviv today instead of cowering in the sands of the Sinai.

Thoughts of Aziza intruded. His impending marriage. Oma Kamil's querulous imprecations. "*When* will you set the date, Hafez?" Aziza's father, Abdou Daoud, his beady eyes peering through thick glasses, scowling and asking, "When should we announce the wedding, Hafez?" A pox on them all. There was time enough to settle down later. He shook his head and forced himself to pay attention to the briefing.

An hour later, Hafez sought the shade of his Spitfire's wing. Sitting with his back to the left landing gear, he noticed that the red, white, and blue RAF roundel beneath the wing was still faintly visible. The Brits had made a big thing of "giving" two squadrons of the swift fighters to their former allies. Actually, the planes were of an older vintage. Leaving them in Egypt merely saved the time and expense of returning them to England, where they would have been junked. The supply of spare parts they left was nearly exhausted, and the English were absolutely churlish about providing more. Only eight of the original twenty-four Spits were still operational.

Restless, Hafez stood and inspected for the tenth time the ugly snouts of the left wing's four .303-caliber Browning machine guns. It would be another thirty minutes before the slower Dakotas, with their cargoes of forty-kilogram bombs, would reach the rendezvous point at Port Said. Hafez could feel his excitement build as he pictured the attack. The Spitfires would first sweep the target and silence what few antiaircraft guns the defenders were known to have. The Dakotas would then drop their loads at leisure. Tel Aviv would be burning rubble by sundown. His promotion to colonel would follow almost immediately, he felt certain.

A slight frown creased his forehead as he pondered the report that the planes used to strafe the army at Ashdod were German Messerschmitts. He dismissed the idea with a shrug—where on earth would the Jews get Messerschmitts? Some fool, panicked and crouched in a foxhole, couldn't tell a fabric-covered trainer from a first-line fighter plane. Hafez glanced at his watch and signaled impatiently to the ground crew. It was start-engines time.

1345 Hours
Tel Aviv

Ross awoke from an uneasy doze as a voice drawled, "Sleeping Beauty, as I live and breathe." He jerked upright to regard a grinning Hank Wallace.

"No room at the inn," Ross mumbled. "I sleep anywhere I can these days."

Wallace eyed the parked airplane, its useless starter sitting atop the maintenance stand. "Problems?" he inquired.

"Yeah. The crew chief is trying to salvage a starter from a wrecked bird across the field. When we get this plane glued back together, I'm off for the land of mom's apple pie."

"You don't say. I take it you decided not to hang around for the main feature."

"Not much point in it," said Ross. "I turned over all of Allied Air's planes to the Israeli Air Transport Command—except the DC-3 and Norseman back in the States. I'm out of business here. Only reason I'm working on this one is because it's my ticket out."

"No job offers?"

"I didn't apply. I'm trusting you to get the U.S. attorney general's people to ignore what I've been up to. I *don't* trust you to fast-talk the air force into keeping a mercenary soldier of fortune in their ranks. Now, what the hell brings *you* to this place?"

"Oh, we reporters get some strange assignments," Wallace responded.

Ross snorted. "'Reporter,' my ass. Who are you snooping on?"

Wallace's lips curved into a derisive smile. "You have an inquisitive mind, Colyer. That's good. Are you ready for a new assignment?"

"No way." Ross's voice was firm. "My job is finished. I'm not renewing my contract."

"Oh?" Wallace raised his eyebrows. "Are you displeased with our arrangement?"

"No more so than I was to begin with. I don't see that I accomplished a damn thing, except to develop a guilt complex."

"Don't give me that holier-than-thou business, Colyer." Wallace's bantering demeanor changed abruptly. "Surely you know that President Truman recognized Israel less than twenty-four hours after Ben-Gurion read the proclamation. Didn't you think to ask yourself why?"

Ross laughed, a short, harsh sound. "I hope you aren't going to tell me that the dope I gave you had anything to do with that."

"I judged you wrong," Wallace said coldly. "You *are* stupid. That 'dope' you speak of so slightingly had a great deal to do with our position. In fact, a small, closed-door ceremony is laid on for you when you return—if you can bring yourself to accept a personal 'thank-you' from the director."

Ross blinked. "The hell you say."

"Yes, I do say. And before I get completely pissed off with your attitude, I'll give you something else to think about. Not long ago, the director had a meeting with a certain senator in a certain smoke-filled hotel room. A certain letter, written by that senator to his son during the war, was discussed. When the men left the room, the senator had the letter, and the director had a smile on his face. If you care to check your personnel records, I think you'll find that congressional flag has been pulled. It has also come to my attention that the senator has reconsidered his plans to run for president. He has a health problem, I understand."

Ross closed his gaping mouth. "I can't believe it," he whispered. "I'm sorry I ever doubted that clout you claimed, but . . ."

"Believe it." Wallace relaxed his belligerent attitude. "Now, about your future with the agency—"

Wallace broke off his speech as Ross raised a hand, palm out. "I don't want to hear more. Really, I figure the books are balanced as far as our deal goes. I'm going home and try to put Allied Air on the map. The air force? I dunno, I'll have to think about that. I'd about given up, you know.

"I got a letter from Panama. The FBI is running wild. Julius and the Jewish nationals are on the run; the office at Forty-four Water Street is closed. Murtaugh wants Eddie, Jake Trask, and me to hide out in Panama and operate Panama World Air from there until—if—things cool off. They don't know I've been covering my ass all this while," he added bitterly.

"Ross," Wallace said, his voice taking on an edge, "the need for international intelligence will grow as the world settles down after the war. New threats are showing up every day—the Russians, the Chinese . . . Who knows what else? I don't believe the agency is ready to terminate your contract."

Ross leaped to his feet. "What the hell are you talking about, Wallace? I didn't ask if *you* were willing to terminate our arrangement: I'm telling you that *I'm* breaking it off."

Wallace chose his words carefully. "Agencies such as ours are like jealous lovers, Colyer. We don't easily accept rejection. But," he continued briskly, "we're quibbling about something that may never come to pass. What I was about to say is, you're being placed in the inactive file. You're still subject to restrictions on what you can say, but you won't have a specific assignment. If the need to activate you arises, well, we can negotiate then—okay?"

"Why, you underhanded bastard," Ross said softly. "I should've run, not walked, from that goddamn meeting in that stinking theater—the time you hinted that walking away from this deal might not be easy."

"Maybe you should have," Wallace agreed. "But let me finish. That dope you gave me in New York—" He stopped in midsentence as the air-raid siren moaned to life.

Ross watched the activity on the airfield freeze. Heads rose, conversation ceased, wrenches dangled from inert fingers. A mangy, dun-colored dog trotting across the dusty parking ramp constituted the only visible movement. As suddenly as the hush descended, it was broken. Hoarse shouts, the sound of engines revving, and the pounding of booted feet replaced the unnatural silence.

"Oh, m'God," Ross muttered. "*Why* did these idiots bunch half their entire fleet of planes on this, of all fields?" He galloped toward the ops building for no specific reason. Maybe the intruder is just a single straggler taking a look, he thought. God help 'em if it's a raid in force—and after the effort that went into collecting even this motley assortment of aircraft. . . .

The gaunt-faced ops officer stood outside the building, shouting orders to an anxious crowd. "It was a good-sized formation. A ship loaded with immigrants off the canal entrance radioed the sighting." The officer glanced at his watch. "They're roughly an hour out—if they're headed this way, and you can bet they are. Maybe a dozen twin-engine types with a fighter escort. Get everything that will fly into the air; disperse the rest to remote locations. Drape camouflage over anything that can't be moved. I need pilots. Can anyone here fly the Harvard?"

A scattered response of "Yeahs" filled the air.

"All right. We have three loaded and ready to go. Get 'em airborne. The twin-engine planes are bound to be Dakotas with bombs on board but no guns. Go after those first. Any Beaufighter pilots?"

A single response prompted, "Okay, we have one for you. Get going."

Ross felt his guts contract with a sickening wrench. Three Harvards—a British name for the old AT-6 trainer he'd flown at Kelly—armed with a single thirty-caliber gun intended to provide gunnery training, and a clumsy Beaufighter. That was *it?* Perhaps they could break up the bomber formation, he thought, but that fighter escort? They'd be Spits—the only fighters the Egyptians owned. Ross made his way toward the front ranks. He hardly recognized his own voice yelling, "What about the Avia that made it back from Ashdod?"

The ops officer glanced in Ross's direction. "Grounded. There's a problem with the landing gear. We'll cover it up and hope for the best."

Ross wheeled and raced toward where he recalled seeing the battered fighter parked. A half-dozen mechanics struggled to roll the plane away from the parking ramp. It was moving at a snail's pace. "What's wrong with the gear?" Ross asked breathlessly.

A dejected-looking man dragged an arm across his grease- and sweat-streaked face. "Hydraulic leak. Can't keep fluid in the landing gear system. Just cycling it once drains the system."

Ross's mind raced. He recalled some ways that B-24s returning with battle damage dealt with shattered hydraulic systems. "Are the ammo cans full? This *is* one of the birds with a working synchronizer, isn't it?"

"Yeah, for what it's worth," the mechanic replied. "Full loads for both the cannon and machine guns."

"Good," Ross said crisply. "Fill that hydraulic reservoir with anything you can get your hands on: hydraulic fluid, radiator coolant—even water. The pilot can retract it after takeoff, then belly the thing in on the beach."

"*What* pilot?" the exhausted man asked. "All the fighter pilots are over at Ekron, helping assemble the last shipment from Czechoslovakia."

"Shit!" Ross pounded his thigh with his clenched fist. "This is the only plane you have that stands a prayer of breaking up that attack."

The semicircle of dog-tired faces regarded Ross with dull, blank looks. So what? they seemed to say.

"Preflight that bird—have it ready for takeoff in ten minutes. You have a pilot." He turned and dashed toward the ops building.

The operations officer, Eli, scratched his chin as he listened. "It's your only chance," Ross insisted. "Those Spitfires are going to slaughter your Harvards and the Beaufighter—they won't even get close to that bomber formation. So what if I wipe out the Avia? It's a small price compared to what that formation will do if they get overhead and there's no resistance whatsoever."

Eli took a deep breath, then nodded. "I don't think your chances are much better," he said apathetically. "But you're right—there won't be enough left to sweep into a bucket if they get through. Go."

Ross almost collided with Hank Wallace as he turned to leave. The agent wore a twisted, ironic smile. "I can't cover for you on this one, Colyer," he said. "The gyppos are going to scream bloody murder when they learn an American officer is flying combat for the Israeli air force. And they *will* find out—bet on it."

About to utter a scathing retort, Ross hesitated. Christ, what *am* I doing? he wondered. I'm not getting paid by the Israelis . . . the CIA has cut me loose. . . . Ross surveyed the frenetic efforts to save the dozen or so aircraft still on the ground. Memory of the long, back-breaking hours they represented—the men who had lost their lives—rekindled his anger. To see these planes go up in flames . . . no goddamn way, not if he could help it.

Chapter 29

Ross slung his seat-pack chute into the Avia's bucket seat and scrambled into the cramped cockpit. He heard two crewmen winding the inertial starter while he attempted to adjust the borrowed oxygen mask. A filthy, unshaven face appeared at his shoulder.

"You got guts, mister," the man said as he helped Ross strap in. "We'll have a crew waiting for you on the beach . . . when you come back."

Ross allowed himself a mirthless grin. Had the man been about to say, If you come back?

"Clear," Ross yelled to the ground crew before he engaged the starter. The Jumo, as if to apologize for the plane's cantankerous ways, came to life with a smooth, ear-shattering roar.

Ross ran a quick cockpit check while taxiing to the runway. The metric instruments all seemed to have normal readings. He double-checked the fuel tank selector and armament switches; they were, after all, the only really essential items.

Ross felt the Avia break ground, and he yanked the gear control lever to the UP detent. After what seemed ages, he heard a gratifying double *thunk*. He realized that he'd been holding his breath, and released it with a gusty sigh. He grinned. "Okay, you're airborne with a clean bird," he muttered aloud. "Now what?"

Where are the Harvards? he wondered. They'd departed at least ten

minutes ahead of him. And the enemy formation? He tried to mentally calculate their dead-reckoning position. They would stay close
to the coastline, he figured. He reached toward the rack at his right
elbow for a map. The metal tray was empty. Idiot! he berated himself; you're getting careless. Oh, well, fly south along the coast—you'll
find them. And then?

His thoughts drifted back to the hot, hostile skies over East China.
He recalled tactics that the slower P-40s, flown by Chennault's Flying Tigers, had used against the speedier, more maneuverable Jap Zeroes—
an apt comparison between the awkward Avia he flew and the British Spitfire. The Americans would climb as high as they could go and
wait until the Jap formation passed beneath them. Then they'd dive
at full power and make a slashing attack out of the sun through the
fighter cover, continuing directly toward the lumbering bombers. Ross
added power and hauled the nose above the horizon.

The radio. Good God, he hadn't taken time to find out what frequency the Israeli Harvards were on. You're really asking for it, Colyer,
he thought disgustedly. He fiddled with the unfamiliar switches until
he heard his headset crackle to life. No voices, just static. Were the
Israeli pilots maintaining radio silence? He couldn't imagine why. More
likely the radio was still tuned to the tower frequency. Oh, well . . .

He watched the altimeter wind past the eight-thousand-meter mark—
almost twenty-five thousand feet. The Jumo was howling at top climb
power, but the controls were growing mushy. This would have to do.
Ross leveled off and scanned the hazy, dust-laden air below. C'mon,
he mouthed savagely. You have to be down there *someplace*. Had he
missed them? Instinctive calculation of time and distance said he had
not. He commenced sweeping the shoreline in a disciplined, sector-
by-sector search.

There! An insect-sized dot crawled across the reddish-brown terrain. Concentrating on the featureless desert, Ross detected another,
then another, three more. . . . Hot damn! he exulted. Those had to be
the Dakotas. Now to find their fighter escort. Five eye-straining minutes passed before he spotted the pattern of dots formed by the Egyptian fighter craft. He frowned. They weren't where they should be.
Instead of holding in lazy S turns behind and above the bombers, they
were at least five miles in front. He was almost even with them.

Okay, he thought, they plan to lead the attack; go in and silence
any antiaircraft batteries. The arrogant bastards; they're ignoring the

threat of an airborne defense. We'll see about that. He nodded grimly and nosed the Avia into a forty-five-degree dive. He decided to make a wide, circling approach, hit the fighters first from an angle, and then pick up the bombers.

Ross hurtled earthward, engine screaming at max revs. He felt the controls start to shudder and glanced at his airspeed; it registered past the redline and he backed off the throttle. Even with a shallow bank to turn into the formation, g forces made his jowls sag. Hauling back on the stick, he forced the Avia's ungainly nose through a 180-degree turn. Don't you flip out on me, you bitch, he grated. A high-speed stall would be fatal. At last, eight black crosses were visible through the windshield. He held the turn to approach the loose formation head-on.

1445 Hours
Abeam Ashdod, Israel

The V formation wasn't bad, Hafez decided. True, his pilots didn't have the flying skill he possessed, but they hadn't had an opportunity to train under RAF veterans, and none had ever flown in combat. The fishing village he'd marked on the map as a turning point flashed beneath the plane's nose. Hafez waggled his wings—a signal for the formation to take up in-trail positions. He turned thirty degrees onto a course leading over the sparkling blue Mediterranean. He would make the first pass from over water, staying low to avoid detection as long as possible.

About to roll in forward trim and set up a gradual descent, he detected a shadowy blur pass behind and to his left. While he was still trying to decide what it was, he heard a startled, "A fighter plane! It hit Sayyid's ship. He's on fire—he's breaking up!"

Hafez froze momentarily. A *fighter* plane? Attacking? Impossible. About to reprimand the green pilot for breaking radio silence, he paused. Could that report of German Messerschmitts be true? He couldn't take a chance; the slow, ungainly Dakotas would be cut to ribbons. "Reverse course, Green Flight," he barked. "Locate the fighter and attack. It must *not* find the bombers."

Ross streaked toward the bombers with grim satisfaction. He had selected a straggling Spitfire and blown him out of the sky without being spotted. Now, he almost felt sorry for the Dakota pilot ahead. There was nothing the poor bastard could do to avert disaster. The snarling fighter raced toward the lumbering, bomb-laden transport like a hungry shark closing on a school of mackerel.

Ross selected the twin 7mm machine guns; he'd save the cannon for the Spitfires. Within seconds he was close enough to see the crew wrestling to get their ship out of the Avia's path. He fired three short bursts. The Dakota's port wing, in the process of lifting into a turn, separated from the fuselage—its main spar shattered. A figure tumbled from the open cargo door.

Ross rolled into a climbing turn. Have to get above and ahead of them, he thought. Get as many of the bomb carriers as possible, then worry about taking on the fighters. During the two minutes required to turn around and jockey back into position for another attack on the bombers, he anxiously scanned the northern horizon for their fighter escort. But the Spits seemed to have vanished. Meanwhile, the scattered Dakotas were diving toward the desert floor. Smart move, he observed. I'd do the same. They want to get down there so I can attack only from above. Then they'll slow down and make a series of tight turns inside my turning radius, hoping I'll stall out.

The Avia moaned in protest as he racked it into a steep turn to line up a target. He blinked. A pair of mosquito-sized shapes had the transport bracketed—the Harvards! He gave a triumphant whoop, and sought another victim. Seconds later, he saw his tracers rip through the starboard engine of his second target. As smoke and flame erupted from its engine nacelle, the plane fell off into an uncontrollable turn. Inverted, it plunged to earth.

He hauled back on the stick. Okay, he thought, let the Harvards take on the unarmed, bomb-laden Dakotas—I'd best locate those damn Spits.

They were right where he'd expected them to be: slightly above and to his front, headed back toward where Ross and the Harvards were wreaking havoc on the Dakotas. He continued his climb, hoping to come up on them from out of the haze. Maybe I can get two of them if I catch 'em by surprise from below, then do a 180 and come in on their tail, he thought. His blood racing, he crammed the throttle forward and prayed they wouldn't spot him before he got into range.

Immediately upon learning of the enemy fighter's presence, Hafez had racked his Spitfire into a tight turn and headed toward where he judged the bomber formation to be. He saw the rest of the formation streaking in the same direction and added power to catch up. Farther ahead, he could see smoke spiraling up from the desert floor. A cold fist clutched at his guts; the bombers were already under attack. He searched the empty sky, seeking to locate the marauder. Squeezing the mike button, he shouted, "Green Flight from Green Leader. Break formation. Climb and—" He stopped in midsentence as he saw a Spitfire spew white coolant vapor, then burst into flames. A gray-green shape hurtled past going in the opposite direction. "Enemy fighter at six o'clock, Green Flight. Re-form on me for attack."

The disorganized string of Spitfires held its southerly heading. Damnit! thought Hafez. Was his radio not working? "Green Flight, Green Flight. . . ." Realization dawned. The others heard him, all right. They were *running away!* Hafez squeezed the stick-mounted mike switch in a death grip and screamed, "Anyone who doesn't return immediately will be court-martialed and shot!" Not a single ship altered course.

The disaster's full extent became clear. Total defeat—by a *single* enemy plane . . . treasonous flight by men whom *he,* Hafez Kamil, commanded. He wouldn't just be the butt of officers' club jokes, he'd be discharged in disgrace! His career was finished. A red mist of rage partially obscured his vision as he yanked the nimble Spitfire into a screaming turn. When he straightened out, the hated Messerschmitt was there filling his windscreen. He clenched his teeth and pressed the attack.

Ross caught a glimpse of flames erupting from the Spitfire he'd just riddled with cannon fire as he streaked through their formation and flung the Avia into a gut-wrenching turn. The g forces hammered him into his seat and his vision blurred. He straightened out and his eyes focused on the nose of a lone Spitfire headed straight for him.

He held his speed and course. Meeting a head-on attack could be dicey. Break too soon, and you're dead. Wait too long, and you're going to fly into the bullets from eight wing-mounted Brownings, even if you *do* luck out and get a hit with your longer-range cannon. The guy had guts—and confidence—to challenge the enemy this way.

Every nerve stretched to the breaking point, Ross waited. His 20mm cannon had roughly a five-hundred-yard advantage, he knew. If he lobbed a few of those golf ball–sized tracers from about two thousand yards, maybe he'd rattle the pilot into breaking off his attack.

They were closing at roughly eight hundred miles per hour. Now! Ross squeezed off two short bursts. The orange tracers arced lazily beneath the out-of-range Spitfire. The pilot never deviated from his headlong attack.

"She-e-i-t!" Ross exclaimed softly. *He's no green bean.* This could be close. Ross saw sparks dance along the leading edges of the Spit's wing and he stood the Avia on one wing. The two planes passed within inches of each other. *In this situation the book calls for an immediate loop to get above and behind the quarry. This guy will have read the same book,* he thought, *and he has both speed and maneuverability on me. Okay, let's see how he does with a tail chase.*

Ross reduced speed slightly and searched the sky to his rear. Sure enough, the Egyptian pilot rolled out of the top of a tight half loop and zeroed in on the fleeing Avia; he closed swiftly from behind. *C'mon, c'mon,* Ross urged silently. *You got yourself a sure kill, now set up your pursuit curve.* The Spitfire pilot, as if tuned to Ross's thoughts, moved into position above and to Ross's right rear.

Seconds later, Ross saw the Spitfire's elliptical wing dip and its nose swing into a firing pass. *Hold it, hold it,* Ross admonished himself— *now!* Yanking the Avia's stick back and to the right, he mashed the left rudder with a silent, fervent prayer. *Okay, you miserable excuse for an airplane, do what you're supposed to do . . . just don't come apart on me.*

The fighter's nose flipped up like a startled horse's head. It shuddered and hesitated. *C'mon,* Ross urged, *roll, damnit!* Without warning the nose whipped through the most vicious snap roll he'd ever experienced. He barely had time to shove the stick forward and recover when he glimpsed the brown and green Spitfire zip past his nose. Before the surprised Egyptian pilot could take evasive action, a withering hail of 20mm slugs transformed his cockpit into a twisted, riddled coffin.

1700 Hours
Tel Aviv
Ross collapsed on the bed and flung a forearm across his eyes. The hotel room was hot and close. He tried to sort his jumbled thoughts: the dogfight, the gear-up landing on the beach, a jubilant gathering of Palmach troops hoisting him out of the cockpit and into a canvas-covered weapons carrier. He found little to rejoice about; Wallace's words were burned into his memory: "I can't cover for you on this

one, Colyer." This, after telling him that Senator Templeton's noose had been removed from his neck.

So what had he done? He'd let blind rage urge him into blowing any chance he had of returning to an air force career. Wallace's last admonishing words were like a bone in his throat: "The gyppos are going to scream bloody murder when they learn an American officer is flying combat for the Israeli air force—and they *will* find out." Oh, well, what the hell? Ross thought wearily, there's always Panama. He stumbled to the window and threw it wide open. On the way back to the bed, he retrieved a grimy water tumbler from the bathroom and poured a good four fingers of Scotch.

Propped against the bed's headboard, the glass of warm, undiluted liquor resting on his stomach, he regarded the immediate future. The repaired C-46 would leave for Ajaccio in the morning. From there, a Pan Am flight to New York. Get in touch with Jake Trask. If Wallace could be believed, they would be free to start making Allied Air into another TWA.

Janet. Ariel's advice that morning was to "Go home—to the Janet you talked about in your sleep. . . ." Do you suppose? Ariel. Damn, he'd promised to check on Dov and let her know if the rescue was successful. A staccato rapping on his door interrupted his musings. "Yeah?" he called.

"This is your room clerk, Mister Colyer. I didn't see you come in. There was a trans-Atlantic phone call for you earlier. You're to call overseas operator number thirty-nine. You'll have to use the booth in the lobby, sir."

"Okay, thanks," Ross mumbled. Heaving himself off the bed, he considered showering and changing. Oh, screw it. . . . He tossed back the last of the Scotch and stumbled toward the door.

The tiny phone cubicle was hot and stuffy. Ross left the door open while he listened to the static-filled background of the undersea cable connection. The voice, when it came, boomed from the receiver. "Ross? This is Ted Wilson. I've had one helluva time tracking you down."

Ross held the squawking receiver away from his ear and shouted back, "Hey, Colonel Ted. This is a pleasant surprise. To what do I owe the honor?"

Wilson's voice faded but was still distinct. "Get your ass home, guy. I just discovered that the PI flag in your records has been yanked. I have your application for a regular commission filled out—all it needs is your signature."

Ross felt the raw Scotch churning in his gut. He grasped the receiver in a white-knuckled hand and gulped. About to explain what he'd just done, he hesitated, then said weakly, "That's great news, Colonel Ted. I—I'm on my way. See you in a few days—and thanks." He started to hang up when he heard, "And there's a certain redhead who says to tell you—" Further conversation was shut off by a crackling crescendo of static, then the line went dead.

Ross hung up slowly and sank onto the booth's tiny bench seat. His dejected introspection was broken by the sight of Hank Wallace leaning against the registration desk. The agent's face wore a sardonic smile. "I couldn't help but overhear," he said. "Was that the news I think it was?"

"If you came here to gloat—to say I told you so—you can go straight to hell," Ross snapped. "And you can forget about your fucking contract, too. There's no way you can force me to do any more of your dirty work."

"My, my, but aren't we testy today." Wallace observed mildly. "And you don't seem overjoyed at your good fortune. Does a return to active duty, as a regular officer, no longer appeal to you? I didn't get to finish telling you how it came about before you went charging off to do battle."

"It doesn't make much difference how you pulled it off, does it? I just blew the entire ball game. But okay, I've got nothing better to do—tell me."

"Your girlfriend deserves most of the credit," Wallace said. "She dug up that donation to the senator's campaign fund—the one you asked me to trace."

"And?"

"Funny thing. It wasn't from a New York Jew; it came from her old boss—Nate Green, owner of the *Chicago Globe*."

"Green? Hell, I thought he hated Templeton for being anti-Semitic."

"Not really. Remember, one of the things the president asked us to find out was, who will end up leading a Jewish nation? Okay, Green was an Irgun supporter; he wanted a president who would back Begin. Truman made no bones about liking Ben-Gurion. *That's* why the profile your girlfriend wrote was killed. It showed Templeton to be a strong anti–Ben-Gurion candidate. We figure Green was worried that his faction's role might be exposed if that aspect of Templeton's campaign was played up.

"Of course she also came up with the letter to his son. That was the clincher. Now c'mon, I'm here to collect you and join the party."

"Party? You're sick, Wallace. I'm grateful for what you did, but I don't have anything to celebrate. I'm going up to my room, get drunk, and have a decent night's sleep before I wave good-bye to this place."

"Not so fast, Ross. Dov Friedman will be disappointed if you don't show up."

"Dov? Do you mean they got him out? Is he okay?"

"Not a scratch on him. C'mon, he's the guest of honor. There's talk of nominating him for sainthood."

Ross brightened. "I'll get changed and be right over. He deserves congratulating—I understand the Egyptian army is sitting there with its tail between its legs."

"You'd better believe it. And him shooting down two bombers and three Spitfires with a crippled Avia; it kept the Tel Aviv airfield on the map."

"Come again?"

"Yeah. He got back in time to take the last fighter on the field—with a landing gear that'd retract but not extend—and he chased the entire gyppo air force all the way back to Cairo. They're drawing up the commendation right now, complete with statements from the ground crew that pulled him out after he crash-landed on the beach. He'll get a damn gong that's six inches across, I'll bet."

"What the hell are you talking about, Wallace?"

"Your buddy, Dov Friedman. The whole world will know about his heroics after I file my story. And to think that all the time that was going on, you and I were out there working on that busted C-46—*all afternoon.*" Hank spoke slowly, placing heavy emphasis on his last two words.

Ross's face went slack as he realized what the CIA agent was telling him. "Wa—Wallace"—he could barely form the words with vocal cords that felt like cotton—"like I said before, you are a totally unscrupulous, devious bastard. I have no idea how you pulled it off—I don't think I *want* to know. Now, wait here. I'll get changed and be right back. Hell, I'll even buy you a drink."

20 June 1948
Base Chapel, Bolling Field, Maryland
Ross's hands trembled ever so slightly as he slipped the plain platinum circlet on his new bride's finger. His svelte, auburn-haired betrothed had chided herself for the same display of nervousness only hours earlier: after all, Janet Templeton, you're a widow, she'd observed wryly; this is your second time around. But she'd never felt the same emotional depths with BT that Ross stirred. She chortled to herself as she saw him falter: the big, strong combat veteran has butterflies too. A warm glow engulfed her.

Their wedding day was also Ross's first day of active duty. Following a long weekend for a honeymoon, he would report to Langley Air Force Base, Virginia, for assignment. After that? . . . Janet pushed the future from her mind. Ross was her husband, and they loved each other; what more was there? Tears filmed her eyes as her six-foot two-inch mate tipped his face to bestow the traditional nuptial kiss. The blinding pop of a flashbulb captured the scene: a beaming chaplain and the newlyweds bathed in the light of a stray sunbeam peeking through the overhead stained-glass window.

Ross steered Janet to a position just inside the officers' club ballroom, where they joined the Wilsons to form a receiving line. Janet giggled. The plans for a simple ceremony, a drink with friends afterward, and a quick departure had obviously gotten out of hand. Doris's work, she surmised. The Wilsons were dear friends; it was appropriate that they had "stood up" for Ross and Janet.

Ted Wilson had never ceased his efforts to have Ross returned to active duty. Yet a nagging question returned fleetingly to Janet: what had *really* made the senator withdraw that political interest flag from Ross's personnel records? It was out of character for the arrogant old bastard to do anything benevolent, voluntarily at least. When Janet had asked, Ross was blandly evasive, as were Colonel Wilson and Ed Adair.

The article exposing that mysterious contribution to Templeton's campaign fund had been killed with an offhanded: "Inconclusive—no second source." That decision was passed on to her when Adair announced her new status as a permanent associate editor. There were other puzzling developments: Adair's lack of concern that the Jewish Relief Foundation exposé had come too late to create the anticipated explosion; Ross's bland dismissal of a possible grand jury summons. It was all just too damn slick and pat.

Janet's lips tightened. And whatever happened to the letter and other information she'd given Ross? I'll get to the bottom of this someday, Ross Colyer, she vowed. Pillows are good for things other than resting your weary head on.

The foursome took places beside the doorway, and Janet watched the fifty-odd guests straggle away from the punch bowl to form a line. She recognized a sizable contingent from her office at the International News Service office. Things could get rowdy with that crew having access to free booze. She accepted Doris's congratulatory peck on the cheek, made sure that her pale green tailored suit was straight, swept an errant lock of hair from her oval features, and smiled widely.

Ed Adair was the first to appear. He squeezed her hands and muttered an inanity. She introduced him to Ross and the Wilsons. He was followed by a couple of lieutenant colonels from Ted's office—Ted did the honors. Then came a dangerously handsome Kyle Wilson— new silver bars on his shoulder and a willowy blond on his arm. So it went.

Less than a half-dozen people passed who didn't require introductions to one or more of the wedding party. Janet's new husband smiled bashfully when Lieutenant Colonel Deckard told the group about Ross's rescue mission during the Missouri flood. Deckard then passed a muttered aside to Ross that a colonel named Prine couldn't make it—he had received orders for Japan. Both men seemed inordinately amused.

Suddenly Janet experienced a poignant yearning to see her parents in the line of smiling faces. A flurry of airmail special delivery letters had established the impracticality of their making the long journey from Colonel Richards's retirement home in Honolulu. Janet knew that her mother's heart condition, unmentioned, was responsible. Still . . .

Janet recognized the handsome Latin features of Ross's new boss, Col. "Cappy" Cipolla, and chuckled at his courtly gesture as he bowed from the waist and kissed the back of her hand. Cipolla turned to a dark-haired captain beside him. "Major and Mrs. Colyer, I'd like you to meet Captain Chuck Yeager. Chuck was at Langley Field on TDY and I thought you should get acquainted."

Janet met the man's appraisal—a lazy summing up from pale blue eyes framed by deep squint lines—and murmured a pleasantry. She felt Ross stiffen. "*The* Chuck Yeager?" she heard him stammer. Janet couldn't recall ever hearing such awe in Ross's voice. "I'd sure like to talk with you later," Ross added. Janet marked the incident as something else to quiz her new mate about and turned to the next guest.

Ross led her out for the first dance—Ted Wilson had claimed the next. Janet found herself thoroughly enjoying herself, feeling more uninhibited than she had in years. Then Doris murmured that it was time to open gifts. Janet and Ross crossed to where a corner table displayed a surprisingly large mound of gaily wrapped packages.

Janet opened all but one. Larger than the rest, it was saved until last. The paper was expensive and the box was heavy. She slipped the card from its envelope and stopped dead still. Ross saw two scarlet patches form on her cheeks and reached for the card. In elegant, Spencerian script it read, "A token of my admiration for a job well done. Broderick Templeton."

Janet stripped away the wrapping to expose a silver punch bowl of Olympian proportions. She and Ross exchanged startled glances. She saw his jaw muscles bunch. "Send it back," he snarled under his breath. "Now, this very evening—by special messenger. I won't have it in my house."

Janet laughingly glossed over the incident, and the happy newly-weds rejoined the festivities. That bastard Templeton, she seethed privately. He knows how much I detest him. Is this his sick version of a joke? Well, I'll be damned if I'll give him the satisfaction of returning that ostentatious trinket. I don't know how, but I'll convince Ross to keep it. If nothing else, we'll have a conversation piece for a trash can.

Janet eased from the aft cabin's lower bunk, careful not to disturb her softly snoring husband. The idea of sleep was unthinkable. She wanted to savor the prolonged session of lovemaking, tender at times, approaching savage abandonment at others. She slipped into a robe and stole toward the short ladder leading to the yacht's open deck, pausing to retrieve the half-empty bottle of flat, warm champagne and a pack of cigarets.

The sleek craft bobbed at anchor, the shoreline an indistinct blur across Chesapeake Bay's placid surface. She curled herself into a sheltered corner of the spacious cockpit and lit a cigaret. Well, old girl, she thought, you have it all, don't you? You have the man of your dreams, and he has a brilliant career ahead of him. You're safely established in the sanctity of marriage, and you've proved that you can compete with the best of them, men included, in the rough and tumble world of business. She grinned into the darkness. *And* we're pretty damned good in bed together.

Janet tipped the champagne bottle and took a long swallow, giggling slightly as she realized she was something less than stone sober. What's ahead of us? she wondered. Ross will get his assignment when he reports to Colonel Cipolla on Monday. A set of government quarters on one of the old established bases, she supposed—Langley, Mitchell, Kelly. It would be as it was when she was growing up before the war—her mother busy with the officers' wives, parties at the officers' club, gossip and sherry over bridge. Babies. Babies? Well, not right away, maybe. She drank more of the flat champagne and lit another cigaret.

Ross would get his promotions on time. There was no war to yank him away from her. Could things get any better? Well, there was the matter of money. Ross had refused to even consider spending any of BT's six-figure life insurance policy; he'd insisted she put it in a trust for their children. She had—most of it, anyway. Damnit, they were broke, and she would no longer have a salary. Ross's money was tied up until he could liquidate Allied Air; and a major's pay wasn't exactly a king's ransom. She'd told him that this yacht she'd chartered for their honeymoon was a wedding present from her mother—after carefully briefing Mrs. Richards. Well, she'd tell him everything someday, at the right time.

Or would she? A long-ago conversation between a newly engaged girlfriend and her aunt surfaced. Her friend had just terminated a heavy affair with a married man. "Should I tell Jack?" she'd queried.

The aunt, a divorcée, had advised, "What happened in the past should remain there. You don't gain a damn thing by baring your soul; men just don't understand. Trust me—I'm speaking from experience."

Janet decided to finish the champagne and return to bed. A farewell drink to her job, she decided. Ed hadn't been pleased when she'd told him of her wedding plans. "You're good at your job, Janet. Damn good. I hate to see you waste that talent chasing some hotshot aviator all over the world. If you ever get tired of ironing shirts and washing diapers, let me know. There'll always be a job for you here as long as I'm around."

And follow Ross around she would, she conceded wryly. The message was pretty clear this afternoon. As they drifted lazily down the Potomac, she'd asked, "Just who is this Yeager person? I thought you would maybe dance with him—you spent most of the reception with your nose in his face."

Ross's features had gone slack with astonishment. "Yeager? Chuck Yeager? Ye gods, Janet. Do you mean you don't know who he is? He was the first guy to fly faster than the speed of sound. He's just the hottest pilot in the world, that's all. And you're in the news business?"

"I'm not on the aviation desk," she'd answered crossly. "Anyway, he practically undressed me with his eyes, right there in the reception line. I don't suppose you noticed though; you were too busy blushing and stammering like a schoolboy." With that brief exchange between Janet and Ross, the fact that their future revolved around airplanes— and the men who flew them best—was chiseled in stone.

Well, she mused, so be it. You thought it all through before you said yes. She watched a pair of red and green lights, flashing alternately, materialize above the horizon. When the plane's sound reached her, it was muted—not the snarling thunder she was accustomed to hearing, but more like a teakettle boiling. It was one of the new jet-powered fighter planes Ross spoke of in glowing terms. She realized it was her first sighting. A twinge of pride swept aside her pensive introspection.

An omen? she wondered. Janet suddenly longed to be up there, sharing its majestic passage. She raised the champagne bottle in a silent salute. Words to the closing number the combo played that afternoon came to mind. Those guests wearing uniforms stood, resplendent in their formal dress blues, and sang, "Off we go, into the wild blue yonder . . ."

That pretty well sums up my situation, she mused. I should have joined in—I believe I'll drink to that. She discovered that the bottle was empty. Holding it overboard between thumb and forefinger, she consigned it to the dark depths of Chesapeake Bay. Janet chuckled. A fitting end to a past life, she thought. It was fun, but the future is in that wild blue yonder.